WORDS
OF FAREWELL

STORIES BY KOREAN WOMEN WRITERS

by Kang Sŏk-kyŏng, Kim Chi-wŏn and O Chŏng-hŭi

translated by Bruce and Ju-Chan Fulton

Seal Press

Publication of this book was made possible in part with support from the National Endowment for the Arts, The Wheatland Foundation, and The Korean Culture and Arts Foundation.

"Lullaby," "A Room in the Woods," and "Words of Farewell" first appeared in *Korea Journal*, and "Days and Dreams" was first carried in the *Korea Times*. We gratefully acknowledge the editors of these publications.

The cover painting is by Shin Pong-ja.

Library of Congress Cataloging-in-Publication Data

Kang, Sŏk-kyŏng, 1951-
Words of farewell : stories by Korean women writeres / Kang Sŏk-kyŏng, Kim Chi-wŏn, and O Chŏng-hŭi : translated by Bruce and Ju-Chan Fulton.
  p. cm.
Contents: Days and dreams: A room in the woods / Kang Sŏk-kyŏng – A certain beginning: Lullaby / Kim Chi-won – Chinatown : Evening game : Words of farewell / O Chŏng-hŭi.
  ISBN 0-931188-77-6. –ISBN 0-931188-76-8 (pbk.)
  1. Korean fiction–20th century–Translations into English.
2. Korean fiction–Women authors–Translations into English.
3. English fiction–Translations from Korean. I. Kim, Chi-won.
II. O, Chŏng-hŭi III. Fulton, Bruce. IV. Fulton, Ju-Chan.
V. Title.
PL984.E8K56 1989   89-10860
895.7'34089287–dc120   CIP

Printed in the United States of America by Epac
First printing, October 1989
10 9 8 7 6 5 4 3

Distributed to the trade by Publisher's Group West.

Translators' Acknowledgments

Several individuals and organizations have contributed generously to the publication of this book. The translation was made possible in part by grants from the Korean Culture and Arts Foundation, the National Endowment for the Arts, the Wheatland Foundation, and the Committee on Korean Studies of the Association for Asian Studies. We are especially grateful to Kim Chong-un and Kwŏn Yŏng-min for their assistance in securing support from Korea.

Special thanks go to Steve Hopkins and our editor Faith Conlon for their critical reading of the entire manuscript, and to Marty Holman for his extensive comments on a draft of the title story. We also wish to thank Fred Lukoff for his assistance with the note on romanization of Korean words.

We are indebted to Hwang Sun-wŏn for introducing us to the works of all three authors represented in this collection, and we are grateful to the authors themselves for their cooperation during the translation process.

Finally, we wish to thank our parents, who have contributed more than they realize to this project.

CONTENTS

INTRODUCTION

It is an irony of Korean history that the culture of Korea has come to the awareness of the West mainly in the wake of the Korean economic miracle; in traditional Korea, artistic accomplishment was esteemed over commercial success. To Koreans, who for much of their history have fought for cultural as well as political autonomy from their stronger neighbors, this culture has been a source of intense pride. One of the more surprising developments in Korean culture since the opening of Korea to the outside world in the late 1800s has been the emergence in the present century of a literary tradition that shares many characteristics with the literatures of the Western world. Young Korean men and women who studied in Japan after Korea's annexation by that country in 1910 were introduced to the authors of Russia, France, and other European countries in Japanese translation. Adopting the literary models of those countries, primarily realism, Korean writers had by the 1920s begun producing stories whose forms and techniques are familiar to the Western reader but whose atmosphere and themes are often uniquely Korean.

Traditionally, women writers in Korea have labored in relative obscurity. Despite the literary contributions of women such as poet Hwang Chin-i (c. 1506–1544) and Lady Hong (1735–1815), whose *Hanjungnok* (A Record of Sorrowful Days, 1796) is the best-known example of court literature in Korea, belles lettres was primarily the avocation of the cultured gentleman. And even in the twentieth century, it has been only recently that women have received recognition for their literary accomplishments. Such recognition is due in part to Pak Kyŏng-ni's (1927–) roman fleuve *T'oji* (The Land, 1970–), one of the great achievements of modern Korean literature. It is also due to the emergence in the 1970s and 1980s of a talented group of women writers including Pak Wan-sŏ (1931–), Sŏ Yŏngŭn (1943–), Yun Chŏng-mo (1946–), Yang Kwi-ja (1955–), and the three women represented in this anthology.

There are several reasons for this late blooming of women's writing in Korea. One is the patriarchal nature of traditional Korean society. Like many East Asian cultures, that of Korea has been heavily influenced by Confucian precepts. One of the most enduring of such precepts is the separation of public from domestic life; men reigned in the former, women in the latter. This concept is embedded in Korean language, where the wife is commonly referred to as the *chip saram* ("house person") and the husband the *bakkat yangban* ("outside gentleman"). And insofar as literature was a public, recreational activity, typified by gatherings of literati for the exchange of verses, it was the domain of men.

More recently, women such as Kim Mal-bong (1900–1951), Pak Hwa-sŏng (1904–1988), and Ch'oe Chŏng-hŭi (1912–) were among the first generation of twentieth-century Korean writers. But it was perhaps their misfortune to have been active at the same time as the twin patriarchs of modern Korean literature, Hwang Sun-wŏn (1915–) and Kim Tong-ni (1913–). These two men are generally regarded as the finest writers of fiction that twentieth-century Korea has produced, and they overshadowed not only this first generation of twentieth-century women writers, but a subsequent generation comprising such women as Son So-hŭi (1917–1987), Han Musuk (1918–), Kang Shin-jae (1924–), Han Mal-suk (1931–), Chŏng Yŏn-hŭi (1935–), and Pak Sun-yŏ (1928–).

That the current generation of women writers of fiction in Korea is emerging from this tradition of obscurity is a measure of the increasing sophistication of their craft. In terms of style, technique, plotting, characterization, and subject matter, the contemporary writers have built on the accomplishments of their predecessors. But it is also in their less sentimental, less deterministic outlook that these younger writers, and especially the three represented in this collection, stand apart from the earlier writers. A streak of fatalism and passivity may be detected in the works of earlier Korean authors of this century, both men and women. This should come as no surprise in view of the traumas sustained by twentieth-century Korea—colonization by the Japanese (1910–1945), political turmoil during the period 1945–1950, and devastation wrought by civil war (1950–1953).

But contemporary Korean women writers differ in outlook in another important sense as well. Korean women have begun to break out of the confines of the domestic sphere and take a more active role in Korea's rapid modernization, and their ways of thinking have gradually become more expansive as well. Korean women have traditionally been seen, and have seen themselves, first as someone's daughter, then as someone's wife, and finally as someone's mother. Indeed, in everyday speech they are referred to in these terms, as in the case of Ki-yŏng's mother in Kim Chi-wŏn's "A Certain Beginning," who is never called by her own name. It is no exaggeration to say that even today in Korea a married woman may be addressed by her own name no more than a handful of times in a year. Such traditions have proved resistant to change, and the conflicts of independent-minded women in a male-oriented society are evident in the works in this volume.

Of the three women represented in this collection, Kang Sŏk-kyŏng is perhaps the most outwardly concerned with social problems. Kang was born in the city of Taegu in 1951 and currently lives in Seoul, where she graduated from the College of Fine Arts of Ewha University in 1974. Also in 1974 she won the first Newcomers' Prize awarded by the journal *Munhak Sasang* (Literature and Thought). But it was with the publication of her short-story collection *Night and Cradle* (Pamgwa Yoram, 1983) and her novella "A Room in the Woods" (Supsogŭi Pang, 1986) that she consolidated her reputation as a writer having both a popular and a critical following. Before writing "Days and Dreams" (Natkkwa Kkum, 1983) and the title story of *Night and Cradle,* she spent time near an American army base in Korea researching the lives of the prostitutes depicted in those stories. Not surprisingly, the resulting works, like many of Kang's stories, are written in a reportorial style that lends a sense of immediacy to the events. Moreover, in the dispassionate account of the narrator of "Days and Dreams" we see a departure from the sentimentality that has often characterized portrayals of outcaste women in Korean fiction. In the best-selling "A Room in the Woods," Kang not only struck a chord among young people with her description of the Seoul street scene but illuminated the consequences of the failure to compromise with the tradition of male dominance that lingers in Korean society.

At first glance, Kim Chi-wŏn may seem a more traditional writer in terms of theme and narrative outlook. Kim was born in 1943 in Kyŏnggi Province. She comes from a literary family: she is the daughter of Ch'oe Chŏng-hŭi—one of the most popular women writers in twentieth-century Korea—and her sister, Kim Ch'ae-wŏn, is also a writer. She graduated in English literature from Ewha University in 1965 and made her literary debut in 1974. The women in "A Certain Beginning" (Ŏttŏn Shijak, 1974) and "Lullaby" (Twimmun Pakken Kallip Norae, 1979) see themselves as failures because of broken relationships with their husbands. But if they lack the resourcefulness of the women portrayed in the works of Kang and O Chŏng-hŭi, they are sophisticated enough not to ascribe their circumstances to fate, and they are strong enough to insist on retaining their dignity in trying situations. Since the 1970s Kim has been living in the New York City area, and many of her works describe the tribulations of Korean immigrant women in an American metropolis.

O Chŏng-hŭi (1947–) is one of the outstanding Korean writers of fiction of this century. A native of Seoul, she studied creative writing at Sŏrabŏl College of the Arts. While still an undergraduate, she retrieved the manuscript of a story she had thrown aside and entered it in the annual literary contest for aspiring writers held by the *Chungang Daily*. The story was "The Toy Shop Woman" (Wan'gujŏm Yŏin, 1968), and it won first prize. Since then,

O has published thirty-two stories and a novella—a meager output in comparison with that of many of her contemporaries. But these few works are consistently rich, provocative and carefully crafted; much lies beneath their surface. O's stories are difficult, even for Koreans. Her command of language is formidable, and she frequently uses flashbacks and stream-of-consciousness technique. Her characteristically detached narrative stance ("Words of Farewell" is a rare exception) has bothered Korean critics, who seem to expect a gentler, more empathic treatment of character and situation by women writers. O is intensely concerned with family life, and especially the strains imposed on the traditional Korean family by modernization. Many of the families O describes are shockingly at odds with Korean standards; the absence of the family head in "Words of Farewell" (Pyŏlsa, 1981) and the abandonment of the mother to a mental institution in "Evening Game" (Chŏnyŏngŭi Keim, 1979) are only two examples. Darkness is a physical presence in many of O's stories, representing, among other things, this gap in the fabric of the family. In "Evening Game," for instance, memories of the abandoned mother and the lost brother are barely held at bay by the light of a single lamp as the father and daughter play their nightly game of cards. The women in these stories are made more vulnerable by the loss of a family member. Perhaps more important, their bonds of family obligation are loosened, and we sense that they, like the narrator of "Chinatown" (Chunggugin Kŏri, 1979) and the central characters in the Kang and Kim stories, can chart their own future, independent of their status as someone's daughter, wife or mother.

Bruce and Ju-Chan Fulton
Seattle, Washington
July 1989

WORDS OF FAREWELL

Days and Dreams

Kang Sŏk-kyŏng

A SPRING SCENE of an ancient palace with forsythias in full bloom had replaced the mountain villa with smoke coming from its stone chimney; and so winter was torn from the calendar on the wall in the corner. A week later, I flunked my checkup. That happens a lot in this part of town, but I was really sore about it.

Sure, you can pick something up while you're on the job, but who ever heard of a person failing her checkup while she's living with someone? I'd been living with Overton for two months, but that didn't stop him from playing around and making me eat my heart out. This time he'd picked it up from another woman and shuffled it off on me.

It was bad enough having to be faithful to my new man. But an infection and a trip to the Monkey House? And right at the beginning of spring? That was too much.

The first thing I did after leaving the health center was call the Fire Brigade and let Overton have it—told him I was sick and tired of him playing around.

But Overton's a sly one. "Every man feels like playing around for a while," he said. "You can understand, can't you?"

I snorted. "You think men are the only ones who play around? Women are just the same. Wait until I make eyes at another fellow while I'm living with you."

Then I told him about the checkup, and he finally owned up. Maybe he'd had a checkup too. He told me in that sulky tone of his that he'd get in touch with the woman he'd caught it from. He kept saying he was sorry, but I figured I'd put the screws to him, so I said "This is it!" and hung up.

The more I thought about it, the more steamed I got. In a month Overton would wind up his tour of duty and head back to the States. He could have been faithful, figuring this would be the last time he'd live with a woman in Korea, but it was the other way around. Let's play with the girls to our heart's content—that was his philosophy. Hadn't he acted like we were a heavenly match when we met two months ago? He lay there on the bed, bouncing up and down in excitement, saying we'd met at the last minute through a whim of fate, and some other bull.

On my way home from the health center I bought thirty sleeping pills and a bottle of *soju*. I tossed off twenty of the downers with a glass of the liquor and passed out on the bed.

When I woke up I saw the sun shining through the window. It was the next afternoon. A transparent IV bottle was hanging in the air and I had a needle in my arm. Overton's blond hair brushed my eyelashes, and I grabbed the needle and pulled it out.

Overton took my arm and started wailing: "Honey, I was wrong. I won't play around anymore. Go ahead and take it out on me, honey."

I managed to keep from laughing. It was the first time I'd heard "honey" from him since we'd started living together. He looked pretty scared. But I figured that since I'd started in on him, I might as well go ahead and teach him a lesson.

I closed my eyes and asked him for a drink of water. When he reached over with it, I lurched out of bed and opened the nightstand drawer—still ten sleeping pills left. Overton stuck out his hand, but I stashed the pills under my quilt.

"Don't try to stop me. I'll have to get high before I can go to the Monkey House."

At ten that night I left for the Monkey House. The way I was feeling, I couldn't walk there in broad daylight. The pills made me feel like I was walking on air. I started humming to myself, like a soldier heading home on leave. I turned down a big, quiet alley, passed some walls, and there it was. It's two stories—just like any other public building, except for the lights showing on the second floor. The small iron gate was locked. Not surprising—my watch said it was close to eleven. So I tossed my bag over the wall. It rose like a heavenly body in the darkness, then disappeared. There was a lion's head on the handle of the gate. I got one foot up on it and was just able to grab the iron fence on top of the wall. Since I was still feeling light on my feet, it wasn't hard to climb over the wall and jump down.

I had to wake up the custodian, and he was griping when he opened the front door. But that wasn't the end of the day's commotion. I was assigned to the Chrysanthemum Room, and while the other girls were crowding around me and giggling, we heard voices from the hall. One of the girls, Yŏng-ja, flung open the door and said, "What the fuck is it this time?" Mousie, the housemother, and two policemen were coming out of the Iris Room down the hall. The three of them went into the Rose Room next door and made sure all the girls were there by calling off their names one by one.

Two of the Iris girls came out in the hall, and Yŏng-ja hollered again, "What the fuck's going on this late at night?"

"Someone escaped," a girl answered. "One of the night guards saw someone climb over the wall and run away."

The policemen looked through all the rooms, but no one was missing. Finally they took a head count in the Chrysanthemum Room; nothing unusual there either. Just imagine, someone escaping in the middle of the night! We'd heard about a girl who went out through the window like Tarzan on a rope made out of ripped quilt casings; she was a legend in her own time. Now there was a grate over every window.

The policemen checked their head counts, but they still weren't ready to leave. I guess they didn't want to give up.

Mousie, who got her nickname because her face was pointy like a mouse, tilted her head in thought, then pointed me out.

"This one climbed over the wall to get in—maybe she was the one the night guard saw. In the dark he might have thought she was running away."

"You came in over the wall?" one of the policemen asked me with a look of amazement.

As she escorted the policemen from the Chrysanthemum Room, Mousie added, "You didn't want to come here sober, so you popped some pills—that's why you pulled that stunt." Mousie had all the answers.

The girls started giggling again and one of them, Toma, yelled to Mousie's back, "Seems to me people *like* coming here. After all, someone climbed over the wall to get in."

We often put on this kind of show when a girl comes in because of how awful she feels. But once she's here she usually finds something interesting to do. The day starts early. At home the girls can toss and turn in bed all morning, but here everyone gets up at seven and cleans her room from top to bottom while the girls whose turn it is are making breakfast. When we're done cleaning we all flock downstairs. All we have with our rice and soup are vegetables such as soybean sprouts—no meat—but we still have a pretty healthy appetite right from the morning.

Except for mealtime, room cleaning and penicillin shots we're mostly on our own. Sometimes we read old magazines or watch TV, but mainly we pass the time playing flower cards and talking about this and that. Naturally we get to know all about each other. When I was in the Chrysanthemum Room there was Yŏng-ja, who started and ended every sentence with a swear word; and Toma, always ready to tell about her several "first" loves. Then there was Ch'u-ja, who always went around with artificial eyelashes that looked like bristles, but never washed her face. The youngest, Tina, was nicknamed Rattles because she couldn't sit still for a minute. And there was Sunny, who wanted to have her wedding in the mountains even though her luck was so wretched she had to sell herself to the first man she ever had a crush on—thirty-year-old Sunny, her face already blue all over from years of wearing lead-based makeup.

The oldest one in the room was Sun-ja, who was thirty-four. She looked gentle with her long face and the corners of her eyes hanging down. There wasn't anything special about her appearance, and she didn't talk much, so at first scarcely anyone looked twice at her. Sun-ja crocheted from morning till night. All she did was sit against the wall like a shadow, her hands moving like a machine. The other girls seemed used to this. When they played cards or talked, nobody tried to include her. And so the lace streamed into Sun-ja's lap like a bubbly little waterfall all day long.

The first day, I didn't give her crocheting a second thought. But the next morning she started in as soon as she got back from breakfast. That's when I started to get curious. I lit a cigarette and sneaked up beside her and just stood there.

Sun-ja wasn't even aware of me. She sat poker-faced, eyes down, just moving those hands of hers automatically. Her thick hair spilled down both sides of her face, almost blocking her vision. The coarse hair didn't go well with her gentle face. I tested her with a question, as if I were prodding a worm.

"What kind of fun do you get out of that? Just looking at you always crocheting makes my bones ache."

Sun-ja didn't respond right away. She had to finish the row she was working on before she could look up. Then she gave me a brief smile that seemed to say she knew me.

"I don't do it for fun. It's like busywork, that's all."

"Did someone ask you to do it?"

"No. Maybe I do it like some people count their prayer beads."

I kept standing there, and then out of nowhere Sun-ja asked, "How old are you?"

"Twenty-six."

"That's a good age. I had my second baby when I was twenty-six. If I'd known better, I wouldn't have done it. I wonder how those kids are doing now."

Her hands stopped for a moment, then began crocheting again. I asked where she was going to use the lace. It looked like a tedious business, like trying to dig dirt with a spoon.

"It's going to be a bedspread. I've knitted a lot of things—a table cover, curtains, cushion covers. I can use them when I get married, you know."

"You're. . . going to get married?"

"Someday."

I smirked. Sun-ja jerked her head up, like a fish jumping out of water.

"You'd better believe it," she said, dead serious. "I'd marry a black guy—I'd marry his grandfather."

Now aren't people the most interesting thing in the world, I said to myself. I've always thought so. Ordinary humans all have their own little quirk when you look at them up close. It can be given to them at birth or created by their circumstances. And isn't that quirk the thing that makes a person what she is?

Living around the army base I meet all kinds of people. I look at this as an education in life, and maybe that's why I've had more unique experiences than others. Thanks to this education, I have plenty of things to talk about. And maybe because I know how to talk—after all, I spend my days wagging my tongue—I tend to be popular when people get together. The Monkey House was no exception.

On my fourth day in the Monkey House, once again some interesting stories popped up in the Chrysanthemum Room. When it comes to fun, there's nothing like dirty stories, and this time it was Yŏng-ja who started in. She had just taken her turn in a game of flower cards.

"Fuck! Look at you rake in the dough with those shriveled-up little hands," she said to Ch'u-ja, who already had two thousand-wŏn bills in front of her. "I know a small pepper is supposed to be spicier, but give us a break."

Ch'u-ja wiggled her little toes and grinned. "This GI told me I'm small all over. I'm short, my hands are small, and so is my mouth. So I said to him: 'That's right, I'm small all over, but there's one thing that's big, and you'll find it when you get in bed with me.'"

Toma played a red bush-clover card, which wasn't worth any points, and screwed up her face. "All that talk about big and small is making my asshole ache again. I was having diarrhea like a faucet, and the day before I came here I picked up a GI who wanted some anal sex. Bad luck. It felt like a billy club. No wonder my rear end got torn. I kept saying I'd have to see a doctor about it, so I got another ten dollars out of him."

"I thought only homos did that sort of thing," said Sunny. "I wonder whether it hurts *them*. Just thinking about them makes me laugh. I'd say lesbians are better. They look better, too."

"You think so?" I responded. "Well, I know a lesbian. She's a real beauty. I can see where even a woman could fall for her. But I have to admit it felt creepy when she touched me."

"You mean you slept with her?" Toma asked. She put her cards down and looked up with a scowl.

"I even had a marriage proposal," I said, nonchalantly playing a card.

"From a woman?"

Now they all put down their cards. Yŏng-ja threw hers down and took a cigarette.

I'd met her the week before I came to the Monkey House, I began, as if I were playing a card I'd been keeping up my sleeve. Overton was working the graveyard shift, and for the first time in ages I was able to be a lazybones during the evening. It was about eight, I guess, when someone knocked on the door. It was An's old lady. An runs the club where I work. Next to her was a beautiful young black woman. She had a slender, oval face and thin lips that weren't like other blacks'. After An's old lady made sure Overton was working the night shift she told me why they had come.

The black woman was a soldier who had come to Korea from Japan for some emergency training, and she wanted to be introduced to a Korean woman. An's old lady told me she seemed to be looking for someone friendly who could show her around. Before I could say anything, the woman gave me a smile and introduced herself as Barbara. I looked at her evenly spaced teeth, and since I wasn't sure what to say, I simply told her it was nice to meet her.

At first I didn't know what Barbara was really like. She'd brought a bottle of cognac, and we drank and talked till midnight. She asked me this and that. She wanted to hear about the difficulties I'd had in making a living, and I got to talking about my past—about my high school days, when I ran away from home because my family was poor and didn't get along; about the tough life I'd had since then.

Barbara seemed to care about what I was saying. I could tell by the way her expression changed, depending on what I was talking about. After I finished she asked, "Are you satisfied with your life now?" I just said, "I know what I have to do, and I do it."

"Barbara's twenty-two," I continued. "Even though she's younger than me, we could communicate just fine because we're both women; we were tuned in to each other. I opened the wardrobe to hang up her coat, and we started putting down the rotten men we've known. She could see Overton's leather jacket and his two suits. But I didn't tell her I was living with a man—told her I'd grabbed them from GIs who slept here and didn't give me enough money. That does happen now and then, right? So she curled those thin lips like a German shepherd and said, 'Those stingy bastards!' like she was spitting. She didn't have much sympathy for them. I got a kick out of that, and I added my two cents' worth.

"But when it comes to going to bed I get kind of particular, even though I'm basically a free and easy sort. Except for business, I can't sleep with people I don't know, especially since I sleep in the nude. So I just sat there for a while. But Barbara got undressed in no time. All she kept on was a slip, and it showed everything. Her body looked smooth and slippery, like a seal's. She asked me why I wasn't undressing. That was my style, I told her; it wasn't anything to worry about.

"Maybe ten minutes after I lay down, I felt like I was sinking because of all I'd drunk. Fortunately, I'd almost forgotten there was somebody next to me, I was that high. But then it felt like my quilt was being lifted. I wondered whether I was imagining things, so I perked up a little and listened. Then I felt a soft touch on my waist. She's just trying to find out whether I'm asleep, I thought. But before I had a chance to do anything she lifted my shirt real gently. It was a strange feeling, so I held my breath. She felt my waist and then went toward my chest. Her hand was warm, but it gave me the shivers because it was smooth like a snake. So I whipped over on my side.

"That wasn't the end of it. It couldn't have been five minutes later when she started feeling me up again. Normally I would have yelled at her and got up to turn the lights on. But I didn't feel like budging because I was drunk. So I pretended I was talking in my sleep and told her I wanted a good night's rest."

While I was taking out a cigarette, Ch'u-ja and Sunny spoke up one after the other:

"You probably felt strange because it was a woman's hand, right?"

"Black women are sexy, aren't they?"

"Maybe I'm prejudiced," I said. "She's beautiful, all right, but I'm sorry, she doesn't turn me on at all."

Everybody giggled, and then Yŏng-ja said, "Fuck! I'd rather be a lesbian than get pushed around by all these stupid bastards. Did she say how you two were going to get married?"

Everyone's eyes were shining with curiosity, so I continued.

"She came back the next night. I hadn't slept well the night before, and as soon as she left that morning, Overton came home, so I didn't have any time to relax during the day. After dinner that evening I sent Overton off to work, and then Barbara knocked again. Instead of coming in she suggested going to one of the clubs. I was exhausted, but I said okay since I was still curious about her. We headed toward the black clubs. A couple of years ago when I was going out with blacks, that was my territory. So it was no problem showing her around.

"We went to the Blackjack Club and had ourselves another night of drinking. Barbara wanted to do some slow dancing, and you know, when two women hold hands and dance slow, everyone starts looking their way. I'm pretty tough inside, and even *I* got embarrassed. But Barbara didn't mind. In fact, she was downright bold the way she glided over the floor with her arm around my waist. As soon as we sat down, this black man comes up to us chewing on a cigarette filter. The way he walked was enough to make me sick. He started to put on the make: 'Lonely, sister? How'd you like me to be your partner?' Barbara made short work of him: 'Sister? Forget it!' Barbara doesn't like blacks. But then we don't always like Koreans either."

"Maybe that's why she's a lesbian," Toma interrupted breathlessly. "Besides, it's hard for a black woman to marry a white man."

Then Yŏng-ja chimed in: "Fuck! She probably has a big ax to grind against men. You can take only so much from them. Like they say, a woman's spite can make the earth turn cold in June. We could do a lot worse than being lesbians. I think I can understand her."

"I can understand her feelings too," said Sunny. "But how can a woman sleep with another woman? That's what I want to know."

"I'll get to that," I said, gesturing to Sunny to be patient. "We left the club, and two black guys hanging around the entrance started whistling at us. One of them yelled from behind, 'Hey, tall girl, show me how long your tongue is!' I had no idea what he meant. When we got home, Barbara started off by giving me forty dollars—for the time I'd spent with her. And then out of the blue she said, 'I like you. Why don't we get married?' I couldn't believe it. I thought she was a little weird. How could two women get married? And then without batting an eyelash she said, 'I can satisfy you more than a man can. I can't explain it now, but I can make you crazy; you won't even need the likes of a man.' That's when I remembered what the black guy had yelled at her. Then she said something even more interesting. If I agreed to marry her, I'd first have to find a GI here—a man I could marry officially. She said she'd stake me to a thousand dollars as long as I divorced the guy when I got to America. She told me to look for a white man, since whites are more likely to fall for something like that. Then she'd give me the money. And that wasn't all: she'd send me two hundred dollars a month to live on until I found someone."

"Fuck," Yŏng-ja broke in. "That's just a big con game."

"Now who would believe that," Tina agreed with a sneer. "Really!"

None of this fazed me. I smiled and said, "Barbara expected there'd be some doubters, so she had an explanation ready: 'The last thing I'd do is double-cross you. We're both women, so believe me,' she said."

"Even if I went along with that, I still couldn't live with her," said Sunny. "Oh, sometimes we say we don't like men, or we hate them. Still, women are supposed to live with men."

"But if two women see eye to eye, there's no law that says they can't live together," said Toma. "So what if they're lesbians? People live the way they want to. And so what if we're whores? Except for worrying about money, it's great living around the base. No husband to treat us rough, no kids to worry us, no one interfering with us."

"That's right," said Sunny.

All this talk about Barbara had led us to accept our own lives, and without such thoughts to make us feel good, how could we live? We women were facing up to life with our bodies as our only asset. We may not have smelled like roses, but we got to learn all about life and freedom in our own way. We were all on the same wavelength as we sat around and smoked, and then Sun-ja surprised us all.

"So what happened between you and Barbara after

that?" she asked, holding her crocheting and looking at me. No doubt she had been listening all along.

"She'll look for another woman. I don't have any mind to marry a lesbian. But if there's anyone who's seriously interested, tell me, because Barbara's only going to be here for a couple of weeks."

My experience with Barbara seemed strange even to these women, who had had all sorts of experiences. Even I didn't know what to make of it. But as far as I was concerned, it was something to talk about and nothing more. You can never tell what will happen in the future, but I didn't want to be a lesbian. I wanted to be a woman who wanted a man—that was the natural thing to do. I had said that to Barbara too. "I understand you," I had told her, "but I can't accept your offer."

I never would have thought that Sun-ja would be the one to show an interest in Barbara. It was the day I went home from the Monkey House. I put on my makeup a little early and left for the club around six. I wondered whether Overton would drop by while I was out. Ae-ja from next door had told me that he'd come around the night before. But I decided I didn't want to stay home.

The club was deserted. I was sitting over a martini when someone behind me called my name. I turned and saw two women several feet away. One of them was Su-jin, who also worked at the club. "Somebody's looking for you," she said, motioning to the other woman.

In the dim light, the second woman's white dress seemed to be floating in the air. An expressionless face came toward me like a mask and stopped.

"Wow, I thought you were a ghost," I said.

"I went to your place, but they said you'd left for the club. You're here early," said Sun-ja.

"Being locked up five days made me itchy, I guess. And seeing you leave yesterday didn't help matters. I just couldn't wait any longer." Before I knew it Sun-ja had taken a seat. "What brings you here?" I finally asked.

"Well. . . I wanted to ask you something. How could I meet Barbara?"

I had no idea what her intentions were. "How come you're looking for Barbara all of a sudden?"

"Introduce me to her, will you? Tell her you know a good woman who could be her friend."

"What's this all about?" I gave her a suspicious look.

"Help me out, will you?" Sun-ja's voice was subdued, but her face was cold and determined.

"How?"

"I have to get to America. You think I came to this god-forsaken area for my health? At my age? I'm not going to live in this country anymore. I want to leave any way I can."

"And so you're going to marry Barbara?" I asked, shaking my head. "It's not going to be that simple."

"It won't be any easier marrying a GI. There's lots of pretty girls around; who's going to propose to someone like me? I've heard talk about the GIs being pulled out of Korea, and if that happens there's going to be even more women around. I have to get going on this. Just introduce me to Barbara. I'll take it from there."

Before I knew it Sun-ja had grabbed my wrist. Her hand was warm but sticky. I tried to pull free. In a softer voice I said, "So you've got your heart set on being a lesbian?"

She snorted. "I'd be a monkey in a circus if I had to. It'd be better than living around here. I get more scared every day—it's like hell."

I gave up trying to talk her out of it. Sun-ja was all hot and bothered, like someone possessed. I was amazed at the blindness of her obsession, and I snatched my hand away.

"Even if I arrange for Barbara to meet you, I'm not going to be there. I'm not a pimp and it's not going to do you any good if I get involved. What's Barbara going to think if I show up acting like a marriage broker?"

"Then just let me know where I can get in touch with her. I'll do the rest myself and see what happens."

Sun-ja was so insistent, I felt like banging my head against a wall. I sighed and said, "Don't be in such a hurry. I think An's old lady could introduce you. She's the one who brought Barbara over to my place. I'll tell her about you. She won't have anything to lose, so I'm sure she'll do it."

"Then... let's go. There aren't any GIs here yet. For all I know, it might be too late already," said Sun-ja.

And so we carried it out on the spot. Like they say, strike while the iron is hot. I felt ridiculous introducing Sun-ja to An's old lady, but then I couldn't just turn my back on her. If Sun-ja had simply gone there without an introduction and started pleading her case, An's old lady probably wouldn't have taken her seriously.

Anyway, An's old lady went right along with my request, and it looked like things were going to work out. She wasn't surprised when I told her Barbara was a lesbian. Maybe she knew it from the beginning.

When I told her what Sun-ja wanted, she didn't seem particularly surprised about that, either. Half joking, I said, "It's about time she got sick and tired of men."

After she had heard me out and looked Sun-ja over, she asked, "So, all I have to do is introduce her to Barbara? And you'll pay me a commission if it's a good match?" Then she chuckled. A couple of years ago she was some hayseed's wife who couldn't even keep the family finances straight; now she was a skilled madam.

Sun-ja's appearance at the club had taken me by surprise, but by the time I got back there I'd forgotten about it. I was working again for the first time in two months. I went to the ladies' room and put on a fresh coat of lipstick. I hadn't worn makeup in a while, and I felt like my face was a rusty dish that had been polished into something quite serviceable. Also, I'd been going around in jeans all the time, but now I had a dress on that was open down the front. I looked like a different woman.

I found a table in the middle of the club, and before long a blond-haired GI with a lot of freckles approached me—I felt like my cheeks were on fire. For a second I thought it was Overton, but except for his blond hair he didn't really resemble Overton at all.

This fellow Freckles kept silent to the point of making me yawn. All he did was keep time to the music with his hands and watch people dance. His face was kind of ugly but it had some cuteness to it. Whenever I took out a cigarette he'd almost jump at me with a light and grin. He looked like he had a screw loose.

All I did was blow smoke and stare into space. Suddenly I caught sight of another blond head, and my heart started jumping. I decided to improvise, so I held my glass out and asked Freckles for more beer. He gave me another grin and poured until the head ran over the side. I gave a cheer and sucked up the foam. He filled his glass and I clinked it with mine. "Bravo!" Then I tilted my head back and started posing coquettishly.

At that moment the large hand of a strong man snatched my left wrist. Freckles' eyes opened wide in surprise. I glared at Overton and tried to shake free. He stuck his face in front of Freckles, completely ignoring me.

"Hey, friend, you're blond like me. This lady likes blond-haired men. Her fiance is blond too. Unless you have some objections, I'll be off with my lady."

"My lady!" I snorted as Overton hauled me away by the wrist. And that's how I started living with that exasperating playboy again. Actually, if it was just exasperation I felt, I couldn't have lived with him—even if he had hauled me away by the *neck*. But to tell the truth, I liked him. Although he did what he wanted, he was a cheerful type. And he was man enough to be able to grab me by the wrist and get away with it. I'd light into him for being a playboy, but I can't say I disliked that part of him.

When I first met him he was losing his head over a woman named Mi-na. Strangely, it captured my heart the way he sat in front of the dance floor all by himself and watched her dance. He was like a little boy who had lost his senses. I hung around and pestered him and finally brought him home—success! Mi-na was the best looker in the Hilltop Club, and I wasn't about to take a back seat to her. He kept saying, "I'm waiting for Mi-na," so I teased him and asked if she was his old lady. I'd gotten on his nerves needling him like this, but finally he burst into laughter and said, "Then are *you* my old lady?"

Now that we were together again, Overton was much more affectionate. He came straight home after work, and he kept us supplied with cookies and canned goods. And there were no more excuses about going out to meet a buddy—he seemed to have given up skirt-chasing for the time being.

The days he worked the graveyard shift he'd remind me to call him at work. It was funny to see him fussing like a little kid, so I did it. He always sounded happy, and I could hear him over the phone drumming on his desk while he questioned me: "No guys chased you home? No one picked a fight with you?"

It was seven days since we'd started living together again. I'd sent Overton off to work and was lying down when Ae-ja called me from next door:

"Are you sleeping?" Before I could answer, the door opened and she stepped in. "Did you hear about Mi-ra? She's dead."

I was puzzled.

"She used to come over and see Chin-hŭi once in a while. Had a smile that lit up her face, remember?"

"The tall one, right? She wore baggy clothes like a hippie—they looked good on her. She was cute. How come she's dead all of a sudden?"

"A Korean man killed her early yesterday morning. A pimp. He stuck a pair of coal tongs between her legs. Korean guys are really vicious!"

Ae-ja frowned and I shut my eyes tight. We get suicides and murders around here now and then, so those kinds of things tend to bounce off us. But this one was so brutal it made my heart ache. Mi-ra was someone I knew. I kept quiet for a while, and then Ae-ja started talking—it was an effort.

"They'll get the son of a bitch, and soon. He can run, but he won't get very far. He takes tickets at the Tae-yŏng movie theater. He's been convicted twice—drug addiction and gang fighting. They'd known each other about two years. Seems everyone around her tried to talk her out of it. But when it comes to a relationship with a man, that doesn't work. All the girls know what pimps are like, but they can't get away from them."

"She must have been lonely. You can't communicate very well with GIs."

Ae-ja glanced at me as if I'd said something strange. Damn it! I said to myself. Don't I feel lonely? Sure I do—I just don't advertise it.

Ae-ja would unravel her tale of woe about as often as she ate, and now once again she spelled out her version of the truth.

"Who can understand our loneliness? Fuck! All people think about is how to use us. Hasty has this classmate, a girls' middle school teacher, who's always coming over to see her. She always asks Hasty to get her something made in America. If I were Hasty, I'd grab that bitch by the hair and kick her out. And I've heard that some of the girls are squeezed for money by their own families. If their families can't pity them, how can they take money the girls make by having their crotches ripped open and then use it for someone's tuition? Family, friends or whatever—they're all a big headache."

Three days later we heard the murderer had been caught. Chin-hŭi, who had been pretty close to Mi-ra and had visited her house that day, told us the news. The man freely confessed his motive, saying that all Mi-ra gave him was leftovers.

"She'd live it up with the GIs and then give him leftover sex. She gave him plenty of money and secondhand clothes from the GIs, but they were leftovers too. All the bitch gave him was some damned foreigner's leftovers. That's what he told the police," Chin-hŭi said.

"The lousy son of a bitch," said Ae-ja. "He's nothing but a pimp who tried to drag down a defenseless woman. Is he the only one who's eaten leftovers? This whole country's been living off other countries' leftovers."

"What he did was hateful, but the guy had his pride," I said like a smartass. But actually the murderer's remarks hit home. Ae-ja was right. My mother told me that when I was a kid during the American military occupation I used to suck on hard candy from the relief goods until my tongue turned red. So she made me spit out any candy that colored the inside of my mouth. She'd get mad and say, "Do those little sugary things fill you up?" When I think about it now, it was our poverty that made her angry.

When I was little, the five of us in our family had to sleep under a single quilt, and we were always wrestling for a piece of it. And I grew up on leftovers from relief goods. Cornbread was what we had at school, but even before I started school I used to eat it almost every day. Since there was nothing to eat at home, I went to my sister's school at lunchtime. Next to the custodian's room was the kitchen where the yellow cornbread was baked and piled as high as a house. The custodian's wife was a generous woman, and she used to let me snoop around in there and sample the bread.

When it comes to English, I don't feel inferior to anyone around the base. I've been good at it ever since middle school. I didn't have much interest in other subjects, but English would get me excited and I worked at it without anyone forcing me. My English ability was the one thing I took pride in. Maybe it was a way of making up for being poor. When I passed the church in our neighborhood, I would sometimes see American missionaries. The white faces along with the Bibles in their hands seemed like peace itself. English was a symbol of peace and wealth to me.

I left home after running into a middle school classmate who was working at one of the American army bases. That was ten years ago, when I was an eleventh grader. Several months later I got money from a GI for the first time, and suddenly I rememberd the cornbread I ate when I was young. I realized vaguely that I'd gone back to where I started from, and I felt ashamed of myself.

By a strange coincidence, Chin-hŭi brought up the subject of Sun-ja the same day she told us about Mi-ra's murderer. Actually it's not so strange, considering what a small world it is around the base. While we were talking about Mi-ra and what a terrible shock her death was, Chin-hŭi mentioned the girls who had lived with Mi-ra.

"There were four of them," she said, "and today one of them named Sun-ja moved out. I heard she cried like a baby at Mi-ra's cremation. She said she couldn't stay there anymore because she kept hearing laughter from Mi-ra's room. She looks kind of old. By the way," she asked me, "do you happen to know her?"

"Which one?" There are more Sun-jas than you can shake a stick at, and besides, the Sun-ja I had met at the Monkey House was disappearing into the farthest corner of my memory—that's the indifferent part of me. So I was more surprised than anybody when Chin-hŭi started talking about lesbians:

"This Sun-ja seems to be a lesbian. She looks like a nice person, but there's something gloomy about her. Until a few days ago there was a black woman who was in and out of Sun-ja's room all the time. She came to Korea for emergency training, and the two of them apparently hit it off and decided to make a go of it together. Don't you remember that black woman?"

"I'll bet it's Barbara!" I exclaimed in a low voice. Chin-hŭi and Ae-ja, living under the same roof with me, knew about my experience with Barbara.

"I don't think Sun-ja told her housemates much about Barbara," Chin-hŭi went on. "She only shows off the things she wants to. The day before Barbara left for Japan the two of them went to a department store in Seoul and brought back a bunch of stuff. Having a woman's point of view, Barbara picked out things Sun-ja really needed, like a pair of tweezers. Sun-ja was amazed. Besides that, Barbara gave her a month's living expenses—two hundred dollars." Chin-hŭi tilted her head to the side in thought. "You know, I can't figure out why Barbara took up with Sun-ja. I'm afraid you lost the pot of gold at the end of the rainbow."

I knew it was a joke but I shook my head. "I don't believe in that. I can always catch the real McCoy."

I can't explain it, but from that moment, this business with Sun-ja started bothering me. When I talked with An's old lady I had made a point of telling her to go ahead and introduce Barbara to Sun-ja—but only if Sun-ja really wanted

it. And now to find that this crazy dream of hers had come
true just like she wanted—it blew me away. I had never expected it to work out so easily.

An's old lady seemed to have figured out Sun-ja's relationship with Barbara some time ago. When I asked if she'd
heard anything from Sun-ja she quickly replied, "Didn't
you know she's been coming to our club?"

"The Hilltop?" I didn't show any more surprise after
that. An's old lady was wearing a gold ring I hadn't seen before, and I guessed they'd already left me out in the cold.

Two days later I saw Sun-ja at the Hilltop. A bunch of
us were throwing a birthday party there for Harrison, one
of the gang in the Fire Brigade.

I left home before six. I'd set aside plenty of time to buy
a gift for Harrison, but I found something at the first place I
went to, a folk art shop. I picked out a long Korean traditional pipe; it seemed like a good thing for him to remember
Korea by.

I was supposed to meet Overton at the club at seven. It
would have been a pain in the neck to go back home, so I
went straight to the club even though I had some time to
kill. It was a little after six, and none of the GIs had showed
up yet. Several of the girls were sitting around a table near
the entrance. A husky voice came to me clearly as I approached the table.

"You can say what you want, but Mi-ra's more pitiful
than us. She couldn't give all her love to a Korean, or to a
GI either. A Korean man took her for all she was worth,
and she ended up dead. And what a way to die—it's too
cruel."

"Fuck! As long as we've got to die, what difference does
it make how we go?" said another girl.

"But this isn't just Mi-ra's story. The Koreans don't accept us, and neither do the Americans. Over and over we
sacrifice ourselves for dollars and we end up foreigners'
girls. Knocked around like fish on a cutting board. When
life's as hard as this, dying young just isn't fair," said someone else.

Mi-ra was the topic of conversation wherever I went. And always she represented how bad women had it.

Sun-ja was sitting at the next table chain-smoking and watching the others. She was dressed in black, and her tangled, wiry hair was held on each side by a white pin. It was a mourning outfit, but strangely enough it radiated vitality. Again the husky voice sounded.

"The first thing we should do is wake up. Why should we sacrifice our money and hearts to these Korean pricks? What good are they? GIs are cold as ice when they turn their backs on you, but they'll propose if they like you. Basically they care for women. Can you think of a Korean man who would propose to one of us?"

"The problem is that feeling doesn't always go along with thinking straight," said Chŏng-sun, one of the other girls. "I get frustrated when I see girls kept by a pimp, but I can understand them. Let's be honest: Is there any one of us who doesn't want to get along with a Korean man? At least it'd be nice to have a man we could communicate with as a friend. I wish I had a man I could see once a month—to take a trip and talk with. That's how I feel."

While Chŏng-sun was talking in her unique way, unrefined but measured, everybody became quiet. Both the girl with the husky voice and Chŏng-sun with her straight talk were right.

I was just about to sit down when I saw a man come through the door. I took a better look and saw he was Korean—a short, young fellow with ordinary features. He scanned the interior, then went straight to a table in the middle of the club. Soon we were all staring at him, but he remained composed even after glancing at us.

"He's Korean, isn't he?"

"He must be crazy. What's he doing here?"

Koreans aren't allowed in the clubs around the base. Since it was still early, perhaps the bouncer had stepped out for a moment and not noticed him. The man gestured to one of the waitresses. She walked over to him with a sassy look and took his order. A moment later she plunked down a bottle of beer on his table and left. The man ignored our stares and filled his glass.

A girl with an acne-ridden face was the first to approach him. She was the one with the husky voice. The others giggled. The girl stood in front of him, her hand on her hip.

"Hey, you, what do you think you're doing here?"

The man looked up slack-jawed, blinked, tossed down his beer and refilled the glass. He didn't seem to be fazed.

Chŏng-sun and another girl approached him. Chŏng-sun started making snide remarks: "Look at you, so calm and collected. How about passing the glass and sharing instead of drinking by yourself, Mister Stone Heart?"

"What's a Korean man doing here?" said the other girl. "You don't even think we're human outside the club."

Then I heard a high, shaky voice: "There's the door. Get out!" I looked up. Before you could snap your fingers, Sun-ja had moved right in front of the man. With her hair and her black clothing trailing behind her, she looked like a witch. "Get out!" she shouted again, pointing to the door.

The rest of the girls joined the crowd and took turns making fun of the man, who sat there like a stone Buddha. Finally he emptied his bottle and got up, with Sun-ja still standing over him. He gave her a stony look and walked toward the door. Laughter broke out behind him. The man brushed past me and spit out two words in a low voice: "Fucking bitches." It was his way of calling us whores.

When you think about it, the area around an American army base is like an island between Korea and the U.S. An island is only an island—not part of the sea, not part of the mainland. And those of us on the island are only whores for Westerners. Ignored by our motherland, we're temporary sweethearts, nameless "honeys" for the GIs.

Since the GIs are stationed in Korea "as a right, not a duty," as the Americans would say, the island around a base is not genuinely Korean. And when that political tidal wave they call troop withdrawal surges over us, the island becomes a wasteland in a second. That's what happened in Unch'on, the first island I landed on. The GIs were pulled out of Camp Kaiser Number One and overnight Unch'on was ruined. "Out of Business" signs were everywhere and the clubs were nailed shut with two planks in the form of an X across the doors. Hundreds of girls were scattered like dandelion spores.

Since these islands have no roots, the girls living on them have no roots there either. They know full well they can't rely on the islands, and that's why they have a pimp— or long for a one-way ticket to the U.S. Mi-ra and Sun-ja were just extreme cases of this.

Sun-ja had quite a past. Here was a woman who did day labor for other families from the time she was young, only to grow up to be a housekeeper who was raped by her employer. It sounds like a common enough story, but she was treated like an animal by the family. The man of the house slipped into her room whenever he was feeling his oats. As a result, Sun-ja had two children by him while living under the same roof with his family. The man's wife put up with it all in order to keep Sun-ja tied to the family and working like a slave. Sun-ja washed their college-age daughter's clothing, even her underwear, and practically ran their rice mill by herself. Meanwhile, her older child lost four fingers playing in the mill.

Her rude, ignorant life was the reason Sun-ja had this wild dream about going to America. She lost her love for her motherland, and the dream became an obsession. Ultimately this thick-headed blindness carried her to her death.

That night at the Hilltop Club was the last time I saw Sun-ja. A week and a half later I heard she had fallen down the stairs from the second floor of the club and died of brain damage. Her poor, ignorant parents were called to the scene and asked about surgery, but they sneaked away without deciding what to do. An, the owner of the club, contributed some money for her medical expenses, and then washed his hands of the affair. According to the doctor, she would have been a vegetable if she had lived. In this meaningless way, she left the world of the living for the eternal America of her dreams.

The circumstances of Sun-ja's life came to light the day after she died. The girls who lived with her thought she was just another divorcee. They hadn't been aware of the in-human treatment she had suffered. Having finally found out, they could only nod their heads in wonder.

Her housemates knew only two sides of her: the way she sat and crocheted all day without budging, and the way she looked when she was drunk. When she drank, as one of the girls at the club put it, she drank until it came out her ears. Then she went around the tables badgering the GIs to buy her another drink. "She didn't attract GIs," the girl continued. "She drove them away." Maybe she was having that kind of a night when she fell down the stairs.

As the news spread about Sun-ja's death, the GIs stopped coming to the club. This was the only real effect of her death that I could see. I went to her cremation and with my own hands sent her ashes floating down the river. Before they could call to mind her face, the ashes had slipped between my fingers and disappeared without a trace.

The same day, a letter for Sun-ja arrived from Japan: "I love you and your agony. I hope I can be your savior. Think of our meeting as a blessing and please plan for our future."

Enclosed was a photo of Barbara showing her evenly spaced teeth in a smile. She looked as beautiful as a black pearl. I couldn't believe Sun-ja had tried so frantically to get this miraculous pearl that seemed sent by the gods. But then she had believed in that dream of hers, and perhaps she had been happy during her brief time with Barbara.

Everything returned to normal. An's old lady kept saying what lousy luck it was, but she continued to wear the gold ring. The club recovered. Everybody forgets as time wears on.

Sun-ja's landlord could breathe easy. He said her death had prevented a disaster by drawing Mi-ra's spirit away from his house. He claimed that if she and Mi-ra had both died there, the place would have been haunted.

A "Room for Rent" notice was posted on the gate of the house Sun-ja had moved to so recently. Spring became balmy and from one day to the next, dark pink blossoms spread like a watercolor over the wall of the house.

It wasn't long before Overton would return to his homeland. On Friday, four days before his departure, he came home from the base and asked me for a camera I'd been keeping for him. He said he was going out to take some photos with a buddy.

I gave him a hard look and told him I'd left it at a friend's. It was a lie, of course. I didn't plan to lie, but then I didn't feel like handing over the camera without a fight.

Overton shook his head. "Come on now, don't act like that. I promised this guy."

"The only people who go around with a camera at night are the ones who take nude pictures. Is that what you're up to?"

"What the hell's the matter with you?" said Overton.

"You should have told me before. It's Friday night— my friend went out somewhere."

"Bullshit!"

Suddenly his face was all twisted. I was sitting nonchalantly on the edge of the bed, about to pour myself another glass of peach champagne. He came toward me with big strides. His mouth was clamped shut and his eyes were hard slits. I scowled at him and moved near the head of the bed. He stuck his hand out.

"I'll ask you again. Give me the camera."

"I told you, I don't have it. It's in the pawnshop. Give me some money if you want it back."

He lunged toward me, and instinctively I threw the champagne bottle at him. He dodged it and the bottle flew into the mirror on the dresser. There was a sharp crash, and I could see glass splinters glittering behind him.

He was on top of me before I could escape—one hand holding me down by my hair, which was spread out on the bed, the other hand on my neck. Since I couldn't move my head, I tried to squirm free with my legs, but then he squeezed them between his knees and I was trapped.

I felt like I was being tied up. "Son of a bitch!" I shouted. He started choking me. I saw stars, and then I couldn't breathe and my insides felt like they were about to explode. My body started shaking, and his hands finally loosened a bit. I yanked my head to the side and bit his arm. He howled and rolled off me. I sprang up, climbed over him, and jumped down from the bed. The silver bits of the mirror seemed to be flowing in front of me. I was about to kick open the door when a piece of the bottle flew by me, grazing my leg and shattering a couple of steps ahead. I skipped across the mess and got away.

As I ran toward the neighborhood police station I felt something missing near one of my knees. I stopped for a moment and looked down. The right knee of my jeans was ripped; I had nearly been cut.

The first thing I did in the police station was look in the mirror. My neck was already discolored. It looked as if black petals had been printed on it. I showed the marks to an MP.

"Look at this. One of your damn men tried to choke me. I want to press charges."

The MP studied my neck and gave me a knowing smile.

"If he used a deadly weapon against you, you could demand compensation. But marks like that'll be gone in no time. No way you'll be able to collect."

"Can't you put him in jail?"

"If you press charges, he'll be deported."

The MP just kept on smiling, so I gave up and left. I went straight to Chŏng-sun's, and ran into Overton in front of her gate. Whenever I had a fight with him, I'd run over to her place and hide out. He knew that, and there he was waiting for me. I started shouting as soon as I saw him.

"I pressed charges. You're going behind bars. We'll see how you like rotting away in jail for a while."

"You know, I really liked you. I never thought about you as a business girl—but you acted like one, lying to me about the camera. I felt betrayed. But it's okay now—you don't have to return it."

He looked like he was about to cry, and his arms hung loose as if he was exhausted. I smiled complacently. I'd been growling at him the past few days for no good reason, and the fight today was more of the same. Maybe I was raising more of a fuss because his day of departure was approaching. It was my way of loving him.

The day before he left, Overton asked me for an address where he could get in touch with me. He told me he had come to Korea two months after getting married, and the idea of having a wife hadn't seemed very real. Now he felt as if he was leaving his real wife, and he promised to write from the States.

I started giggling and told him I didn't need his letters. If he could just give me ten dollars, I'd call his name even in my dreams. It goes without saying that I didn't give him an address.

The next day, Overton called me before boarding the plane. He told me to come over to the base and he'd give me some money. I ran there like the wind, and he stuffed two hundred dollars in my hand saying, "Pay off what you owe your madam." I gave him a violent kiss. I'd paid off my debt to the madam a long time ago, but I still had plenty of places to spend the money.

A Room in the Woods

Kang Sŏk-kyŏng

1

ONCE AGAIN my younger sister So-yang hadn't come home. That made two nights in a row, and not a word from her. Not so long before, in cases like this she would have had a friend call home for her and ask Mother if she could stay out. Mother would in effect say yes by asking the friend's telephone number. But then So-yang announced she was leaving school and proceeded to surprise us with one thing after another—not only staying out as she pleased but refusing to explain, even after being slapped by Father.

The news that So-yang had dropped out really shocked us. I was the first to know, and the events of that night a month ago have become vivid in my mind. So-yang had left that day to pay her second semester's tuition. It was sultry from early morning, and the heat seemed to collect in my lower back. It was nearly eleven at night when So-yang finally returned.

Everyone must have been asleep downstairs; no one stirred even when the bell from the front gate rang for the third time. Our baby brother, Chŏng-u, who stayed up late studying, usually answered the bell at that hour, but he seemed to be asleep as well. I clicked my tongue as I went downstairs, annoyed with So-yang before I had even opened the gate.

I wasn't in a very good mood. I'd had a slight disagree-

ment with my fiancé after work that day, and I arrived
home to hear Mother and Grandmother arguing.

"And it's not just the black beans—all the other side
dishes are sweet too," Grandmother was complaining.
"You're not thinking about my health. Older people are
liable to develop diabetes if they take in that much sugar."

Mother countered that as far as she was concerned,
Grandmother was overly sensitive about her health—if she
wouldn't worry about every little thing she'd easily live to a
hundred.

Instead of responding to this, Grandmother started in
on So-yang: the girl was always flitting about and coming
in late without permission. This wouldn't happen in a good
family.

This indirect attack on Mother was unreasonable of
Grandmother, and the squabble between the two women
intensified. I had often witnessed these childish scenes, but
still, my dinner sat like a rock in my stomach, and I couldn't
get to sleep.

Anyway, I went outside, and by the time I'd reached the
gate I was scolding So-yang out loud for being late. But
there was no response from the other side, so I asked who
was there.

"It's me." So-yang's voice was subdued.

I opened the gate without thinking twice about this, and
was startled to see an adhesive bandage on her nose. She
brushed past me, then went in the front door and straight to
her room. I glanced at the window of our parents' room. It
was dark. I tiptoed inside and went upstairs.

I found So-yang, her skirt thrown aside, pacing about
her room in her T-shirt and panties. She wasn't tall, but
from childhood she had developed her body through dancing, and her legs were long and wiry like a bird's.

"What happened to your nose?" I asked right off.

So-yang looked at me calmly, but her eyes were
gloomy. "I got hit," she said offhandedly as though she
might have been whistling.

I was at a loss. Was this the way kids talked these days?

Did this mean that she—a girl, no less—had gotten into a fight? I looked more closely and saw that one of her nostrils was stuffed with cotton.

"Are you an alley cat or something, getting a bloody nose? Just look at yourself."

"A pickpocket did it. I caught him with my tuition money and this is what the guy did to me. My blood's all over the street."

So-yang removed her T-shirt and flung it beside me. A sour, sweaty smell filled the air. Wearing just her under-clothes, her nose bandaged, So-yang resembled a boxer's mistress who had taken a beating.

"Really?" I asked skeptically.

"Can't you see?" she retorted bluntly, thrusting her head through a sacklike cotton crepe nightie.

"Good lord, when did this happen? Did you get the money back? You should have called home first, but instead you go traipsing around until all hours of the night looking like that."

So-yang whirled around and flew at me: "Sister, can't you even ask how badly I'm hurt? Can't you see I'm in pain?" It was venom and not just irritation that filled her expression. Her teeth were bared like those of a dog.

I recoiled and lowered my voice. "And what about school? Did you go anyway?"

"I'm dropping out. I'll tell Mom tomorrow." She stuck a comb in her short, thick hair and gathered some fresh underwear.

All I could do was stare at her as she left for the bathroom. Her defiant tone had made me shrink, and I gathered from her words that she had nothing more to say to me. Then I realized I hadn't seen So-yang face to face like this for some time.

The next morning So-yang didn't come down for breakfast. I had intended to give Mother a hint of what had happened, but I decided to wait until after work. I wasn't sure if So-yang had been telling the truth, and I wanted to be certain I had understood her correctly.

What So-yang had told me weighed on my mind throughout the day. Then about three Mother called. She immediately asked if I would be seeing Mr. Ch'oe that evening and coming home late. Mr. Ch'oe was my fiance. Our wedding was approaching, and in a few days I would be leaving the bank where we both worked, so we were going out almost every day after work.

"What is it?" I asked.

"Oh my," said Mother with an odd sound that was different from a sigh. I suspected it was because of So-yang.

"I'll be home as soon as I finish work, Mom." I was not usually that friendly and informal in my speech with Mother. My spirits lifted when I recalled that she always consulted me about serious matters, even if Father was there. I became sentimental at the thought that I would soon be leaving home.

As I had expected, Mother began talking about So-yang when I returned. "I always tell myself three daughters is just right, and when one of them marries the house will seem big and empty. These days I feel as if something is missing. Why can't So-yang realize that and stop worrying me so much?"

"Did she say she'd left school?" I asked abruptly.

"She told you?" Mother looked surprised.

I told her about So-yang coming home with the bandage on her nose and about what she had said to me. "Did she say she'd lost her tuition money?" I added. This was the biggest question in my mind.

Mother clicked her tongue. "I asked her if that was why she was leaving school, but she said no."

That meant she really *had* lost the money.

"Then what was the reason?"

"I don't understand it either," Mother asserted. "She says it's because of scarlet sages."

"Scarlet sages?" I pressed Mother for an explanation.

"Well, I'll tell you what she told me."

Apparently So-yang had felt a sudden impulse to leave school. Clearly she had left home the previous day intending to pay her tuition. True, she had wasted one semester of school, and she realized that the semester about to begin would be just as tiresome. But these weren't the thoughts that had aroused her unusual urge.

So-yang had fallen in with a large group of students who were also going to pay their tuition. She felt as if she had been squeezed among them. As soon as they entered the campus, a bed of scarlet sages caught her eye. The scarlet was so intense that it seemed to pour into her. The flowers appeared to be dripping fresh blood beneath the late summer sun. Her only feeling was that she was drowning in a surging throng of crimson flowers.

"And so she dropped out of school," Mother concluded. "That was her reason."

I gaped at Mother. Was So-yang that strange? I tried to imagine what incident was entangled with the scarlet sages. A bed of scarlet sages blazing under the late summer sun—was that all there was to it? And fresh blood dripping? I couldn't identify in the slightest with an expression like that!

I frowned and cocked my head in thought. "The kids these days, really!" I muttered, clicking my tongue. "Did something happen to her?" I asked Mother.

Then it occurred to me that So-yang might have spent the tuition money. Because I worked at a bank I was well aware that once people get their paws on money there's no stopping them. I remembered a teller who had begun removing one bill at a time from bundles of money—first a thousand wŏn and then five thousand. She had ended up pocketing customers' deposits. If the tellers, who ought to have been precise as clockwork, could do such things, then how easy for So-yang to have spent the tuition money she had in her hand.

Next I tried to imagine what she might have done with the money. Normally So-yang liked to spend money and pretty herself up. But she wasn't the sort to throw away her tuition on luxuries or amusements. Perhaps she had spent it on someone else?

My impoverished imagination settled on a man as the recipient, and I wondered if he was one of the college students we often read about in the newspapers who were being sought by the authorities for participating in the antigovernment movement.

Mother, for her part, seemed to be reasoning out the situation. She had taken a sounder approach than I, asking So-yang if she had been expelled because of a student demonstration. "She told me she would have been happy to have such a good reason for leaving school," Mother continued. "I just can't understand it. But then the fact we're trying so hard to understand her proves she's hard to figure out, doesn't it?"

It took me an instant to fathom Mother's meaning, and then I glanced at her. She liked to think of herself as clear-headed, and so she talked just like a grade school girl reading a book out loud. I secretly disapproved of her cold, heartless analysis, which seemed so unlike Mother.

Why in the world was So-yang dropping out? I asked myself. There was no good reason. Whether she was looking for a job or getting married, the first thing to do was finish school.

I argued that we should first persuade So-yang to change her mind about leaving school. That scarlet sages could have such an impact on her—it was not as if she were a Spanish bull! As one who detested anything illogical, I spoke decisively.

But once the withdrawal form was submitted, Mother replied, it was impossible to retract it. This was a letdown.

"Shouldn't the school check with the family if a student has reached the point of dropping out?" Mother asked with resignation in her voice. "Are colleges just supposed to let students go their own way?" Now she was blaming the innocent schools.

Not until then did I ask Mother if she had called the school.

"Do you think she would say she dropped out if she hadn't? More likely the other way around," she said stiffly.

But then she revealed the true reason: "If I called, don't you think they'd say, 'You're her mother and you don't know?'"

I had become quite frustrated. You're thinking only of yourself, I nearly told Mother. Instead I said emphatically, "We have to take matters into our own hands and see if we can change her mind. Why do we need parents and brothers and sisters, anyway? What are families for? If a child wanders, or stumbles, we have to help her along."

I decided to call So-yang's school. Mother felt terribly awkward talking with strangers, and so the burden fell on me. I would meet with So-yang's French professor and figure out a way to retract that withdrawal form. Persuading So-yang would come next.

I made the call at lunchtime the next day. I reached the French Department and asked the office assistant if the department chairman was in. I had no choice but to pose the question that way, for I didn't know the professor's name. He wasn't there, and when the woman asked my name I had to reveal that I was the older sister of a sophomore named Yi So-yang.

"Yi So-yang, Yi So-yang... oh yes, the one who left school."

The idea that So-yang was a dropout made me uncomfortable, so I said hesitantly, "So-yang said she turned in a withdrawal form yesterday...." Then I told her why I had called. Like other young people these days, So-yang was acting independent, so to speak, and without any warning she told us she had dropped out of school. But she hadn't obtained her parents' consent, and therefore we wanted to find out if there was some way to reverse her action.

I heard nothing at the other end, and had to say "Hello" before I could get a response.

"You say you're Yi So-yang's older sister?" she queried tentatively. Then her tone changed and she quickly asked, "You say she turned in a withdrawal form yesterday? Actually she dropped out during spring semester."

It was my turn to be speechless. What on earth was she

talking about? Wasn't she mistaking So-yang for another student?

"It was Yi So-yang who dropped out in the spring?" I asked.

"There's no one else in the department with that name. She kept her hair short, right?" the office assistant said, putting an edge to her words.

I closed my eyes tight, feeling as if the roof had caved in. Whatever else I had to say was lost, but I felt I had to say something. I was barely able to ask where I could confirm So-yang's dropping out.

"Try the Student Affairs Office."

"Mmm, could you tell me if she's been in any trouble—a demonstration, perhaps?"

"If she had, I'm sure the family would have known."

If the office assistant had been the least bit cordial, I would have asked more about So-yang and then visited her professors. But having lost face, I ended the conversation there. The girl had been out of school for several months now, and we hadn't known about it.... If Mother had called, she probably would have been troubled more by her shame before the office assistant than by So-yang's having left school in the spring.

As long as I had gone this far, I decided to call the Student Affairs Office. But as the office assistant had said, there was only one Yi So-yang in the French Department, and she had withdrawn from school during spring semester. I inquired about the date, but it seemed the school had no more time for me: I was told to come and find out for myself, and the line went dead.

For the rest of the day, my mind wandered from my work as I thought about So-yang. The afternoon was a disaster. I would count a sum of money twice and still not be sure I had it correct, and I misread the amount on a withdrawal slip as 3,000,000 wŏn instead of 300,000.

What troubled me the most was what a sharp little kid she'd become. That talk about scarlet sages and a pickpocket was all lies. All this time she'd completely deceived the family. I suppose I had an excuse, because I went to work every day. But Mother was home all the time, and to think she hadn't known! That was how superb So-yang's performance had been.

I remembered So-yang coming home late several times, her book bag over her shoulder. Last May, after a spell of this, I encountered her on the veranda one night and told her coldly not to come home so late. "I've been at the library studying for exams," she had said, rubbing her eyes wearily. And I remembered the book she had dropped as she entered her room. It was by Camus, in the original French. I was proud of her, and I told myself I would give her some pocket money the following payday. Unlike So-yang and our other sister Hye-yang, an honor student from grade school through high school who now attended medical school, I didn't have much interest in studying. Mother detected this early, and thanks to her I was able to study piano. Even so, I always respected learning, though I did not admit this to anyone.

How to tell Mother—this was what agonized me about So-yang. To Mother, who was so proud of herself, being taken in by her own daughter would feel more like betrayal than anything else. I wondered if Mother's reaction might cause her to push So-yang farther in the wrong direction, instead of trying to understand and reason with her.

After all, this was the same woman who had given me the cold shoulder for two weeks after I tried to quit piano in middle school without telling her. Unable to endure this treatment, I had burst into tears, pleading with her that I had made a mistake. If I had continued to stand up to her, who knows how long the cold war would have dragged on. As I thought of that incident, bitterness toward her welled up in me anew.

It occurred to me that rather than tell Mother, it might not be a bad idea to try to persuade So-yang to reregister. I could say to So-yang, "I'll tell Mother and get the money for you." If that didn't suit her (the women in our family hated asking favors), I could loan her the money. I'd even tell her, "I'll steal it from the bank if only you'll go back to school."

Such thoughts quickly made me realize that I had been neglecting So-yang to the point of forgetting she even existed. So-yang's deception was a measure of our lack of attention to her. It was not that we didn't love her, but even so I felt apologetic toward her.

I hurried home that day after telling Mr. Ch'oe over a cup of tea that I had something to do there. Father had already returned and was reading the paper. I went upstairs, but before going to my room I tiptoed to So-yang's door and put my ear to it. Light came from under the door to Grandmother's room at the head of the stairs, but there was not a sound from either room. The second floor was quiet.

I stealthily turned the doorknob, but it stopped partway around. Perhaps she was asleep, I thought, but when I knocked there was still no sign of life. She was gone, it seemed.

I was somewhat surprised: the four of us children were not in the habit of locking our doors. I wasn't sure how long So-yang had been doing this, but the previous year, at any rate, I had used her room several times on Sundays when she was gone. It was a good place for a nap because it faced the north and didn't get the sun.

That evening I made a point of eating by myself. When I was called for dinner I said I'd come down after taking a bath. It was not that I didn't know how to begin talking about So-yang; rather, the words would stick in my throat with Chŏng-u and Grandmother there. And hot-blooded Father's first reaction might be to throw his spoon.

When I went downstairs, my hair still wet, Father and Chŏng-u were in the living room watching television and Mother was just finishing the dishes. I went in the kitchen, closing the door after me.

Mother, who was about to clean some bundles of young radishes on the table, glanced at the closed door. "Why are you doing that? It's hot in here."

I took a seat and asked if So-yang had returned.

"She was here during the day, but when I came back from the market she was gone. No one else was home, and she didn't even lock the gate."

I stirred the chilled seaweed soup in front of me and then said all at once, "So-yang dropped out of school some time ago."

"What do you mean?" Mother fixed her eyes on me.

Naturally she didn't understand. I ate calmly and told Mother what I had found out at So-yang's school.

Leaving the radishes piled on the table, Mother listened to me, her mouth open. Her eyes had a strange look, as if she were trying to detect whether I was lying. I told Mother everything, including my embarrassment at having to question the office assistant about a member of my own family. I concluded that the only thing to do was to confirm the facts with So-yang.

Mother took a gulp of my barley tea, then inadvertently tipped over the glass, spilling the rest of it. "I've had all you children and now one of you turns out peculiar," she said, wiping up the tea mechanically. Her voice was trembling. No doubt the news had shocked her.

To give Mother some time to calm herself, I asked if Father knew.

She shook her head. "I was intending to tell him after hearing the details from you, but your father will never understand this business about scarlet sages and such. . . . "

"Mom, why didn't you sit So-yang down today and talk with her? Do you know what she's talking about when she says she's leaving school because of scarlet sages? Does it make any sense to you? Whether it does or not, it's not the truth, is it?"

"I meant to talk with her," she said in a low tone as she began trimming the roots from one of the radishes, "but I was afraid."

"Afraid of what?" My eyes pressed her for an answer.

Mother pretended in vain to be cleaning the radishes, but then, as if short of breath, she heaved a great sigh. "I don't have the confidence to talk with her face to face. I tell you, the way she looked with her nose black and blue when she told me about those scarlet sages. . . when she looked right at me and said I wouldn't understand even if she told me a hundred times. . . I just stared at her in a daze and wondered if this girl was really my own flesh and blood."

It had chilled her, Mother added, even more than the time her second brother, whom I had never met, suddenly joined the Communist party and began calling his family members "Comrade" during the violent split between rightists and leftists following Liberation in 1945. I felt the comparison was slightly exaggerated, but such was the shock So-yang had given Mother.

"Well, Mom, are you going to just look on throughout this affair?"

Instead of answering, Mother said, "So So-yang left school last spring. Why would she have deceived me? My heart is pounding." She pressed down on her chest with her hand.

Seeing Mother so agitated after her composure of the previous day, I realized that this matter was more important that I had thought. A black cloud seemed suddenly to have descended upon the family. And when I thought about my wedding, two months away, I became anxious.

"Mom, how did this happen?" I asked abruptly, looking at her intently.

"It's not as if I did something wrong. . . . " Biting her fleshy lower lip, Mother began breaking the stems off the radishes. For the first time in my life she looked feeble to me. Deep wrinkles had appeared beneath her eyes. I felt a warmth for her that I hadn't experienced in a long time. Even if it was just until my marriage, I wanted to be a source of strength for my mother, to have a mission or duty as the oldest daughter in the family. I came to regard this problem with So-yang as the final task given to me.

So-yang didn't come home that night. I stayed up until two, waiting for her and thinking about her. First I tried to find out why she had cut herself off from everyone. The problem, I came to realize, lay in our family's individualistic lifestyle.

As adolescents we took care of our own business and never interfered with each other. This individualism was made possible by the fact that each of us had a separate room. I had had my own room since I was young; Hye-yang and So-yang had shared a room through middle school, but when we moved to this two-story house five years ago, they had moved into rooms of their own.

I remember vividly how happy So-yang was with her new room, and Hye-yang with hers. The first thing So-yang did was hang a poster of the Beatles on her wall. Then she pestered Mother and had the old record player in the parlor moved to her room. Every day after that the sound of pop music came from her room, and in no time she was coming home with flowers and candles. It seemed most of her pocket money went for such things, and within six months her room was filled with dried flowers and colored candles. She was in high school then, and just at the age where girls did such things, but in satisfying her aesthetic taste she was like a starving person eating: she didn't know when to stop.

One evening I heard a song by Leonard Cohen, a folk singer I liked, coming from So-yang's room. I decided to pay a visit. The room was lit by a dozen or so candles that looked like little spirits, and the shadows of the flowers that covered the ceiling gave the effect of frost on a window.

I entered the cavelike room cautiously and discovered So-yang lying toward the wall, her back to the candlelight. Something resembling a bat was huddled above her head. It was a black umbrella. The sight of So-yang lying under that umbrella was grotesque, but it also seemed mystical, perhaps because of the candles.

The light from the flames glanced off the black cloth of the umbrella and scattered. So-yang was motionless, her eyes closed. Having lapsed into a world of her own, she was unaware I had entered her room. But that's it—a world of her own! Only now has the right expression for it come to mind. Unable to endure the light from the candles burning like a charm, which she herself had lit, she was intercepting it with the umbrella.

My impression of that night makes me shudder. Without So-yang knowing it, I slipped out of her room. So-yang seemed to be living in a different world. But by recognizing the age difference between us I could easily acknowledge the space she needed.

After that I didn't have the chance to observe So-yang carefully. I didn't worry about her because she remained an honor student as always, whether or not she lit the candles and used the umbrella in her room. In short, I believed in So-yang and secretly I expected more of her than Mother did.

Much earlier I had been truly affectionate toward this sister who was so much more talented than I. Her artistic sense was extraordinary, to the point that she learned to play piano by looking over my shoulder as I practiced. From childhood she was so good at dancing that her instructor, ignoring the jealousy of the other students, would always have her demonstrate in front of the class. Her supple movements were delightful, as was her dancing, which, unlike that of most children, was imbued with passion. Whenever I had the time I would accompany her to class and help her on with her ballet shoes.

While in middle school So-yang caught the eye of her physical education instructor, who had her begin figure skating. I was never busier than during my first year of college, but I would occasionally skate with So-yang at the East Gate Rink, where she practiced. Deft as a bird, she traced circles on the ice, her arms spread. Although her looks didn't equal her sisters', when she danced on the ice she was so beautiful she captivated me.

Our estrangement surely started when our family moved to the two-story house. So-yang was able to have her own room, and around that time I was experiencing the greatest agony of my life. I fell into a severe depression, and for almost a year my conversation with the family was barely worthy of the name. And after I graduated from college the job at the bank fell into my lap and I became busy adjusting to life in the real world.

Throughout high school So-yang would poke around my room and wouldn't hesistate to borrow my Brahms and Bach records, but after she unexpectedly failed the entrance examination at the college she wanted to attend, her visits became infrequent. Like me during my depression, she felt it was too much of a bother to talk with the family, and so she shut herself in her room, even on Sunday. Now and then she would come home smelling of liquor, but none of us scolded her because we assumed she was discouraged at having to wait a year before she could apply to college again. Fortunately, So-yang was accepted the following year at the school she chose, and she seemed to find a new life for herself, wearing cheery clothing and joining various campus circles.

The break in our relations was not unrelated to Hye-yang's tendency to be a bookworm. Hye-yang was the kind of girl who would practice writing words in English in the film of water inside the lid of her rice bowl before beginning her meal. While still in high school she would write in English on any available surface, such as the top of the dining table where water had spilled or a bus window covered with frost. When Grandmother asked us to say grace, Hye-yang would reply in English, "I am an atheist—a-t-h-e-i-s-t." Grandmother and the rest of us, who didn't understand English, became fed up with her behavior and didn't try to communicate with her.

English nearly caused Hye-yang to be put on probation by the Christian high school she attended. Every morning she left home at daybreak and waited outside a missionary's house so she could speak English with this teacher on their way to school. She did this rain or shine, and eventually the rumor spread that Hye-yang was having an affair with the man. The rumor came to the attention of the school authorities, and Mother was called to school. Some time later Hye-yang's homeroom teacher revealed to her classmates the truth of the matter: Hye-yang's affair was not with the missionary but with the English language.

Hye-yang was such a tenacious student that she would sleep at her desk. Sometimes, in spite of my requests to use the bathroom, she would sit on the toilet reciting the process of digestion from the esophagus to the large intestine, adding the appropriate chemical symbols. This irritated me to no end.

It was no wonder that So-yang, after freeing herself of Hye-yang's influence, became absorbed in music and began buying candles and flowers as if she hungered for them. I was aware that So-yang had once dreamed of becoming a biologist. She was excited by Mendel's theories of genetics and said she would become a genetic engineer and develop good genes.

Artistically talented So-yang may have been influenced by Hye-yang in her dream of studying. The two of them got along quite well, but they seemed to have grown apart after they began using their own rooms and after Hye-yang went to college.

There is no denying that in one sense our family's individualism began with Mother. She was a woman of intense self-respect, proud of having graduated from a top-flight girls' high school. She had been a good student, and she excelled at sewing women's summer clothing with silk gauze linings and elaborately seamed hems. I was told that before marriage she had been besieged with women offering prospective suitors. It is quite possible that Father's family, which was newly wealthy from a mining enterprise, became infatuated with Mother, who, though poor, was equipped with brains, beauty and manual skill.

Father had avoided studying like the plague and had not finished the five-year secondary school instituted by the Japanese. Instead he helped Grandfather in his business. He was always proud of our intelligent mother and devoted to her. It was clear to my sisters and me that the common element in our given names—Yang, meaning sheep—was meant to reflect Mother's birth in the year of the sheep.

Even now Mother turns out casual outfits on her sewing machine. She has made Father enough dressing gowns and bathrobes for a fashion show, and when my sisters and I were young, everything we wore was made by her— dresses with crimson pockets resembling strawberries, and overcoats with a big round collar like that of a nun's habit. I

remember even now that those clothes of mine, so un-
conventional then, always attracted the stares of the other
children.

I alone inherited this talent of Mother's, but although I
could knit sweaters and make simple outfits merely by
looking at the patterns, I could never equal Mother's handi-
work.

Mother was so flawless that she could never be happy
with anything less than perfection, and so she rarely com-
plimented her daughters. This point distinguished her from
other mothers and aroused our displeasure. It prevented us
from expecting praise from others or becoming caught up
in ourselves, but on the other hand we felt we received none
of the little kindnesses that mothers usually show their children.

As I grew older I happened to discover something else
about Mother that displeased me: she kept me at a certain
distance, as if I were another woman instead of her own
daughter. This occasionally made me feel awkward. For example, one day I was talking with Mother in our parents'
room on the ground floor. I got up to use the adjoining
bathroom, but Mother said, "There's some laundry in
there. . . . " Then she added coldly, "Why don't you use one
of the other bathrooms?" I realized, of course, that this was
the bathroom Mother and Father used, but she had looked
at me with distaste as if I were a stranger.

After that I generally steered clear of their room, and if I
did happen to go there I would glance at the bathroom and
imagine the two of them in there naked. "You think you're
so high and mighty, but you're animals," I would grumble,
feeling vengeful. In any event, the memory of this incident
would upset me from time to time.

And that was not all. Mother was incomparably laughable in one respect: she was extremely shy. During our
graduation festival, for example, the students in the College
of Music held an art show, for which I submitted some calligraphy. Naturally I invited Mother, and when the day
came she was giddy as a child about everything, even the

clothes she would wear. But she never appeared at the exhibition, having heard that parents would be expected to write some comments in the guest book with a traditional writing brush.

And in this matter of dealing with So-yang, Mother's passive attitude upset me. When I called her the next morning from work, all she did was gripe.

"So-yang had one of her friends call this morning to explain, but it won't do her any good. Last night I told your father about her, and there won't be any peace in the house this evening."

"Did you tell him she left school?" I asked cautiously.

"Of course," Mother replied unconcernedly.

I wish she had had a serious talk with So-yang before informing Father, I told myself. The fur is going to fly, and there's nothing I can do about it now.

The next day was my last at the bank, and so that evening I was to join the women from the other departments for dinner. Occupied though I was with So-yang, this appeared to be my only opportunity to have dinner with my co-workers. So instead of canceling the engagement I explained to them that something had come up at home, and they were understanding enough to cut short our evening.

It was not quite nine when I reached the front gate of our house.

"Who is it?" Mother asked over the intercom.

"It's Mi-yang," I answered immediately. "Did So-yang come home?"

"Wait," Mother said, and the intercom went dead.

Mother herself opened the gate for me. As I heard her come out the front door, I sensed something had already happened inside. Just as I suspected, anguish showed on Mother's face.

"Try to be quiet. Father's giving So-yang a scolding. And she hasn't even eaten yet."

The muffled sound we heard at the front door became clearer as we went inside. So-yang was sitting on one of the sofas, facing Father. Father, sitting upright on the edge of the other sofa, looked unsteady. So-yang, in contrast, buried in the plush sofa, loked comfortable, like a reclining cat.

"There's no excuse for deceiving your parents. I know that kids these days don't listen to their parents and do whatever they want, but you've gone too far—you deceived us. Don't you know any better than to make fools out of your parents? Is this the kind of thing they teach you at college?"

Father glanced at me as he was talking, but So-yang kept her eyes on the coffee table between them and remained silent. Except for her immobility, I wouldn't have known she was receiving a scolding, she appeared so nonchalant.

"I'm home," I said. I went upstairs, quickly changed, and came back down. I had already eaten, but I thought I would have a few spoonfuls of something in the kitchen. That way I could listen to Father and So-yang.

"How are we supposed to know what's going on inside that head of yours if you don't talk to us? What's your complaint? What's the problem? I'll tell you what your problem is—luxury!"

I walked by them as Father plied So-yang with these questions, but she ignored me as before. She was still buried comfortably in the sofa, her head propped against one of her palms.

The kitchen table was set for two.

"So So-yang hasn't eaten yet?"

Mother shook her head and placed soup and rice in front of me.

"Your mom lied to me at first," Father was saying. "Maybe she was ashamed that her daughter had deceived her so badly. She knew you'd left school, but she didn't tell me until now because she thought I wouldn't understand. I had to keep after her and finally I got her to tell me. It was already several months, she said. I couldn't believe it. I had no idea—I was completely taken in. I'm amazed."

I could hear Father clicking his tongue as I drank a glass

of water. "Does So-yang know I called her school and found out she left?" I pressed Mother. I was hoping So-yang didn't know this yet. I hadn't been showing much interest in her, and so I felt guilty about having checked up on her the minute she warned me she was leaving school. Now I wanted more than anything else to talk with So-yang alone.

"What's there to hide?" Mother said. "It's natural that older sisters should be interested in what their younger sisters are doing."

That word *interested* felt like a worm crawling across my face. I forced myself to eat some of the unappetizing soup. I heard Father's voice again.

"What the hell have you been up to? Let's face it—you did something wrong and you spent the tuition money to cover it up. And you deserve a scolding for that to begin with. But do you think we'd let you drop out of school just because of a few hundred thousand wŏn? And did you do something so awful that you had to hide the fact that you left school last spring? Been looking after some boy, having a hot time with him?"

I scowled upon hearing this indecent language. Next I heard the nasal sound of So-yang's voice.

"I'm not going to say anything, because you wouldn't understand. What you just said proves it. It's true I spent the tuition money, but at first I thought of returning to school with it."

"So I can't understand. Well, we gave you an education, and listen to how you answer your parents."

This was the tired expression Father used when he criticized us. As Hye-yang put it, it reflected the inferiority complex of an unlettered man.

"People think they are so great," Father continued, wheezing, "but they're no better than the proverbial monkey in Buddha's hand. You think you're sitting pretty? How long have you been alive? Worthless brat!"

Father's speech became rougher and rougher, and I became more anxious.

So-yang, though, continued to stand up to Father. "I'm not saying you can't understand because I'm someone special. I myself can't explain in concrete terms why I had to do what I did. I feel like I'm living a pseudo life, and school is like a shell. . . . Anyway, I can't go back."

"If you talk like that, no parent could understand. You deceived everyone in the family, and that's unforgivable. I'm so mad I'm shaking, and I haven't been able to sleep."

Without my knowing it Mother had prepared some iced ginseng tea, and now she took it into the living room. As always, she had kept out of the way so that Father could exercise his authority, only to step in at the critical moment. I watched her set some tea in front of So-yang and then sit down next to Father.

"At any rate, register for this semester," Mother told So-yang. "I found out from your school today that it's not too late."

"Registration's not over yet?" I went into the living room to confirm this solution we seemed to have discovered.

But So-yang replied that she had no intention of registering.

If only the events of that evening had ended there. The scene that followed was not very pleasant. Thinking perhaps that his first attempt in a long while to stand on the dignity of our household had been met with silent contempt by So-yang, who remained recalcitrant and unrepentant, Father gave her a look of hatred. "Crazy girl!"

Brats these days cause problems because their stomachs were too full, Father went on. His generation had survived a war, stepping over the dead bodies of their buddies. After the war he had wandered the mountain villages of Kangwŏn Province with a rucksack searching for food for his family. He had then started a factory that made nylon socks, and now he owned a factory that produced sweaters for export. In all that time he had never been able to stretch his legs and relax. And so Father recited the history of his life. He hated to see the cheeky mugs of these little brats with their make-believe ideologies and useless demonstrations, doing whatever they wanted. "Get out of my sight!" he finally shouted at So-yang.

Even while receiving this abuse from Father, So-yang sat buried in her comfortable sofa without budging. Her bored look told us it would be an effort for her just to stand up.

I resented Father, who had no thought of looking into the spiritual world of his children and tried instead to judge everything in materialistic terms. But I was also angry with So-yang, who was making no attempt to understand Father.

I was the one who directed So-yang upstairs that evening. I took her by the wrist, and she sprang up lightly.

"I think I'll get along just fine without your help," she said to Father, as if she felt obligated to respond to all she had heard from him.

Fortunately Father did not hear this; he had turned up the volume on the television in a fit of anger. I don't know about the heads of other households, but our father was intensely proud of steering his family's course.

As soon as So-yang had gone upstairs I went in the kitchen and warmed up the soup. I set a meal on a tray, complete with barley tea, and set off for So-yang's room. From the bottom of the stairs I heard the faint sound of music. It was a Leonard Cohen song So-yang often listened to. The sound of the women singing in the background spread throughout the dusky second floor and draped itself heavily across my chest like the shadow of a sorrow.

I tapped gently on So-yang's door and turned the knob, but it was locked.

"So-yang, open the door!"

There was no response, so I knocked again.

A moment later the door opened. The sound of the women's chorus poured out, and So-yang's frowning face appeared in the gloom.

"What do you want?" she asked bluntly. Then she glanced at the tray.

Could her raised eyebrows have meant she wasn't expecting this? Lately, I realized, I hadn't so much as brought So-yang a cup of coffee.

"Mom asked me to bring this up," I said, ill at ease. I thrust the tray at her before she could refuse.

2

It was after I left the bank that I became more aggressive in tracing So-yang's activities. Having never considered my bank job permanent, I thought it natural to resign before getting married. My spending money had come from home, so I had managed to accumulate six million wŏn through a five-year payroll savings plan, some time deposits, and my retirement pay. And after meeting my husband-to-be, I had no further attachment to the bank.

An uncle who owned a large textile mill and used this bank had obtained the job for me five years before. I gained experience, and eventually I was serving one of the bank's most important customers—a professor who paid twenty million wŏn a year in property taxes alone. The big piles of money took my breath away when I first saw them, and after the bank was closed for the day my face would be screwed up in concentration as I squared the accounts and wondered what new mistake I had made.

There were numerous discrepancies of less than 10,000 wŏn. Convinced I wouldn't find these sums, I would make up the difference with my own money rather than filling out an accounting form explaining the loss. But then one day my accounts were off by 360,000 wŏn. Apparently I had mistaken a 40,000 wŏn check for 400,000 and paid out the latter amount.

Some of my colleagues joked that I'd be better off not working at a bank. And I had a serious conflict with some of the tellers who had only a high school education. They thought I was having it easy because I was a college graduate. But at that time I was keen on having a regular job, and so I persevered.

Like any other organization, a bank is a small society, and there I learned not to trust people. There were frequent attempts at fraud. A man who looked down at the heels would deposit, say, 900,000 wŏn and come back the next day with his wife insisting he had deposited a million. Or two people would jointly deposit the money and one would shortly reappear alone to withdraw it.

Because of these incidents I always felt tense at work. In addition, we in the bank could victimize each other, and so I had to be friendly with my co-workers yet keep my distance. Sometimes a teller would receive a deposit from a customer and use the stamp of the teller next to her on the deposit slip. She could then do what she wished with the money and shift the blame for the loss onto her co-worker. One of the tellers actually used such a deposit to help her lover's failing business. I too was a victim of such actions, and I made sure to take my stamp with me if I left my window for even a minute.

Wanting a life completely different from that of music, I chose the bank, but at times the tension I felt there put me in a daze. If I hadn't met Mr. Ch'oe, I probably would have become manic-depressive or have quit the bank much sooner.

At first Mr. Ch'oe didn't catch my eye at all. Because I was a newcomer to the real world, his title of assistant manager made me feel apart from him, and I must have unconsciously avoided him. In addition, I was not interested in men at the time.

Mr. Ch'oe began to attract my interest by becoming a source of moral support whenever I was caught in an awkward situation. Sometimes I was aware of his help, sometimes not. In any case, this was how romances among the employees generally came about. Whenever the allowance in my cash drawer didn't square with the deposit and withdrawal slips for that day and I became perplexed, he would advise me to judge whether the discrepancy was large or small and then act accordingly. And he would stay with me until I had achieved a balance. The accounting that took place at the end of every month required the members

of our department to take a late meal and stay up through
the night. At such times Mr. Ch'oe joined us. Not surprisingly, the two of us became closer as a result. The day I
swallowed my anger and decided to pay the bank the
360,000 wŏn I had mistakenly paid out, he said he would
cheer me up and proceeded to buy me a drink.

I wasn't very good at keeping my wits about me on the
job, and that day I disliked myself. My pride was wounded,
and I was in no mood for being consoled. So before Mr.
Ch'oe could say anything, I told him that I would make up
the difference out of my own pocket rather than filling out
an explanatory accounting form. Since anyone who would
blithely walk off with 400,000 wŏn rather than 40,000 could
not be expected to return the extra money, I decided to take
on the entire responsibility myself.

Mr. Ch'oe did not oppose me. He merely suggested
that since the amount was so great, the responsibility was
shared by my supervisor—that is, himself. But I rejected
this, saying I couldn't shuffle off such a burden even on my
father, not to mention my superior.

At that point Mr. Ch'oe suddenly adopted the expression of an elder brother. "You seem to be working at the
bank out of a sense of pride and stubbornness. What made
you think of counting money, of all things, rather than
playing the piano? Didn't you turn down a job as pianist for
the bank?"

It was true. Every bank hired a graduate of a music
school to play piano for special occasions in addition to performing regular bank duties. But through a special selection
process, thanks to my uncle, I had chosen to work at the
bank as a teller, and I had prepared myself to be treated as a
high school graduate.

I told Mr. Ch'oe that I would work at the bank until I
had saved a certain amount of money. Since we can never
tell what other people are going to do, I would use that
money to build an independent life in case my husband
turned out to be a failure or ran away with someone. I then
realized I was unburdening myself to Mr. Ch'oe, and I began to feel that I trusted him quite a bit.

Mr. Ch'oe didn't ask any more questions. Instead, trying to suppress a laugh, he said that if I kept losing money the way I did, I wouldn't get married until retirement age.

I couldn't help laughing, and when he suggested seeing me home, I accepted. That was our first date.

Finding out about So-yang's problems the same time I gave notice at the bank, two months before my wedding, created some unexpected worries. On the other hand, leaving the bank seemed to have given me the opportunity to devote more time to her.

It had never been my intention to reason with So-yang tactlessly. For some years now we had each been living inside a wall of our own. As for So-yang, her castle wall was solidly constructed, its gate seemingly not easily opened.

I decided first of all to see Myŏng-ju, So-yang's high school pal, who had also failed the college entrance examination the first time around. They were close enough to have entered the same university, though in different departments, and until last year, at any rate, Myŏng-ju had been a frequent visitor at our home. She, if no one else, had probably known some time before about So-yang's departure from school. They believed, as I had at their age, that they communicated better with their friends than with their family.

I found Myŏng-ju's telephone number and dialed it, only to find that it hadn't been in service for at least a year. Evidently her family had moved. No more than two months previous, So-yang had called Mother and said she would be sleeping at Myŏng-ju's. Mother, trusting So-yang, must not have called Myŏng-ju's house to confirm this, and so had not learned about the new number. So-yang had done a beautiful job of deceiving Mother, as she apparently had done since leaving school.

The morning after my last day at the bank, I lay wiggling beneath my quilt, savoring my new leisure, but soon, at the thought of seeing Myŏng-ju, I jumped out of bed. To ask So-yang for Myŏng-ju's new telephone number would have made me appear like a detective tracking down a suspect. So I decided on the spur of the moment to visit their university. That way I would probably be able to learn something, even if I was unable to see Myŏng-ju.

So-yang's room was quiet when I passed it on the way to the stairs. Grandmother and Hye-yang were eating breakfast in the kitchen. Grandmother was wearing a lavender blouse, and her hair was enclosed in a gold hairnet. From the smell that greeted me when I sat beside her, I could tell she had applied a pack of sliced cucumbers to her face.

Although I had eaten breakfast with Hye-yang three days earlier, it seemed like a long time since I had seen her.

"No classes today?"

Only then did Hye-yang remove her eyes from the newspaper she was reading. "Sister, is it true you're not working at the bank anymore? Why don't you stay on after you get married? It's no fun not having a job."

"I agree," said Grandmother. "Even if Mr. Ch'oe wants you to quit, you should think of transferring to a different branch. It won't do to sit back and take it easy when you're still young. It's nice to have a man providing for you, but a woman can't speak out unless she has some economic power of her own."

Grandmother was an example of what she preached. The land she had inherited in Maljukkori had soared in price, and she had sold some of it and used the proceeds to have rental property constructed.

"You didn't know that I've been working till now so I wouldn't have to live off a man?" I asked Grandmother. "Don't worry—I'll manage to feed myself even if I have to play the piano to do it," I continued bluntly. This connection between marriage and livelihood was not to my taste. "Hasn't So-yang come down yet?"

Hye-yang immediately frowned. "She's been springing too many surprises on us lately. I said to her, 'How could you pull such a clever stunt?' And all she would say was, 'It was something I had to do—a bookworm like you probably wouldn't understand.' Kids these days act like there's no one above or below them. They're the only ones who are right."

"So-yang is possessed by Satan," declared Grandmother. "She's being tested by the devil. I asked her to go with me to see a minister I know and have him lay his hands on her head, and she lost her temper."

This was absurd. "Since you've received the grace of Jesus Christ, why don't you lay hands on So-yang yourself?" I asked Grandmother cynically. Then I asked Hye-yang if she had time to join me in taking So-yang out to lunch the following Sunday.

Hye-yang was less than enthusiastic. "She's impossible to figure out. And she's so clever it scares me. She's not about to talk with me, and she walks off wearing my shoes whenever she feels like it. Then she comes back, kicks them off, and leaves them where they are, all covered with dust."

True, Hye-yang had enough shoes to fill the family shoe cabinet all by herself—more than ten pairs of dress shoes and half a dozen pairs of sneakers. This was her only extravagance. But this was the first time I'd heard of So-yang borrowing them.

I scowled gently at Hye-yang. "You have a lot of shoes, don't you?"

"But So-yang has her own."

"She probably thinks you're close to her, and so you're an easy target. She's never once worn my shoes."

Despite my attempts to mollify Hye-yang, she continued to grumble. "It would be good if the closer we became, the more we minded our manners."

That morning I also exchanged ideas with Mother about So-yang. Mother believed we should register So-yang in school even if she didn't want to go back, but I thought we should respect her feelings. So-yang had decided on her own to leave school, and even if we forced her to register, she probably wouldn't attend.

"If that's the way it's going to be, then the first thing we should do is try to persuade So-yang to see things our way," I said.

Then I began to persuade Mother that we should let So-yang do as she wished for the time being. After all, the sensibility of people in their twenties was keen as a knife, and everything appeared unmanageable to them. With So-yang at that age, it would be preferable to help her relax and get her life in order.

Mother had been insisting that So-yang reregister since she had acted rashly in leaving school, but when I pointed out that the tendency to overreact was characteristic of young people, I sensed she was changing her mind. I thought of myself at that age, and then realized it was not impossible to communicate with Mother. After all, she had been a great fan of James Dean in *Rebel Without a Cause*.

The same morning, I hurried to So-yang's school in search of Myŏng-ju. As I entered the campus an old stone building came into view—it seemed to soar up from a grove. It had a holy, dignified appearance, different from that of the outside world, and it made me feel as if I were in a sacred precinct. It had been several years since I had walked through a campus, and a strange sentiment was revived in me.

It was after eleven when I arrived at the Department of History. I first looked at the class schedule, and fortunately a course required of Myŏng-ju and the other history majors had started at eleven. I decided to wait.

I slipped down a dim hallway resounding with amplified voices from the classrooms and stepped outside, where I was dazzled by a bed of scarlet sages. In the blazing sun, the flowers suddenly seemed to be spreading like blood before my eyes. I almost felt dizzy.

A bench caught my eye to the left of this flower bed. I approached it, walking beneath a sycamore, and came upon two bulletin boards crammed with posters and notices:

Fabricated Values

Oppression by the Masses

A Call to Conscience

Advance sale of tickets for Arthur Miller's The Crucible

Announcing the presentation of a thesis: "Technical Independence or Technical Dependence?"

Festival of the Great Land of the East, on the 30th anniversary of the founding of the University of Foreign Studies

A unification ceremony on behalf of democracy, the masses and the liberation of the Korean people

Students! Don't you hear the sound of the opening of a new day?

Warning! Do not remove. Be on the lookout for those who would invade our campus.

The thick gothic letters competed for my attention. Somehow they were like blood, and they made me feel dread and compassion at the same time. The campus was a sanctuary, a privileged land whose inhabitants had been given a reprieve. Because when they took just one step out into the world, the shields of outsiders lying in wait would stifle their youthful breath.

While sitting on the bench I heard a guitar. The music sounded like a Spanish dance, but was cold and tedious.

Gentle laughter came from students among the trees, and a girl walked briskly in front of me in high heels and baggy, calf-length pants. Her triangular earrings, hanging almost to her shoulders by a long metal chain, were ludicrous; perhaps this too was an image of youth.

As I listened aimlessly to the guitar, contemplating the scene around me, I suddenly felt old. My upcoming marriage, perhaps? No, that wasn't it. If I hadn't been injured in the springtime of my life, I probably would have wanted to enjoy that period for as long as I lived. I would have yearned for it, this springtime of life that was like a transparent green balloon, and I would have become endlessly expansive among my reminiscences.

I had no problem finding Myŏng-ju after her class. At first she was puzzled, but after learning I had come to see her she seemed to be trying to guess the reason. I decided to treat Myŏng-ju to lunch, so we fled the campus and went to a Western-style restaurant.

As soon as we sat down, Myŏng-ju inquired about So-yang.

"How long has it been since you've seen her?" I countered, recalling the change in her telephone number.

"A couple of months—it was before finals."

"That's right. So-yang was at your house. You called us then, didn't you?" I was relieved that So-yang hadn't lied about this.

"Yes... she left about four in the morning. It was if she'd been waiting for the end of curfew."

"Curfew? There's no curfew these days."

"But four a.m. is the most dramatic and effective time to take action," Myŏng-ju joked. "We were up all night talking, but we couldn't agree on anything. As soon as the clock struck four So-yang stomped out, as if there was nothing to keep her there any longer. 'I'm going,' she said—didn't even look back. She can be a cross one, can't she?"

These young people are more than I bargained for, I told myself as Myŏng-ju laughed hesitantly. As I recall, So-yang hadn't returned home by the time I left for work that day. Where could she have gone on that dark dawn road?

I was anxious to hear what Myŏng-ju and So-yang had talked about that night.

"Well, we talked about our notions of truth," Myŏng-ju began. She was very interested in the problem of social inequality. Because of the structure of the country's transitional industrial society, the political or economic triumph of one group was obtained at the expense of another group. Every social class resisted oppression from above but bore the seeds of oppression of those below. It was only natural that those with a disadvantageous position in society should try to establish a system of rules that would promise them a better income.

Myŏng-ju then turned to the student movement. Students were privileged people, she said, and as such they had to take the lead in working for social progress. Once people became established, they corrupted themselves into petit-bourgeois to preserve their comfortable lifestyles—they adjusted and compromised with reality. Who else but the students could carry on the pure fight? "Isn't that an elitist way of thinking?" I argued. "An avant-garde way of thinking," Myŏng-ju corrected me. All the students did, she continued, was play a middle role by educating the oppressed classes in the contradictions of the social system. The main body of the labor movement would always be the workers—the students *knew* that.

To reapprehend through firsthand experience the theories and notions they entertained, Myŏng-ju and some other students had gone to work in a factory during vacation. Myŏng-ju had been an apprentice in an export-zone factory, earning 80,000 wŏn a month for such things as ironing collars and folding inseams. And because she wanted to do the same work as her co-workers and enjoy a rapport with them, she was currently being tutored in the use of a sewing machine.

I had finished my meal, but Myŏng-ju, spewing her impassioned speech about inequality, had scarcely touched hers. I urged her to eat, recalling the year she had studied for her second try at the college entrance exam, her long hair tied in a ponytail like that of a country girl.

"You know, it feels funny using a knife like a bourgeois in a place like this," she said. Then she resumed her account.

"That's mainly what I talked about with So-yang. Her response was, 'Are you that concerned about these things? It sounds like pseudoelitism to me. You don't even know who you are, and you're going to raise people's consciousness and help lead popular movements?' And then she really lit into me. 'Movements are fine, but you have to recognize other kinds of suffering and conflict. You think you and your friends are the only ones who are enlightened, the only ones who have a sincere cause? If you do, you're pretty arrogant—you're as inhuman as the system you're opposing.'"

That was enough to give me a sense of the situation between So-yang and Myŏng-ju that night. This was the Soyang who had told Mother that she would have been happy to have felt a clear moral obligation to participate in a demonstration at the risk of expulsion. But at that moment I was more curious about Myŏng-ju's transfiguration than So-yang's departure from school. I had the urge to say— half as a joke—that I felt a generation gap sitting across from someone who had changed so much in a year. But instead I said, "You're lucky to have established your values that quickly."

Myŏng-ju stopped as she was cutting a piece of meat and became more earnest.

"It's not the kind of luck you have when a winning lottery ticket falls in your lap. A way opened up for me because I was serious about finding it." After a brief silence she continued. "The year after I failed the entrance exam I felt really discouraged and left out. I did a lot of spiritual wandering. But when I got over these feelings and finally entered college, I got away from thinking so much about myself and became aware of some important social realities." She made it sound so logical. I felt like giving her a pat on the back.

Finally I asked if she knew that So-yang had left school.

"Of course. She told me she was going to, and I heard later on that she handed in a withdrawal form the very next day."

"And when did she tell you?"

"In the middle of April, when the magnolias were withering. There was a cold snap that day, and it was really windy. So-yang was waiting for me under one of the magnolia trees. Her face was drawn, probably because she was cold. When I saw that small figure sitting under the large magnolia with its yellow, withering blossoms, I somehow felt sorry for her. Of course her face was larger than those blossoms, but on that particular day it looked smaller. Anyway, that was the day—the day she told me she was leaving school."

What she had told Myŏng-ju was no different from

what she told us. So-yang said she had been living falsely. School was just an empty shell, and she felt empty too. There was nothing there for her to grab on to.

These words were still too abstract for me. I wasn't quite sure what So-yang was talking about. I tilted my head in thought and asked Myŏng-ju what So-yang had been trying to find.

"She was probably trying to find the truth."

I snorted. I recalled Myŏng-ju having mentioned at the beginning "our notions of truth" and such. Perhaps this word *truth* was their common denominator. *Truth*—how vague and obscure! So she was going to grab for the truth. Wasn't that like saying she was going to grab for thin air? I sighed gently.

Myŏng-ju's plate was empty, so I called our waitress and asked for coffee. The waitress asked what kind we wanted, reciting a list that included vienna and mocha.

I ordered vienna.

"I don't like Western things," said Myŏng-ju, but she orderd mocha anyway.

I looked intently at Myŏng-ju, and suddenly I understood why So-yang had left her house that morning in the darkness just before dawn.

My coffee arrived, and I asked Myŏng-ju if their meeting that cold spring day was the last she had seen of So-yang.

Myŏng-ju reticently said yes, hesitated, then told me something unexpected. "I told you I worked in an industrial complex this summer. When I mentioned this plan to So-yang, she gave me this smart-alecky smile and said she was thinking about working at a bar."

My head jerked up as I was about to take a sip of coffee. "What was that?"

"She said she was going to be a hostess." Myŏng-ju dropped her eyes to the table. "And she probably did it. She worked for a month as a waitress at a noodle place the year after she failed the entrance exam."

"She did that too? Why?" My sadness must have shown in my face.

Myŏng-ju was lost in thought for a moment. "She's probably drifting. I had a bad case of that myself. ... "

This was a tremendous blow to me. A waitress at a noodle house? I could forgive her for that, but I couldn't imagine So-yang as a hostess at a bar. Would she call that a case of drifting?

A rash thing for a daughter of a wealthy family to do, Myŏng-ju had said sarcastically to So-yang. But then she added to me, "I shouldn't have said that, because I sensed a kind of urgency in her." But Myŏng-ju's qualification, far from lessening my worries, added to my confusion.

I mentioned that I had been thinking vaguely of dropping by the French Department, but had given up the idea.

"You mean you were going to see So-yang's professors? They're nothing but professionals whose futures are guaranteed. If you're lucky, they might recognize her name."

Myŏng-ju was being too harsh, but in truth I had no great urge to visit So-yang's department. I could think of only one or two professors I respected during my four years of music school, and I couldn't remember a single one I could speak with as a human being.

Myŏng-ju then said it would be much more helpful to see So-yang's close friend in the French Department than to visit her professors without knowing exactly what to ask them. So I jotted down in my address book Myŏng-ju's new telephone number and the name of this classmate of So-yang's, Shin Kyŏng-ok, whom I remembered having heard of.

At the campus entrance Myŏng-ju left me with this parting shot: "Try to understand So-yang. She doesn't like her family, but if they warm up and take an interest in her she'll probably give up keeping that depressing diary of hers."

Depressing diary? I repeated to myself. Without waiting for a reply Myŏng-ju tossed back her short, straight hair, turned and left.

So-yang was gone by the time I returned, and her door was locked. Grandmother had also left, and the second floor was still. The early autumn sunlight seemed to seethe soundlessly.

I turned the doorknob to So-yang's room back and forth a few times, then went downstairs. Mother was in the kitchen pickling some food. Without a word I began rummaging through some drawers in the living room in search of the room keys.

"What are you looking for?" Mother asked.

I had no choice but to tell her—the chain with the room keys. "I want to get a record from So-yang's room," I explained too hastily.

The rusty keys turned up in the drawer next to the kitchen sink. There were two keys for each room except So-yang's.

"Could she have taken both of them?" Mother said, cocking her head skeptically.

No doubt So-yang had done exactly that. She had enough secrets to warrant her keeping those keys.

Without a word I went to the neighborhood marketplace and returned with a locksmith. The door was unlocked without difficulty, but having a duplicate key made would mean removing the lock temporarily. I asked the locksmith to do this, and he left with the lock, saying he would return in two hours.

I rushed into So-yang's room and found her desk unlocked. I began rifling the drawers, but the diary was nowhere to be seen. A pad of note paper, an old address book, photographs, postcards, and a songbook were scattered at random. I finally discovered it in an unlikely place—among some college notebooks in the bookcase.

The notebooks were all the same size but different in color—orange, green, blue, brown. So-yang had chosen the plainest one, brown, for her diary. The first few pages contained notes for an ethics course; if I hadn't leafed all the way through, I probably would have returned the notebook to its place on the shelf.

The diary took up about half the notebook. The first entry was dated June 2, but it told me So-yang had been keeping a diary long before:

I've burned all the old diaries. I like a perfect crime and a perfect performance, and I was afraid of the childishness that appears in those entries.

But now it's time to toughen up and start the diary again. No more infantile, morbid self-discovery. Instead I'll sight in the best I can on my target—the truth that brushes past the hunting ground of my soul.

Again today my head feels as though it will explode. It's just before midnight when I turn out the light and go to bed, but I can't hypnotize myself to sleep. After a while I reach beneath my pillow, take out my harmonica, and start playing. I recall a fragment of a song I composed and sang in English long ago—something something castle. It was about a girl who lived in a castle.

I'm a castle now. I've broken off relations with others. There was a time I suffered because I could never be understood by others. But now I can add a rather elegant commentary on this: I'm not one of the "common people." Could it be that the fact I am called "I" is the only reason I'm considered different from others?

June 4
Hŭi-jung kept frowning and didn't smile the whole time we were together. This unfeeling expression was not to my liking, so after mumbling along by myself for a while I rubbed the back of his hand and asked what the problem was.

"Nothing to do with you. It's my problem, and I'm not going to talk about it with a woman."

I snorted. This is the crudest thing he's said so far.

Hŭi-jung, quickly sensing the significance of my laugh, and raising his smokescreen of self-defense: "You don't know me very well. I'm a frightening person. Women in love are blind."

Me: "I want to look into the spots where you hurt and tingle. Like a microscope would. That's what love is."

At that moment the thin white scar above Hŭi-jung's lip resembled a sea gull dropping, and I felt forlorn at my trivial wordplay.

June 9
The middle-aged women who came this morning to help with the cooking for Grandmother's birthday made me heavy at heart,

and I ran out of the kitchen before finishing breakfast. Their faces looked unlucky, their expressions servile. One of them, frying some lentil pancakes: "My husband's from P'yŏngyang, so I've been served plenty of these in my time. . . . "

Right now that same woman is probably cooking that stuff at someone else's house and showing off about how happy she used to be. She sat at our table and said in this tiny voice, "Mmm, I don't seem to have a spoon. . . . "

Grandmother, to the church friends who came to visit her in the afternoon: "I wish I lived in a house without a lotus pond. Feeding the fish is so bothersome."

Rejects of the leisure class, trying to escape the loneliness of life through narcissism. What's the use of corsets and pink lace parasols at their age? But then at their age they won't commit suicide even if they confront the fact of their loneliness.

I read the first page of the diary straight through with a mixture of interest and tension. If I continued to read, I thought, I would learn more about So-yang. And so I pored over the diary until the locksmith returned.

The diary was like a great harvest. Reading it allowed me to discover and observe various aspects of So-yang and to find out how she viewed the people around her, including this boyfriend Hŭi-jung and her family. Portrayals of the family appeared in a few other places; the descriptions were scathing.

The mountains and streams are unchanging: my family's snobbishness becomes more graphic with time.

I don't want to walk barefoot anywhere outside my room, even in the hallway.

There was also this line:

Someone said that humans are, after all, just animals, and Mother and Father are an animalistic couple.

I remember Father once saying that every one of those demonstrating brats should be sentenced to death. So-yang

was repelled by this statement and by Mother's calm attitude as she poured carrot juice for Father:

*He probably said that because the sweater-exporting business
is slow. Whatever the reason, Mother doesn't bat an eyelash—just
feeds him more carrot juice. Kyŏng-ok once told me after dropping
by our house, "Your parents get along so well," but then, as if she
felt alienated from us, she asked in a roundabout way, "Your
house is kind of big, isn't it?" If only big, tall Mencius had appeared and whisked me over our fence and away in his arms. . . .*

So–yang then jotted down some thoughts about Father's
sweater factory as seen through the awakening eyes of college students these days. The conflict within her was evident:

*Granted, up to now I've been able to live materialistically,
free of inconveniences, thanks to Father. But if I look at this
through Myŏng-ju's eyes, I owe it all to the blood and sweat of the
workers. That's probably true. It's like America's wealth, which
was obtained through the exploitation of blacks. Behind prosperity
there are clearly some victims.*

*But as long as I'm living like a petit-bourgeois thanks to Fa-
ther's Yudo Trading Company, I'm afraid to look at how the
workers live in the factory dorms. I'd like to put this problem aside
for the time being. Even thinking about it gives me a headache.*

So–yang's intense dislike for the family jarred me. I had
never thought our family had any major problems—except
for Hyŏk, that is. Hyŏk was Grandfather's youngest son,
born of a young *kisaeng**, and he lived in the half basement
of our house. Athough I considered him my uncle, he was
younger than So–yang. He had also failed the college
entrance exam. We didn't like him because of the wild
drumming that came from his room and because his clothing always had a strong odor. This boy's existence
seemed a dark shadow over our family.

**kisaeng:* the Korean counterpart of a geisha.

I too had felt that Mother and Father's amicable relations were based on sex, but somehow it was appalling to
see it in writing—So-yang's conclusion that their union was
animal-like.

What Myŏng-ju had called a depressing diary was to me
a diary of startling revelations. There were two entries concerning a bar called the Icy Road, confirming what Myŏng-
ju had said about So-yang working there.

The name Icy Road seemed to have drawn So-yang. She
wrote that the woman who owned the bar had a higher-
than-normal body temperature and had gone to a professional name maker, who had given her a name including
Ping, meaning "ice."

*But I'm the one who has a high body temperature. My blood is
always hot. It gathers only in my head, and the pain is terrible—as
if my head will explode. If I were to add this Ping to my name so
that the blood in my head would cool off, it would be fine with me.
Ping-yang—Frozen Sheep, Frozen-to-Death Sheep. . . .*

That was So-yang's first day at the Icy Road. There
were few customers, and so it seemed So-yang didn't have
to join any of them at a table. She detailed the strange rituals
she underwent in accordance with bar custom.

*As soon as ten o'clock had passed, one of the hostesses told me
to do as she said without any questions, and took me to where the
other women had gathered. One of the women put some salt on her
palm and ate it, and then each of the others took turns doing the
same. I too joined in this strange ritual.*

*From what I heard right after that I gathered that there aren't
any customers the day a new girl begins. It's as if they all agree to
stay away. I wondered if the women ate the salt to prevent themselves from rotting like fish.*

The next day So-yang scrawled, "I was depressed, and
drank myself silly." The diary then skipped three days, and
the next entry contained some lines on prostitution, which
she had perhaps read in a book.

Because it appears in human nature, and since there are per-verts who can't help abandoning themselves to it, people say prostitution is a practice that can't be stamped out. But prostitution is a social system and not just a system bestowed on us by nature. It is accelerated by war and economic depression, and women are its victims.

In any event, it's terrible that women can become objects, dehumanized things, through sex. A creep put his hands inside my blouse to give me a tip. I took out the money right there and ripped it up.

Myŏng-ju was dead wrong to say that my becoming a hostess was the rashness of a rich family's daughter, nor did I do it to be a loose woman, to squander a youth as burdensome as a chain. Just let me fall to the bottom, as far down as I can go.

What I want most to do—the only thing I want to do—is smash this class consciousness, this bourgeois mentality of mine.

I felt like slamming the diary shut. I couldn't comprehend these outrageous actions, but more than that I was troubled to have discovered these facts about So-yang. It had been my aim to get close to her by referring to her diary, but now it seemed a deep river that couldn't be crossed was passing between us. I felt that So-yang was being swept away by the torrent and all I could do was watch, stamping my feet in frustration.

I had been in So-yang's room about two hours. I took a cigarette from her desk and lost myself in thought while smoking it. The locksmith returned with the duplicate key. While the doorknob was being refitted, I replaced the diary, opened the window to freshen the air in the room, and removed all traces of my presence. Now I could enter So-yang's room anytime I wanted.

Although I had left the bank, I had less free time than I expected. Every day I played the piano, which I had been neglecting, and I continued giving weekly Korean harp lessons to the women at the bank. I took up piano again thinking I would teach the neighborhood children after my marriage, but in truth I was considering graduate school. I was highly motivated to improve on the piano, but I also felt that adding one more feather to my cap in this society based on ability might help me someday.

I spent the rest of my time with Mother buying the things I would need after marriage. Also, I was seeing Mr. Ch'oe every other day. But So-yang never left my mind amidst all this. Fortunately, around this time there was a call from Kyŏng-ok, So-yang's friend from the French Department.

As luck would have it, So-yang was out. At that moment all my thoughts were of her, and when I heard Kyŏng-ok's name I was delighted.

I told Kyŏng-ok who I was. I said I had wanted to see her a while ago and asked straightaway if she could spare some time.

Kyŏng-ok consented at once, seeming not to have wondered what I had in mind. She then asked if I could come to the Wooden Horse, a cafe near the university where she worked part-time.

It was not quite six o'clock when I arrived at the cafe. Kyŏng-ok would be working there until seven that evening. If we ended up in a long conversation, we could go somewhere else for dinner, I thought.

The Wooden Horse was suitably comfortable for a place near a univeristy, and its checkerboard tablecloths and other furnishings gave it a cheery atmosphere. It was fairly large, maybe thirty *p'yong* or more, but there were only three empty tables. I sat at a table facing the kitchen and watched the waitresses. They all seemed to be college students, and they looked trim in their green aprons.

I ordered a bottle of beer from a waitress with short hair and asked her to call Shin Kyŏng-ok for me. She gave me a friendly smile and went in the kitchen, where I heard her say, "Interview for Brooke Shilbap."*

A long-haired waitress who was making toast in the kitchen turned her head toward me. Her pointed chin and bright, lively face made her resemble Brooke Shields. She

---

*shilbap: bits of thread.

squinted at me for a moment, then gave me a look of recognition.

She had willingly agreed to see me, but not until the end of her shift did she join me. I could have counted the number of new customers on one hand, but Kyŏng-ok stayed in the kitchen all the while, frying eggs and brewing coffee. In the meantime I observed some other waitresses leisurely washing dishes, and I counted the number of dried Chinese lantern plants hanging from the wall. A young couple sat side by side at a corner table facing me. The man, whose hair was permed, had his arm around the woman's shoulders and kept putting his lips to her cheek. As I was trying to avoid this embarrassing sight, Kyŏng-ok came to my table.

"Sorry to have kept you waiting." She wrinkled her nose charmingly.

The hour-long wait had tired me out. "I feel kind of uncomfortable among these young people," I said, indicating with my eyes the couple in the corner, who by then were virtually embracing.

"Don't think badly of that. It's the generation gap—really. They love each other, so why should they be aware of others?" Kyŏng-ok's blinking eyes seemed to be saying that I was the strange one.

I was taken aback at the comment about the generation gap, but it spurred me to bring up the business at hand.

"I'm afraid I came at a busy time for you." Although I was wondering if she had been avoiding me, I put on an apologetic expression.

"We can still talk for a little while," Kyŏng-ok quickly said. Then she told me she had an appointment at seven-thirty and stole a glance at her watch.

This was a letdown, but I couldn't allow even this small opportunity to slip by. I began by asking about So-yang.

Kyŏng-ok answered calmly, as if she had been expecting this. When I asked if she had known from the beginning about So-yang's leaving school, she responded "Of course" and added that she had accompanied her when she turned in the withdrawal notice.

"Have you been able to figure out what made her drop out?"

Kyŏng-ok replied with a question of her own: "Wasn't it because she couldn't adapt? As far as I'm concerned, it doesn't matter whether someone joins the demonstrations or not. So-yang did at first, but then she got away from it. After that she felt mixed up whenever there was a demonstration. It bothered her not to be joining in anymore."

"Are the demonstrations that important? Does she think she's supposed to be a militant?"

"What I'm saying is that she's mixed up about everything."

"I wonder if she feels alienated." These words flew out of my mouth before I realized it. I felt as though a shadow had brushed past my heart. I had a vivid memory of feeling isolated while watching the young people play guitars and laugh on So-yang's campus. And I remembered the pain I felt during times of isolation from others. . . .

I wanted to know how often Kyŏng-ok and So-yang saw each other. Kyŏng-ok informed me that So-yang had come by the Wooden Horse every other day during summer vacation but rarely touched base there these days. It had been over two weeks since she had seen her. "She must be enjoying herself," she said.

I said nothing for a moment, then sounded out Kyŏng-ok about So-yang's boyfriend, Hŭi-jung. I felt that as her older sister it was all right for me to know about So-yang's private affairs.

"Does she talk about him?" Kyŏng-ok asked with a look of surprise. She told me that So-yang and Hŭi-jung had met at a small Western-style restaurant called Something. She had been with So-yang at the time. "I'm surprised they've been together this long."

"And how long is that?"

"Since spring, right after she dropped out of school."

I laughed in amazement. It was autumn now.

That was a long time, considering where they had met, Kyŏng-ok elaborated. Again I sensed that to Kyŏng-ok I was the one reacting curiously.

Naturally I wanted to hear about Hŭi-jung, but Kyŏng-ok would tell me only that he was a junior majoring in chemistry.

I learned that Something was located in the second block down Chongno, an area containing several study centers for entrance-exam repeaters. According to Kyŏng-ok, So-yang hung out in that area, like other young people. She had been doing so since she failed the entrance exam. The restaurant was frequented by a young crowd, who had fun *cholt'ing*—calling one another over the intercoms located at all the tables.

I took an interest in this slang word *cholt'ing*, but then Kyŏng-ok looked at her watch and I realized she couldn't stay any longer. I rose, asking her not to mention to So-yang that I had visited her. "So-yang seems to be drifting these days, and I just want to help."

"Isn't drifting the privilege of youth?" Kyŏng-ok suggested after looking into a hand mirror she had extracted from her apron.

I didn't go home immediately but instead called Mr. Ch'oe at the bank, as I had agreed to do after seeing Kyŏng-ok. I told him I had taken care of my business, and he said he would be at the Sunnyside Tearoom, our usual rendezvous, in twenty minutes. "I made it a point not to eat yet," he added.

His deliberate tone calmed my jumbled nerves. I wanted to see him soon, and took a taxi to Kwanghwamun.

I had been astonished at Myŏng-ju's transformation into an activist, and now, having met Kyŏng-ok, who seemed cheerful yet self-centered, I felt So-yang's loneliness all about me, like a second skin. *I'm trying to follow the ideas of people like Myŏng-ju but the actions of people like Kyŏng-ok and Hŭi-jung,* So-yang had written in her diary. *Because I respect rationality but find instincts comfortable?* But it seemed to me she had no one to follow. *I used to be proud of this diversity—it reminded me of the breadth of humanity—but now it makes me feel unsteady.*

I firmly believed tht Hŭi-jung was not someone So-yang shared her inner self with. So they had met at Something? I smiled bitterly. I felt compassion for So-yang, twenty years old. Drifting was the punishment rather than the privilege of youth.

3

When I was twenty I was like virgin soil. Mother enjoyed dressing me in embroidered blouses and in Chinese styles, braiding my glossy hair, and decorating me like a holy maiden, but in reality I was a maverick—sneaking cigarettes, eating a sweetened cherry to hide the smell, and whistling innocently.

Father had an inferiority complex about cultural things, and he treated me, a music student at a prestigious women's university, as a treasure second only to Mother. For the most part I lived up to his comparison. At an early age I was vaguely aware of the exquisiteness of Bach's music, which had seemed like mathematics at first, so cut and dry, but a musical conversation once I understood it. And so I heard from my music teacher that I had a talent for music. My enthusiasm for the piano extended throughout college, where I practiced to the point of collapse. Every year the music school chose me through an audition and sent me to the national Newcomers' Music Festival. I was a student of great promise, armed with a "precise, forceful touch." If only I could reinforce my technique with a subtle lyricism, the critics added, there would be nothing to find fault with.

But my ambition to succeed as a pianist was not so great. For one thing I had a practical side to me, and rather than being a pianist I had the concrete dream of graduating from college and being a bride as beautiful as a June rose. Wasn't that the road women took? The woman who gave rubdowns at the public bath treated me like a girl and rubbed me a little more gently than others. But the youth and beauty that I tried to preserve by growing up unstained were by no means for me alone. In my room with its piano and its lamp with the orange shade I stored away a dream of a glass slipper and waited for the prince who would make the dream come perfectly true.

Among all the men I saw during that time I found not one who resembled the prince I was awaiting. But this is not to say I expected anything of the man I will now tell you about. Indeed I was not even conscious of him. I first saw him at a calligraphy studio introduced to me by a painter friend, and I was as indifferent to him as if he had been a mere object.

Having never heard this man talk with anyone at the studio, I knew nothing whatsoever about him. He didn't seeme to have a regular job, because he came to the studio at all hours, and although the college students were on winter vacation, he didn't appear to be a student either. Despite his neat apearance, his drooping, lifeless hair and the expressionless eyes behind his glasses seemed to have robbed him of his youth.

What first caught my eye about him was his clumsy handwriting. One day, about two weeks after I had begun going to the studio, I noticed a red notebook on the table near the window where I practiced. It was about half the size of a college notebook. I was about to set it aside, but first I opened it out of idle curiosity. A quick scan was enough to show me that the owner's small, uneven writing was extremely crude. It was ugly.

I asked the middle school girl who tended the office in the evening whose notebook it was. I would not have been surprised had the writing been hers, but I could tell from the contents that it was an adult's. The girl looked at the notebook and said it belonged to a man who was going to America. It appeared from the contents that the man was attending the class that all emigrants take before going abroad.

At that moment the door opened and a bespectacled young man entered. Speak of the devil. The girl giggled, and the man looked at us uncomprehendingly. Ignoring him, I candidly told the girl, like a child who has not yet learned to be tactful, that this was the writing of a retarded boy.

Although I was not near the man, I distinctly remember

tumultuous holiday mood had left me depresed; I had quarreled with Mother all day and was out of sorts.

Mother wanted to introduce me to the son of the president of a trading company with whom Father did business. The son was working toward a doctorate in business administration in the United States and had come briefly to Korea during his winter vacation to find a prospective bride.

I flatly refused. Winter vacation was a lonely time without a sweetheart, but it wasn't that bad. I was vaguely waiting for someone, but until I graduated from college I didn't want to participate in a marriage interview, which to me was about as romantic as weighing something on a scale.

But Mother kept trying. Annoyed, I left home shouting that from now on I'd take care of my own affairs. This was a hangup of mine. During high school I had been taught by my parents to call home immediately if I was staying late at school. And in college I had to return by ten in the evening without fail. Hye-yang and So-yang were not treated that strictly, and it appeared my parents were overprotecting me because I was the oldest daughter. I was sick and tired of this.

If memory serves me correctly, I had almost a whole bottle of wine that night. The man had two bottles of beer but didn't touch the wine. The dinner was accompanied by a recital of recent lyric songs by a music-school graduate. The chandeliers in the dining hall were dazzling and every seat was occupied. I found the extravagant atmosphere suffocating.

As soon as I sat down the man handed me something wrapped in red. I balked at accepting it.

"They're only some stockings. I wanted to get something better, but I was afraid you wouldn't take it." His voice seemed to be crawling from his throat.

I reluctantly opened the package, wanting to set him at ease. It contained seven pairs of stockings in a flower pattern.

"An expression of my gratitude," the man said, still looking uncomfortable.

I nodded the way a big sister would.

Explaining how I was drawn to an unfamiliar place that night is like boring a hole in my heart. But the stockings had dispelled my tension, and I sat there drinking until the songs were over. It was almost eleven when we got up to leave, but I had no thought of calling home. And when the man offered me a ride I gratefully accepted. With the people pouring out of the hotel, I wouldn't have been able to catch a taxi anyway.

Everything had been planned. The car sped toward Pulkwang-dong as I had directed, but then flashed by my neighborhood. It took me a moment to realize what was happening, but by then the man was no longer talking. The traffic was moving swiftly, so no one paid any attention to me pounding on the window and shouting.

The man drove to the outskirts of the city, and when the car turned down a driveway toward a secluded grove, I almost gave up hope. The horn sounded, and an old man who appeared to be a caretaker opened a gate and nodded in greeting. It was like a scene from a cops-and-robbers movie. We drove along a path lined with fruit trees and arrived at a villa. Even if I had yelled, no one could have heard me.

I tried to spring free the moment the man got out of the car, but instantly a hand caught my wrist. The windows were brightly lit. We passed a deserted living room, went upstairs, and entered a room at the end of a hall. The first thing the man did was lock the door. Then he shoved me toward a chair, telling me to sit down, and gazed at me with his expressionless eyes.

"Where are we? What's the meaning of this?" I shouted, looking around. With its tiger-stripe bedspread, gaudy rococo sofa, and inlaid wardrobe, the room vividly displayed the tastes of a nouveau-riche. Next to the bed were a Marantz audio system and a white porcelain vase filled with dozens of roses. I turned my back in contempt on all these things and approached the window.

"You can't escape. Might as well give up the idea."

I flung the curtain aside. The window was locked, and

iron bars were set in the darkness outside. The pane felt cold, but moisture was condensing on it. The man must have had the heat turned on.

I scowled fiercely at him. I had resigned myself, but strangely, I had also become bold. "If you touch me, I'll stab you with a piece of glass."

He gave me an insinuating smile and loosened his belt. "I won't touch you—promise. As long as you kneel down in front of me I won't touch a hair of your head. Just strip naked in front of me—now. I think that'll be enough to cut you down to size. You're just too proud."

He said I had rejected him. I replied coldly that I had had no interest in him, but he nailed me down by saying that too was a kind of rejection. "Sure, it's because I'm like a retard," he mumbled.

All the energy drained from me. I was stunned that my heedless remark at the calligraphy studio had led to this.

The man removed his clothes, starting with his jacket. They were shed like sloughed-off skin, and presently his naked body was before me. His reddish-black organ rose from his pubic hair. I was dizzy with terror.

It was then that I discovered that men too had pubic hair. It was no different from the hair of an animal. This was a shock to me, for I had always imagined nude men as resembling sculptures by Michelangelo.

The man ordered me to undress. I stared at him, my face frozen. "You're worse than a dog. I've never seen a male dog act violently toward a female," I said, recalling our family's good-natured shepherd.

But the man was not dissuaded in the least. He seemed bereft of everything human. He took a step toward me, and I unfastened a button of my overcoat. It was a dead end; there was no way I could escape this horror. Even my eyelashes were trembling.

Just then I remembered a sentence from the journal of a veterinarian: People should teach animals that humans are also animals. All right—by taking off my clothes I'll be teaching this animal that I'm an animal too. Although I felt

wretched exposing my untouched body in front of this im-
becilic creature, in my mind I had suddenly turned into a
warrior to defend myself.

The man's face convulsed for a moment, as if he had lost
his senses, and then he stared at me. His face lacked any
trace of vulgarity; it was the countenance of an idiot. I
stared at him in disgust.

A moment later, the man's face became expressionless
again and he started walking backward toward the bed.
Then, like a robot, he lay down and began fondling himself.

"Once I was in love with a woman. But she had a
change of heart while I was in the army. I practically begged
to see her one last time. We met at a tearoom and she told
me she was getting married soon. Then she took off. When
I went to pay, I found that her half of the bill had been taken
care of. That's when I learned how cold women can be
when they change their minds. Afterwards I seduced three
of her friends, one by one, and made them submit to me.
Then I tricked them all into seeing me together. I had a
good laugh telling them I was getting even with women."

The man was submerging himself in the past, as if sinking into sleep. His face contorted as he relived the torment,
and he groaned and panted like a beast. Finally, excrement
spilled from his malevolently swollen organ and he fell back
exhausted.

Although his eyebrows twitched from time to time, his
nude body had already been released from his pain. When I
saw his soulless face, I could no longer hate him. He was a
weak human being. While losing his love for others he had
lost himself, and his feeling of betrayal by women had stuck
to him like plaster. He had moved his past into the present
and was obsessed with escaping reality. He had blinded
himself to the present—to moral principles, will, everything. His growth had been arrested and he was spiritually
deformed.

I escaped from that nightmarish house early the next
morning, making my way through the darkness. I felt I had
lost everything. Because the villa sat apart from other

habitations, I had to walk for a while through the woods before emerging in a field.

No lights were visible. The houses were buried in darkness, and there was only the cutting winter wind, grazing
my cheeks. I had left my scarf behind in my haste to slip
away, but I would not have looked back even if I had been
barefoot. Now and then the crescent moon, cloaked in
clouds, showed its face and lit the way. I marched forward,
no longer afraid.

Although I had no external wounds, this event shook
my life. Most important, I lost my passion for music. Before, I had believed that music and the other arts gave relief
to my soul, but now I realized music's limits. Even the great
Bach could not save me. Of course the problem was in me
and not the music.

A newspaper photo of the Apollo spaceship landing on
the moon comes to mind. Though I was young at the time,
it was so miraculous to me. And the sun: what kind of energy could burn and glow and never cool off? These
mysteries of the universe transcended religion and the arts.
Though people say the arts are magnificent, they belong
only to humans.

Around the time I was losing my passion for everything, a friend I had once dated notified me of his engagement to the daugher of a national assemblyman. I proceeded
to seduce him and throw away my virginity at a seashore
near Inch'ŏn. He was the sort who could talk about Freud at
a soccer match. In addition to being scholarly he could
move people with his singing. But because his family was
poor he had made up his mind to marry into a wealthy family, and so I had restricted our relations to a friendship.

He was genuinely happy at my unexpected suggestion
to go to Inch'ŏn. But the next morning in a hotel bathroom
I looked down insensibly at my white handkerchief stained
with blood. It no longer had any meaning for me, and in
throwing it away like wastepaper I was also throwing away
my dream of the glass slipper.

A friend once told me that I lived in a world that was

immune to misfortune. Another friend would escort me home each time we met but then lope away as if escaping. I was like someone who lived in a different world, he once said. Then he went in the army.

In a sense he was correct. You might say that my circumstances allowed me to enjoy all the things a person was capable of enjoying. My intelligent mother saw to it that I received an education befitting the daughter of a solid middle-class family, and I grew up without insufficiencies or special hardships. When I thought about how much pain was spread about the world, I clearly realized that I had received my share of benevolence, and that according to the principle of distribution I was indebted to the world in return. But even if I had been ignorant of that principle until my horrible experience with that man, I still would have thought that life had been very ungenerous to me. Shouldn't I have been given an opportunity to pay my debt first?

The winter I graduated from college I happened to read a book of essays by an English author. One of them brought tears to my eyes. One day the author saw a boy of about ten leaning against a tree trunk and crying in a secluded place near the entrance to town. The boy had been sent by his parents to pay a sixpence debt but had lost the money. To think that this boy, who should have been suffused with childlike delight on this glorious spring day, was crying his eyes out. . . . The author, a compassionate man, was poor, but he emptied his pockets, provided the boy with sixpence, and sent him on his way.

I was this very boy who was crying over the lost sixpence. The money with which I was to pay my debt had been lost in the wrong place. If there is a God, he too would have been heartbroken at this, but the powerless have only their tears with which to confront life.

I told Mr. Ch'oe this story the day we were engaged. "You're the one who gave that boy the sixpence," I said.

"Well, aren't you a strange one today." But he didn't question me.

That is one of the things I liked about him—even though engagement did not break him of the habit of calling me Miss Yi.

4

Opportunities to talk with So-yang were few and far between even after I left the bank. She seemed to be avoiding me, going out almost every day I was home and returning late. I sometimes prepared a snack and waited up for her, thinking it would be better to talk at night, but she would invariably come upstairs after a scolding from Father. Even a knock on her door irritated her then. Once during this time I went into her room and read more of her diary.

September 17
I went to a tearoom near school to see Hŭi-jung. My pores felt plugged, my face prickly. He saw my bloodshot eyes and said, "Cry your eyes out, and next time join the demonstration." This was the Hŭi-jung who had been nicknamed Papillon for his skill in cutting classes and slipping away from his demonstration group. Yet he claimed he didn't want to escape the tear gas. "When the neighbors start bitching about the tear gas I feel like rapping them on the head. Must be my conscience at work."
"So, a two-faced outsider."
"Hey, analytical lady, time out for a short laugh. Here's to your sweet sorrow."
We finished our sport in just twenty minutes again. Same time, same place. Kind of like playing ping-pong. When I think about you, I find no fragrance. No aftertaste. Now I know. You're a male animal. Nothing but an animal.
Despite that, I won't forget that he once called me a deer, and another time a dagger.

September 19
I went to the public bath today and played Gas Chamber in

*the steam room again. I held my breath awhile and honestly felt I
was dying, so I jumped out.*

*Next it was Goo-Goo Eyes with a newborn next to me. But
as I looked into its innocent eyes, I could feel the tears flowing from
my own eyes. The purity of its being filled me with reverence. But
what about me? . . .*

September 21
*I went with Hŭi-jung to hear a divination instructor lecture on
acupuncture. Later the man told us our horoscopes based on the
principles of yin and yang and the Five Elements. Hŭi-jung's personality turned out to be two parts water, two parts metal and one
part fire. I was four parts metal and one part wood. The instructor
said "Good heavens!" and shook his head. "That's too strong a
conflict for a good match."*

*Someone whose personality is dominated by the metal element
and grips a knife tends to judge and condemn. I'd be a great success
as a judge or a doctor, he said. How about that.*

*Hŭi-jung was talking to himself as we left: "That's right,
you're like a child who's holding a knife—you're dangerous,
but. . . . " Children injure themselves without being aware of it,
but I judge and condemn myself more than I do anyone else.*

September 23
I'm nowhere. Only headaches to prove I'm alive.

Hŭi-jung's name had appeared a couple of times, and
now I could see how close he and So-yang were. Even so,
the expression "our sport" startled me. To compare sex to
ping-pong. . . . And this game in the steam bath made me
worry about So-yang's mental state.

The evening before Harvest Moon Day, late in September, So-yang returned home at midnight. I opened the front
gate for her and was overpowered by the smell of alcohol.
She went straight to the upstairs bathroom. I heard the
sound of vomiting, and a few minutes later she emerged,
her face wan. I had been standing outside the bathroom as if
I had something to see her about, and I asked if she had an

upset stomach. She nodded, perhaps lacking the energy to answer, and went into her room.

So-yang made at least two more trips to the bathroom that night. Her stomach still seemed to be bothering her in the morning, because she didn't get up. Mother wanted all of us to eat breakfast together because of the holiday, but So-yang simply shook her head and stayed in bed. I told the others that So-yang was sick, and after we had eaten I soaked some rice and made gruel. I filled a tray with a bowl of the gruel, fried bits of fish, and some half-moon rice cakes and carried it up to So-yang's room. Perhaps in repentance, So-yang sat up and thanked me. I could still smell liquor on her breath. I joked that I could make gruel and rice cakes every day, now that I no longer worked at the bank. It had been so long since So-yang and I had sat face to face and laughed; it was like old times.

I started eating one of the rice cakes, urging So-yang to do likewise, then had some water kimchi. "Where have you been hiding these days?" I tried to sound as nonchalant as possible.

"I feel like I'm suffocating when I'm home. So I try to find myself outside." She didn't appear to suspect anything.

"Aren't people supposed to look inside to find themselves?"

"You sound just like Confucius."

I apologized, then smiled, and So-yang laughed lightly. I asked her some questions. Didn't she regret not registering for the current semester? Didn't she want to go to school? Did she see her friends very often? But each time I received a curt response: "Not really."

I was temporarily at a loss, but then I decided to unburden myself: "Frankly, I want to understand you, and I feel badly that I've neglected you all this time. Maybe it's because I'm getting married soon, but our family feels more valuable to me now, and you've been on my mind more than anyone else. Why didn't you tell anybody you were dropping out of school? Was it so much of a secret that you couldn't communicate with anyone in the family?"

"It wasn't a secret. I just didn't feel like going to all the trouble of explaining," So-yang answered reticently while spooning herself some of the cold gruel.

It was like playing tennis with an unenthusiastic partner. Nevertheless, I persisted in saying what I had to say.

"When you get a taste of college you find it's nothing special. That's how it was with me, too. And I know you've put out more effort and had higher expectations than people who didn't fail the entrance exam, but then you probably ended up with a more hollow feeling than the others, too. And so you probably suffer because you think school is a facade and you start wondering about your values."

"Suffer?" So-yang murmured, knitting her brow. "Yesterday I was walking through an underpass with a friend, and a man selling cigarette lighters called out, 'Student, how about buying one?' I guess I'm still a student, even though I've dropped out, but I felt strange being called one—like an old woman might feel if she were called "Miss" from behind because she had long hair. But this fellow called every young person who went by 'Student.' My friend said that everyone likes to be called a student. So why would I have given up this title that people like so much? What do I want to be? Not knowing what I want—that's suffering."

For a moment I didn't know what to say. So she didn't know what she wanted. But didn't we discover our immediate wants as we went through life? And aren't those wants variable rather than absolute? Because once we've satisfied some of them, we end up with other ones.

Perhaps So-yang was talking about having an ideal rather than a want. Even if she hadn't been able to discover this ideal, this want, the anxiety of not yet having one is a more future-oriented worry than the immediate suffering we feel when an ideal is smashed. This is because not yet having gives us the desire and the urge to create. As I gave this poor excuse for advice, I recalled having read such a statement in a book.

In the meantime, So-yang had finished the gruel. And now, after putting a rice cake in her mouth, she pushed the tray from her lap onto the floor. "Words are so empty compared with thoughts. And as far as appetite is concerned, it's animal-like."

"You look settled when you eat, you know."

So-yang laughed. Seizing this opening I asked, "Are you really working at a bar?" I raised my eyes to her face. So-yang stopped eating the rice cake and glanced at me.

I had met Myŏng-ju by chance, I lied. "I said I was worried about you, and that's what she told me. Why a bar, of all places?"

To my surprise, she candidly said, "It was only for four days. No big deal."

"Did you need the money?" I asked, beating around the bush. I knew this was probably not the reason.

This time So-yang did not answer me directly. "This bastard stuck a tip in my bra. So I took it out and ripped it up right there. And then I quit." As if she were hot, So-yang swept back the hair streaming over her face. Down still covered her forehead, like that of a child, and the sight of it called to mind something that happened when she was young.

We were on our way home from the dance studio. We were walking along a sidewalk, and a bicycle brushed past So-yang, ran into a tree and toppled over. Though she wasn't injured, So-yang moved to the other side of me, away from the street, and said peevishly, "If you're going to protect a child, shouldn't *you* be the one closer to the street?"

"Do you remember that?" I asked her. "I even remember the yellow ribbon in your hair."

"Did I say that?" she said without emotion.

I couldn't believe that this So-yang was the child with clever, twinkling eyes that I remembered from childhood.

We heard Grandmother calling, and I picked up the tray and stood up. "We're supposed to visit the family graves today. Aren't you going to get ready?"

"I'm not going."

So much for that, I thought. I stood there a moment, than asked, "You don't have any money these days, do you? Shall I give you some spending money?" I felt as if I were offering her a baited hook.

"Money?" So-yang gave me a piercing look, then nodded. "If you've got some, sure. Why not?"

So-yang stayed out twice that week. The first time was the day after Harvest Moon Day. Mr. Ch'oe joined us for dinner the next evening, and the family glossed over the problem of So-yang's staying out. Four days later, So-yang again failed to come home. Early that afternoon I had gone out with Mother to look at furniture, and that evening I saw Mr. Ch'oe, so I was late getting home.

According to what Grandmother said the following afternoon, So-yang had left after receiving a call from a male friend about three the previous afternoon. Upon learning that So-yang not only had failed to call home the previous evening but also had not returned the next morning, Grandmother, as the oldest member of the household, did not miss this rare opportunity to deliver a sermon:

These days girls and boys were all alike. They both had their hair fried, walked around in baggy pants, and were always ready to demonstrate. And that wasn't all. According to a church member she knew, who ran a pharmacy near a university, it was common for girls to smoke. And young hoodlums would come in the pharmacy in broad daylight to buy those condominiums, or whatever they were called. There could be no worse doomsday than this, Grandmother concluded.

Mother, whose nerves were on edge to begin with because of So-yang's staying out, thumped down her spoon at the reference to condoms and got up from the table. She had a hot scallion cake in the frying pan, and now, lifting the pan high, she was trying to flip it without a spatula. The cake, only half cooked, ended up on the floor.

Pretending not to notice, Grandmother made one more pronouncement, which sounded like a line from a play. "The wings of youth are easily injured—indeed they are."

After finishing the breakfast dishes, I again unlocked So-yang's door. I closed it soundlessly, afraid Grandmother might come out from her room, then took out the diary. I looked at this record of a soul as if on a search. But I must also admit that I enjoyed playing Sherlock Holmes. There were three new entries:

September 25
I was imitating the wretched voices of the elderly ladies from church as they sang hymns, and believe it or not I ended up singing them. Like a brainwashed girl.

I was drawn to the Bible for the first time in a long while. I read Genesis 47, and the words of Jacob pierced my heart. Asked his age by the Pharoah, he replied, "The days of the years of my sojourning are a hundred and thirty years."

The days and years of my sojourning are now twenty years. But I feel like I weigh a ton, as if it's been a hundred and thirty years. All the Jewish people spent forty years wandering the desert, but they were promised by God that they could endure their suffering.

I don't believe in God, but even if there were a God, I wouldn't have any desire to be one of his flock. It would be a hypocritical compromise.

October 2
It's the middle of the night, and suddenly I'm awake, with everything so far away. I'm being thrown into darkness all by myself, and far, far away all the people I know are turning their backs on me and lying down.

I wandered along Chongno in vain again today. Had a smoke in the Bluebird. Somebody brushed by me, glanced at me, kept looking back. He finally caught my eye. "You look familiar."

An awkward attempt to pick me up? But we're always hoping to discover a familiar face. Because unfamiliar faces, no matter how many, are like masks, making us lonely. A familiar face would be someone I could share an umbrella with when it rains.

October 7
There are many definitions of love, but one, more straightforward than the others, appeals to me: "A profitable exchange between a man and a woman, each wanting to obtain to the maximum what he or she expects of the other."

Is it sex that Hŭi-jung wants from me? And wasted hours that I want from him? Space Cadet is more tolerant and intelligent than others, but somehow he gives me the feeling he's impotent, and that bores me.

There's no one I long for. . . .

Mother was in and out of the kitchen all morning in a somber mood. In the afternoon, wanting something else to do, she turned on her sewing machine and made me some seat-cushion covers as a wedding present.

In the meantime I practiced a piece by Chopin, but I couldn't concentrate and wore myself out trying. In the end I quit. Some friends of Grandmother came to visit and poked around my room, asking me to play some hymns. Even a book couldn't amuse me, so I went to the public bath.

It was a weekday, and the bathhouse was quiet. Instead of applying egg yolks to my scalp and doing the other things I usually fussed over, I found a woman to give me a rubdown. I hadn't indulged in such luxuries when I worked at the bank, and so it had been a long time since I had lain down on the blue vinyl cot.

The young woman was sturdy like an athlete. She soaped my body gently and shampooed me, and I entrusted myself to her like a girl would. While I lay there I completely lost track of the time. I remember only that I was in an agonizing, stifling space.

Long ago I had enjoyed losing my sense of reality like this. It had been a fantasy of hopelessness. And now when I saw the swinging breasts of the woman who was rubbing me down, and when I focused my eyes in the steamy vapor, the ceiling of the bathhouse appeared high above me like the huge ceiling of a temple. When I looked down on myself again, I saw not a soapy body but a leaden body. I was heavy, and I felt I was sinking and sinking.

The woman let my hair down over the end of the cot and shampooed it again. With my head bent back I could see the window in the door to the steam room. A young woman with short hair and a towel covering her mouth was standing inside in the steamy vapor. Perhaps because of my uncomfortable position the woman looked distressed— gagged and imprisoned in the vapor.

Or maybe it was because I thought of So-yang pretending that the steam bath was a gas chamber. Warm water poured over me, and again I felt stifled. So-yang had written that there was no one she longed for, but she was always trying to find something in people. Myŏng-ju had called it "truth," but couldn't it be a tangible, familiar face So-yang was seeking? The wounds received from humans are healed through humans. But So-yang's drifting seemed like reckless dissipation to me.

So-yang hadn't returned by dinnertime that day. I was supposed to meet a magazine reporter friend at seven, but as I was preparing to leave, this friend called. She had just been assigned to a story, and asked if we could get together another time.

Hye-yang and Father had come home early, so except for So-yang we were all able to eat dinner together. As soon as Father sat down at the table he learned that So-yang hadn't returned, and he lost his temper.

"So, quite the free-spirited filly, isn't she? I thought I'd seen everything, raising four kids," he said, constantly clicking his tongue.

Grandmother, who had gotten on Mother's nerves that morning by talking about So-yang, kept silent, and this made the rest of us feel awkward. Mother, who was at the stove fumbling unnecessarily with some side dishes, told Hye-yang that she had received a phone call. "It was a fellow."

It appeared Mother was trying to change the subject, but Hye-yang merely answered, "Is that so," and continued eating.

"If you have a fellow," Father then said, "why don't you bring him home and introduce him? How can you kids know whether someone's decent or not? I'm sure So-yang got mixed up with a guy—otherwise she wouldn't act so strange."

Father seemed all puffed up to have established a link

between a man and So-yang's dropping out of school. I responded that girls these days were not so foolish as to go astray merely on account of boys. So-yang was much more intelligent and critical in her judgment than Father gave her credit for. It was just that she had some problems.

"Being smart is a problem? The problem is she's not so smart. If she was really smart, she'd never pull something that would make her fall behind her peers in the competition."

Father's talk of "the competition" irritated me, and I challenged him by asking if college was supposed to be a training school for industry. But then his steely expression convinced me that I had best leave it at that.

"College *is* competition. You think it's a training school for pleasure? Why do you think I sent you kids to college? It's so you'll have a better marriage than others, a better job than others."

This was something he could say as a father.

With my appointment postponed and So-yang still out, I felt restless. And there would likely be a fuss when So-yang returned. Father had gone into the living room to watch television while he kept a vigil for her.

I paid a rare visit to Hye-yang's room. There was nothing different about it, with the anatomical chart on the wall, the metal bookcase lined with medical texts in English, and—the only decoration—the calendar with landscapes.

Hye-yang was reading *Madame Bovary*.

"Now wait a minute—is that really a novel you're reading?"

"It's the season for it," she replied, sticking out her tongue at me.

"How about going downtown for a change?"

"It's already after eight, isn't it?" Hye-yang was confused at this sudden proposal.

I told her I was feeling stir-crazy and urged her to take a taxi with me to Chongno for a gin and tonic. "Pretty soon we won't be able to do this anymore."

Perhaps because I sounded so earnest, Hye-yang gave in and changed her clothes.

From the time we set foot on Chongno I poked about as if we had entered unfamiliar territory. It had been a while since I had last come here at this hour, and seeing the swarms of young people in their distinctive clothing made me feel like an outsider.

Sitting in front of a watch shop, on the steps of a building that had closed for the evening, or at the entrance to a beer hall, or eating hot dogs on the sidewalk, or going here and there in groups—the young people commanded the streets in this area. They were a mass unto themselves, an extraterritorial enclave that rejected the establishment.

Two busloads of riot police had been posted at the entrance to a side street, but no one paid any attention to them. Not far away a group of people stood in a circle shouting their high school song.

We plowed through this forest of young people, rubbing shoulders with them, and walked down a side street. A group drinking draft beer at a wooden table was visible through a large window; the scene reminded me of an aquarium. The games in a video arcade produced a jumble of sounds. Bright lights drew my eyes one level above the street to a wire-mesh batting cage with several pitching machines. A line of youths, each in turn, were lashing at the ball with all their might.

We continued down the street and came upon some lit-up portable stalls, lined up like ships in the night, that sold liquor and snacks. Hye-yang, her curiosity aroused, suggested trying one of them. I told her I had a place in mind, and we moved on.

It was just after nine when we arrived at Something. The place served drinks and snacks, and it had the unusual feature of tinted windows. It was hard to see the customers because the interior was dark and high partitions surrounded the seats. The music was loud.

I found a table, and a red intercom on the wall caught my eye. The letters CC were imprinted on it. Everything was as Kyŏng-ok had said.

I called a waiter, ordered two gin and tonics and asked how to use the intercom. He genially explained that if I lifted the receiver I would automatically reach the disk jockey, who would play a song I requested or connect me with another booth.

"How did you find out about this place?" Hye-yang asked me with a suspicious look.

"You're in college and you've never been to a place like this?"

The only opportunity we had had to drink together recently was a night when Mr. Ch'oe and I had invited Hye-yang and So-yang out to dinner. So now I asked Hye-yang various questions as they came to mind: Did she have a boyfriend? Was anything troubling her? What did she think of the rest of the family?

Hye-yang's answers were simple and to the point. She had a close male friend, but he was an only son, his mother was widowed, and his major was German literature. Their circumstances were so different that she had no thought of marrying him. So she kept a certain distance, insisting on going dutch with him on their dates. The kind of man she was thinking of marrying would be a natural sciences major, someone who could help her in her study of medicine. She had no great worries because her plans for the future were clear. And she had no dissatifactions with Mother and Father because her expectations of them were no greater than they should have been.

"How can you be so on top of everything? You treat life as if it's a business." Even if law students had the wherewithal to cram day and night without distraction and to memorize the law codes, I continued, they would have to experience life's many agonies if they were to become good judges. Wasn't it the same for doctors too?

Hye-yang, who had been rolling a grape around in her mouth, spit out a seed and turned more serious.

"You think I've never had any agony? To me, you're the one who's lived like a flower. And look at how you're ending up—happy just to be someone's wife." No matter how she tried to talk about the conflicts within her, Hye-yang continued, I wouldn't be able to sympathize. So she would merely tell me about her dreams for the future. She then described her motive for entering medical school.

Some time ago she had read *Memoirs of Hadrian* by Belgian-born Marguerite Yourcenar. This epistolary novel concerned an outstanding general who became the Roman emperor and blessed his land with freedom and peace but was then confronted with death. It contained a scene in which the emperor, tormented by a painful illness, appealed to a young doctor named Iollas to prepare poison for him. Although Iollas sympathized with Hadrian, he had to refuse on account of the Hippocratic Oath he had taken. The emperor repeatedly implored Iollas and finally persuaded the doctor to do his bidding. But that night the doctor's corpse was discovered in his laboratory. Unable to refuse the request of the emperor, he had chosen death in order to remain loyal to his oath.

"You thought I went to medical school because I was a bookworm, didn't you?" Hye-yang said with a purposeful look.

Deciding to go to medical school because she was attracted to a character in a novel was a part of Hye-yang I had never known. Just as Hye-yang didn't know about my suffering, I hadn't been aware of her dreams. Since these things were not visible, perhaps we had no choice but to keep them to ourselves. And for the same reason, So-yang's suffering could not penetrate me. I was trying to help So-yang by peeking in her diary, but she alone was afflicted. Was there any other way but for her to cure herself?

Almost all the couples vanished after ten o'clock, leaving many empty tables. Hye-yang, who enjoyed drinking so much that she had drunk with Father at mealtime since high school, was on her third gin and tonic when our intercom buzzed. Puzzled, I picked up the receiver.

Was this table CC? a man's voice inquired. He enjoyed the sight of two ladies sitting quietly and drinking gin and tonics. After a few more such remarks he asked, "Would it be all right if we talked a little?"

So-yang had probably received a call like this, I thought. A good opportunity seemed to have come our way. In fact, I had been about to try this intercom myself out of curiosity. I asked the caller if he was a college student, and he launched into a spiel.

"I go to Democracy University. I study math, natural sciences and anticommunism. I know how to report a spy. H_2O is water. I drink while I'm studying chemistry. I study trigonometric functions while I'm playing billiards, and I go dancing for my phys ed class."

His wordplay was like a riddle. I asked him some random questions, starting with what he had done that day.

"I washed my face, ate some ramen, moseyed around for a while and came here. I spend all my time away from home. Yesterday I pulled an all-nighter with some friends."

"Why do you stay out like that all the time? Do you tell your family when you spend the night out?" This was something I was genuinely curious about.

"Sure. Only I tell them lies. I say I'm staying with a friend."

"How many times a week do you come to Chongno?"

"Eight. And sometimes twice a day."

I burst into laughter and suggested he join us. His polished wit didn't mark him as a high school student; he was a college student, I guessed. He didn't want to show his ugly face, he said, but a moment later a tall, neat-looking young man arrived at our table. Pretty cagey, I thought. Although his hair was long and he was smartly dressed, he still had a boyish look about him.

My guess was correct. He introduced himself as a college senior majoring in electrical engineering. He was with two friends, he said, looking back at a table near the entrance. I responded that I was soon to be married and that my younger sister and I had come here for a change of pace. He must have been disappointed that I was old enough to be his big sister, I said, but if they didn't mind, I'd buy them a beer.

We all left Something together. Hye-yang, who had been watching me in disbelief, followed silently, perhaps thinking it wasn't a bad idea to be drinking with people her own age.

It was late by now, and trash was strewn along the side

street. One of the others, a swarthy, determined fellow, kept kicking pieces of trash as he walked.

"Why do people have to throw things away wherever they want?" I said to myself.

"They're dissatisfied, that's why," shot back the same fellow, who had overheard me.

"They're dissatisfied, so they throw garbage around?"

"They don't have any self-control—they're young." This time he kicked an empty liquor bottle.

We took a table in a nearby beer hall. Five mugs of draft beer were brought to us. I had ordered a half liter, the others a liter. While tearing open a packet of snacks, the electrical engineering major introduced his two friends, starting with the trash kicker.

"This is Twenty-five Hours, the gateway to dissatisfaction. He's a business administration major, and he studies, he demonstrates, he sees women and he's so filial to his widowed mother that he goes straight home at dawn after staying out all night. Twenty-four hours a day aren't enough for him, so we call him Twenty-five."

The fellow with the big eyes sitting across from me was Buzzer. Whenever a professor ran overtime in one of his worthless lectures, the first student explained, Buzzer's role was to inform him that class was over by saying the buzzer had sounded.

Buzzer then gestured with his chin toward the electrical engineeering major. "His nickname is the best of the bunch. His name is Ha and he really gets into porno, so we call him Harno."

Hye-yang giggled, then introduced herself as a fourth-year student in the basic medical course, thereby inflating her standing by two years. I changed the subject to school life. Twenty-five spoke first, in a heated voice.

"Before I went to college, I thought it was a wonderland—purity itself. But what I've learned in my three years there is that it's all a sack of lies. Integrity alone doesn't make it. You can study yourself into the ground, but it's the guy who cheats who gets the A. And you have to be strong. When we demonstrate against the idea of sending students out to branch schools in the countryside, the administration sicks the upper-class phys ed students on us, and they don't give us any mercy. You can't survive if you're weak, even in the ivory tower."

As an example, Twenty-five continued, the hero of a current bestseller was a master of karate. A person just couldn't promote himself unless he had power, money and prestige. People couldn't live any other way, because that was what the world was like. He himself had chosen money, he asserted, because once he had grabbed power through money he would help everybody live a better life. "What do we go to school for? To make a living, right? The quest for truth, the quest for academia—all a sack of lies," he snarled.

Though Hye-yang the bookworm was usually indifferent to almost everything, she listened attentively, perhaps agreeing. So-yang, who had said she had nothing to grab hold of—could this kind of disappointment and resentment have prompted her to leave school?

"Do you know why there are so many kids in Chongno?" Twenty-five asked. "It's because they need an outlet. Nothing is established here. It's a mess, but it's also a lifeline. Coming here is something they do to soothe themselves."

These acrimonious remarks fascinated me. I opened up and said I was wondering how deep their friendships were with women.

"Frankly, this is what turns us on," Twenty-five answered. "We drink when we come here, but the main thing is hunting girls. It's obvious what they're up to, the girls who go around late at night."

I realized he was talking about one-night stands. This was difficult for me to accept. "Don't you have any human feelings toward these girls? Don't you feel any compassion for them when you think of your own sisters?" These silly questions were inspired by my thoughts of So-yang.

"If you're not going to take care of yourself, who is?" Twenty-five snapped coldly.

Harno was more direct, as if Twenty-five had been unable to get through to me: "When a man and a woman get together, it's constant bickering. And where am I supposed to find purity? In a sweetheart? I don't have time to think about things like that—I'm going in the army soon."

5

It was after midnight when Hye-yang and I returned. Mother opened the gate for us without a word and we went inside. The living room was brightly lit. Father was shouting at So-yang, who was leaning against the sliding door to the kitchen. She merely stared at the wall as we entered.

"You're a grown-up girl, and you stay out all night without a word of explanation? Who do you think we are, anyway? Your mother's so ashamed she doesn't even want to talk about you."

Hye-yang went upstairs with only a glance at So-yang, but I hid against the wall of the stairwell. Father continued to upbraid So-yang in vain: Where had she spent the night? If a friend's house, which friend?

As Father began to repeat himself, So-yang cut him short. "What's wrong with staying out?" she spat. "I'll take care of my own business."

"Taking care of your own business, eh? Well, look how well you're doing. Are we just supposed to stand by and watch?"

"Isn't there a limit to what parents can do with their children after they're grown up? I've had enough—I'm going to bed," So-yang said.

I heard simultaneously So-yang's footsteps and the sound of Father getting up. I stuck my head toward the living room just in time to see Father smack So-yang across the cheek. So-yang staggered, but soon righted herself. Father then threw a punch at her, but she ducked and walked to the stairs.

"You little brat!" Father shouted, his nose twitching. "You're still wet behind the ears and you come home after spending the night out and talk back to your own parents. Instead of respect, it's backtalk!"

I followed So-yang up to her room, but she locked the door behind her and wouldn't respond to my knocking. Hye-yang came out of the bathroom after washing her face, and the two of us called So-yang. A few minutes later she finally opened the door. She had changed into a white nightgown and was brushing her hair.

"What's going on? What's the matter with you two?" she asked nonchalantly, as if nothing had happened.

Having come upstairs to console her, I stood there at a loss. Hye-yang, though, was not about to gloss over the incident.

"Let's settle down a little. You're always welcome in my room, you know."

"The best way is just to leave me alone," So-yang replied in a low, husky voice filled with annoyance. The door shut right in our faces.

A week later So-yang declared war by staying out yet again, this time for two nights. Mother was openly disgusted, and I ate later than usual to avoid Father.

The day So-yang left, I stayed at my future in-laws' house until Mr. Ch'oe returned from work. Not until the following morning could Mother and I sit down by ourselves and talk. Mother asked if So-yang had a boyfriend.

I hesitated, unable to tell her about Hŭi-jung. Would Mother ever understand? I myself found it hard to accept.

So-yang was at that age, I replied. She appeared to be seeing a fellow from time to time, but I didn't think their relationship was serious. Rather than attributing So-yang's nights out to a boyfriend it would be better to look at them as part of the ordinary lifestyle of young people. The disco clubs and all-night video tearooms were swarming with people her age, I explained.

"Why do they stay up all night at places like that? Don't they get tired?"

"It seems they prefer them to home."

"They must have problems with their families,"

Mother said perfunctorily, as if confident there were no problems in our family. "Why does So-yang keep going off on the wrong track?"

I fixed my eyes on Mother, then shook my head. "I don't know—she's not an easy one to figure out. But it's wrong to think we can handle a girl like her by hitting her," I said with a frown.

"He's quick-tempered, your father, but he's also old-fashioned," Mother said, half supporting Father yet nodding in approval at what I had said. "Now and then when I go into your rooms I smell cigarettes. I told Father this once, and he said kids were all like that these days. He even told me to smoke one myself if I got to feeling frustrated. At times like that he seems modern, you know."

I nodded. Temperamental Father did keep up to date in this respect at least. "I don't dislike Father."

After breakfast I went directly upstairs to So-yang's room. It reeked of cigarette smoke. I discovered her ashtray heaped with cigarette butts, and opened the window. Her quilt lay unfolded on her sleeping pad, and her clothes were strewn about. Two books were lying on the floor—a collection of poetry by Baudelaire and Darwin's *Origin of Species*. The most recent line in So-yang's diary began with her being slapped by Father:

The commotion has passed, and now it's calm, as if nothing has happened. But within this tranquillity, something is penetrating keenly to my fingertips.

This room of mine isn't a room. I need a room that will make this little bleeding sheep sleep, that will ease the heart of this startled deer, that will caress the steel-blue blade of this dagger.

Perhaps such a room will never exist for me. Even van Gogh's Bedchamber of Vincent, *depicted so vividly in his uncomplicated fashion, gives a feeling of anxiety rather than repose. The rough wooden floor a faded reddish brown; the mirror glaring but empty, nothing shining there. The crimson blanket. . . .*

So-yang must have felt dejected that day. Even so, her

description of her room pained me. In comparison, the next entry, written several days later, was light as a soap bubble.

I wash my hair, lie down with it still wet, and eat some ice cream. No artificial constraints—just basic human nature, and I'm comfortable like a baby.

I just discovered the words "vanity case" on a makeup kit. I like this word "vanity," in the sense of being in vain. Among the things that are in vain, the most useless is sensation. It's like the fragrance of a skin toner. In the end, being alive is such a sensation, and nothing more.

So-yang then skipped a line and briefly jotted down a passage from *The Tale of Shim Ch'ŏng*. She had been reading an illustrated version of the story in a children's magazine while eating ramen late one night. The scene in which Shim Ch'ŏng parts from her blind father brought a flood of tears from her, she wrote.

How in the world could someone's personality be so inconsistent? To cry at her age upon reading a story everyone knows! I sat blankly for a bit in So-yang's room, then left to call Myŏng-ju. Luckily she was home; perhaps she had no classes that morning. I asked if she had seen So-yang lately.

"No, not since last time."

I sighed.

"Did something happen to her?" Myŏng-ju asked after a pause.

"We haven't seen or heard from her in two days, and now I feel like talking with you some more." There was another silence, and I added, half to myself, "Maybe it'll make me feel better."

Myŏng-ju then said that since she didn't have a two o'clock class that day, we could meet then at the Cordwood Tearoom, across from school.

I passed a stone lion at the entrance to the tearoom and stepped inside to the slow rhythm of a folk song from one of the northwestern provinces. A wedding costume from long ago mounted on the wall caught my eye. Kites ornamented the ceiling—a unique sight. With its wooden chests serving as tables, its candlestick holders shaped like butterflies, its framed folk paintings and such, the tearoom was cozy and classic. I took a seat, and just as I was ordering some sweet rice drink, Myŏng-ju sat down opposite me.

"I like it here," I greeted her. "It's comfortable, and it's really Korean."

Myŏng-ju responded with a fleeting smile. She said she and So-yang had practically lived there around that time the previous year, and that recordings of the oral narratives known as *p'ansori* would be played for So-yang.

So-yang liked *p'ansori*? My face must have registered my surprise.

"Last fall So-yang joined a *p'ansori* club that met once a week," Myŏng-ju continued. "Didn't anyone at home know?"

Just then our waitress arrived with my rice drink and Myŏng-ju's peacock tongue tea, so named for the shape of the young green leaves used to brew it. I tasted the rice drink and tried to remember if I had ever heard *p'ansori* coming from So-yang's room. Yes, I had heard it, once, on a Sunday—I was cleaning the hallway and I heard "The Song of the Red Wall." Without thinking anything unusual about this at the time I opened So-yang's door and looked inside. She seemed to be asleep, her head near the door and her feet extending into the middle of the room.

"What could have gotten her thinking about *p'ansori*?"

Myŏng-ju warmed her porcelain cup with a little hot tea, then filled it up.

"She said that when she was young and taking dancing lessons she felt an affinity with the melodies of traditional music."

That was probably true, I thought.

"And when she sang those tunes she felt she was unburdening herself."

"What made her feel burdened? And now she doesn't have any interest in it?"

I asked myself what I was doing asking someone else

about my own sister—someone I lived under the same roof
with.

Myŏng-ju drank some tea, cleared her throat and continued: "She quit going to the club before the semester was
over. She got disgusted with the other kids making a big
fuss over tradition. To her this was sentimentalism, and she
didn't like it. She accused the others of studying tradition
while carrying on about independence of mind and such,
when they themselves lacked a spirit of independence."

I understood. These days music school students are taking more pride in things Korean, and many of them choose
to major in court music. One might call it a movement toward cultural uniformity. So-yang seemed to have turned
up her nose at this overenthusiasm, but couldn't she too
have begun studying p'ansori on account of this movement?

I had been tracing So-yang's state of mind by myself,
and now Myŏng-ju was helping me along as best she could,
as if she were cooperating in an investigation.

In the spring So-yang had enthusiastically joined the
theater and broadcasting clubs, but before the semester was
over she had quit them too. Myŏng-ju thought it was because she had clashed with the other club members. The day
new members were welcomed to the club, for instance, So-
yang, nonchalant as could be, had surprised everyone by
smoking. I was startled to hear this.

Myŏng-ju also told me she once saw So-yang wran-
gling with a male student in a dive across from school. The
fellow had started the argument because So-yang, a
woman, was drinking in broad daylight.

"Most girls just smirk and let it pass, but So-yang
wouldn't stand for it. She told me she'd never heard that
kind of garbage when she was growing up. She wanted to
slap any son of a bitch who carried on about how women
should behave."

"That's So-yang, all right," I sighed, nodding in agreement.

So-yang had made a mistake in coming to a coeduca-
tional school, Myŏng-ju intimated. At a women's college

women are their own masters, but in a coed school women who are exceptionally bright or who disregard the expectations of others have a difficult time accomplishing anything on their own. And of course the club presidents are always male, she added.

I cocked my head, wondering if a women's college would suit So-yang. When she first took the entrance exam, Father and of course Mother had urged her to go to a women's school. It was Father's cherished opinion that in this age of men and women contending with each other, women who went to coed schools would become competitors with men and the object of their hatred. This was farsighted of Father, but So-yang made clear her views: she didn't like the kind of flashy, all-girl school that Sister had attended.

"She couldn't put up with that kind of school, and she couldn't put up with this kind either," I couldn't help concluding.

Seeing Myŏng-ju again helped me understand So-yang better. I had known nothing about So-yang's school life. And to think that while she was studying *p'ansori* she had said nothing about it to me, a music school graduate.

Myŏng-ju went so far as to skip a class in order to continue our conversation. I was interested in Myŏng-ju's activities, and questioned her about this and that.

Using terms such as *economism* and *reformism,* Myŏng-ju explained how the nucleus of society—those who controlled the means of production—were actually excluded from society, and what the struggle of these workers was like.

"Mi-yang, even if you accept this in theory, you probably can't feel it in your heart," she said. Then from out of the blue she asked, "What would you do if you were a magician?"

"Well. . . . " It was an interesting though fanciful question. As a child I had had such wishes as wanting to walk on the ocean and wanting to be transformed into smoke so I could seep through the cracks around the window of a sleeping friend's room and surprise her. But now. . . .

Myŏng-ju looked at me as I entertained these dusty dreams. "I'd like to use magic for the sake of justice," she said animatedly. Her childhood dream had been to become a magician and punish the wicked people who trampled the weak. Comic-book versions of traditional tales had been a big influence on her. In addition, the dream was not unrelated to her disposition. After all, in middle school she had been nicknamed Yu Kwan-sun, after the heroine of the March 1, 1919 movement for independence from Japan.

"The word 'justice' was probably buried deep in my subconscious all along, and ten years after I got that nickname I happened to meet up with the word again. When I entered college I decided I would devote my youth to the most beautiful thing in the world. At the time I didn't know what that was. Later I discovered it within myself—justice, the most beautiful thing."

These words rang truer than any theory about justice. So Myŏng-ju had this attractive side to her, I thought, looking at her out of the corner of my eye.

"It would do her good to take an interest in things like the women's movement," Myŏng-ju said, returning to So-yang. "She's aware of women's problems because she's faced them herself. But she lacks perseverance. Maybe it's her circumstances. She despises her nouveau-riche grandmother, and she rebels against her parents and rejects their bourgeois ideology. On the other hand, she can't help having a complacent streak because of all the things she's been given."

This was the first time I had heard the term *bourgeois ideology*, and it got me to thinking. According to her diary, wasn't it for just such reasons that So-yang disliked her family? The philosophy of life that governed our family *was* this bourgeois ideology, to borrow Myŏng-ju's expression.

"There's a part of So-yang that doesn't see reality," Myŏng-ju continued. "She's always in conflict. She has the will to change, though she doesn't express it. The body can energize the spirit, but I don't know whether she really has a vision of change for herself. All I know is that she's headed for destruction. I'm always criticizing her about this because of my expectations of her, but there's not much she can do."

"You two are just too intelligent for your own good." I couldn't contradict Myŏng-ju, but there was something I wanted to say. Though she attached great importance to those who are isolated by their own materialism, wasn't she ignoring those who were spiritually isolated as well?

As if reading my mind, Myŏng-ju said in a softer tone, "So-yang is an outsider. She always keeps her distance from human relations and events and just looks on."

This I acknowledged. Even the relationship with Hŭi-jung was something So-yang had never jumped into. Only then did I ask Myŏng-ju if she happened to know Hŭi-jung—his relationship with So-yang was what I really wanted to know about.

"So-yang has never told me about a boyfriend, but even if I said I knew him, what use would that be to you?" Myŏng-ju countered.

"Well, I'm not sure. It's just that I'm frustrated. And Kyŏng-ok said she knew of him. . . . "

"I'll bet she does. She and So-yang are always together. But she's not my cup of tea," she said disdainfully.

"I see what you mean," I said hesitantly. I was about to end the conversation there when Myŏng-ju hurriedly continued.

"So-yang's not some wayward high school girl, so what's the use of meeting the people around her? Why not just start talking with her." After a pause she added, "She's not some idiot who's turned strange because of her friends; she's so good at analyzing people."

I concurred. Although Myŏng-ju was being outspoken, she wasn't wrong. Even if I met Hŭi-jung, what would I say to him?

Father's voice sounded throughout the house when So-yang returned from her two nights out. The house always seemed noisy then because of her.

Convulsed with rage, Father drank whiskey as he

waited for So-yang. It was just past eleven when So-yang returned. She smelled of liquor. As before, So-yang, by keeping silent, stood up to Father as he tried to exercise his authority as the family head. This angered him even more.

"If you can't listen to anybody you're an animal. You call yourself elite, you worthless brat?"

"Elite? Are you kidding?"

Although So-yang was scorning herself by saying this, her attitude still seemed arrogant.

Finally hot-blooded Father cursed her and jumped up with such force that the footstool bumped against So-yang, toppling her to the floor in surprise. Then Father, who had extended a leg to block the rolling footstool, accidentally kicked So-yang's leg. There was nothing I could do.

It wasn't deliberate, but now that it had happened, Father shouted even more spiritedly, "If you pull that kind of stunt once more, don't ever come home again! Because if you do, I'll break those pretty legs!"

Probably because of the alcohol, So-yang's body felt heavy and feverish. When I tried to help her up she became annoyed and tried to brush me away, and when we reached the second floor she threw my hands off and went into her room.

Then the music started. First there was the noisy sound of drums, like that coming from Hyŏk's room in the basement, as I had a cup of tea. Then I heard Mozart's Requiem. The record played over and over, and I couldn't get to sleep. I started out for the upstairs bathroom but ended up downstairs, as if my mind had gone blank.

So-yang's door still hadn't opened late the next morning. Eleven o'clock passed, and when I knocked there was no response. I shouted two or three times for So-yang to come and eat. She answered curtly in a sunken voice that she wasn't eating. Around noon the telephone rang. I happened to answer, and instantly recognized the voice as Kyŏng-ok's. Instead of calling So-yang I exchanged greetings with Kyŏng-ok. "Do you have something going today?"

"No. I just wanted to let her know she left her appointment book at the cafe the day before yesterday. She's probably been looking for it."

"I'll tell her." Then, feeling for some information, I calmly asked if they had had a good time the other night.

"Did she tell you we went to a disco?" Kyŏng-ok promptly responded.

"I had a hunch."

I asked no more questions, and hung up after informing Kyŏng-ok that So-yang wasn't feeling well.

I made a sandwich and a cup of coffee, took them upstairs and knocked again on So-yang's door. Still no sign of life. I told So-yang she had a phone call.

"You aren't going to take it?" I asked. So-yang's door finally opened.

I practically shoved her aside as I stepped into her room. I told her about the call from Kyŏng-ok and set the tray on the floor.

"Sister, why are you acting like my private nurse?"

So-yang leaned against the wall with a bitter look. Although her eyes were puffy, her face was hard.

"Did you go to see Kyŏng-ok?" she asked unexpectedly. "Why did you do that?"

Embarrassed, I offered her the coffee. "Because I don't know what's been going through your mind."

"Is Kyŏng-ok supposed to know?" She set down the cup with a clink and snorted.

This rubbed me the wrong way, and I made some cutting remarks. "Since she goes around with you, there must be some similarities between the two of you." If Kyŏng-ok and So-yang had something in common, it was probably their sensuality.

I became more serious. "You've been acting very strange lately. I know staying out all night with friends seems to suit young people, but can't you let the family know in a nice tone of voice that you'd like to spend the night out? We've all been on edge since we found out you dropped out of school, so you should be able to understand why Father gets so furious."

Before I realized it, So-yang had gotten up and was pacing about as if looking for something. My words were going in one ear and out the other.

Finally I spat out petulantly, "You went to a disco? For two days straight?"

"So I went somewhere—what's wrong with that?" she shouted, as if she had been waiting for that question. Then she took a record lying on the stereo and slammed it against the desk again and again. Black fragments littered the floor. I was stunned.

A blue flame flashed in So-yang's eyes. Her body shook, and she thrust both hands through her hair. Not until then did the white handkerchief binding her left wrist come into view. It was soaked with dark red blood that looked like the petals of a flower. I reached for the hand, but So-yang retreated a step and quickly stuck both hands in her pockets.

"There's blood on your handkerchief."

So-yang stubbornly kept silent.

"Why'd you do a thing like that?" My voice trembled.

So-yang threw herself down on her sleeping pad and buried her face in the quilt. "I feel like an island, and it's just me and the waves washing over me," she mumbled.

As she lay there in a heap, her pale, bare feet and her arms limp, she looked like an abandoned woman. I was about to tell her I wanted to help her, but my mouth wouldn't come unglued. Deep inside me I felt her loneliness, and my heart ached. But all I could do was sweet-talk her as I would have a child, suggesting we go downtown the next day and see a movie, eat some sushi and walk around for a change. So-yang feebly pushed at the sky-blue quilt under her foot, and I saw blood sprinkled there.

We never did go downtown together. I guess I was the one to blame. The next day I received an unexpected call from Yŏng-suk, a classmate who had actively encouraged me to enter graduate school. She now worked in the office of our music school. She suggested that we call on the chairman of our department of instrumental music, who was celebrating his birthday that day.

I had never taken a course from this professor, but since I had cut my contacts with my alma mater, this seemed like an excellent opportunity to say hello to him. I felt hesitant about seeing the professor, but Yŏng-suk, who had been invited for lunch, pieced together a scenario for us.

"Why don't we say that you dropped by to see me, and we happened to come together?"

We arranged to meet in Shinch'on at eleven-forty at a tearoom opposite a university near the professor's house.

My plan was to call So-yang after leaving the professor's house. I asked Mother to tell So-yang to wait for my call and suggested that the two of them have lunch together and try to talk.

Mother showed little interest in this as she cleaned some cabbage, but she didn't seem to mind having a good excuse to go up to So-yang's room.

Mother had remained in her room when So-yang was slapped by Father. In fact she had avoided confronting So-yang since learning she had left school. She was afraid that her intelligence might be interpreted by So-yang as merely the insignificant common sense of the older generation, and this fear was greater than the effort she put into understanding her daughter.

"If I have time this afternon," I told Mother, "I'm going to a movie with So-yang." I didn't mention So-yang's wrist. It had been a terrible shock to me, and I didn't want to tell anyone. I wanted to forget that it had ever happened.

I left the house a little before eleven and arrived early at the tearoom. It was on a main street only a few steps from the bus stop in front of the university. An even row of shields lined one of the sidewalks opposite the entrance to the university. Behind them, as if in ambush, stood riot police. This was a familiar sight, since demonstrations had been occurring day in and day out at universities throughout the city.

I went inside and was about to take a seat by a window facing the street when I suddenly heard a commotion. I looked around, thinking the noise was coming from the radio or the television, but just then the waitress set a glass of barley tea in front of me, clicking her tongue.

"More tear gas—I'm so sick of it."

I looked toward the street and saw a crowd of students, arms around one another's shoulders, swarming like bees from the campus entrance. Those in front ran forward, some throwing rocks at the riot police and others, wearing masks, hurling torches and Molotov cocktails.

"Go away! Go away!"

This battle cry, started by one of the students, sounded again and again. It was an angry wave, a clamorous forest of youth. The rocks, torches and Molotov cocktails continued to fly, and reddish-black flames rose here and there on the street.

"Go away! Go away!"

Tear-gas canisters burst, producing a hazy smokescreen in which the wave dispersed, but angry voices continued to flare up. Some of the stones rolled onto the sidewalk in front of the tearoom, and the students tugged and pushed a bulletin board into the middle of the street and set it ablaze.

My skin felt as though it were shrinking and my face prickled, as if sparks were flying up at it. I covered my teary eyes with my handkerchief. It wasn't just the tear gas that was making me cry; although these students were acting on their convictions, their troubled youth oppressed my heart.

Why did these young people have to shout? Why did they have to wear masks in broad daylight having committed no crime? Why did they have to throw flames toward an indifferent world? Would they knock at the door of this iron-walled government until their fragile fists were shattered? It was the springtime of their life, but instead of being exhilarated by their youth they were shedding their own blood. From So-yang's hand, scattered fragments of a record, splashes of blood on a quilt. I had the illusion that blood was spreading through my field of vision, that I was shedding bloody tears.

I was glad that I went to the professor's house. Not only did he recognize me but he mentioned that I had played the difficult Hungarian Rhapsody of Liszt at our graduation recital with extraordinary clarity. He encouraged me, pointing out step by step the preparations necessary for entering graduate school and stressing the importance of not giving up music even if I didn't become a pianist. In truth, I had considered teaching part-time, and I would have been satisfied to have been treated as decently as any other Philistine. After seeing this professor I was ashamed of yielding to such complacency, and my passion for music sprouted again.

We left the professor's house at two. I saw Yŏng-suk to the entrance of our alma mater and then dropped by the Granary, a tearoom I had frequented in college. I found my old table. It was on the second floor next to a window with poplars outside. The blue window frames, which reminded me of a ship's cabin, were still there.

I had intended to call So-yang and ask her to meet me here. I felt I could tell her about the year I was twenty, which seemed like a limpid, emerald-green sphere. And I felt I could tell her about the mire of ugliness that I had fallen into that winter because of a single human—that the springtime of my life had been painful as well. That, as a poet had once said, life begins when its indignities are ready to challenge you.

But So-yang had left by the time I called. I asked Mother if she had given her my message, and she replied brusquely, as if no answer were necessary, "Who does So-yang listen to these days?" The reluctance evident in her voice told me she had not seized this opportunity to talk with So-yang. I asked how So-yang was.

"She seemed quite good. Grandmother's church friends came over, and So-yang sat with them. And she ate two bowls of rice. I was so impressed I gave her some spending money."

I hadn't expected this. The instant I hung up it occurred to me that Mother had been taken in. To think that a girl who had slit her own wrist had sung hymns and eaten two bowls of rice the very next day! But then she might have skipped most of her meals the previous day. If not, were her extreme mood shifts an indication of manic-depression?

So-yang seemed to be in such danger that I could leave

nothing to chance, and so I decided again to see Hŭi-jung. So-yang was like a girl standing at the edge of a cliff, with nothing but straws to clutch at. If the person she saw most frequently now was Hŭi-jung, then perhaps he was the one who could help her out of this situation.

I had no problem obtaining his phone number from his school. It was just after nine the next morning when I called him—a little early, I realized. The courage to call didn't come readily when I tried to imagine what his reaction would be, but I couldn't give up without trying to put my plan into effect.

A young woman answered in a high, bright voice. When I asked for Hŭi-jung she asked who was calling. I replied very precisely that this was So-yang's family calling.

"So-yang?"

From the way she asked, I gathered this was the first time she had heard that name.

"Big Brother!" she called.

So he has a little sister too, I thought, more or less relieved.

When Hŭi-jung answered I excused myself for troubling him and told him I was So-yang's older sister.

"Older sister?" he said, his voice rising.

I had heard about him from So-yang and had told her to invite him over sometime so we could meet him, I began. Then I got to the point: it was nothing special, but I wanted to ask his advice about something concerning So-yang.

As I had anticipated, Hŭi-jung remained silent for a moment, mulling it over. I realized that if I were in his shoes, I would be suspicious too.

To put his mind at rest I said that I had also seen So-yang's friends Myŏng-ju and Kyŏng-ok some time ago. I explained that since her friends were the only ones who knew about her having left schol, I had no choice but to ask them about it.

Finally, as if it were a burden, he said, "All right, then, you set the time." We agreed on eleven that morning.

I was nervous, unlike the times I had met Myŏng-ju and Kyŏng-ok, and I paced uncertainly until I left. Fortunately,

So-yang, who had returned late the previous night, had not stirred from her room.

Perhaps because I had imagined from So-yang's diary what Hŭi-jung looked like, I recognized him at first glance. When I entered the bake shop in Kwangwhamun that Hŭi-jung had picked for our meeting, I took a seat facing the door. I was brought some barley tea, and five minutes later Hŭi-jung walked in.

His sweater, with its buckskin patches on the elbows and shoulders, and the gray scarf draped over a shoulder, gave him the jaunty appearance of a young ice skater. As he looked about the interior, his brow became furrowed as if he were nearsighted. Thinking he had penetrating eyes, I raised my hand to signal him. He saw me and came over.

"How did you recognize me?" he said with a trace of a smile. He took a seat and called a waitress. He ordered a citrus soda, saying he was thirsty, and I ordered the same.

"Put some ice in mine," he told the waitress as she was leaving. His use of plain rather than polite speech forms with the waitress seemed natural.

I sipped my barley tea, wondering where to begin. Hŭi-jung seemed to be the uncomfortable one, but instead of making idle talk—remarking, for example, that I didn't resemble So-yang—he didn't say a word. He wouldn't be easy to deal with.

I opened by saying that he must have been surprised that I called. He had probably guessed, I said, that So-yang had left school without checking with anyone in her family. Since then we had been puzzled by her behavior. So my seeing him was kind of like gathering intelligence.

Hŭi-jung, still wearing his muffler, chewed on an ice cube. "To be honest, I don't know So-yang very well," he replied gravely.

"You haven't known her very long," I exclaimed knowingly.

"If I had known her for three years, it would be exactly the same," he said, gently shaking his head.

After a pause Hŭi-jung said that the So-yang he knew was given to extremes, had no patience and was negative toward everything. She seemed to be waging a demonstration of her own, because she was more radical than the students who demonstrated.

I found this interesting, and asked him to continue.

Hŭi-jung gave an example. One day they met in a tearoom and So-yang was smoking. A waiter approached and told her to put out her cigarette. The owner couldn't stand the sight of women smoking, he explained, and had directed him to tell women not to smoke.

"So-yang told the waiter to call the owner. They kept arguing about this for a while, and then she got tired of it and put out the cigarette. We had already paid for our tea, so we drank it and left. But as soon as So-yang got outside, she sat down on the steps and lit up. There she was smoking right on the street, just like an old lady!"

So-yang and Hŭi-jung had then had words. So-yang had quit arguing, she told him, because he had kept silent, as if taking sides with the waiter. If she couldn't make her case with the man she was with, how was she supposed to convince a waiter?

"And so?"

Hŭi-jung looked intently at me, wanting to know what I wanted to hear. "I begged her not to smoke on the street, but she wouldn't listen. The people passing by were staring at us. I wanted to break her of her stubbornness, but finally I just left."

Hŭi-jung took out a cigarette, and I decided to have one too. It was my first cigarette in a long time, and my head began whirling. To hide any signs of this I looked squarely at the wall.

Sensing that what he had just told me was not to my liking, Hŭi-jung gave me his point of view. So-yang was acting like a feminist, but this was Korea with its Confucian society. These days women were making a big fuss over women's liberation and blaming men as if they were their enemies, but the union of men and women was the beginning and the end of everything. Such was Hŭi-jung's pet theory.

"The world doesn't operate through racial harmony but

through men and women," he continued. "When I told that
to So-yang, she said it was just an excuse for men to sub-
ordinate women. But it's natural for the world to operate
through men and women. Subordination? What's that?"

Hŭi-jung also told me of a time So-yang drank to her
limit and proceeded to lie down on Chongno. "She's a
smart kid, but every once in a while she does something un-
controllable. It must be madness."

Madness? The word echoed in my mind as I recalled So-
yang shattering the record a few days before. Hŭi-jung,
seemingly lost in thought, had lowered his gaze to the table.
Although he had a good grasp of So-yang's personality, he
wasn't mature enough to defend her. And So-yang wasn't
mature enough to defend Hŭi-jung.

The first thing I did was criticize Hŭi-jung's statement
that So-yang was acting like a feminist. The world had
passed through industrialization, I argued, and was now entering an information-oriented era. Like a certain song said,
the world is one. In such an age, it was anachronistic to talk
about whether women should smoke or not. If Hŭi-jung
really thought of women as independent individuals, then
how could he say such absurd things? And remaining silent
when the waiter told So-yang to put out her cigarette made
it clear whose side Hŭi-jung was on. If Hŭi-jung had told
me he was conservative, I would have said nothing more.
But in any event So-yang was not incorrect. I then attacked
Hŭi-jung by saying that society inflicted many dehumaniz-
ing sanctions on women, and that statements such as "Men
and women make the world work" are nothing more than
sweet talk.

Hŭi-jung had been watching me as I spoke. He crushed
out his cigarette without smoking much of it, then took a
sip of his soft drink.

"When I first saw you I thought you were different
from So-yang," he said with a bitter smile, "but you resemble her in the way you talk."

Wanting to know more about Hŭi-jung, I casually
asked him how many brothers and sisters he had, whether

he had any problems at school, whether his major suited his talents, and so on.

There were three boys and a girl in his family—just the opposite of our family. Hŭi-jung was the second of the four.

"As far as school is concerned, I go to college because I need to, so I'll put up with it until I graduate—why not?"

He seemed to have clear aims, so I asked him what he wanted to do after he graduated.

He said he had thought of becoming a professor when he started school, but no more. He now wanted to use his major to do something productive, he said calmly. "Being a professor is nothing special. Professors take useless knowledge and get paid for talking about it."

Hŭi-jung then mentioned that he had spent the summer studying in Taiwan, and he told me a surprising story. He had brought back from there some essences that he had used to develop a ginseng gum. He had taken this product to a large, well-known company and had met the president himself. The president's reaction had been favorable, and a decision about production was expected soon.

"At my age, what's the use of thinking about my talents? Effort is what's necessary."

I was surprised to see this side of Hŭi-jung—what I might call his realistic perceptions. He was like a refined master with a touch of callousness—this was the attractive thing about him—and he was taking care of what he had to do. As I was thinking what a great deal of backbone he had, So-yang came to mind, and soon I was feeling gloomy. Others had found and paved their own way; how long would So-yang continue to drift? Myŏng-ju had sacrificed her youth for her ideology. But what was So-yang shedding her lifeblood for?

Only then did it occur to me that So-yang had fallen behind. Father had talked once about falling behind one's competition and so on, and I had challenged him. But before I was aware of it, I too had become one of the older generation.

We talked for about an hour, and Hŭi-jung, turning down my offer of lunch, left for school. He said he had eaten a late breakfast, but in reality he seemed to want to avoid spending more time with me.

I hadn't asked him any uncomfortable questions, such as how he regarded So-yang. Nor had I adopted the grandmotherly approach and asked him to be a good friend to So-yang. I requested only that he not tell So-yang of our meeting, since she rebelled so easily. He too had a younger sister and could probably fathom my state of mind, I said. Hŭi-jung couldn't very well tell me whom he had met for the first time that day, about the "sport" he and So-yang shared, but there would be another day to talk about more personal things such as that.

In any event, I didn't think that seeing Hŭi-jung would do So-yang any harm. Hŭi-jung told me candidly that he was going to see So-yang after class that day. And that evening So-yang returned home earlier than usual.

Mother had made a blue-crab stew and, thinking of her future son-in-law, had asked me to invite Mr. Ch'oe. Coincidentally I had been thinking of having So-yang join me in seeing him that evening, and just as we were finishing dinner, in she came with a gay face.

So-yang greeted Mr. Ch'oe politely, and while we were drinking tea in the living room she ate dinner with Mother and even helped her with the dishes. Then she brought tea for Mother and herself into the living room and sat on the same sofa with Father and Mr. Ch'oe. The evening overflowed with geniality, for our marriage would take place within a week.

Mr. Ch'oe spoke of his plans for a constructive life for us as newlyweds. He was a business administration major and a dull banker, but after marriage he would take piano lessons from his wife for thirty minutes a day. Moreover, he was thinking about studying French—something he had always wanted to do. Mastery of a foreign language in this age of internationalization was a great asset, he continued, and not just useful for watching foreign movies.

"You've picked a good major, so work hard at it," he implored So-yang.

I was stung by this mention of school. Mr. Ch'oe didn't know that So-yang had dropped out. I wasn't trying to keep it from him. Rather, I had wanted first to arrange my thoughts about So-yang. But in the meantime I had lost some opportunities to tell him. Also, with our marriage so close, I didn't want to reveal our family's problems to him.

So-yang read the situation and tactfully changed the subject. Influenced by books, she said, she had originally wanted to do genetic engineering, which was at the frontier of modern technology. To make a green barley field out of a desert or to manufacture growth hormones from intestinal bacteria would be to realize a miracle. If we could make a plant that was barley from the ground up and a legume underneath, and if we could develop a barley that could be grown without fertilizer, food crises would disappear from the earth.

But apart from solving these practical problems she had some wild dreams. She would make acacias bloom on oak trees, removing their roots, which were not suited to the mountains, so that their lantern-shaped blossoms might open. And she would make a different flower bloom every season on a tree. Stitching together the genes of organisms to make a new organism, as one would alter a suit to one's satisfaction, was truly a frightening thing, she continued. She was afraid that we would go as far as creating the ideal superhuman. We would then be advancing full speed toward remaking humans. We had already replicated rats and created a mosaic animal containing human and rat blood, but these were debasements of nature. When So-yang saw the presumptuousness of this advanced technology, and the mistakes of technology, she had switched her course of study to the humanities.

"I assume, of course, that people want to live a long life and to have cures for their illnesses, but they should also know how to die with courage. But in science, which does not agree with this, I see instead an ugly side of humanity.

To put it more radically, people should know how to kill themselves."

Speaking her mind, her eyes shining like those of a bright student, So-yang was an entirely different person. Father, who had kicked So-yang three nights earlier, looked on in wonder, and Mr. Ch'oe passed his beer glass to his future sister-in-law, this romantic erstwhile aspirant to the sciences, and filled it.

So-yang then pleased Mother by serving us some fruit she had sliced into attractive shapes. She had placed the slices with their red skin facing up and had laid two wild chrysanthemums at the side of the plate.

"I thought you couldn't do anything, but look at you," Mother said.

"Well, look whose daughter I am," So-yang quickly responded. Father, who adored Mother, was delighted.

So-yang did not budge from the house for four days. She helped with the dishes, but apart from mealtime she confined herself to her room, reading or listening to music. She seemed more at peace with herself, more normal, than in recent days.

When I came back from shopping, I would knock on her door and give her some cream puffs or show her what I had bought. This was a pretext for talking with her. One day I returned with some new slippers and clothes to find So-yang reading a women's magazine in her room.

"I didn't have anything else to do, so I got this from your room," she reported, not lifting her eyes from the magazine.

I moved closer and saw a heading "Universities of the World." This was the pictorial section of the magazine, and below the heading was a scene of students leaving a campus, books under their arms. A classic stone building occupied the background, and several couples were courting on the grass bordering the walkway. I wondered if another change had come over So-yang.

I had a sudden thought. "I ran into the younger sister of a friend on the street today. After she graduates next year she's going abroad to study. She's a French major too, and so I thought of you." I talked as if I were speaking off the cuff. "You dropped out of school because you were confused about your values, but life isn't something you can apply cut-and-dry solutions to. There's never an end to the questions. And whether or not you drop out won't affect the school or anything else; they'll always be the same. It's been almost a year now that you've been taking it easy, so how about getting ready to go back? You'll realize that school life isn't so bad after all. Even if it doesn't seem so great, I'm sure you'll be able to do what you want after you graduate, whether it's finding a job or going abroad to study. Even if you're going to be a hippie, you've got to be a college graduate in a society like this."

So-yang responded to this earful by mumbling in a tone of self-scorn, "I guess the problem lies with me."

Was this a reply? I asked myself. I couldn't tell whether it was her way of saying she wasn't returning to school or whether she was talking sarcastically to herself.

"If you know the problem lies with you, isn't that grounds enough to solve it?"

So-yang remained composed at this attempt at humor. "What I meant is that everyone *says* the problem lies with me."

Relieved that So-yang had not responded with a sharp look, I started talking about myself.

"Maybe it's because I blocked out studying by telling myself I had to play the piano, but if I could be a college student again, I'd devote my time to absorbing all kinds of knowledge. I'd go to the library. Imagine the world that would unfold in all the books there. But we don't live long enough to read them all. When we're suffering, everything about life seems painful, but if we open our eyes wide, there's an infinite world out there—an infinite reality. Don't you want to know about that world?"

So-yang had been studying me, and now she drew her knees up and circled them with her arms. She sat mum like that for a moment, then said simply and without expression, "I'll probably end up going back. I'm already worn out."

I concealed my delight at this response and finally showed her the slippers and clothes. I had bought them in It'aewŏn, where the prices were cheap. So-yang particularly liked a one-piece olive business suit that resembled an astronaut's jumpsuit. I willingly offered it to her, but she held back, saying it was too large.

The next day I bought the same outfit, but in a black color, and gave it to her. It was the only color left, but fortunately So-yang was quite content with it, saying it looked like a fighting man's uniform.

6

Marriage didn't seem real to me when I became engaged, but with the arrival of the gift chest from Mr. Ch'oe's family, two days before the wedding, its significance touched me deeply.

The masked gift bearer arrived in the evening, the chest strapped to his back. He carried before him a candle lantern draped with red and blue gauze. There was quite a commotion as the man haggled over his pay with every step he took, and just outside the front gate three of my cousins lifted him high and carried him into the house.

My cousins placed the chest on top of an earthen rice-cake steamer on the table near the front door. When the time came for Mother to choose some colored fabric from the chest, sight unseen, she glanced at Mr. Ch'oe.

"Whichever you choose is fine." Mr. Ch'oe gestured with his eyes toward the chest but indicated no preference between the blue and the red fabrics that lay inside.

Mother's selection turned out to be the red fabric, which signified that our first child would be a girl. I felt no regrets whatsoever—why should I have to prefer a son to a daughter? A smile covered Mr. Ch'oe's face. The second of four sons, he had told me after our engagement that two daughters was all he wanted for children.

The gift bearer had received a white envelope stuffed with money when the chest was deposited on the steamer, and now, as custom dictated, he attempted to return the money to the family. But Father good-naturedly indicated with a wave of his hand that the man should keep it.

"When I got married my mother-in-law pulled out a crimson skirt. She was about to start wailing, but I told her not to worry because I had nothing at all against daughters. I ended up consoling her with a drink," Father said, showing Mr. Ch'oe that he wasn't disappointed. With the amber studs dangling from the outer jacket of his traditional attire, Father seemed more dignified to me than ever before.

We didn't learn of So-yang's absence until everyone had gathered to open the chest. All the women, including Hye-yang, enjoyed looking through the gorgeous fabrics. Remembering that she would have her turn someday, Hye-yang took an obvious interest in this ritual, to the point of memorizing the names of the fabrics.

No doubt So-yang had left the house while I was at the beauty parlor. I guess she didn't like all the commotion. It was past midnight when Mother's sisters and Mr. Ch'oe and his family left. I went upstairs and sat up indolently until after one. My room was cozier than usual with its wisteria bed, the nightstand lamp with its orange shade, the Bach records, the Korean harp and the green curtain hiding the cracked window. This snug room was an agreeable space that defended me from the world. It was like a mother's bosom that had eased my pain, even during the most agonizing period of my life.

So-yang stayed out the entire night, apparently bored after several days at home. I didn't give much thought to this, but the following morning I couldn't resist the temptation to visit her room.

The room was neater than before, and the diary had been moved to the bottom drawer of her desk. I sensed she had discovered my little trick, but I told myself I wouldn't have this opportunity after marriage.

The new entries were undated.

I don't know what I want. And there's nothing I particularly desire. A trivial, meaningless greeting card, a satiny white candle

with a top like a flower, a pure wool scarf in a check pattern. I
peek into the shops on the street and look at the things I might like,
checking them off in my mind with a sense of obligation, only feel-
ing more intensely the poverty of my soul.

What I'd really like is to write poems, but my thoughts always
whirl and scatter. They're desultory—no continuity. And so, like
a student of Zen I stare at candles or bury myself in darkness. But
inside me is another me that gazes steadily at me and constantly
rises in revolt, saying, "Meaningless, powerless."

This seemed to have been written the night she was
kicked by Father. Some of the writing was feeble and airy,
some so forceful and exact it dug into the paper. I found this
unsettling, like the sound of drums that night.

The places where the paper was scored were the
sentences about poems. I hadn't realized So-yang wanted to
write poetry. If I had, I would surely have encouraged her.

What I wanted to see was something related to the two
nights in a row she had spent out. The next entry allowed
me to guess what had happened.

It's addicting, but Chongno is tedious like an aquarium—it al-
ways has limits. This is the place where young people enthusiasti-
cally spew their pent-up resentment and the dregs of sensation. I
only pretend to do that.

Yesterday I ran into C. I didn't recognize him because of his
frizzy hair, which turned out to be a wig. I spent time with him to
remove that wig—no, to share our wounds. At first he was dis-
dainful:

C: So what have you been doing since you dropped out?
Hanging out on Chongno?

Me: You've got your demonstrations, but what could I do?
(Then I laughed at myself.)

Afterwards he said, "The only reason you're doing this is be-
cause I'm going around in hiding."

C, I'm not a whore and I'm not the virgin Mary. All I'm
doing by holding you in my arms is repaying a tiny bit of the debt I
owe all of you.

But this too was a meaningless encounter. We became like

Adam and Eve, but even removing our clothes merely confirmed the existence of the wall between us.

So-yang had then skipped a line and written the next entry in green ink.

The body that confirms the despair in my soul is a river I can never cross, no matter how I try
The most useless, meaningless thing it is, eventually rotting, burdening me, not allowing me to cross
I reject the small consolation, illusions, deceptions it tries to bestow on others, and others on me.
Today everything makes my head ache, makes me sick
Strangely, the smell of the burning candles makes me sick
It's because of this body, unable to fly
Once I had wings—when I didn't recognize my body.

So-yang had written this the four days she had stayed home. Her face had been so peaceful, convincing me she had had a change of heart the day after she slit her wrist. But now a black cloud gathered in my heart again. There was something menacing about her having stayed out the previous night, and I grew anxious.

So-yang still hadn't returned by the time we finished dinner that day. I sensed that Mother considered it ominous for a family member to be absent on such an occasion, but because of the happy event that lay ahead she didn't mention So-yang.

Around six o'clock I called the Wooden Horse and asked Kyŏng-ok if So-yang had dropped by. She said she was still expecting So-yang to come for her appointment book, then asked if she had said anything about it. It was clear she knew nothing of So-yang's sojourn the previous evening.

Mother then talked with me about entertaining the wedding guests, preparing for my honeymoon, and other such matters, but the words went in one ear and out the other. I kept checking my watch needlessly. At about nine I went upstairs for a while, then slipped out of the house.

As always, Chongno was packed with groups of young people. They were camped at every side street, and I bumped shoulders with them as I emerged from a pedestrian underpass. They crowded the snack stalls that lined the side streets here and there. Some were eating roasted silkworm larvae, some deep-fried sweet potato sticks. I noticed two couples turning sticks of cotton candy and licking the white and pink confection.

I entered an alley and peeked into the establishments that lined both sides. I came upon a beer hall whose interior was entirely visible from the outside. Mounted on a wall was some diving apparatus. As I was inspecting the interior through the window, a waiter came out and urged me to go in. The owner was president of the Coral Aquatic Club, he obligingly informed me, and if I were interested in scuba diving he would be happy to introduce me. I gave him a smile and moved on.

So-yang would enjoy the sight of that diving gear, I thought. She was particularly fond of the sea. The summer of the year she entered high school, the whole family had visited a secluded beach on the east coast. The sea was like everlasting youth, she had said as she watched the ocean. She had dreamed of how wonderful it would be if she were a sea captain spending her life on the sea. She said she would like to go to a school of oceanography and study underwater life. So-yang was full of dreams of the many things she wanted to do. Was five years such a long time that these dreams had died?

I walked aimlessly down the alley, passing the clustered businesses, and found myself at Poshin Pavilion. For a fleeting moment I saw someone lying on the dimly lit grass inside the pavilion's iron fence. Perhaps he had fallen there drunk.

A few steps farther along, two girls were leaning against the fence and singing a lyric song. How strange to be singing at this hour here on the corner of Chongno, I thought. Because their young faces suggested they were high school girls, I felt like encouraging them. They sang well, I told them. One of the girls, who had long hair, smiled, forming a dimple.

"We like it here—we can sing where there's some atmosphere. We get kind of giddy and it clears away our depression. It feels good to know it's just us kids here."

I smiled and turned away. I knew they hadn't come here because they had no place to sing. When kids gathered with kids, it was like a haven in the woods. They found comfort together and realized they weren't the only ones who were confused.

Having covered most of Chongno, I returned to Something. I hadn't been able to find the Bluebird, mentioned in So-yang's diary. I didn't expect to find So-yang in either of these places, but I did feel a step closer to her.

As I was about to go in Something, a young man in a flashy ivory-colored suit caught my eye. It was Harno. His brow furrowed, he was looking nervously in all directions, as if awaiting someone. His dress shirt was unbuttoned at the collar, revealing a metal elephant hanging from a chain around his neck. I pointed to it as I approached him.

"Well, hello."

"That's some chain—did someone make you an African chieftain?"

"On your way to the beauty parlor for a facial?" He patted his smooth face in imitation of a massage.

I laughed. "Waiting for someone?" I casually asked.

"Have you seen Twenty-five? I've got to get going. We've got some business to take care of, but I need some cash to do it." Harno looked fretfully up the alley.

"How much?" I asked amiably.

"Five thousand." He passed a hand through his hair.

I took a five-thousand-wŏn bill from my purse and gave it to him. Harno put the money in his pocket and was about to walk away when a familiar face approached. It was Twenty-five.

"Hey, just a minute," Harno said as Twenty-five raised a hand to greet me. He led him several steps away and briefly explained something to him. Twenty-five nodded, and Harno pushed him toward me and then set off up the alley toward its intersection with Chongno.

"Looks like you've got a good thing going tonight. You're both all spruced up." I eyed his dazzling crimson pullover.

Twenty-five pulled up his sleeves. "This is Friday, you know. We've got to pull off a bunch of schemes this weekend. If Harno can swing this one, we'll have some money for our dates tonight. He gets a hundred thousand wŏn if he finds a college girl for someone."

A group of girls in tight pants passed by. After looking them up and down, Twenty-five craned his neck and kept watch over the intersection where Harno had disappeared. I was curious, and asked what they were doing. Twenty-five freely explained.

An older man, a company president, had come to Something and offered to pay the owner if he would introduce him to a college girl. The owner had asked Harno to take care of it, and it was agreed that Harno would receive one hundred thousand wŏn for his efforts. So he had gone out looking for a girl. Twenty-five's tone was very matter-of-fact, his expression unchanging.

"There are girls like that around—all you have to do is look for them. We'll get some money, and she will too. Not bad, eh?"

I stood there with my mouth open. Harno was using my money to angle for a girl to bring to an old man.

Before I knew it, Twenty-five had struck up a conversation with a girl in bobbed hair who was buying some sweet potato sticks at a cart nearby. Speaking too familiarly, he repeatedly asked the girl to meet him an hour later. The girl studied him and smirked, not seeming to mind his brazenness.

My eyes met the girl's. I hardened my expression and gently shook my head. The girl got the message, and shrewdly suggested to Twenty-five that she wait for him with her friends.

Thirsty and wanting to sit down for a moment, I decided to go in Something for the time being. I pushed open the door to the dizzying sound of rock music. It reminded me of popcorn popping. The place was much more noisy this time.

The lower level was full, so I went upstairs. Green light from the disk jockey's booth lit the stairs. The disk jockey wore a white turtleneck and his hair was permed. I watched him turn toward the stairway and reach for a record from the record cabinet next to the window. His sluggish, mechanical movement was just like that of a robot. I couldn't remove my eyes from him until I reached the second floor.

The upper level was less crowded. The bar at one end and the low tables with their white vinyl chairs gave it a cozy appearance. The atmosphere here was different. There were some young white-collar types at the tables, and a middle-aged man with his hair neatly combed back sat at the bar.

I sat where I could look down at the disk jockey. He was stiff and deliberate in everything he did—selecting a record, replacing the previous one with it, answering the intercom. His turned his head ninety degrees to the side, as if it were disengaged from his body, and reached straight out to change the record. He repeated these simple motions. His lack of expression numbed me. He was like a robot in a fish tank, and this made me feel odd.

I ordered a beer and continued to gape at the disk jockey. Then I saw Harno's ivory-colored suit. He came upstairs, went straight to the bar, and sat next to the middle-aged man, his back to me. They exchanged some words, and Harno pointed outside. The middle-aged man reached into his pocket and took some money from his wallet.

Harno left, and the man finished his beer and stood up. I too emptied my glass and got up. The clock in the green disk jockey booth read ten-fifty. It was time to go home, but I was anxious to see how this affair would be accomplished.

Harno had vanished by the time I emerged through the tinted glass door. I followed the middle-aged man up the alley toward the intersection. He walked into a parking garage and shortly reappeared at the wheel of a cream-colored Hyundai Stellar.

The car stopped at one of the broad corners of the intersection. Harno emerged from the entrance to a building across the street and signaled the man. The Stellar glided in that direction.

Harno turned to a woman standing behind him, then walked up to the driver's side of the car. I focused on the woman, who had remained in front of the entrance to the building, one hand stuck in her jacket pocket. She seemed to be studying the Stellar, where the two men were talking in low voices.

I couldn't believe my eyes. Despite the handsome, mature appearance that her crimson lipstick and gray jacket gave her, this woman in short hair was clearly So-yang. I was too stunned to move as Harno returned to escort her to the car.

Harno opened the door. So-yang nervously threw back her hair and stooped to get in. I ran to the car on trembling legs, pushed Harno aside and grabbed So-yang's arm.

"What are you doing? Get out, quick!"

So-yang glared at me and tried to lunge free. Despite my quaking voice, the reality of my sudden appearance didn't seem to have sunk in to her.

"I said get out, quick, you crazy thing." I pulled so hard that her jacket began to rip.

"Close the door and leave me alone!" So-yang shouted. Then, to the man: "Let's go!"

The car began moving, but I held onto the door. Harno tried to restrain me. I smacked his face with my purse. "Bastard!"

Passersby began gathering around the car.

"I told you to leave me alone, you idiot!" So-yang screamed. Then she tumbled out of the car. Pushing Harno and me away, she ran toward the main street. Drained though I was, I slammed the door and set out after her. She ran desperately and erratically, like an injured bird, bumping into other people. She was buried in the tide of humanity, her gray jacket fluttering like a torn wing. I had

almost reached the main street when I collided with a man.
There was no time to apologize, and I ran on. But the bird
had flown, and I couldn't catch her.

I combed the streets like someone bereft of her senses,
colliding with the sea of humanity. I wanted to collapse.

I ended up in front of a video arcade. It was late, and
many of the games were not in use. Bruce Lee's Homecom-
ing, Animal Farm, Vietnam War—I looked among the
games and hesitated. The bright colors on the screens, the
rat-a-tat sounds and all the complicated controls dazzled my
eyes. I stood there blankly, then finally sat down in front of
a screen that showed Tarzan swinging on a vine through a
green jungle. It appeared to be the simplest of the games.

But it wasn't easy to control Tarzan. Although I kept
my eyes on the screen and pressed the buttons every time
Tarzan leaped, he always ended up falling from the vine.
Because I was trying too hard, my hands moved too
quickly or too slowly. The boy next to me was playing
Animal Farm, lassoing one animal after another in a peaceful, lime green field. My Tarzan had become a constant
straggler in the woods, and not until I had donated a thousand wǒn worth of coins to the machine did I shake off my
inertia and stand up. I had worked five years for a bank but
was not in the least suited to the computer age.

Many places had closed for the night, and the alley was
less crowded. Most of the street stalls had been wheeled
away. The second-story batting cage was still lit up. Only
two batters were left, and they took turns swinging. The
hollow sound of bat against ball echoed in the alley. Here
and there small groups of people emerged from doors like
matches spilling from a box, and headed for home.

As I left the video arcade I noticed a sour smell coming
from a truck parked nearby. Several barrels occupied the
bed of the truck, and two young men in jeans were hoisting
another drum up. They were collecting swill from the res-
taurants at closing time.

I brushed past the truck and saw several steps ahead a
half dozen young people clustered together and singing,
each waving an arm:

When I was young I had love and affection,
But now I have a living to make.

Two more youths were sitting beneath a building shuttered up for the night and looking vacantly at the street scattered with litter. They didn't seem to be waiting for anybody, nor did they seem about to go home. I wondered if they, like So-yang, lacked a room they felt comfortable in.

Just before reaching the main street I turned and walked back up the alley. It was impossible to find So-yang now, but I had no desire to return home, even though I would be a bride the next day. The sight of So-yang getting into that car had staggered me, as if a pillar that I had leaned against had suddenly toppled over, and I wanted to be swept away by the wind like a falling leaf. Perhaps it was because I felt empty. I had decided to marry to unburden myself of the springtime of my life, and on this last night perhaps I wanted to break free of the stifling web of expectations that everyone held for me.

I passed through this alley of dark, quiet buildings and emerged on a side street. The crimson border of a neon sign at the entrance to a disco in an alley stretching toward Kwanggyo seemed to move in circles. A few young women in miniskirts were gathered like moths under this light. Viewed from the dark alley I had just traversed, the scene was like a picture of a different world. I set off toward the disco, and the music from inside grew louder.

The music surged out of the darkness and into my eardrums when I entered. The dance floor was filled, and two young women in thick makeup and bobbed hair were dancing in the aisles, their sweaters tied around their waists.

Most of the tables were occupied, and I was about to suffocate in the heat, so I sat down on a long sofa near the entrance. Most of the people looked no older than college students. They danced as if they were trying to expel the dregs that had settled inside them. Whenever the strobe lights flashed, their writhing, spellbound expressions seemed to gloat in the air like death masks. A teenager with short hair and sunken eyes was shouting along with the music, his body quivering.

The disk jockey changed to a slow tune. As I was emptying a glass of beer and eating some snacks, a man in a white dress shirt dyed purple by the disco lights approached and asked me to dance. I refused, saying I was waiting for someone. I had come here with no objective, but I didn't feel at all like dancing—especially with a man I didn't know.

I glanced idly to the side and saw a young man sitting by himself. He had long hair, but the large collar of his shirt reminded me of a sailor's uniform. A glass of citrus soda was on the table in front of him. He would watch the people dancing, get bored, sip some soda, then repeat the process.

I was curious. Neither of us had a companion, and I was sure he was younger than I. This gave me the courage to approach him.

"All right if I sit here?" My ready use of plain rather than polite speech surprised me.

The young man, who had been staring dully at the dancers, was too startled to refuse. I brought my beer and sat across from him.

"How about some beer?"

He eyed me intently, then reluctantly nodded. I passed him my empty glass and filled it for him.

"I'm by myself too. Nothing else to do, so I felt like talking with someone. Shall I try to guess your age? Twenty?"

He shook his head. "I'm twenty-two."

"I'm twenty-seven."

He cocked his head and looked me over. "I would have guessed twenty-five."

I followed up immediately: "When did you get here?"

"I sneaked out of the house sometime after ten. My mother probably thinks I'm home in bed."

"Why did you sneak out here?"

This time he didn't have a ready answer. "Why do you ask?"

"Oh, no special reason."

He was on guard again, like a porcupine raising its quills. "What do you want from me?"

"Nothing. I was thinking of my little sister and I felt like talking with you. That's all."

The young man lowered his guard. He naively admitted that he had come here to make friends with a woman.

Though older, he was like a boy in comparison with the precocious So-yang. I found it interesting that he talked straightforwardly about women.

"What kind do you like? Pick one out."

The young man looked at the dancers for a time, then pointed to a young woman in a maroon sweater. She was pert, with short hair, not big and not too small. Her way of moving very little as she danced struck me as excessively coy. She would be a tough one to deal with. I shook my head slowly.

"Can you really make friends with a girl at a place like this?"

"I guess my chances would be better in the clubs at the YMCA, wouldn't they?" He seemed to be changing his mind.

I agreed, saying it would be much easier to make friends with a girl at the Y because of the various activities in which to meet.

He listened attentively, then said abruptly, shaking his head, "No, that's a pain in the neck too."

It was past one when we left, having finished barely a bottle of beer. When I looked at my watch and stood up, he did the same, as if by prearrangement. The alley was dark save for the spinning neon light. Nauseating piles of garbage dotted the way.

The autumn wind blew among the grove of buildings, scattering pieces of wastepaper. The young man kicked the ones that came to rest at his feet. In this empty alley there were only our two long sticklike shadows walking along.

"You come to Chongno very often?"

My voice sounded louder than usual. A tin can clattered along.

"When I'm feeling lonely. But it's not much fun going to a disco all the time, is it?"

"Not so much that. . . . "

"Usually I'm by myself. I like it when it's quiet."

He kicked another piece of newspaper. I asked if he had any younger brothers or sisters. I had guessed he was the youngest, but it turned out he had a younger brother.

"My big brother went in the army. I miss him every now and then and write him a letter, and when he's home I try to be good to him."

I nodded. "Now that it's time for me to be getting married, I feel the same way toward my family."

As we were crossing the street a man in white toting a large athletic bag at his side overtook us. I had seen him at the disco. He was a professional dancer. Finished for the night, he was on his way home.

The young man recognized him too. "You must be happy," he ventured.

"Why is that?" The dancer looked back, passing a hand through his permed hair.

"Because you can dance every night."

We kept walking aimlessly down the third block of Chongno. The trash scattered beneath the pallid light of the mercury street lamps made the avenue seem like virgin land that had been neglected. An occasional car sped by, but virtually no people were to be seen. From somewhere came a cool, gentle breeze.

"It must be an awful pain being a garbageman," the young man said to himself as he kicked a cluster of plastic wrapping tape lying in his path.

"Mmm, so filthy."

The young man started talking about his hometown of Ch'ŏngju.

"It's a clean city. But there are a lot of rules, and that's not so hot. The upper-class people are always telling us what's right and wrong. But there's a lot to be learned. Nothing wrong with knowing about things."

"What do you want to do? There must be something."

"I don't think about that at all. I don't feel like making money, and I don't have any goals."

He stopped in front of a wall poster advertising the play *A Taste of Honey* and looked at it for a while. A piece of paper blew toward me end over end. It was an advertisement for a cabaret. The young man picked it up and studied it. His curiosity was genuine.

Three canvas-covered snack stalls on wheels were lined up beneath the Seun Building.

"Want to sit down for a while?"

The young man readily agreed, and we ducked into the middle stall. The owner of one of the other stalls was gathering the leftovers in preparation for wheeling his stall away. In the third stall, a drunk was egging on the proprietor. We couldn't understand his blather, but his curses were clearly audible. The young man gulped the glass of liquor in front of him.

"I don't go for that sort of thing—I'm not very tough, I guess."

"But you can't get away from it."

The young man bowed his head, as if trying to ignore the drunk, then changed the subject. "You must have had fun going around like this all night when you were going steady."

"I never had the opportunity. But aren't you tired?" I looked at my watch—half past two. I stopped drinking, fearing a wave of fatigue, but the young man didn't look the least bit tired.

"Once I stayed up three days in a row without a wink of sleep—just for the experience."

Not until then did I notice the Korean University Student Association badge on his shirt pocket. I immediately recalled having seen a notice to join this club posted on a crammed bulletin board when I entered college. This refreshing memory gave rise to a wave of nostalgia.

I took apart a large, freshly grilled clam to make it easier to eat, and set it in front of the young man. "How do you spend your time at home?"

"I like listening to the radio. I don't watch television, but the radio's fun. I try to imagine what the characters are like from their voices. And whatever happens one day, I think about it several days afterwards. Some things are like dreams. Like right now. Tonight ought to leave me with some good memories."

He was an odd boy—like the one in the children's story who looks at the world's affairs through a window. Buried in a precious world of his own, he seemed to be dreaming dreams of the unknown. It was a world uncontaminated by knowledge or ideology, entirely different from that of other college students.

We wandered the streets until daybreak, roaming where our feet led us. We watched a kung fu movie in a video tearoom, drank coffee in a music tearoom with a disk jockey booth that resembled a spaceship. We saw people sleeping propped up against street lamps, people leaving discos and eating bean-curd stew at the streetside stalls. We observed these scenes as if for the first time.

Several groups of people were camped in a pedestrian underpass. We walked by half a dozen college students playing poker there. I turned and asked them why they weren't going home.

"No bus fare," said one. "Want to join us?" he asked, waving us over.

We emerged from the underpass to see an occasional bus going by. The streets were still dark. Rats poked their heads out of wastebaskets, then disappeared into gutters. A bus pulled up beside us and released a stream of boys and girls with book bags. Chŏng-u went to a study hall at daybreak from time to time. This realization was like waking from a dream. Like other boys, Chŏng-u left home at dawn to study. Maybe he too would be playing poker in an underpass several years from now.

A street cleaner sweeping the illuminated alley across the street came into view. And wouldn't So-yang, like that street cleaner, be sweeping up after her children in another ten years?

I heard the sound of static and glanced at the young man to find he had put a transistor radio to his ear. Just then came the announcement that it was five o'clock, followed by music.

"The music they start off with always gives me a lift."

His expression was bright as the music. My tension had been drained, and suddenly my eyes felt heavy. I longed for my cozy bed. I had to go home. I rubbed my eyes and smiled. "Thanks for being with me till now."

"I wish there were more people like you. Can we get together again?"

I didn't answer. We wouldn't be meeting again. We would have to treasure the innocence of this night in our dreams. The young man put the radio in his pocket, comprehending my silence.

A taxi approached. I waved to the young man and ran to catch it. I felt his lonesome gaze, but I didn't look back as I got in. The taxi pulled away, and I leaned back in the seat and closed my eyes. The image of the young man standing in the gloomy dawn, his face showing he had awakened from his dream, rose distinctly before me. It was a part of me I had lost. Will your innocence prove powerful or powerless as you make your way through life? I silently asked him.

7

"Peter Ch'oe and Yi Mi-yang, do you enter into matrimony of your own free will, without the compulsion of others?"

"I do."

"Will you love and respect each other in marriage throughout your lives?"

"I will."

"Will you willingly accept the sons and daughters that God will entrust to you, and will you educate them properly according to the teachings of Christ and the laws of the church?"

"I will."

"The Lord of Heaven himself solidifies the mutual consent that the two of you have professed in this church, and he gives you his bountiful blessings. What he has joined let no one put asunder."

Six candles were burning on the altar. The faint scent of lilies wafted about as I reverently made these vows before the priest. It was a beautiful, solemn wedding mass. I was not a believer, but according to the dictates of my husband's religion, the ceremony was held in a Catholic church. I had never become used to the word *God*. I believed instead in a certain Absolute—the laws and order of the universe—and it was before this Absolute that I took my oath: I would love him and be faithful to him for the rest of my life, in happiness or in suffering, in sickness or in health.

Our exchange of rings, which had been consecrated by the priest, was truly a holy covenant—a covenant to share our love and pain, our loneliness and responsibilities, a covenant to create a family.

Together we partook of the host and the wine, affirming their link with our flesh and blood. The wedding guests, witnesses to our covenant, blessed and encouraged us with their applause.

I felt that everything had gone well. The others told us we were like a brother and a sister and hinted that ours was a match made in heaven.

The ceremony over, we threw off our wedding clothes in favor of jeans, retaining only the flowers, and climbed into a van. Mr. Ch'oe had remembered that I liked riding in trucks, but had rented the van to provide his bride with a more comfortable honeymoon.

We sped toward the East Sea. At one point we crossed the yellow line and zoomed by a clumsy driver at a hundred kilometers an hour. Our excitement was tempered by the sight of a policeman stopping a car ahead of us. We had also run a red light upon leaving Seoul, but luck was with us that day, and we were not pulled over for our violations.

We met no delays, and eventually the limpid turquoise sea unfolded before us. We stopped at a hotel in the foothills of the Sorak Mountains as twilight was settling in. At my suggestion we took an hour-long walk to a Buddhist hermitage after dinner. Although the dark path was lit by our flashlight, I stumbled time and again on the jagged rocks.

"It'd be easier if we came in the morning," Mr. Ch'oe said, taking my hand. The outline of the hermitage nestled beneath a magnificent, towering peak reminded me of a mysterious woman. I was captivated by the wind bell and the tile roof gently upturned like the toe of a Korean sock.

It would be fine if we spent the night there, a young monk suggested. He happened to be alone, and apparently found it admirable that two newlyweds had sought out the hermitage at night. But we politely declined, saying we already had lodgings. In any event, we were unsure whether an offering was expected. I felt regretful.

"Your place for the night is wherever you stop," said the monk, and he left it at that.

We returned to our hotel. "You're my home, darling," I said impulsively. "A traveler can put up anywhere for the night, but I'll always come back home."

Mr. Ch'oe put an arm around my shoulder and pulled me close.

Everything went smoothly on our honeymoon except for a downpour on the fourth day. At first we thought it was romantic to be traveling in the rain, but the water fell with such force that it blanketed the windows of the van. We couldn't see the ocean or stop and poke around. After settling for lunch in the van we drove south toward Samch'ŏk, then turned toward Seoul late in the afternoon.

On the way home we stopped at a rest area, and the first thing Mr. Ch'oe did was buy a newspaper. As if by tacit agreement, we hadn't seen a paper or heard a news broadcast since leaving Seoul. He opened the paper, and a photo of smoke billowing from a campus building caught our eye. "Police Quell Student Riot with Tear Gas, Water Cannons... ," read a large headline, and below that in smaller type, "70 Injured, 2 Critical after Self-Immolation." The picture showed several students making a stand on the flat roof of the building. A headline on the city page read, "Slogans, Building Occupation, Tear Gas: 3 Days on a College Campus," and under it was an on-the-scene report of the student demonstration. We could tell from all of this that something big had happened.

Mr. Ch'oe frowned. "Twenty-two schools, and over two thousand students—all hell's broken loose in Seoul," he muttered.

Awakened from the reverie of our honeymoon, I slowly looked through the paper. I found that the day we left Seoul, left-wing students from schools throughout the country had gathered at International University for a rally —"Students United in Struggle against Foreign Influence and Dictatorship," they had called it.

I skimmed the article and gently closed my eyes. It's an age of youth going to extremes, I thought—So-yang running down Chongno as if she were out of her mind, plowing through the surge of humanity; the young activists massing like clouds, shouting slogans, burning effigies of President Reagan and Prime Minister Nakasone; the campus building being retaken by the police, with the students emerging from it waving white flags of surrender. The attempt at self-immolation made me shudder. I recalled the description in the article of a burning mattress, and imagined the flames surging and ebbing like waves.

I noticed the smell of Mr. Ch'oe's cigarette and looked up to see a troubled expression on his face.

"The students are getting more radical by the day—it makes me wonder," he said.

"People wouldn't have to get hurt if the authorities showed some flexibility." I responded. "In any country, what happens in the society affects the nation as a whole, so if the government uses force, then there's bound to be a violent streak swelling up in the society. I read about a survey that a social psychologist did. He found that when people think the government values human life cheaply, then the society itself begins to do likewise."

Mr. Ch'oe also criticized the establishment, but at the same time, he was pessimistic about the display of radicalism among the students. The present sorry state of affairs was of course the responsibility of the administration, he said. But if you asked anyone in the older generation, they'd tell you it was dangerous for students to be establishing extremist ideologies and thinking of becoming revolutionaries when they still had so much to learn.

Then he brought up the student occupation of the American Cultural Center in Seoul the previous year. The students had held a three-day hunger strike there. When some of them weakened, a request was made to the Americans to supply some sweets. How childish to think they had to have chocolate, as if they were war orphans, Mr. Ch'oe chided them. He concluded that no matter what kind of ideology they cloaked their radical behavior in, they couldn't disguise the fact that they were acting their age.

Although I agreed with him, I admired the students' passion in tirelessly challenging the system, and I defended them.

"First of all, the older generation have only themselves to blame. The students don't trust them because of their compromises, and so they've decided to act on their own. They're not always right, but if they don't demonstrate, then who will? They're radical because they're young, but they're also capable of sacrificing themselves for an ideal."

"Do they have to set themselves on fire for an ideal? Is that really their goal in life?"

"Then what's the life goal of those of us in the middle class? A promotion to department head or manager? Having children and passing on the family name? Someone who lives comfortably like me and people in the older generation who've adapted to the system are in no position to talk to the students about life goals."

I was surprised at how my voice had risen. Mr. Ch'oe said no more. Since we were still on our honeymoon, perhaps he was afraid of irritating his bride, but I chose to interpret his silence as agreement. I sensed that he respected my thoughts, and realized once again what a good companion he was.

"Darling, you have what it takes to love someone," I reassured him.

It was after nine when we arrived at the house. The rain was just ending as we stepped inside. We wondered if the showers had been concentrated over the entire country. Mother was surprised to see us; our plan had been to return the following day. She welcomed us by reheating some soup and leftovers. She and Father took turns keeping us talking about where we had gone, but when they noticed the fatigue on my face they told us to open our wedding presents.

The gifts had been piled in a corner of the living room. I hadn't been able to greet our wedding guests as I should have, and as I opened the presents I recalled the friends who had attended the ceremony. There were quite a few of them, from elementary school classmates to co-workers at the bank. My best friend in college, Hyŏn-sun, whom I hadn't seen much of recently, had knit a lace doily for my piano. I was ecstatic at the sight of the frothy white lace.

Another gift that surprised me was So-yang's. I hadn't expected anything special from her, but here was a book of van Gogh's paintings. Printed in French, it was a large-format volume—about four times the size of a college notebook. Inside the cover was a dedication written with a felt-tip pen: "Best Wishes for a Peaceful Life—So-yang." The ink was a vivid red.

"Why the red ink?" Mother complained as she looked over my shoulder. "She knows it's bad luck."

The paintings ranged from van Gogh's early works with their stiff, broken lines to his late works, in which feverish, eddying whorls dominated the canvas. I felt somehow uneasy as I looked at such paintings as a self-portrait in which individual brush strokes were woven together about the artist's face. *Cafe at Night*, with the orange lamps suspended from the green ceiling, disturbed me too. Below the painting of an ocher-colored bed frame on a sienna floor was written "The Room of My Soul" in So-yang's scrawl. This was *The Bedchamber of Vincent*, mentioned by So-yang in her diary.

I came to van Gogh's portrait of himself smoking a

pipe, his ear bandaged.

"Isn't that the painter who cut off his ear?" asked Mr. Ch'oe.

I closed the book.

"Has So-yang been going out these days?" I asked, wondering if she had gotten involved in the demonstration I had read about in the newspaper. Mother hesitated because of Mr. Ch'oe. But I had talked briefly of So-yang during our honeymoon, and there was nothing to hide. I tried again: "Did she go out today?"

"She went out yesterday, supposedly to a friend's, and came back around dawn," Mother answered calmly. "Today she took me to see a movie. I don't know what was on her mind."

This startled me. I couldn't believe So-yang had asked Mother to go to a movie. The movie, *Sunflower*, was an old one I had seen. Mother smiled feebly at Mr. Ch'oe as she told us how So-yang had cried and cried while watching it.

"She was crying?" I almost shouted.

I remembered Sophia Loren roaming a plaza in front of a train station in Russia holding a picture of her husband, who had disappeared in the war; the tears pouring from her eyes at the sight of two pillows on the bed in the house where her husband lived after he remarried; and her showing her husband a baby in a cradle upon his return to Italy and saying, "You understand, don't you?" Such scenes had raised a lump in my throat too. The movie portrayed the fate of the victims of unrequited love. But I couldn't believe So-yang had wept so much at a love story such as this.

Mother thought likewise. "It wasn't a movie to cry over, but cry she did. . . . "

Mr. Ch'oe and I went upstairs. The whole floor was dark and ghostly still. Grandmother had gone to a prayer meeting, and Hye-yang's room, normally lit until two or three, was also dark.

So-yang was probably asleep. She had intended to turn in early to fight off a cold, according to Mother. There was no sound from her room.

Thinking I would have thanked her for her gift had she

been up, I went in the bathroom. Some laundry caught my eye. It was So-yang's nightie and underwear. The vivid whiteness of these clothes, hanging like pennants, reminded me of purity, and this gave me a sense of relief. I looked at them awhile, then, afraid of waking So-yang, I tiptoed back to my room.

It was a dream of hell that woke me that night. I was wandering in a cave I had never seen before. I saw a pit of steaming water. Strange people were sitting here and there, caressing their wounds. I walked by a man with bald spots on his scalp. I was about to look into his face out of pity, when he picked up a cactus and threw it in my face.

I bolted up and covered my face with my hands. I thought I was bleeding, but I felt nothing sticky. I finally woke up, but I couldn't erase this terrifying scene from my mind. I gazed for a time at the dim outline of my husband's face in the darkness, then reached out and touched his cheek.

I got up with a sigh of relief, went to the window, and lifted the curtain. The sky was like thick black ink. I saw a sprinkling of stars and heard the faint sound of traffic. It was when I headed for the bathroom that the smell hit me. It was a woody smell but fishy enough to make me dizzy. I glanced at the hall window, wondering if the night air was carrying in the scent of the shrubs in the garden, but the window was shut.

The instant I left the bathroom something flashed through my mind. It was the smell of blood that was making me dizzy. My face stiffened and my eyes began twitching. I inched toward So-yang's room.

"So-yang! So-yang!"

I pounded on her door but there was no response. After calling her several more times I went to my room and grabbed my handbag. I found the key to So-yang's room in the light from the hall and opened her door, my hands trembling.

I was reeling from the bloody stink as I groped along the wall and turned on the light. The interior of the room opened up like a scene in a wide-angle lens.

My knees buckled. The floor was mottled with red. So-yang lay there in the black outfit I had bought her. Soaked with her blood, the clothing had a reddish tinge. So-yang's face was pale, her lips slightly open, her fingers spread. She looked like a revolutionary sleeping on a scarlet map.

I stepped back, my hand tight over my mouth, and stumbled on something. It was So-yang's blood-smeared diary. I rushed back to my room.

"Let her live!" I shouted. Then I buried my face in my husband's chest and burst into tears.

This isn't a dream.
No wings, just a body in a sterile world.
I'm not a bird, not a butterfly, but a crawling snake chafing all over against a filthy world. Wings are an illusion.
The illusion shatters and I'm an aching, suffering, ugly body.

A world in which people fight for the sake of business is alien to me, a scene in a bell jar.
The glittering slogans are for someone else.
I'm an island, an island that traps me and touches nowhere.

My tears fell on the page, blurring the bloodstained paper. From behind me came Mother's muffled, intermittent sobs. Hye-yang gazed at So-yang's motionless pupils with an air of resignation. As she gripped her sister's left arm, which was still constricted by a rubber band, she heaved a sigh mixed with weeping.

"We spent our lives raising these kids the best we could, and now look," said Father on our way to the hospital. His first reaction at the house had been to cry out. Now he looked back at So-yang's body in disbelief, wiping his tears with his fist.

The previous day Mr. Ch'oe had been full of excitement driving the van in the rain, but now he kept a ponderous silence. I sat between him and Father, my heart bursting.

Like a foolish girl you're trying to find yourself beyond the world. If you'd only given in a little, you wouldn't have had to go around butting up against the world; you wouldn't have had to spill your blood. You would have found that the springtime of life isn't a chain; it's a pair of wings.

To the end So-yang had not been able to find a haven. Nor was there a room in the woods for her—only confusion and mazes.

Before we knew it the morning sky was draped with its first tinges of blue. The clear, cold air of dawn that followed the end of the rain tingled inside my chest. The streets with their closed doors were gradually coming to life. On our way down a hill I saw in the distance a crimson spear flickering high among some trees as though on fire. At first glance it resembled a will-o'-the-wisp, but in the dawn light it weakened and faded like a devil's soul. My eyes pierced the emptiness outside and I saw it was the neon cross of a church.

A Certain Beginning

Kim Chi-wŏn

YUN-JA FLOATED on the blue swells, her face toward the dazzling sun. At first the water had chilled her, but now it felt agreeable, almost responding to her touch. Ripples slapped about her ears, and a breeze brushed the wet tip of her nose. Sailboats eased out of the corner of her eye and into the distance. She heard the drone of powerboats, the laughter of children, and the babble of English, Spanish and other tongues blending indistinguishably like faraway sounds in a dream. Her only reaction to all this was an occasional blink. She felt drugged by the sun.

Yun-ja straightened herself in the water and looked for Chŏng-il. There he was, sitting under the beach umbrella with his head tilted back, drinking something. From her distant vantage point, twenty-seven-year-old Chŏng-il looked as small as a Boy Scout. He reminded her of a houseboy she had seen in a photo of some American soldiers during the Korean War.

"Life begins all over after today," Yun-ja thought. She had read in a women's magazine that it was natural for a woman who was alone after a divorce, even a long-awaited one, to be lonely, to feel she had failed, because in any society a happy marriage is considered a sign of a successful life. And so a divorced woman ought to make radical changes in her lifestyle. The magazine article had suggested getting out of the daily routine—sleeping as late as you want, eating what you want, throwing a party in the middle of the week, getting involved in new activities. "My case is a bit different, but like the writer says, I've got to start over again. But how? How is my life going to be different?" Yun-ja hadn't the slightest idea how to start a completely new life. Even if she were to begin sleeping all day and staying up all night, what difference would it make if she hadn't changed inwardly? Without a real change the days ahead would be boring and just blend together, she thought. Day would drift into night; she would find herself hardly able to sleep and another empty day would dawn. And how tasteless the food eaten alone; how unbearable to hear only the sound of her own chewing. These thoughts hadn't occurred to her before. "He won't be coming anymore starting tomorrow," she thought. The approaching days began to look meaningless.

Several days earlier, Chŏng-il had brought some soybean sprouts and tofu to Yun-ja's apartment and had begun making soybean-paste soup. Yun-ja was sitting on the old sofa, knitting.

"Mrs. Lee, how about a trip to the beach to celebrate our 'marriage'? A honeymoon, you know?"

Yun-ja laughed. She and Chŏng-il found nothing as funny as the word *marriage*. Chŏng-il also laughed, to show that his joke was innocent.

"Marriage" to Chŏng-il meant the permanent resident card he was obtaining. He and Yun-ja were already formally married, but it was the day he was to receive the green card he had been waiting for that Chŏng-il called his "wedding day."

Chŏng-il had paid Yun-ja fifteen hundred dollars to marry him so that he could apply for permanent residency in the U.S. Until his marriage he had been pursued by the American immigration authorities for working without the proper visa.

"Americans talk about things like inflation, but they're still a superpower. Don't they have anything better to do than track down foreign students?" Chŏng-il had said the day he met Yun-ja. His eyes had been moist with tears.

Now, almost two months later, Chŏng-il had his permanent resident card and Yun-ja the fifteen hundred dollars. And today their relationship would come to an end.

Chŏng-il ambled down the beach toward the water, his smooth bronze skin gleaming in the sun. He shouted to Yun-ja and smiled, but she couldn't make out the words. Perhaps he was challenging her to a race, or asking how the water was.

Yun-ja had been delighted when Ki-yŏng's mother, who had been working with her at a clothing factory in Chinatown, sounded her out about a contract marriage with Chŏng-il. "He came here on a student visa," the woman had explained. "My husband tells me his older brother makes a decent living in Seoul. . . . The boy's been told to leave the country, so his bags are packed and he's about to move to a different state. . . . It's been only seven months since he came to America. . . . Just his luck—other Korean students work here without getting caught. . . . "

"Why not?" Yun-ja had thought. If only she could get out of that sunless, roach-infested Manhattan basement apartment that she had been sharing with a young Chinese woman. And her lower back had become stiff as a board from too many hours of piecework at the sewing machine. All day long she was engulfed by Chinese speaking in strange tones and sewing machines whirring at full tilt. Yun-ja had trod the pedals of her sewing machine in the dusty air of the factory, the pieces of cloth she handled feeling unbearably heavy. Yes, life in America had not been easy for Yun-ja, and so she decided to give herself a vacation. With the fifteen hundred dollars from a contract marriage she could get a sunny room where she could open the window and look out on the street.

And now her wish had come true. She had gotten a studio apartment on the West Side, twenty minutes by foot from the end of a subway line, and received Chŏng-il as a "customer," as Ki-yŏng's mother had put it.

After quitting her job Yun-ja stayed in bed in the morning, listening to the traffic on the street below. In the evening, Chŏng-il would return from his temporary accounting job. Yun-ja would greet him like a boardinghouse mistress, and they would share the meal she had prepared.

Her day was divided between the time before he arrived and the time after.

Thankful for his meals, Chŏng-il would sometimes go grocery shopping and occasionally he would do the cooking, not wishing to feel obligated to Yun-ja.

Chŏng-il swam near. "Going to stay in forever?" he joked. His lips had turned blue.

"Anything left to drink?" she asked.

"There's some Coke, and I got some water just now."

Chŏng-il had bought everything for this outing—Korean-style grilled beef, some Korean delicacies, even paper napkins.

"Mrs. Lee, this is a good place for clams—big ones too. A couple of them will fill you up—or so they say. Let's go dig a few. Then we can go home, steam them up and have them with rice. A simple meal, just right for a couple of tired bodies. What do you think?"

Instead of answering, Yun-ja watched Chŏng-il's head bobbing like a watermelon. "So he's thinking about dropping by my place. . . . Will he leave at eleven-thirty again, on our last day? Well, he has to go there anyway to pick up his things." While eating lunch, she had mentally rehearsed some possible farewells at her apartment: "I guess you'll be busy with school again pretty soon," or "Are you moving into a dorm?"

Yun-ja was worried about giving Chŏng-il the impression that she was making a play for him. At times she had wanted to hand Chŏng-il a fresh towel or some lotion when he returned sopping wet from the shower down the hall, but she would end up simply ignoring him.

Yun-ja thought about the past two months. Each night after dinner at her apartment Chŏng-il would remain at the table and read a book or newspaper. At eleven-thirty he would leave to spend the night with a friend who lived two blocks away. Chŏng-il had been told by his lawyer that a person ordered out of the country who then got married and applied for a permanent resident card could expect to be investigated by the Immigration and Naturalization Service. And so he and Yun-ja had tried to look like a married couple. This meant that Chŏng-il had to be seen with Yun-ja. He would stay as late as he could at her apartment, and he kept a pair of pajamas, some old shoes and other belongings there.

Tick, tick, tick. . . . Yun-ja would sit knitting or listening to a record, while Chŏng-il read a book or wrote a letter. Pretending to be absorbed in whatever they were doing, both would keep stealing glances at their watches. . . . Tick, tick, tick. . .

At eleven-thirty Chŏng-il would strap on his watch and get up. Jingling his keys, he would mumble "Good night" or "I'm going." Yun-ja would remain where she was and pretend to be preoccupied until his lanky, boyish figure had disappeared out the door.

It hadn't always been that way. During the first few days after their marriage they would exchange news of Korea or talk about life in America—U.S. immigration policy, the high prices, the unemployment, or whatever. And when Chŏng-il left, Yun-ja would see him to the door. The silent evenings had begun the night she had suggested they live together. That night Chŏng-il had brought some beer and they had sung some children's ditties, popular tunes and other songs they both knew. The people in the next apartment had pounded on the wall in protest. Chŏng-il and Yun-ja had lowered their voices, but only temporarily. It was while Chŏng-il was bringing tears of laughter to Yun-ja, as he sang and clowned around, that she had broached the subject: Why did Chŏng-il want to leave right at eleven-thirty every night only to sleep at a friend's apartment where he wasn't really welcome? He could just as easily curl up in a corner of her apartment at night and the two of them could live together like a big sister and her little brother—now wouldn't that be great? Immediately Chŏng-il's face had hardened and Yun-ja had realized her blunder. That was the last time Chŏng-il had brought beer to the apartment. The lengthy conversations had stopped and Chŏng-il no longer entertained Yun-ja with songs.

Yun-ja had begun to feel resentful as Chŏng-il rose and left like clockwork each night. "Afraid I'm going to bite, you little stinker!" she would think, pouting at the sound of the key turning in the door. "It's a tug of war. You want to keep on my good side, so you sneak looks at me to see how I'm feeling. You're scared I might call off the marriage. It's true, isn't it—if I said I didn't want to go through with it, what would you do? Where would you find another unmarried woman with a green card? Would you run off to another state? Fat chance!"

The evening following her ill-advised proposal to live together, Yun-ja had left her apartment around the time Chŏng-il was to arrive. She didn't want him to think she was sitting around the apartment waiting for him. She walked to a nearby playground that she had never visited before and watched a couple of Asian children playing with some other children. She wondered if being gone when Chŏng-il arrived would make things even more awkward between them. She wanted to return and tell him that her suggestion the previous evening had had no hidden meaning. Yun-ja had no desire to become emotionally involved with Chŏng-il. This was not so much because of their thirteen-year age difference (though Yun-ja still wasn't used to the idea that she was forty), but because Yun-ja had no illusions about marriage.

The man Yun-ja had married upon graduating from college had done well in business, and around the time of their divorce seven years later he had become a wealthy man, with a car and the finest house in Seoul's Hwagok neighborhood.

"Let's get a divorce; you can have the house," he had said one day.

Yun-ja was terribly shocked.

"But why?. . . Is there another woman?"

"No, it's not that. I just don't think I'm cut out for marriage."

In desperation Yun-ja had suggested a trial separation. But her husband had insisted on the divorce, and one day he left, taking only a toiletry kit and some clothes. Yun-ja had wept for days afterward. She was convinced that another woman had come on the scene, and sometimes she secretly kept an eye on her husband's office on T'oegye Avenue to try to confirm this.

"Was there really no other woman?" she asked herself at the playground. "Did he want the divorce because he was tired of living with me?" Their only baby had been placed in an incubator at birth, but the sickly child had died. Being a first-time mother had overwhelmed Yun-ja. "Maybe he just got sick and tired of everything. Or maybe he just wanted to stop living with me and go somewhere far away—that's how I felt toward him when he stayed out late." She had heard recently that he had remarried.

"Are you Korean?"

Yun-ja looked up to see a withered old Korean woman whose hair was drawn into a bun the size of a walnut. Yun-ja was delighted to see another Korean, though she couldn't help feeling conspicuous because of the older woman's traditional Korean clothing, which was made of a fine nylon gauze.

Before Yun-ja could answer, the woman plopped herself down and drew a crimson pack of cigarettes from the pocket of her bloomers.

"Care for one, Miss?"

"No thank you."

The old woman lit a cigarette and began talking as if she were ripe for a quarrel: "Ah me, this city isn't fit for people to live in. It's a place for animals, that's what. In Korea I had a nice warm room with a laminated floor, but here no one takes their shoes off and the floors are all messy."

"Can't you go back to Korea?"

"Are you kidding? Those darn sons of mine won't let me. I have to babysit their kids all day long. Whenever I see a plane I start crying—I tell you! To think that I flew over here on one of those damned things!"

The old woman's eyes were inflamed, as if she cried every day, and now fresh tears gathered. Yun-ja looked up and watched the plane they had spotted. It had taken off from the nearby airport and seemed to float just above them

as it climbed into the sky. Its crimson and emerald green
landing lights winked.

"I don't miss my hometown the way this grandmother
does. And I don't feel like crying at the sight of that plane,"
thought Yun-ja. Her homeland was the source of her
shame. She had had to get away from it—there was no
other way.

It was around seven when Yun-ja returned from the
playground.

Chŏng-il opened the door. "Did you go somewhere?"
he asked politely, like a schoolboy addressing his teacher.

Yun-ja was relieved to have been spoken to first.

"I was talking with an elderly Korean woman."

"The one who goes around in Korean clothes? Was she
telling you how bad it is here in America?"

"You know her?"

"Oh, she's notorious—latches on to every Korean she
sees."

This ordinary beginning to the evening would eventually yield to a silent standoff, taut like the rope in a tug of
war.

Chŏng-il's joking reference to "marriage" the evening
he had offered to take Yun-ja to the beach had come easily
because his immigration papers had finally been processed.
All he had to do was see his lawyer and sign them, and he
would get his permanent resident card.

Though it was six o'clock, it was still bright as midday.
It was a muggy August evening, and the small fan in the
wall next to the window stuttered, as if it were panting in
the heat of Yun-ja's top-floor apartment.

Realizing that Chŏng-il was only joking, Yun-ja
stopped knitting. She got up and put a record on. The reedy
sound of a man's mellow voice unwound from the cheap
stereo:

> *Now that we're about to part*
> *Take my hand once again. . . .*

Yun-ja abruptly turned off the stereo. "Listening to songs makes me feel even hotter," she said.

Several days later, after Chŏng-il had obtained his permanent resident card, he borrowed a car and took Yun-ja to the beach, as promised. Yun-ja had thought it a kind of token of his gratitude. "Like the flowers or wine you give to the doctor who delivered your baby, or a memento you give to your teacher at graduation."

They stayed late at the beach to avoid the Friday afternoon rush hour. As the day turned to evening, the breeze became chilly and the two of them stayed out of the water, sitting together on the cool sand. Whether it was because they were outside or because this was their last day together, Yun-ja somehow felt that the tug of war between them had eased. But the parting words a couple might have said to each other were missing: "Give me a call or drop me a line and let me know how things are going." Chŏng-il did most of the talking, and Yun-ja found his small talk refreshing. He told her about getting measles at age nine, practicing martial arts in college, and going around Seoul in the dog days of summer just to get a driver's license so he could work while going to school in America. And he talked about a book he'd read, entitled *Papillon*.

"If you have Papillon's will, the sky's the limit on what you can do in America. You've heard Koreans when they get together here. They're always talking about the Chinese. The first-generation Chinese saved a few pennies doing unskilled labor when the subways were built. The second generation opened up small laundries or noodle stands. Buying houses and educating the kids didn't happen until the third generation. Whenever I hear that, I realize that Koreans want to do everything in a hurry—I'm the same way. They sound like they want to accomplish in a couple of years what it took the Chinese three generations to do. . . . When I left Korea I told my friends and my big brother not to feel bad if I didn't write, because I might not be able to afford the postage. My brother bought me an expensive fountain pen and told me that if I went hungry in the States I should sell it and buy myself a meal. And then my older sister had a gold ring made for me. I put the damned thing on my finger, got myself decked out in a suit for the plane ride, and then on the way over I was so excited I couldn't eat a thing—not a thing. The stewardess was probably saying to herself, 'Here's a guy who's never been on a plane before.' That damned ring—I must have looked like a jerk!"

Yun-ja related a few details about the elderly Korean woman she had met in the park. (Why did her thoughts return so often to this grandmother?) Then she told Chŏng-il a little about herself, realizing he had probably already learned through Ki-yŏng's mother that she was just another divorcee with no one to turn to.

The cool wind picked up as the sunlight faded, and they put their clothes on over their swimsuits. Chŏng-il's shirt was inside out, and Yun-ja could read the brand name on the neck tag.

"Your shirt's inside out."

Chŏng-il roughly pulled the shirt off and put it on right side out. Her steady gaze seemed to annoy him.

The beach was deserted except for a few small groups and some young couples lying on the sand nearby, exchanging affections. Hundreds of sea gulls began to gather. The birds frightened Yun-ja. Their wings looked ragged, their sharp, ceaselessly moving eyes seemed treacherous. Yun-ja felt as if their pointed beaks were about to bore into her eyes, maybe even her heart. She folded the towel she had been sitting on and stood up.

"Let's get going."

More gulls had alighted in the nearly empty parking lot, which stretched out as big as a football field.

"Want to get a closer look?" Chŏng-il asked as he started the car.

"They'll fly away."

"Not if we go slow. God, there must be thousands of them."

The car glided in a slow circle around the sea gulls. Just as Chŏng-il had said, the birds stayed where they were.

Yun-ja watched them through the window, her fear now gone.

They pulled out onto the highway and the beach grew distant. A grand sunset flared up in the dark blue sky. The outline of distant hills and trees swung behind the car and gradually disappeared. Yun-ja noticed that Chong-il had turned on the headlights.

"You must be beat," Chŏng-il said. "Why don't you lean back and make yourself comfortable."

Perhaps because he was silent for a time, Yun-ja somehow felt his firm, quiet manner in the smooth, steady motion of the car. She wondered what to do when they arrived at her apartment. Invite him in? Arrange to meet him somewhere the following day to give him his things? But the second idea would involve seeing him again.... The tide hadn't been low, so they hadn't been able to dig clams....

"I'll bet I've looked like a nobody to him, a woman who's hungry for love and money." Yun-ja recalled something Chŏng-il had once told her: "After I get my degree here, write a couple of books, and make a name for myself, I'd like to go back to Korea. Right now there are too many Ph.D's over there. I know I wouldn't find a job if I went back with just a degree."

"And for the rest of your life," Yun-ja now thought, "I'll be a cheap object for you to gossip about. You'll say, 'I was helpless when they told me to leave the country—so I bought myself a wife who was practically old enough to be my mother. What a pain in the neck—especially when she came up with the idea of living together.' And at some point in the future when you propose to your sweetheart, maybe you'll blabber something like 'I have a confession to make—I've been married before....'"

Chŏng-il drove on silently. His hand on the steering wheel was fine and delicate—a student's hand. Yun-ja felt like yanking that hand, biting it, anything to make him see things her way, to make him always speak respectfully of her in the future.

Chŏng-il felt Yun-ja's gaze and stole a glance at her. The small face that had been angled toward his was now looking straight ahead. "She's no beauty—maybe it's that thin body of hers that makes her look kind of shriveled up—but sometimes she's really pretty. Especially when it's hot. Then that honey-colored skin of hers gets a nice shine to it and her eyelashes look even darker." But Chŏng-il had rarely felt comfortable enough to examine Yun-ja's face.

"Mrs. Lee, did you ever have any children?"

"One—it died."

Chŏng-il lit a cigarette. Her toneless voice rang in his ears. "She doesn't seem to have any feelings. No expression, no interest in others, it even sounds as if her baby's death means nothing to her. True—time has a way of easing the pain. I don't show any emotion either when I tell people that my father died when I was young and my mother passed away when I was in college. Probably it's the same with her. But her own baby? How can she say 'It died' just like that?"

He had known from the beginning, through Ki-yŏng's mother, that Yun-ja was a single woman with no money. It had never occurred to him when he paid Ki-yŏng's mother the first installment of the fifteen hundred dollars that a woman with such a common name as Yun-ja might have special qualities. What had he expected her to be like, this woman who was to become his wife in name only? Well, a woman who had led a hard life, but who would vaguely resemble Ki-yŏng's mother—short permed hair, a calf-length sack dress, white sandals—a woman in her forties who didn't look completely at ease in Western-style clothing. But the woman Ki-yŏng's father had taken him to meet at the bus stop was thin and petite with short, straight hair and a sleeveless dress. Her eyelids had a deep double fold, and her skin had a dusky sheen that reminded Chŏng-il of Southeast Asian women. She was holding a pair of sunglasses, and a large handbag hung from her long, slender arm.

As they walked the short distance to Ki-yŏng's mother's for dinner that first night, Chŏng-il had felt pity for this woman who didn't even come up to his shoulders. He had also felt guilty and ill at ease. But Yun-ja had spoken nonchalantly: "So you're a student? Well, I just found an apartment yesterday. I'll be moving in three days from now. We can go over a little later and I'll show you around. It's really small—kitchen, bathroom, living room and bedroom all in one." To Chŏng-il this breezy woman of forty or so acted like an eighteen-year-old girl. "This woman's marrying me for money." He felt regretful, as if he were buying an aging prostitute.

"Why don't you two forget about the business part of it and get married for real?" Ki-yŏng's mother had said at dinner. And when she sang a playful rendition of the wedding march, Chŏng-il had felt like crawling under the table. Yun-ja had merely laughed.

The traffic between the beach and the city was heavy, occasionally coming to a standstill. Among the procession of vehicles Yun-ja and Chŏng-il noticed cars towing boats, cars carrying bicycles, cars with tents and shovels strapped to the roof rack.

As Chŏng-il drove by shops that had closed for the day, he thought of all the time he had spent on the phone with his older brother in Korea, of all the hard-earned money he had managed to scrounge from him (did his sister-in-law know about that?)—all because of this permanent resident card. And now he couldn't even afford tuition for next semester. These thoughts depressed him. But then he bucked up: Now that he had his green card (his chest swelled at the idea), there was no reason he couldn't work. "I'll take next semester off, put my nose to the grindstone, and by the following semester I'll have my tuition." And now that he was a permanent resident, his tuition would be cut in half. He made some mental calculations: How much could he save by cutting his rent and food to the bone? "But you can't cut down on food too much," Chong-il reminded himself. There were students who had ended up sick and run down, who couldn't study or do other things as a result. "This woman Yun-ja really has it easy—doesn't have to study. All she has to do is eat and sleep, day after day." Chong-il felt it was disgraceful that a young, intelligent Korean such as himself was living unproductively in America, as if he had no responsibilities to his family or country. "Why am I busting my butt to be here? Is the education really that wonderful?" In English class back in Korea he had vaguely dreamed of studying in America. Or rather he had liked the idea of hearing people say he had studied there. More shameful than this was the impulse he had to stay on in America. "What about the other people from abroad who live in the States—do they feel guilty about their feelings for their country, too?" He had read diatribes about America's corrupt material civilization. But he couldn't figure out what was so corrupt about it, and that bothered him. He wanted to see just what a young Korean man could accomplish in the world, and he wanted to experience the anger of frustration rather than the calm of complacency. He wanted knowledge, and recognition from others. But this woman Yun-ja didn't even seem to realize she was Korean.

The car pulled up on a street of six-story apartment buildings whose bricks were fading. Children were running and bicycling on the cement sidewalk; elderly couples strolled hand in hand, taking in the evening. Chŏng-il got out, unpacked the cooler and the towels, and loaded them on his shoulder. He and Yun-ja had the elevator to themselves. Yun-ja felt anxious and lonely, as if she had entered an unfamiliar neighborhood at dusk. She braced herself against the side of the elevator as it accelerated and slowed. When she was young it seemed the world belonged to her, but as time went on these "belongings" had disappeared; now she felt as if she had nothing. When it came time to part from someone, her heart ached as if she were separating from a lover. "Am I so dependent on people that I drove my husband away? Nobody wants to be burdened with me, so they all leave—even my baby. . . . I wonder if that old woman at the playground went back to Korea. Maybe she's still smoking American cigarettes and bending the ear of every Korean she sees here. Maybe I'll end up like her when I'm old. Already my body feels like a dead weight because of my neuralgia—god forbid that I latch on to just anybody and start telling a sob story."

Yun-ja unlocked the door to the apartment and turned on the light.

Today the small, perfectly square room looked cozy and intimate to them. They smelled the familiar odors, which had been intensified by the summer heat.

But Chong-il felt awkward when he saw that Yun-ja had packed his trunk and set it on the sofa. If only he could unpack it and return the belongings to their places.

"You must feel pretty sticky—why don't you take a shower?" Yun-ja said.

Chŏng-il returned from washing his salt-encrusted body to find Yun-ja cleaning the sand from the doorway. She had changed to a familiar, well-worn yellow dress. The cooler had been emptied and cleaned, the towels put away. Yun-ja had shampooed, and comb marks were still visible in her wet hair. Chŏng-il tried to think of something to say, gave up, and tiptoed to the sofa to sit down. "She's already washed her hair, changed, and started sweeping up," he thought. As Yun-ja bustled about, she looked to Chŏng-il as if she had just blossomed.

"Shouldn't I offer him some dinner?" Yun-ja thought as she swept up the sand. "He went to the trouble of borrowing a car and taking me out—the least I can do is give him a nice meal. And where would he eat if he left now? He'd probably fill up on junk food. . . . But if I offer to feed him, he might think I had something in mind. And when I've paid people for something, they never offered me dinner, did they?"

"How about some music?" Chŏng-il mumbled. He got up, walked stiffly to the stereo, and placed the needle on the record that happened to be on the turntable. The rhythm of a Flamenco guitar filled the room. Although Chŏng-il didn't pay much attention to the music Yun-ja played, it seemed that this was a new record. "Why have I been afraid of this woman? You'd think she was a witch or something."

"If that woman sinks her hooks into you, you've had it." Chŏng-il had heard this from his roommate, Ki-yŏng's father and goodness knows how many others. "Nothing

happened again today?" the roommate would joke when
Chŏng-il returned in the evening from Yun-ja's apartment.
"When it comes to you-know-what, nothing beats a
middle-aged woman. I hope you're offering good service in
return for those tasty meals you're getting."

The shrill voices of the children and the noise of air-
planes and traffic were drowned out by the guitar music.
The odor of something rotten outside wafted in with the
heat of the summer night.

Chŏng-il began to feel ashamed. Here he was about to
run out on this woman he'd used in return for a measly sum
of money—a woman whose life he had touched. He had
visited this room for almost two months, and now he
wished he could spend that time over again. "Why didn't I
try to make it more enjoyable?" he asked himself. He and
Yun-ja had rarely listened to music, and when they had
gone strolling in the nearby park after dinner he had felt uneasy, knowing that they did this only so that others would
see the two of them together.

Yun-ja finished sweeping the sand up and sat down at
the round dinner table. "If you're hungry, why don't you
help yourself to some leftovers from yesterday's dinner?
There's some lettuce and soybean paste and a little rice too."

Yun-ja's hair had dried, and a couple of strands of it
drooped over her forehead. She looked pretty to Chŏng-il.

"And some marinated peppers," she continued.

Chŏng-il's body stiffened. This offer of dinner was a
signal that it was time for him to leave. He rose and
fumbled for something appropriate to say about the past
two months. The blood rushed to his head and his face
burned. Finally he blurted out, "What would you say if I . . .
proposed to you?" Then he flung open the door as if he
were being chased out. In his haste to leave he sent one of
Yun-ja's sandals flying from the doorway toward the gas
range. Then the door slammed shut behind him.

Yun-ja sprang up from the table. "What did he say?"
Her body prickled, as if she were yielding to a long-
suppressed urge to urinate. "I don't believe in marriage,"
she told herself. "Not after what I went through." She

rushed to the door and looked through the peephole into the hall. She saw Chŏng-il jab futilely at the elevator button and then run toward the stairway.

"The boy proposed to me—I should be thankful," Yun-ja thought. Like water reviving a dying tree, hot blood began to buzz through her sleepy veins. This long-forgotten sensation of warmth made her think that maybe their relationship had been pointing in this direction all along. "It was fun prettying myself up the day I met him. And before that, didn't I expect some good times with him even though we weren't really married?"

Yun-ja turned and looked around the room. There was Chŏng-il's trunk on the sofa. "But he'd end up leaving me too." Suddenly she felt very vulnerable. Everything about her, starting with her age and the divorce, and then all the little imperfections—the wrinkles around the eyes, the occasional drooling in her sleep—reared up in her mind. "But I'm not going to let my shortcomings get me down," she reassured herself. "It's time to make a stand."

Lullaby

Kim Chi-wŏn

It was showing its age, this secluded traditional Korean house, but its pillars were still burly and the thick planks of the veranda had a time-worn luster. A tall tree bursting with leaves cast its shadow over a corner of the roof. The main gate, set behind the house, seemed to tower imposingly over both tree and roof. Viewed from the garden, the roof and the gate seemed to penetrate the sky. A stone stairway sloped downward from the gate to the house.

Down these steps walked a woman toward her husband, who was standing in the yard with an elderly realtor and the old couple who owned the house. Summer seemed to ripen in the luxuriant breeze, and the cicadas were singing. A feeling of tranquility came over the woman, and she lingered on the steps to savor it.

She closed her eyes tight, then opened them. That's where I'd play with Suni, she thought—in the garden, with the sunplants, touch-me-nots, cockscombs and four-o'clocks in full bloom. Just then Suni was probably gathered around a wicker basket full of popcorn with her friends at the landlady's house, waiting for her parents to return. The image of the little girl toddling about this big yard and clambering up the stone steps without first having to search a landlady's face for approval lifted the woman's spirits.

The price of the house was unbelievably low. Because the couple had walked the streets searching for their dream house till their feet were blistered, they had known sight

166

unseen the size and location of the house they could expect at that price. It would be a house barely fit to live in. But the house in front of the woman now was like a paradise. The lot was walled in on three sides, and a large, stagnant pond bordered by a dense grove served as a boundary at one end.

The gracefully aged face of the owner's wife beamed as the woman marveled at the garden, the tall tree, a room whose floor was neatly covered with laminated paper.

"Young lady, if you like the house, you could move in today if you wanted," said the older woman. "Our son and his wife keep telling us to move in with them, but we couldn't because of the house. People think it's a temple, so even the peddlers don't bother coming here."

In a house this big, I'll have a place to hide from my husband, the woman thought. I won't have to sit against him in a tiny room anymore, and I won't need to put up with that hateful look he gives me no matter what I'm doing. When he acts like that, I can hide in the garden—or sit over there in the backyard, catch some sun, and read a book.

The woman adjusted her hairpin. "We have a three-year-old girl, so we should probably fence in the pond," she said, as if the house were already hers.

"Oh, don't worry about that. One of our neighbors is a carpenter. He'll take care of it for you. Last fall he touched up the whole house. Now there aren't any leaks, and everything's nice and clean," said the owner's wife.

Later the woman waited for her husband outside the realtor's office at the entrance to the alley leading to the house. From where she stood, the house couldn't be seen.

Her husband hadn't said a word when they had left to see the house that morning. He was always upset with her about something. Where did she put the shoehorn? Why wasn't dinner ready when he returned from work? Why couldn't she get up earlier? The woman had forgotten what it was like to talk with her husband, and had gradually been reduced to playing the role of a maid. There were times, as when she slid open the door of their rented room and saw the sunlight slant into the garden, that she wanted to leave with her daughter, dressed just as they were, for some back-country place on Cheju Island or in the Ch'ungch'ŏng, or Chŏlla, or Kangwŏn regions. And sometimes she realized with a start that these thoughts of leaving the world behind, of going with her daughter to live beside a stream and watch the water flow by, were frightening. I'd be ruining the girl's life, she would tell herself. I'd be depriving her of a good father, an education, her friends. At such moments she would call Suni, and frantically look for her if she was out of sight. Then, discovering her in front of the gate or in the neighbors' yard, she would take the girl into her arms. Embracing her daughter was her way of apologizing for these thoughts.

"Suni, do you know what Mommy's thinking?"

The girl, held to her breast, would tickle her mother as she laughed.

"Uh-uh."

"Mommy just adores Suni. Isn't that right?"

"Yeah."

Her husband emerged from the realtor's office.

"All right, then, I'll be back tomorrow. I'd like to take another look with a friend of mine," he said to the realtor. "I wish there was an easier way to buy a house."

Thick hair, deep-set eyes, a tall and slim build, limpid white skin and the scholarly look of a man who had graduated at the top of his class—her husband was clearly a handsome man.

"You won't find a comparable house at that price," said the realtor. "Why don't we work out an offer? Those folks have lived there over thirty years, and everything's gone right for them. You wouldn't believe how much money their son has made. People say he's a very rich man."

The woman and her husband left the realtor's office and walked down the street side by side.

"It really has a lot of space."

"Isn't that great!" the woman replied. "And they have a pump in the garden—I loved the taste of that water." She was frustrated that her husband hadn't signed a purchase agreement.

"I'll have to come back tomorrow with Yŏn-ho."

The next day, as the woman's husband and Yŏn-ho took one last look at the house, Yŏn-ho remarked that it sat much lower than street level and that the main gate was at the back instead of the front. And the triangular shape of the yard wasn't a good sign—it should have been nice and square. Even so, he thought it was a beautiful place. As on the previous day, a breeze passed through the tree, the cicadas sang and the flowers were in full bloom.

The woman's husband returned to his office and became lost in thought. He hadn't told his wife this, but the house was supposedly haunted. People said that mysterious voices seemed to come from the pond at night, hearty, youthful male voices chanting, "Your head aches, my head aches" over and over. Several former residents of the house had complained of splitting headaches and then died. The last one to die had been a young boy. One night, so the story went, the boy had developed such a headache that he had begun to moan and bang his head against the wall of his room. Outside, several tall shadows resembling sturdy young men had swayed like comrades-in-arms on the brilliantly moonlit surface of the pond, producing a soft chorus: "Your head aches, my head aches, your head aches, my head aches." The voices had continued until dawn, and at daybreak the boy had breathed his last.

But this was merely a rumor from long ago, and no one knew for sure the boy's name or when he had died. The present owners had lived in the house for over thirty years without mishap, and their son, now such a great success, had grown up there. Even if a boy had complained of headaches and died in that house, the cause might very well have been meningitis or some other disease more deadly before the advances of science and medicine—not an evil spirit. Once born, people are destined to die, whatever the cause. They can die after their allotted life span, or they can die in their youth. So reasoned the woman's husband, a college graduate and an intellectual. And even if the house was haunted, perhaps the evil spirit would spare them, for the brother who had unexpectedly left him the modest sum of money he was using to buy the house had been a minister.

The most important thing was to move; their rented room had become painfully cramped. He wanted to fix a nameplate to the gate of his own house, and with his own hands mount the national flag from the gatepost on holidays.

So, as soon as they moved into the house the woman's husband had an ample nameplate made and attached it to the gate. Next he had the pond fenced off. The water in the pond was turbid, but the natural scene it reflected was more beautiful than reality.

The woman felt peaceful when she walked among the flowers with Suni, when she softly called the cute little neighborhood children to come play with Suni in the yard or when she spread a blanket and sat in the garden under the tall tree. If she was in the mood, she would pick and clean some of the zucchinis and scallions the former owners had planted, grill wheat cakes with them and feed the children. When the leaves on the tree trembled in the breeze, she paused to listen: it was the sound of freedom. When it was time for the children to return home, she would sit them in a row beside the pump, wash their faces, hands and feet, and then send them on their way. But there were also days when the woman felt empty and unhappy. She would feed Suni any old thing and skip meals herself, and neglect the girl if she got dirty.

Whether her day was miserable or happy, she generally sat for a while under the tall tree. Nature was always offering her an escape, and rather than thinking of her mother or friends whenever she was troubled, she longed for the woods, the fields and the mountains. Wherever she lived, nature was there to console her—a wisp of cloud, a blade of grass, a single tree. Lectures, professors and college friends she had virtually forgotten, but the flowers that had bloomed at a certain place on campus and the sunbeams that had dyed the sky at dawn and sunset, harmonizing with her state of mind, these were the memories that remained vivid.

Mommy dear, Sister dear, by the river let's live
With golden sand, golden sand, sparkling in our yard.
That's the song of the reeds out back behind the gate.

This was the lullaby the woman softly sang to Suni when putting her to sleep.

When the girl nodded off on her mother's back, the woman would lay her down and then go outside to the fence and call the schoolgirl next door. The neighbors' house looked down on the woman's, and so the lower house was in full view.

Leaving the neighbors' girl to look after the house, the woman would drop by the market and rush through her grocery shopping, then visit a nearby bookseller's. Going to the bookstore gave her the same feeling of stability that she felt sitting in the shade of the tree. She would browse among the books, but some days she didn't have enough money and would leave without buying anything. And sometimes when she returned home and was preparing a meal, a book she had leafed through in the bookstore would suddenly come to mind, and she would decide to buy it on her next trip to the market. One kind of book would make her want to read another. It was true, she reflected, that books opened up a whole new world.

This habit of visiting the bookstore had begun with the move to the house. Before, in the rented room, she would start the rice and then read a piece of newspaper that had been lying around, or a few pages of a book or magazine that had been pasted together to form a grocery bag. Now and then she felt strength build in her as she listened to the voices of the people in the books she read. But she also felt restless, and she didn't know why.

Her husband had grown cold as ice. The woman had gradually lost her smile and become taciturn. When she did talk, her husband never bothered to hear her out. He tormented her with his pointed silence, giving no reason for the anger it suggested. Was the stew too salty? Were the socks she had laundered too damp for him to wear? Was it the kitchen window she had left open the previous evening, allowing the rain to storm in? In her own way, the woman would try to guess whether it was these or other reasons that provoked her husband's dark moods. She had finally lost confidence and become unsure of herself in front of him.

"Do you ever think about me?" he asked one evening, towering over her. "Do you ever wonder whether I'm hungry, or what I'm in the mood for?"

The blunt words pierced her heart. It was eight o'clock, and earlier he had clearly said he wasn't hungry. She knew that the feet of that towering form promised violence.

"Your dinner's in the kitchen. Help yourself," she said defiantly, slamming shut the book she had been reading. When was the last time they had had a decent conversation? Anger seethed inside her as she thought about their relationship. "How many times did I ask you if you wanted to eat?" she asked.

"That was a while back. You know, I don't like this. All you do these days is sit there high and mighty with your nose in a book."

"When we were in school together, weren't we equals? Didn't we share notebooks? And now what? Meals, laundry, housecleaning! That's all I ever hear from you. You've even made me Suni's errand girl. When have you ever treated me as a mother in front of her? Instead, you tell me, 'Get me some water. . . . Didn't you hear me? I told you to get me some water.'" With a hateful expression she mimicked her husband's tone of voice. "Listen, I'm a good homemaker. Okay, maybe I'm not all that great, but I think I can hold my own with other women! I try to do a good job so we can live like civilized people. I don't want the neighbors thinking we live in a pigsty. Why do you have to compare me with some ideal homemaker? Have I ever compared you with a model husband?"

"Okay, okay, you're right. You're a damn good homemaker."

"Come on—that's not what I meant."

"No, you're right. You *are* good. You're very good—

to yourself. Everything you do for yourself you do well. As long as it's for *your* sake, not mine."

Violence followed, as if they had deserved it for failing to communicate for so long. And then came a night of intense love.

"You love me—you still love me, don't you? Oh, it's so good," her husband gasped.

As the woman looked down at her husband sleeping in the darkness, she realized that he, like she herself, was ever so feeble and lonely. At such times she heard the stream of warm affection flowing in her bosom cry out: I promise to love this man for all I'm worth, to watch over him with a warm heart.

But before long, the reality of the vicious circle of their lives would return. A mistake here, a blunder there—whether the woman could have helped it or not, her husband wouldn't forgive her. He was hurt by the way she made him feel like dirt. And when the woman saw that she had injured his pride, she felt guilty; she felt she was worthless and ill-mannered.

If it was nature that consoled the woman at such times, it was Suni who gave her the strength to live on. The woman took apart the emerald green jacket and crimson skirt that had been part of her wedding chest, measured and fit them to Suni, and dressed her in them. And when she sat Suni on the edge of the veranda, a crimson ribbon holding the girl's hair in a pigtail like a garlic clove, and watched the fiery twilight settle on the stagnant pond, she could feel the tiny existence of her daughter.

Whenever the woman bought a book, she would jot down the date and the name of the bookstore inside it. Someday she'll read it, she would tell herself, expecting Suni to grow into a forgiving and accepting friend of hers. Sometimes she felt a need to pass on to Suni her knowledge of the world, knowledge that had dawned on her when she had stumbled and suffered. It was then that she would lie down with her daughter among the falling leaves under the tree and explain Newton's law of universal gravitation; or if it were raining, she would sit with Suni on the veranda and explain why thunder followed lightning; or she would anxiously tell the girl not to play with fire and to watch out for cars.

And when she thought about her unhappy marriage, she felt like a failure; she hadn't achieved her aims in life. Relying completely on her husband for material support, she felt her married life had been one retreat after another deeper into the home. She convinced herself that she lacked the strength to live alone with her daughter. The woman's spirit kept on shrinking, and she began to dwell on her misfortune. Her husband too grew unhappy; sadness was written all over his slumped shoulders. This sadness would occasionally catch her eye, but she was unable to reach out to him. She felt incapable in his presence.

Longing for something to sustain and steady her, the woman nevertheless tended to doubt the permanence of everything. Do flowers last more than ten days? And floods that look like they'll sweep the world away are gone in a couple of days, aren't they? But her relief that the world was transitory was tempered by the painful realization that society expected marriage to be the most harmonious of human relationships.

The movie showed a cobblestone alley, clean and peaceful. A woman, Woyzeck's mistress, was telling several of the girls in her neighborhood a story from long ago. The mistress was poor, and throughout the movie she wore the same long dress. The movie focused on Woyzeck, with his mistress having only a minor role, but the woman could see herself there on the screen in the gloom of the neighborhood theater. When the mistress knelt to scrub the floor, the woman could feel the restless spirit and the anxiety that the character on the screen suppressed.

While his mistress was telling the story in her monotonous voice, Woyzeck, tormented by her infidelity, came to take her away. To the woman, he looked both kind and angry. He dragged his mistress to a field full of dazzling sunlight and waist-high weeds. There he stabbed her a dozen, two dozen, almost three dozen times. Her body was riddled, her death prolonged.

After the movie, the woman slowly walked home through the alley in the midday haze. But there on the stone shoe-ledge of the house was something that shocked her— her husband's shoes, accompanied by another, unfamiliar pair. Suni and the schoolgirl from next door were nowhere to be seen. What could have brought her husband home in the middle of the day? He had caught her, and she realized that her blunder would bring yet another awful scolding from him. Just then she heard a voice: "Once a month you've got to teach these women a lesson they won't forget. There's nothing wrong with it—it's just something that has to be done." So the shoes lined up next to her husband's belonged to his cousin Kyŏng-hak. The woman hesitated, a faraway look in her eyes, then went back up the steps and over to the neighbors'. She had come to feel that the neighbors' house was a majestic fortress. Her daughter was there, as she had suspected.

"Your husband had some company, so I brought Suni here," said the schoolgirl.

That night the woman's husband acted on his cousin's advice. He gave the woman a brutal beating, as if he intended to correct her once and for all.

"What the hell kind of a wife goes out for a movie without her husband? Ask anybody—they'll tell you. And abandoning the damn kid. . . . "

If a wife is nothing but a slave to you, then I'd like a wife myself, the woman thought.

Her husband was as tormented as Woyzeck plunging a dagger into his mistress. The woman could sense his utter despair in the hands that beat her. Two lonely sailboats adrift, the woman and her husband longed for each other's redemption. But they were unable to unite themselves in spirit, and they fought like a pair of devils. At last her husband began kicking her, and with one final kick he drove her from the house.

The woman's husband slumped against the wall. Suddenly he heard a voice. It sounded as if it were coming from outside, but at the same time it seemed to reverberate inside him: "Do not make your wife into what you want her to be. She is far away now, out of your reach. She is in the dark, in pain. She belongs to us now, not to you."

"Who are you?" the husband shouted.

"Nature—the wind, the water, the clouds."

"But I'm yours, too. I belong to you, too, don't I?"

"Yes. In the end, you're ours, too."

The woman lay in the sloping backyard. The ground was so very hard and damp. In the darkness she could make out the back of the house and the chimney rising from it. No trace of light escaped from inside. The tree swayed in the faint starlight, towering above the roof.

Ǔn-hǔi must be having a terrible time of it, too, she suddenly thought. This college friend of hers had also married, and the woman hadn't seen her since, or heard a single word from her. I'm sure she's had a tough time since her marriage, she repeated to herself. She had never thought this way about the woman next door or the wives of her husband's friends.

The temperature plunged. It was autumn already and the mosquitos had disappeared. "What shall I do?" the woman murmured. "I don't know what's right or wrong, what to do or not to do, nothing! I'm miserable. All I know is that I'm hurt, I'm miserable, I'm unhappy. Oh, my head!"

The woman looked up. She thought she had heard a voice: "Your head aches, my head aches." The woman got to her feet, and the voice sounded again: "Your head aches, my head aches, your head aches, my head aches."

Someone else has a headache? the woman wondered. Who could have a headache like mine? She strained to listen.

"Your head aches, my head aches."

Where was the voice coming from? The tree? She went there and listened.

"Your head aches, my head aches. . . . "

Was it the gate? The woman raced up the steps toward it.

"Your head aches. . . . "

Where could it be? Where? Who else could be complaining of a headache? And who could understand how my head aches? Seeking the voice, the woman wandered through the yard, which was now suffused with darkness.

The following morning several of the neighbors climbed over the fence and retrieved the woman's body from the pond. It was a crisp, cold morning.

The neighbors went to call an undertaker. The sunlight gradually advanced across the veranda, where the woman's husband was sitting. He couldn't believe it. It had to be a dream, he repeated to himself. He looked vacantly toward the pump, which was shimmering gently in the sun. Even now he thought he might see his wife emerging from the kitchen or the back room with a container of rice or greens. If she were to appear now, unsmiling and sulky because of their fight last night, it would be all right. He wouldn't mind it even if she were to fly off the handle, get red in the face and scream at him the way she had then. But his wife was lying dead in the back room. It's real, he told himself. What now? He spread his fingers and with misty eyes studied the lines of his palms.

The girl from next door had taken Suni. The neighbors returned with the undertaker, and the man's family, along with his wife's family and her close friends, flocked to the house by taxi, bus and car. It was a terrible day, one that made him wonder why life contained such moments, but it finally drew to a close. The house, so quiet and gloomy the previous evening, was now brightly lit inside and out. People bustled about within. As the night gathered, those who had come to offer condolences curled up one after another and fell asleep. The woman's husband went into the back room and found his mother-in-law dabbing at her tears. She wearily moved aside and offered him a seat. The stiffened remains of his wife were concealed by a crude folding screen supplied by the undertaker. The screen made him uncomfortable. The fragrance of burning incense filled the room.

He felt like flinging aside the screen, picking up his wife and giving her a good shaking. Had she really killed herself—and over such a trivial thing? She was the one who had caused all this mess. So what if he had kicked her out—even though she was hanging all over him and crying? Even if he had kicked her out a dozen times, shouldn't she have kept crawling back, apologizing and saying she'd listen to him from then on? Wasn't that how a nice, obedient woman was supposed to act? Wouldn't he have gone to his wife as she crawled back inside, gathered her in his arms and showed her how big-hearted he was by saying he'd forgive her? And then they would have gone to bed together. He sighed.

Kyŏng-hak's wife, whose bad habits were corrected once a month by a horrible beating from her husband, appeared with Suni in her arms. She had dressed the girl in her green jacket and crimson skirt, which made her look like a peppermint. She pointed to the girl's father and said, "Look—here's Daddy. See? He hasn't gone anywhere, has he?" Having spent all day apart from her father, Suni looked at him and tried to squirm free. But Kyŏng-hak's wife held the girl tightly, saying, "There we go, that's a good girl. Other children cry, but not our Suni. . . . Bracken-fern hands and cherry lips, bracken-fern hands and cherry lips. . . . " Then she quickly turned and stepped down to the yard, rocking the girl gently. Meanwhile, the dead woman's two sisters-in-law were in the bedroom sorting out her belongings from the dresser and closet.

"Oh God, what am I going to do?" said the man. Suddenly he pounded his forehead against the wall. Frustrated, he did it again.

"What are you doing?" said the dead woman's mother. She had always deferred to her son-in-law, but now she cast propriety aside and grabbed his hand. The man, even more frustrated now, kept ramming his head against the wall—

thunk! thunk! thunk!

"Goodness, what should I do?" The woman called outside: "Come here! Look what he's doing! Hurry!"

The man banged his head against the wall with a frightening, irresistible force, as if this were his sole remaining task in life—thunk, thunk, thunk, thunk! Outside, the surface of the pond, gleaming in the light of the moon and stars, became dappled with shadows resembling a group of sturdy young comrades-in-arms: "Your head aches, my head aches, your head aches, my head aches. . . . "

Evening Game

O Chŏng-hŭi

GOD, I FEEL like I'm on display! I felt exposed in this kitchen that opened onto the living room, and suddenly I resented the "Western-style" layout of our apartment. I'd been scrubbing away at the gas range where the rice had boiled over. I'd tried a wet dishcloth and then a dry one, but a few faint speckles remained sprinkled around the burners—probably the result of Father's carelessness last winter when he was preparing his medicine. Time and again he had mixed angelica roots, red-bellied frogs, black soybeans and toad oil in an army cookpot, boiled it to a brown foam, added honey, and stirred gently until the stuff became thick and dark like coaltar. The medicine would purify his blood and rid him of constipation, he had told me, looking like a medieval alchemist as he stood at the stove in his robe, stirring the coagulating liquid with long wooden chopsticks.

The pungent stink of the medicine had seeped into every nook of the house, and the flesh and bones of the frog had produced an acrid steam that settled heavy and sticky like resin. Sometimes my anemia would make me dizzy and I'd want to vomit from the stench, so I'd go into the bathroom. But there I'd get mesmerized by what I saw in the mirror—my dreadful psoriasis acting up again and the tiny wrinkles in my dry skin.

The speckles, turning into tarnishes on the stainless steel of the range, would be more malignant and enduring than my memory of their origin.

banality

Everything was under control, just like the previous day. The hands of the clock on the kitchen shelf read five-thirty, the rice was steaming away in the cooker, and faint wisps of smoke rose from the seared scales of the fish, which had been broiled to a golden brown.

Sunlight slanted through the west window into the kitchen, subduing the sheen of the chopping knife, seeming to scour the finely carved grooves of the cutting board for the bits of food stuck there, and highlighting the particles suspended in the milky dishwater in the sink.

I could look out this wide, sunny window without having to stand on tiptoe. Today, as usual, I watched the juvenile delinquents troop back to the reformatory through the field after work.

grey?
wind?
wheel w/o axle?

There were easily seventy or eighty of them, wearing their gray work clothes and caps of the same color. The scene always left me cold, as if I had touched the bodies under the loose-fitting garments and found coarse gooseflesh. I wondered if this feeling came from some preconception I had about prison uniforms, or from the wind I imagined to be streaming through the field. The slow procession, with the uniforms fluttering like pieces of ragged fabric unevenly trimmed and joined, reminded me of a massive cement wheel without an axle rolling slowly and ponderously forward, or of someone whistling a melancholy tune.

Two men in jackets who looked like guards were escorting the gray line, a step ahead and behind.

wheel Hades
→

If I hadn't seen the delinquents up close, I probably would have glanced at them indifferently, thinking there might be an army camp somewhere nearby, rather than trying to decipher childish fantasies such as the cement wheel without the axle and the millstones of Hades being endlessly turned by unseen hands as a result of some misdeed committed in a former life.

I first encountered these boys during one of my evening strolls with the dog. At the sight of them I exclaimed in spite of myself, remembering that a reformatory sat on the other side of the low hill nearby. But then I turned away in embarrassment, pulling tight the dog's leash: A surprisingly

young face had stared at me from the line. I couldn't have
guessed the boy's age, but his eyes were clear to the point of
loveliness. Or maybe they just seemed that way because of
the sense of freshness that I felt looking at his uniform, or
because of my sudden awareness that I was not growing old
very gracefully, an awareness awakened by the pale com-
plexion of his round cheeks.

The boy soon passed and I lost him in the pack. Afterward I couldn't really remember what he looked like. If I
had lined them all up, I still wouldn't have been able to pick
out his face. Yet the sensation of his lovely clear eyes remained, prompting me to look out the kitchen window
around this time every day, in a vain attempt to spot him.

They had almost crossed the field when a small dis-
turbance developed in the middle of the line. A boy had
bent over as if to replace a shoe that had come off. Everyone
behind him lurched to a stop, and the man in the jacket approached from the back of the line. Perhaps the boy had
picked up something shiny from the ground and stuck it in
his sleeve, or hidden it in his shoe. . . . The boy straightened
and showed the man that his hands were empty. They
talked on about something, but from my vantage point it
looked like sign language.

The man returned to his position, and the boys in the
rear moved a little faster in order to fill the gap that had
formed in the line. Well, maybe it was nothing. After all,
how could something be shining when the sunlight had
retreated from the field?

The gray line marched over the hill where the field
ended and a housing development began. Some of the scattered units of the development were half finished; others
were receiving last-minute touches before the first cold
snap. As the gray line disappeared, the ponderous wheel
and the melancholy tune vanished as well.

I plucked the stopper from the sink and looked with satisfaction as the water quickly bubbled, swirled and drained.
The plumber had unplugged it earlier that afternoon. The
sink hadn't been draining properly and had begun to smell
foul. A couple of pumps with the plunger, and out came a

lump of vegetable fiber mixed with clotted hair. Father had come up behind the plumber and me before I had noticed, and had stared at the lump with an expression that seemed to be telling me, "I told you so."

It was approaching six. Without thinking, I set three spoons and three pairs of chopsticks on the table, which sat near the kitchen wall. Then, realizing what I had done, I quickly returned the third set to the serving tray. I knew well enough that Brother wouldn't be coming home this evening either. Just force of habit, I told myself. No big deal.

"Dearie, which direction is that magpie cawing toward?" Father asked.

I looked up at a tall poplar in the field where the delinquents had just been. The bird was among the leaves at the very top of the tree, some of which had just started turning a yellowish brown.

"I took out my contacts," I answered with a clatter of dishes.

He knew I was virtually blind without my contact lenses, but he stubbornly persisted: "Spit in the direction it's cawing toward. You know what they say—a magpie in the evening is bad luck."

"I *said* I can't see very well."

"Did you go and lose your contacts again? Haven't I told you to be sure and soak them in water when you're not using them?"

It was a lie; I hadn't removed the lenses. They were centered right over my pupils, and I had a clear view of the magpie cawing toward us from its treetop perch. I could see its feathers, a shiny black in the evening sun, as if coated with oil, and its flapping wings, looking strong as steel.

I scowled briefly at Father slumped in his chair in the dim living room, from which the sunlight had retreated. I wasn't really angry with him. Then I pushed the play button of the cassette player on the shelf, thinking about the first movement of a Kodaly symphony that had been going through my head. All I heard was a slow, faint whisper as the cassette tape wound. I was beginning to wonder whether something was wrong with the machine when the music abruptly started.

I had heard the familiar melody that afternoon during Request Hour on the classical radio station and had been seized by an urge to record it. The old Sony cassette player had belonged to Brother and had been thrown in a drawer long before. By the time I had dusted it off, ransacked the drawer for a blank cassette and started the machine, the first movement of the symphony was over. The music sounded scratchy—it must have been an old record—and I probably shouldn't have bothered recording it, but I was simply too lazy to push the stop button until the symphony had ended. It had all fit on one side of the sixty-minute tape.

I listened to what I had recorded for about ten minutes and then turned the machine off.

"Dinner is ready." My tone was a bit stiff, as I had intended.

Without looking I knew that Father was hoisting himself from his chair after picking his ears with his little fingers and then flicking the nails against his thumbs.

Through the thin wall to the bathroom I could hear water pour into the sink and then drain. I had cleaned the dinner table, but I wiped it again with a dishcloth.

Father appeared, shaking his dripping hands.

"Can I have a towel?"

"What's the matter with the one in the bathroom?"

"It's wet and dirty."

That was a lie. I had replaced the towel the plumber had used with a fresh one.

The magpie was still cawing away on top of the poplar.

Father gazed toward the window. The sound seemed to have gotten on his nerves.

"The more I think about it, the kitchen window looks out the wrong way. It's no good having the evening sun come in," he muttered.

Two years ago more than half of Father's stomach was removed, and since then mealtime has become quite a lengthy affair. Although I reminded myself to eat as slowly as I could, I always ended up finishing my meal before Father was half done.

The sunlight gradually receded, and before I knew it only a thin line on the front door remained. That line would soon disappear into the darkness of the living room.

With a vague anxious feeling, I watched how Father's jawbone firmed every time he chewed and how the feeble, sagging wrinkles of his neck became suffused with shadows.

The days of autumn are short, I thought. By the time you notice the sun going down it's practically dark.

"Shall I turn on the light?"

I pushed a dish of boned fish toward him.

"The soup's cold."

I turned on the gas and put the soup pot on the stove. The even blue light of the burner in the dim kitchen reminded me of a magic flame. Hissing faintly, the flame looked somehow cold, like the reflection of blue steel.

The darkness made Father's face look a bit mournful. The bridge of his nose, which drooped at the end, seemed to lengthen in the shadows. Knowing that my face would look like that someday made me fretful.

I set the warmed soup pot on the table, got up more quietly than necessary, then pushed the play button of the cassette player again. Father lifted his head momentarily at the clamor of the cellos and violins seemingly competing with each other. The andante third movement started. Father ate slowly, like an animal chewing its cud, and spooned his soup little by little.

The music ended but the tape continued to wind. Soon it would stop and the play button would spring up.

Father finished eating and pushed his glass toward me with a belch.

"Give me some water."

As I filled his glass, a deep, composed voice came from the cassette player. I flinched. As if by reflex, Father turned and looked toward the living room.

The voice was husky from an evening of cigarettes, but

the words were distinct: "... He has no hobbies, no fun to speak of. Handguns have been his only pleasure in life. When the world is asleep, he strips naked and sticks a loaded, five-chamber revolver under his ear. He simply loves the absolute freedom and tension of doing this. Or maybe it's not freedom, but just a game. He hooks his finger around the trigger, and when he realizes that he might pull it by reflex—if somebody were to open the door when he least expected it, or if he found eyes observing him from somewhere, or if he were bitten by a mosquito in the small of the back—the blood vessels of his brain are charged with tens of thousands of volts. ... "

The visitor suddenly disappeared. Father and I looked simultaneously at the empty seat at our table for three. The tape, now silent, kept winding, whispering. I finished filling Father's glass.

It had taken me a few moments to realize it was Brother's voice.

I wondered if it was the tape recorder that made his voice sound far away, like a spirit of the dead, but with a strange urgency.

This older brother of mine had occasionally recorded his writings and then listened to them. But I couldn't believe that this one hadn't been erased; he had always done such a good job of disposing of them.

The tape coiled its way to the end and the play button snapped up.

"Shall I turn on the light?" I asked more cautiously, blinking in the sudden darkness.

The table seemed to spring up from the lamp's sphere of light as I turned the switch. The refrigerator, the kitchen shelves and the ko-hemp-papered wall disappeared behind the shadow thrown by the lampshade, like stage props being changed in the dark.

After noisily rinsing his mouth, Father went into his room and came out with the deck of flower cards. Unable to wait until I finished cleaning the table, he started shuffling them nervously. His thick shoulders in his bulky wool sweater cast a giant shadow on the wall.

"It's already dark—what's the use of playing now to tell the day's fortune?" I asked. The dishes clattered together as I scrubbed them.

"It's dark, but the day's not over yet, is it?"

Not over yet! What's that supposed to mean? Even as I asked myself this, I felt ridiculous always trying to unearth some hidden meaning from Father's casual remarks.

I put away the clean dishes, and as I turned around and removed my apron, Father gathered the scattered cards into a pile.

"What did you get?"

"The visitor," he snapped, without much enthusiasm.

"Shall I peel some fruit?"

"No. I'll have coffee instead."

Anxiety glittered in his eyes. He was hoping I'd sit down right away. After putting the teapot on the stove, I sat down across from him.

"Want to go first?" he asked.

"Of course not. We have to cut for the deal."

I cut toward the bottom of the deck; a five-point plum blossom showed. Father turned up a worthless black bush-clover, then pushed all the cards toward me. The forty-eight cards, worn and thick, filled my hand. They lacked the fresh touch and crisp sound of a new deck being shuffled. Damp and sticky, they clung to my skin.

"Give them a good shuffling. They're probably all bunched together from when I was playing for my fortune. . . . That's enough—if you overdo it they'll go back to the way they were, you know."

I set the deck down. Father, who had kept his eyes riveted on my hands, cut only the top card, as if snapping his fingers.

By dealing the cards one by one instead of in the usual two groups of five, I eased Father's worry that he would get a run of useless, no-point cards.

"Water's boiling."

Not until all ten of his cards were lying before him did Father touch them.

Water was spitting from the spout of the pot.

I put down my cards and poured the two cups I had set out. I knew that as I stirred the coffee Father was probably peeking at my hand.

"Saccharine in mine."

"Yes, I know."

Of course, Father knew I wouldn't put sugar in his coffee. The reminder was merely a smokescreen for stealing a look at my cards.

Father had a serious case of diabetes, which required regular injections of insulin. All winter long he took that homemade nostrum of his, but every morning the toilet bowl would be a foamy yellow with his sugary urine, and Father would somberly soak a strip of litmus paper in it.

I returned with the coffee. Only when Father saw me collect my cards did he gather his own hand. He carefully spread the cards one by one as if unfolding an old fan. A smile of satisfaction played briefly about his lips. The eight table cards that I had dealt were spread face up like a gaudy bouquet.

"The flower beds of Loyang! Very fertile, but no seeds planted there. What am I going to do?" Father asked. He kept stealing glances at my hand. Likewise, as I clutched my cards I looked across at Father's hand, held close to the vest. Actually, I didn't have to see what he had in his hand; the backs of the cards told me what they were. It was no doubt the same for him. The card with the slightly slanting crease on the back was a five-point iris, the one with the rounded left corner was a no-point peony, and the one with the split right edge was the ten-point red bush-clover with the wild boar. We were so familiar with the backs of the cards that we could cheat as easily as if we could see the fronts.

"We'll count all three *tan*, three *yak*, seven *tti*, and four *kwang*," said Father, explaining how we would score the game.

"Of course."

From among Father's cards, which included the blue five-point peony and the ten-point Japanese maple, it was the twenty-point full moon with the mountain that his eyes came to rest on. And there at the top of the deck was the no-point full moon with the mountain, waiting patiently to be turned up. Annoyed at having to play his twenty-point full moon right off the bat in order to pair it up with the worthless one, Father started his old routine of mulling it all over before finally playing the twenty-point card, his face telling me how unfair it was to have to dispose of it like that. Then he turned up the no-point card and swept the pair in.

"Twenty points already. Pretty bold, Father." I had wanted to say "shameless" instead. "Got your eye on all four *kwang*?"

Father responded with a childish, slack-jawed grin.

I took the five-point red bush-clover from among the table cards, paired it up, and casually tossed them down.

"You're on your way to seven *tti*," said Father.

"It's just one. Not much I can do about the rest. Nothing to write home about in my hand."

At the same time, I was busy calculating: Got to stop him from getting any more Japanese maples and make him play that blue five-point peony. That way he won't get three *yak*; or maybe I should get those myself.

"How about playing to a thousand?" asked Father.

"Fine by me."

But the autumn nights were getting longer. There was no way a thousand would be enough.

The soft tread of measured footsteps sounded from upstairs. Then I heard the whiny baby crying and the murmur of its mother's soft lullaby as she attempted to soothe it.

The window had become as black as carbon paper. Despite the light above the table, I felt that Father and I were sinking into the darkness. It seemed that we had been sitting opposite each other playing flower cards like this since the distant past. My memories of the time before that were remote and confusing, a mixture of reality and fancy—a childhood dream. Like a gambler who leaves to go to the bathroom when he's in a fix or the cards go against him, Brother had stolen away from his seat to see what his cards had in store for him.

"It's a bad sign when a baby cries at night. When children throw fits, something unpleasant always happens to the family," said Father.

I took a no-point chrysanthemum from the table cards and paired it up.

"Didn't you say I cried a lot too?"

Good night, my baby, sleep tight all night, till morning comes to your window.

"Your mother had a nice voice."

It was true. She had been a kindergarten teacher, and she knew quite a few songs. She enjoyed singing because she knew she had a beautiful voice.

Rockabye, my baby, precious like gold, precious like silver, close your pearly, starry eyes, and off to dreamland you go.

"Your turn," Father said, suddenly sounding fretful as if he too had been listening to the lullaby. The woman above was pacing back and forth on her balcony, precise as a metronome.

I could count on my fingers the times I had seen this woman, who rented the upstairs apartment some four months ago. We rarely ran into each other because the stairs to the second floor were outside and renters were supposed to use the side entry to the building. The baby boy would get peevish before going to bed and start crying early in the evening, and while we played flower cards we could hear the woman's footsteps above our heads as she soothed him with soft, monotonous lullabies well into the night.

I fingered each of my last three cards, then flung down the ten-point paulownia while scowling at the pointless paulownia Father was holding.

"Like they say, when you start off hot. . . . " Speaking with exaggerated joy, Father snatched the card away as if he had been waiting for it.

"The first bite won't fill your stomach," I said.

"This light's too weak. Maybe we should turn on the transformer."

"Maybe it's your eyesight that's getting weak."

Father and I were performing an endless play from a tattered, worn-out script. Firmly entrenched behind our ten cards, we worried about the weather, concerned ourselves with each other's health, wished for everyone's well-being, and deplored the world we saw through the unreliable, slipshod reporting in the city pages of the newspaper or on the TV news.

"Will you look at this! I don't even have enough points to give you what I owe you for *yak*," I complained.

I reached out to count the *yak, tan* and overall points that Father had earned.

Father was appalled. "Look at you, peeking at my points before the game's over. What's there to count, anyway?" he said, pushing my hand away.

"What's wrong? The show's over. Nothing left, see?" I played my last card.

Father grandly threw down the five-point cherry blossom and swept the cards away.

"What's the use of going first if you don't have squat in your hand," I grumbled. "I can't even get anything at the end."

I jotted down the score, gathered the cards and shoved them toward Father. While he was shuffling I went into the living room and turned on the television. The picture was hazy, like smoke. Shadowy outlines of people bustled about, froze for a moment, then disappeared from the screen.

"It doesn't come in good because we don't have enough power," said Father. "Now what the hell are they talking about this time?"

"A fire in an orphanage. They say some babies died."

"What kind of worthless bastards run that place? I never thought I'd see the day," Father said spiritedly.

"Is that our fault?" I muttered between clenched teeth as if to suppress Father's voice. Really—is it our fault? I asked myself. *Baby, our baby, precious like gold, precious like silver,* Mother used to sing, flower-shaped pins decorating her hair. "Having several children was too much for your mother," Father had said. "She was a tiny woman."

"Look at this," I said a bit sharply, pointing to a card

that had slipped inside one whose plastic coating had separated more than halfway.

"We've used them too long. Time to switch to a new
deck," said Father with a grin as he pulled the card free.
"They said she was possessed by the spirit of a baby," Father had told me. What garbage! We never should have left
her with that phony faith healer, I thought to myself. He
wasn't a preacher and he wasn't a shaman, but he sure knew
how to whip her with peach branches. "Save me! Oh, save
me, sweetie!"—even after Mother came home she never got
over her fear of those switches.

"It's because of your father's unrestrained lifestyle,"
Mother had said in a lilting voice to Brother, a precocious
middle school boy at the time, as she pointed to the soft-
boned newborn, whose head was pliant and swollen huge
like a water bag. One day soon after, I came home sulking
because one of the straps of my schoolbag had snapped.
Mother was combing her hair in front of a mirror she had
set next to the window to catch the sun. "Where's the
baby?" I asked. "Don't worry—I'll buy a doll for you," she
said, placing her fingers, cold like icicles, on the back of my
neck. When the van arrived from the hospital, Mother
crawled under the table. "Sweetie, I don't want to go. Stop
them, will you?" And then, as the orderlies whisked her up
by the shoulders, she twisted her head back and shouted till
she couldn't see me any more.

"Why are you laughing? Tell me," Father asked me
long afterward. "Don't you think it was cruel what you did
to her?" I had said. "What do you know? It was the only
way. You were still young, and I didn't know whether she
might cause more trouble. You know how she got rid of
that little baby, don't you? The way you talk, it's all my
fault your mother turned out that way." "Well, you could
have taken better care of her." "Your mother's more comfortable there. She has friends there. A family isn't the big
deal you think it is. And deep down inside, you feel lucky
that you don't have to see her up close, don't you? Because
then you'd complain it was her fault that your marriage ne-

gotiations were always breaking down." I had reacted to all of this by frowning.

Father was trying unsuccessfully to smooth out a crease in the back of a card.

"Go ahead and deal," I said.

"At your service." Father began dealing the cards one by one.

"She showed signs of it from the time you were born," Father had said. "The only thing that saved you was your brother."

"Are they worth playing?" Father looked across at me as he turned up the twenty-point rain card from the deck and paired it with one of the face cards.

"If I were King Midas they might be."

I paired up the pine-and-crane, and as I was bringing them in, I thought I heard someone whistling from across the field. And somehow I could detect the smell of dried flowers carried on a breath of wind. No, it couldn't be. I shook my head.

"What's the matter? Are they that bad?" asked Father.

"It's all right."

Was it ten years ago, or in my dreams long before that, when the boy started visiting me? Late at night, at the sound of the whistle across the field, I would open the door and go out. He would be standing there, smelling of dried flowers. After he stopped visiting me, I often dreamed I was walking side by side with this nineteen-year-old boy above rice fields on a path where Chinese milk vetches bloomed. I was usually wearing a nightgown and had my hair tied with a red ribbon, and there was always a breeze and a delicate smell of flowers. The soft earth under my bare feet was smooth and squishy like earthworms. "The ribbon doesn't become you," the boy would say in my dreams, blinking at the skylarks' song, which seemed to be making him drowsy. "Yes, I guess I'm too old to be tying my hair with a red ribbon. Only a crazy woman or a prostitute would do that. I'm going to catch some butterflies." The boy would look at me with his limpid eyes. "Your mother looked like a butterfly," Father had said.

I noticed one of the cherry-blossom cards turning like a pinwheel between Father's fingers.

"Just raking in the cripples," he said.

"You're merciless. If you keep salting them away like that, there won't be anything left for me."

Once I had wondered out loud where Brother was. Father had flown off the handle: "Don't you ever mention him again! Everything was just fine until he came along." Could Father have been offended by Brother's absence just because playing flower cards wasn't as much fun with only two people?

"This game makes me sick"—one day Brother had jumped up from the table and let go of his end of the taut rope that the three of us pulled on. The triangle was broken, and Father and I were left reeling by the force of the recoil.

Could I just get up and disappear like Brother had? Could I escape like someone in a life vest abandoning a sinking ship? I looked at Father's face, which had tightened while he tried to decide whether to pass up the millet card on the table or prevent me from getting seven *tti*. As his cheeks lost flesh, his long, narrow face and his nose, the tip bent like that of a hawk, seemed to droop even more. "Sweetie, take me home! It's scary here. I'm lonely." "I know, but it's the same everywhere." The cards passed from Father's hands to mine.

I won two games in a row. Father's face turned sulky and he began to get nasty.

"The next thing you know, hell's going to freeze over," he carped.

I disposed of the cards I took from Father as quickly as I could so that I wouldn't have to feel their dampish warmth. Father's hands were always mushy with sweat.

Listlessly I threw down a no-point chrysanthemum, the last card of the hand.

Father raked in the cards with a flourish: "There we go! Four *kwang*! Where have you been all this time?"

I calculated Father's score and recorded the meaningless number. The ten o'clock program, "Show of Happiness," appeared on the television. When Father reached a thousand

I called it a night.

"You'd better take your medicine." I got up feeling wobbly and grabbed the corner of the table to steady myself.

"What's wrong?"

Father put his cards down. He looked strangely old and gloomy. His drooping nose seemed to merge with his upper lip.

"I'm feeling a little dizzy—that's all."

I heard a whistling sound far off. I always thought I was hearing someone whistling. But this time it was real, not a symptom of my anemia, which made me feel dizzy, as though the veins of my brain were emptying out.

"Some idiot whistling in the middle of the night. What in hell is the world coming to? I wish they'd get some families into those development houses. They're crawling with every kind of bum and hoodlum you can imagine. ... "

Father reached for the cards out of habit. Suddenly realizing that I was staring at his hand, he retracted it stealthily, and then took great pains to extract a piece of paper from his pants pocket.

"Look at this electric bill! It's been in the mailbox for days. If we don't send it in when they say, we have to pay extra—you know that. Things should be taken care of on time; then there won't be any trouble. And I don't know why it's so high. If we don't waste electricity, we can save a lot of money."

Father was harping on the time we had to pay a penalty on an electric bill.

"We turned off the refrigerator a long time ago," I retorted, my voice quivering ever so slightly in anger. But I knew it was no use talking to him.

It was because of Father's contrariness that the electric bill had been sitting in the mailbox all that time in the first place. After all, he checked the mailbox at least ten times a day, hovering in front of it with useless gestures. I had often observed him there, empathizing with him yet detesting his behavior and always ready to confront him. The mailbox was wide open as if it were hungry, but it never held any letters—only the electric and water bills, which arrived once a month.

Father threw the bill to the corner of the table and with a grand gesture grabbed the cards. He started to arrange them in a pyramid. I propped up my chin with my palm and watched his hands turn the cards up one at a time. Father knew every game of solitaire you can play with flower cards.

"What did you end up with?" I asked when he had finished.

"The lover and the stroll."

All of a sudden Father was gazing at me with an affectionate but somber look.

"Still dizzy? You look tired. Why don't you go to bed."

The whistle penetrating the darkness from across the field was more distinct now. No way around it, we have to get a new deck, I thought. It's no fun when you know all the cards.

The soft tread of the woman's footsteps in the apartment above halted for a moment, then receded.

"Sounds like she'll put him to sleep by carrying him on her back all night," said Father. "A terrible habit for a boy to pick up."

I gave a great big yawn and rubbed my eyes.

"I'll go to bed first. Don't stay up too late," I said. "Here's your medicine. I'll make sure everything's locked."

I clumped into the bathroom, turned the water on full, and took my time washing my hands.

Though I knew Father would never look up from his cards, I avoided the light from the kitchen as I pressed myself against the living room wall and tiptoed out.

The front door opened silently. I hopped the several stepping-stones one by one and went out the gate. I kept close to the front wall, wondering anxiously which direction the woman might be looking in while she paced her second-floor balcony murmuring lullabies to her boy.

Warming fires were flaring here and there among the housing sites atop the gentle hill at the end of the field. Apparently the construction crew hadn't finished for the day. I wondered if they were pushing to finish the houses before winter.

I urged myself on more quickly, trying as best I could to look away from the fires and the bare light bulbs hanging forlornly amid the construction.

He was standing between a pile of sand and some cement bricks stacked as high as his head, next to a half-finished house.

"I've been waiting. You're a little late," he said as if he had been observing me all along. He was poking the tip of his foot in the sand, not looking at me.

"Just like yesterday," I whispered as if speaking through a veil.

"I figured you might show up, so I finished early."

I could tell from his voice that he had been drinking. Before long I could feel cold, damp air coming from the sand. Could it be the dew gathering? I asked myself. He grabbed my hand, unsure for a moment what to do. The calluses of his palm were as hard as metal. It was a big, firm hand. It would look terribly dirty and rough in the daylight, I thought.

"It's cold here, but the place is empty. The night guards are shooting the breeze down at the bar."

Despite the liquor, he was trembling in excitement.

His palm grew clammy. Led by the hand, I stepped over some broken cement bricks and some pieces of rough-hewn lumber and went inside.

"Shit!"

"What's the matter?"

"The wiring's not done yet."

But it wasn't all that dark, because the roof and two sides of the house were still open. He pushed aside some of the sawdust and pieces of lumber with his feet and made a space for us.

The callused hand drove into my sweater. He was still trembling. He rushed ahead, as if embarrassed at being aroused. But he couldn't unfasten the second button, so he cursed again and pulled the sweater up to my neck. I was breathless, and could feel the goose bumps on the insides of my legs. Naked to my armpits, I curled up against the painful cold of the cement floor. He removed his work jacket and put it under my back. Great pellucid stars descended through the open roof and came to rest above my eyes. There was always the smell of dried flowers in the darkness of night. Andromeda, Orion, Cassiopeia, Ursa Major. "What's your sign?" "Scorpio." "Some day you will have a house with thick walls and small windows and enjoy sex in a car. You are shy and introspective, but you always dream about romantic love." "The flowers don't become you." "Yes, I guess I'm too old to be wearing flowers in my hair. Women don't do that unless they're crazy or they're prostitutes."

"If the days keep getting colder, we won't be able to do it in the open anymore," the man said, fumbling with my hair as if that were the thing to do. "They'll need another couple of weeks to finish up here. But in the meantime it shouldn't get that cold."

"I don't like being cold," I giggled.

"Other than that, everything's okay? Quite the playgirl, aren't you?" He was chuckling too.

A raucous chorus of men's voices came from far away.

"Here they come." He got up, dusted off his jacket, and put it on. "What about tomorrow?" he asked as he stood between the bricks and the sand.

"Do you have a little money you could spare?"

He said nothing for a moment.

"I'm not feeling well so I have to take some medicine. I'm not asking a lot."

He spat between his teeth. "Damn!" he muttered. "Now I see why you haven't made any fuss all along. Well, I'll bet you're cheaper since you're a freelancer."

He rifled his jacket for a cigarette, struck a match as if to light it, but instead put the long flame close to my face. I looked into the flame and gave him a big grin.

"Shit—you've seen better days. Look, I'm broke. The day after tomorrow's payday, so if you still want it come around then."

He spat again, roughly. He was terribly hurt.

I took off. A bunch of drunken workmen brushed by me.

The front gate was still open. The woman on the second floor was still pacing her balcony and murmuring a lullaby to the peevish boy. I stole in through the front door and rubbed myself, trying to get rid of the cold air that had penetrated me. Father was still at the kitchen table, playing solitaire to find his fortune.

"What did you end up with?"

"The lover. Hurry up and get to bed," he said without turning around. The cards slapped against one another as he shuffled them.

I went into my room and turned on the light, looked up for a moment at the sudden brightness, then opened the desk drawer.

"Sweetie, take me away. I'm scared and lonely here," Mother screamed on the paper. The writing was large and crooked, like that of a child just learning to write. And in the spaces between the squares for the letters she had drawn stick figures doing handstands, their heads round like balls and their arms and legs stretched out like branches. I put the bundle of paper to my nose and breathed in the faint smell of dried flowers. When I opened the unadorned locket, the same smell came from the grizzled hair inside. They had been waiting there, and when we arrived they hammered the coffin shut. The sound didn't echo as I had imagined. And the smell of flowers from Mother, who had started turning putrid, was acrid, rather like smoke. "She was filthier than a Chink woman," Father had said. "Wouldn't take a bath to save her life, but she never forgot to spray herself with perfume. She was born extravagant and vain." I wondered if it was the perfume together with the smell of her dry skin that I had noticed then.

I lay down on the cold floor. Remembering that I'd heard no sound of Father going into his room, I pulled up my skirt and rolled up my sweater to my armpits as I had done in the empty, unfinished house. Above me I could hear the tread of the woman's footsteps. She was still trying to put the boy to sleep. *Our baby, like gold and silver, most pre-*

cious in the world. I reached up and turned off the light switch. The room started settling into the still of the night. Soon I felt the whole building sink gradually into a sea of darkness, creaking and groaning. The woman upstairs would flutter all night long like a ragged scrap of cloth, a futile distress signal fixed to the mast of this sinking ship. As I panted from the relentless, pulverizing pressure of the water on my body, I opened my mouth wide in a quick, faint grin, as I had in the light of the fellow's match.

Chinatown

O Chŏng-hŭi

RAILROAD TRACKS ran west through the heart of the city and ended abruptly near a flour mill at the north end of the harbor. When a coal train jerked to a stop there, the locomotive would recoil as if it were about to drop into the sea, sending coal dust trickling through chinks in the floors of the cars.

There was no lunch waiting for us at home during those winter days short as a deer's tail, so we would throw aside our book bags as soon as school was over and flock past the pier to the flour mill. The straw mats that covered the south yard of the mill were always strewn with wheat drying in the sun. If the custodian was away from the front gate, we would walk in, help ourselves to a handful of wheat, leave a footprint on the corner of the mat and be on our way. The wheat grains clicked against our teeth, and after the tough husks had steeped in our warm, sweet saliva, the kernels would emerge, sticking like glue everywhere inside our mouths. About the time they became good and chewy we would reach the railroad.

While we waited for the coal train we blew big bubbles with our wheat gum, set up rocks we had gathered from the roadbed and threw pebbles at them, or hunted for nails we had set on the rails the previous day to make magnets.

Eventually the train would appear and rattle to a stop with one last wheeze. We would scurry between the wheels, rake up the coal dust, and then hook our arms through the gaps in the doors and scoop out some of the egg-shaped briquettes. Usually, by the time the carters from the coal yard across the tracks had made their dusty appearance, we had filled our school-slipper pouches with coal—the bigger and faster children used cement bags. Then we would nestle the coal under our arms and hop over the low wire fence on the harbor side of the tracks.

We would push open the door to the snack bar on the pier and swarm to the table in the corner. Depending on the day's plunder, noodle soup, wonton, steamed buns filled with red bean jam, or some such thing would be brought to us. And sometimes the coal was exchanged for baked sweet potatoes, picture cards or candy. In any event, we knew that coal was like cash—something we could trade for anything around the pier—and so the children in our neighborhood looked like black puppies throughout the year.

Some people called our neighborhood Seashore Village, others called it Chinatown. The coal dust carried by the north wind all winter long covered the area like a shadow, and the sun hung faint in the blackened sky, looking more like the moon.

Grandmother used to scoop ash from our stove, apply it to a fistful of straw, and polish the washbasin to a sparkling sheen before doing Father's dress shirts. But even when the shirts were hung to dry deep inside the canopy away from the dusty wind, they had to be rinsed again and again and starched a second time before they could be worn.

"Damned coal dust! What a place to live!" Grandmother would say, clicking her tongue.

A certain reminiscence would invariably follow. I had heard it so often that I would take over for Grandmother: "Let me tell you about the water from Kwangsŏk Spring. Now this was in the North before the war, you understand. When I used that water, the wash turned out so white it seemed almost blue! Even lye wouldn't get it that white."

When we returned to school after winter vacation our homeroom teacher would take all the Chinatown children to the kitchen next to the night-duty room. There she would have us strip to the waist, assume a pushup position on the floor and take a merciless dousing with lukewarm water. Then she would check for coal dust behind our ears, on the backs of our necks, between our toes and under our fingernails. If she gave us an affectionate slap where the gooseflesh had erupted in the small of our backs, we had passed inspection. We would giggle as we slipped on our longjohn tops flecked with dead skin.

Spring arrived, and with it the new school year. I was now a third-grader. My homeroom had classes only in the morning, and early one afternoon I was on my way home with Ch'i-ok. We had our arms around each other's shoulders.

"I'm going to be a hairdresser when I grow up," Ch'i-ok said as we passed a beauty shop at a three-way intersection.

Her voice reminded me of yellow. It had been worm-medicine day at school, and our teacher had made us come to school on an empty stomach. I wasn't sure if it was hunger, the santonin we took for the worms, or the smell of boiling Corsican weed, but everything seemed yellow—the sunlight, the faces of passersby, the blustery breeze that crept under my skirt and made it flutter.

Except for some makeshift stores, both sides of the street were virtually barren. Here and there the skeleton of a bombed-out building stood like a decayed tooth.

"Somebody said it was the biggest theater in town," Ch'i-ok whispered as she pointed out the one remaining wall of a building in ruins. Plastered in white, it resembled a movie screen or the curtain of a stage. But it too would soon be coming down. A row of laborers was taking aim at it with pickaxes, and in a moment the great white wall would roar to the ground.

Other laborers were removing the reusable bricks and reinforcing rods from a wall already demolished.

"The area was bombed to kingdom come," Ch'i-ok said, mimicking the adults and repeating "to kingdom come" over and over.

Diligent as ants, the residents had reclaimed the devastated areas and were rebuilding their houses. Pots of

Corsican weed boiled on heaps of coal briquettes in stoves made from oil drums.

Ch'i-ok and I constantly stopped to spit big gobs of saliva.

"Feels like the worms took the medicine and went nuts."

"Uh-uh, I think they're peeing."

Whatever it was they were doing, it didn't make us any the less nauseated. The froth from the Corsican weed, the smoke from the coal and the smell of plaster mixed with the seaweed smell of the Corsican weed were one big yellow whirl.

"I wonder why they use Corsican weed when they're building a house," Ch'i-ok said. "One whiff and I get a splitting headache."

The arm looped around my shoulder dropped like a dead weight. I dawdled along, drinking in the smell of the Corsican weed. That yellow smell had been my introduction to this city, the very first understanding I shared with it.

My family had moved here the previous spring from the country village where we had taken refuge during the recent war.

"If your father could only get a job," Mother used to say while she was spraying her tidy stacks of tobacco leaves with mouthfuls of water. She would leave home at dawn, a sack chock-full of the leaves strapped to her back, and return looking half dead two or three days later.

"I don't give up easily, but I've had it with this damn tobacco monopoly. Unless you have a license, you're always getting searched by the police. If your father could only get a job. . . . "

Father's job hunting consisted of looking up friends and classmates from the North who had immigrated to the South or had somehow managed to flee the war. Finally he got a job in the city selling kerosene.

The day the moving truck was to come, we ate breakfast at daybreak and then camped beside the road with our
bundled quilts and our household goods tied up roughly
with cord. Lunchtime came and the truck hadn't arrived.
The endlessly repeated farewells with the neighbors were
over.

Toward sundown, while we were plumped listlessly on
the ground, fed up with playing hopscotch and land baron,
Mother took us to one of the local noodle shops and bought
us each a bowl of noodle soup. The two oldest boys and I
had changed into clean clothes before going outside that
morning, but by now our runny noses had left a shiny track
down our sleeves and on the backs of our hands.

It was dark now, but Mother, sitting on the bundled
quilts with our baby brother in her arms, kept glaring toward the approach to the bridge, waiting for the truck.

Long after sundown the headlights of the truck finally
appeared near the bridge. "It's here!" Mother shouted, and
we children bounced up from our seats on the bundles. The
truck briefly stopped. Mother rushed over, and the driver's
assistant stuck his head out the window and shouted something to her over the roar of the engine. Mother returned
and the truck left. My brothers and sisters and I looked at
each other in bewilderment. The dark outlines towering
above the high railing around the back of the truck were
cattle. We could tell from the sharply bent horns and the
soft, damp sound of their rumination, which flowed
through the gloom.

"They'll be back after they unload the cattle. He arranged it that way because we pay half price if we use an
empty truck going back to the garage," Mother explained
to Grandmother.

Grandmother nodded with a reluctant expression that
seemed to say, "I suppose you two know what you're
doing." We had never seen her disagree with Mother and
Father.

A good two hours passed before the truck reappeared.
After delivering the cattle to a slaughterhouse in a city ten

miles away, the men had had to clean the muck from the truck bed.

Mother and the baby squeezed between the driver and his assistant after the rest of us and our baggage had been piled in back. As the truck started out, we heard the faraway whistle of the midnight southbound train.

I stuck my head out from the bundles and watched our village recede into the night and blend with the hill behind it and its grove of scrub trees. They all undulated together, no larger than the palm of a hand, a darkness thicker than the sky. Finally they converged into a single dot that bounced up and down in counterpoint to the rear of the truck.

We crossed the township line and soon we were barreling along a bumpy hillside road. Those of us in back, stuck among the bundles like nits, kept bouncing up in the air like wind-up dolls. It was as if the truck had lost its temper at the driver's rough handling. I could see Grandmother fighting to keep from crying out because of the jarring. With each bounce I felt certain we would fall headlong into the river below, so I squeezed my eyes shut and drew my four-year-old brother close.

Though it was spring, the night wind prickled our skin like the tip of a knife. It swept across the river, raked my scaling skin with its sharp nails, and gradually removed the smell of cow dung from the truck bed.

I suddenly recalled the soft, damp sound of the cattle chewing their cud in the darkness. "Do you think all those cows are dead now?" I asked my big sister. But she kept her face buried between her raised knees and didn't answer. Surely the animals had been slaughtered, skinned, gutted and butchered by now.

The moon kept us company, and after a while my little brother shook his fist at it: "Stupid moon, where you goin'?"

One or another of us always had to urinate, and so the truck stopped frequently. We would knock on the tiny window between the cab and the truck bed, and the driver's assistant would stick his head out the passenger window and shout, "What do you want!"

"We have to go to the bathroom," one of us would say.

With a wave of his hand the man would tell us to go where we were, but then Grandmother would raise a fuss, and the driver would reluctantly stop. The assistant would lift us down one by one and then bark at us to do our business all together. We shuddered in relief as we squatted at the side of the road. It took us a long time to empty our bladders.

Whenever the truck entered a different jurisdiction, which seemed to happen at every bend in the road, there was a checkpoint. A policeman in a military uniform would play his flashlight over the truck. Mother's tobacco peddling had left her with barely enough spunk to lean out the window and yell, "Help yourself, but all you're going to find are a few lousy bundles and some kids."

All night long the truck hurtled across hills and streams and through sleeping towns, and after stopping once for gas, breaking down twice and going through countless checkpoints, we finally reached the city at daybreak. The streets seemed to perk up at the roar of the truck's old engine.

At the far end of the city we arrived at a neighborhood that seemed to keep the sea barely at arm's length, and here we were lifted down from the truck along with our bundles. After chasing us all night the moon had long since lost its shine and was hanging flat like a disk in the western sky. The truck had stopped in front of a well-worn, two-story wooden house. The first floor had sliding glass doors that opened onto the narrow street like those of a shop. "Kerosene retailer" had been painted in red on the dusty glass.

This was the house where we would live.

The blast of fresh cold air made my teeth chatter. I was supposed to be looking out for my little brother, so I put him on my back.

While the truck had rattled through the city we had craned our necks from among the bundles and gazed out in curiosity and expectation. The city was different from what

I had dreamed of in our country village. When I thought of the city we would end up in, I thought of the rainbow-colored soap bubbles that I liked to blow from the end of a homemade straw, or I imagined the Christmas trees from some strange land that I had dreamed of but never seen.

Our street was lined on both sides with identical two-story frame houses that had tiny balconies. The squeaky wheels of bicycles ridden by seafood vendors on their way to the wharf and the footsteps of people going to work at the flour mill filled the shabby, filthy street with a disordered vigor like that of chickens flapping their wings at dawn. The vendors and mill workers squeezed past the truck, which had planted itself in the middle of the street, avoided our carelessly discharged bundles and headed up the gentle hill that began at our house.

I was lost in confusion. Everything was different from the country village we had just left, but had we really moved? Was this really our new home? It had a dreamlike smell that filled the sky like an evening haze. It was like a once-familiar dream now forgotten, leaving only its sensation. What was that smell?

Father shoved open the door of the kerosene shop and shouted to the driver that he hadn't followed the terms of the agreement. The driver shook his fist at Father and pointed back and forth at the rest of us and our belongings. Curious and apprehensive, we could only gape at them.

You could see the bluish marks where the razor had scraped my neck between my gourd-bowl haircut and the yellow rayon quilted jacket that was losing its batting. A little nine-year-old whose skin was flaking all over, I looked around our future neighborhood with a strangely uneasy feeling, my brother still riding on my back.

The neighborhood had awakened at our noisy arrival, and heads with rumpled hair began poking out through windows and doors.

The dozen or so identical frame dwellings that lined each side of the street ended abruptly with our house. The houses that faced each other on the hill above also had two stories but were much larger. Some were white, others were blue-gray like faded ink.

The houses on the hill were spaced apart, except for the first one, which practically touched our house. A broad wall enclosed the lot of that first house. The door and all the windows I could see were too small and tightly shuttered. I wondered if it was a warehouse—no one could have lived there.

With their steeply slanting roofs and the pinched ridgelines that contrasted with their bulk, these Western-style houses looked strange and out of place to me. Perched on the hill that stood alone like a distant island amid the swarm of people on their way to the wharf, the houses had an air of cool contempt. They faced the sea, their orifices shut tight like shells, but they seemed somehow heroic even in their shabbiness, for they left you wondering how old they were and what their history might have been.

The truck started up but didn't leave. The driver hadn't been paid as much as he wanted, and for a moment he rested both arms on the steering wheel and shut his eyes as if he were about to enter a protracted battle.

"What's all this damn commotion so early in the morning? Are the Northerners invading again?"

A blunt, hard voice flew over our heads, ringing in my ears, and knocked out the menacing roar of the engine with a single stroke. Mother and then my brothers and sisters and I looked up to see a young woman on the balcony of the house across the street. Her legs were exposed to the thighs and an army jacket barely covered her shoulders. Her dyed hair swung back and forth across her back as she went inside.

My big brother was running among the wheels of the truck. Father grabbed him by the scruff, hauled him out and rapped him on the head. Then he took a look at us standing in a bunch. "Well, well, well," he chuckled as if in amazement, "we've got ourselves a platoon here."

Sunlight began to break through the dawn clouds, but still the sleeping houses on the hill kept their shutters tightly closed. The bluish gloom in the sky, driven from here and there throughout the city, gathered ominously above the hill like clouds before a storm.

When the darkness had vanished, the smell I had first noticed began to trickle through the delicate rattan blinds of the night and then rose from everywhere in the streets like a deep breath at last exhaled.

All at once the smell dispelled my confusion and the neighborhood seemed familiar and friendly. I finally understood the true nature of that smell: it was a languid happiness, an image colored by our refugee life in the village we had left the previous night, the memory of my childhood.

Later that year, around the time the dandelions were blooming, I became chronically dizzy and nauseated and had to sit on the shoe-ledge of our house, spitting foamy saliva while my little brother crawled about in the yard putting dirt in his mouth. It seemed Grandmother cooked Corsican weed all spring long. Whenever she forced a bowl of the broth upon me for my worms, I would drink it reluctantly, shaking my head in disgust, and then sink into a strange, languid stupor that felt like spring fever. The whole world was yellow, and regardless of the time, I would always ask Grandmother whether it was morning or evening.

"Are the worms stirring, you little stinker?" she would retort with a hearty laugh.

One day, while I sank into the familiar yellow stupor, as if I were walking into a forgotten dream, the two-story houses on the hill suddenly swooped close, one of the shutters opened and the pale face of a young man appeared.

Mother became pregnant with her seventh child. Only fresh oysters and clams could soothe her queasy stomach, so every morning before school I would take an aluminum bowl and set off over the hill for the pier. I would dash by the firmly shut gates of the houses on the hill, sneaking glances at them out of curiosity and a vague anxiety, for these were the houses of the Chinese. When I had run a mere twenty steps down the other side of the hill, the Chinese district suddenly ended at a butcher shop and the pier unfolded before my eyes. I would stop to catch my breath and look back, and about that time the shutters of the shop would clatter open.

I went to this shop every week to buy half a pound of pork. Mother would place some money in my hand and send me on my way, always with the same warning: "If he doesn't give you enough, ask him if it's because you're a child. And ask him to give you only lean meat, not fat."

The butcher was an unmarried Chinese who had a growth the size of a chestnut on his cheek. It looked as if someone had given him a terrific punch. Long hairs trailed from the growth, as if pulled by an unseen hand.

The first time I went to the shop, I found the man stropping his butcher knife.

"Are you only giving me this much because I'm a child?" I blurted. By standing on tiptoe I was just able to get my chin over the counter as I stuck out the money.

The man turned and looked at me, baffled.

Afraid he would cut the meat before I could finish saying what Mother had told me, I snapped, "She told me to ask for lean."

Stifling a laugh, the butcher quickly sliced the meat for me. "Why only lean? I can give you some hair and skin too."

Next to the butcher shop was a store that sold such things as pepper, brown sugar and Chinese tea in bulk. It was the only general store in Chinatown. The people from our neighborhood occasionally went to the butcher shop for pork, but didn't shop at the general store. We had no use for dyes and firecrackers, and we didn't need decorative beads for our clothing and shoes.

The store's shutters were opened only on one side, and even on bright, sunny days the interior was dark and gloomy, as if enveloped in soot.

But in the evening the Chinese flocked there, creeping like dusk through interlocking alleys. The women had great thick ears and wore silver earrings. They tottered on bound feet, baskets over their arms, and their heads bobbed, the tight buns looking like cow dung.

While the women shopped, the men sat in the chairs in front of the store and silently smoked their long bamboo pipes before creeping back home. Most of them were elderly.

We children parked ourselves in a row on the narrow, low curb, tapping our feet on the street and pointing at the men.

"They're smoking opium, the dirty addicts."

And in fact the smoke scattering from the pipes was unusually yellow.

Now and then the elderly men gave us a smile.

Our families lived right next to Chinatown, but we children were the only ones who were interested in the Chinese. The grownups referred to them indifferently as "Chinks."

Although we had no direct contact with the Chinese in the two-story houses on the hill, they were the yeast of our infinite imagination and curiosity. Smugglers, opium addicts, coolies who squirreled away gold inside every panel of their ragged quilted clothing, mounted bandits who swept over the frozen earth to the beat of their horses' hoofs, barbarians who sliced up the raw liver of a slaughtered enemy and ate it according to rank, outcaste butchers who made wonton out of human flesh, people whose turds had frozen upright on the northern Manchurian plain before they could even pull up their pants— this was how we thought of them. What was inside the tightly closed shutters of their houses? And what lay deep inside their minds, seldom expressed even after years of friendship? Was it gold? Opium? Suspicion?

"Let's do our homework here," Ch'i-ok said when we arrived at her house. She looked up toward the quilt and the blanket stretched over the side of the second-floor balcony. This was a sign that Maggie was out. If she were in, she would have been in bed, beneath the blanket. I hesitated, glancing across the street at our house. Mother and Grandmother referred to Ch'i-ok's house as a whorehouse for the

GIs. Our house was the only one in the neighborhood that didn't rent out a room to a prostitute. These women threw open their doors to the street and thought nothing of letting the American soldiers give them a squeeze. Stained blankets and colorful underwear festooned with lace hung in the sun on the balconies, drying from the free-spirited activities of the previous night.

"Scum!" Grandmother would say, turning away from the sight. To her way of thinking, women's clothes, and especially their underwear, should be hung to dry inside the house.

Ch'i-ok's parents lived downstairs, and Maggie rented the big room upstairs with a darky GI. Ch'i-ok had to go through Maggie's room to get to her own, which was small and narrow like a closet. When I went to get Ch'i-ok for school in the morning I always encountered Maggie lying in bed with her hair disheveled and the huge darky sitting hunched in front of the dresser trimming his mustache with a tiny pair of silvery scissors. Maggie would beckon me in with the slightest motion of her hand, but I always remained outside the half-open door to the room, peeking inside while I waited for Ch'i-ok. The thick flesh of the darky's chest looked like molded rubber and his eyes were smoky. He always mumbled when he spoke, and he never smiled at me. What a gloomy man, I thought.

"Can't you call me from the street?" Ch'i-ok once asked. "The darky doesn't like you going up there."

But every morning I walked up the creaky stairs and called to Ch'i-ok while hovering outside Maggie's room.

"Maggie said she won't be back until tonight. So we can play on her bed," Ch'i-ok cajoled me.

I thought for a moment: Mother had a bad case of morning sickness and was probably lying in the family room, looking vexed at everything. My older brother had likely gone outside to catch mole crickets. And I knew that as soon as I walked in, Grandmother would tell me to piggyback my baby brother, who had just been weaned, and then shoo us out of the house.

And so I followed Ch'i-ok upstairs. Jennie, Maggie's

daughter, was asleep on the bed. Curtains kept the sun out, making the room dim.

Ch'i-ok opened the storage cabinet, located a box of cookies, took two of them and carefully replaced the box. The cookies were sweet and smelled faintly like toothpaste.

"That's so pretty," I said, pointing to a bottle of perfume on the dresser.

Ch'i-ok turned it upside down and pretended to gently spray her armpits with it. "Made in America." Again Ch'i-ok reached inside the cabinet and rustled around. This time she produced two candies.

"It tastes so good," I said.

"Mmm, because it's made in America," Ch'i-ok answered in the same blasé tone.

Jennie was now wide awake and watching us.

"Jennie, aren't you pretty? Now we have to do our homework, so why don't you go back to sleep for a little while?" Ch'i-ok spoke softly, brushing Jennie's eyelids down with her palm, and in an instant the little girl's eyes had closed tightly like those of a doll.

Everything in Maggie's room seemed marvelous. Ch'i-ok let me feel each of the things for just a moment, and every time I exclaimed joyfully as I caressed it. Then we replaced each item, leaving no sign that it had been touched.

"I have an idea."

Ch'i-ok reached inside a cabinet at the head of the bed and took out a gourd-shaped bottle half full of a green liquid. After making a line with her fingernail on the side of the bottle to mark the level of the liquid, she opened the bottle, poured a small amount into the cap and handed it to me.

"Try it. It's sweet—tastes like menthol."

I quickly drank it and returned the cap to Ch'i-ok. She filled it and then gulped it down. The level of the liquid was now about two fingers below the mark, so Ch'i-ok made up the difference with water, capped the bottle and returned it to the cabinet.

"Perfect! How was it? Tasty, huh?"

The inside of my mouth was refreshingly warm, as if I

had a mouthful of peppermint.

"Now don't tell anyone," Ch'i-ok said as she removed a velvet box from among some clothes in one of the dresser drawers.

Everything in Maggie's room was a secret. The box contained a pearl necklace long enough to make three strands, a brooch adorned with garishly colored glass beads, some earrings and other jewelry. Ch'i-ok tried on a necklace made of thick glass beads and studied herself in the mirror.

"I'm going to be a GI's whore when I grow up," she said decisively. "Maggie said she'll give me necklaces, shoes, clothing—everything."

I felt as if I were dissolving and the tips of my fingers and toes had gone to sleep. I was short of breath and couldn't keep my eyes open. Was it the darkness of the room? I imagined that the peppermint was leaving a white trail every time I breathed out. I drew aside the curtain covering the door to the balcony. Seething yellow sunlight entered the room, illuminating the dust and making the room look like a greenhouse. I touched my burning cheek to the the doorknob and peered outside. Once again I saw the two-story house in Chinatown with the open shutters and the face of the young man looking my way. A mysterious sadness, an ineffable pathos began undulating in my chest and then spread over me.

"What's the matter? Are you dizzy?" asked Ch'i-ok, who knew what the green liquid was and how it affected you. She snuggled up beside me against the door to the balcony.

I shook my head, unable to understand, much less explain the feeling I got from that face in the second-floor window, and at that instant the wooden shutter thumped shut and the young man disappeared.

The glass beads of Ch'i-ok's necklace clicked together, their colors dancing in the sunlight. Ch'i-ok took one of the beads in her lips. "I'll be a GI's whore."

I drew the curtain and lay down on the bed. Who could he be? I tried fretfully to revive my memories of a forgotten dream. I knew I had seen him the previous autumn at the barber's. I had had to sit on a plank placed across the chair because I was so short. I had instructed the barber as Mother had told me:

"Please make it short and layered on the sides and back, but leave the top long. I'm ugly enough already, so a gourd-bowl haircut won't do."

But when the barber had finished, I looked in the mirror to find I still had a gourd bowl.

"Too late to complain now. I'll do better next time—promise."

"I knew this would happen! Why can't you concentrate on cutting hair instead of gabbing with everybody?"

The barber jerked the plank away from under me. "What a smart-alecky little girl. That's no way to talk. I'll bet that yap of yours was the first thing that came out when you were born."

"Don't you worry about how I should talk. And I'll bet you're a hair chopper because you came out with scissors around your wrist."

The other customers roared with laughter. I looked around with a triumphant air. The only ones who weren't laughing were the barber and a young man sitting in the corner with a bib around his neck. The young man was studying me in the mirror. He's Chinese, I suddenly thought. Although I had seen him only at an angle from across the street, never close up, his inscrutable gaze had given me that impression. I removed the towel around my neck and tossed it in front of the mirror. Then I stamped to the doorway, put my hands on my hips, and turned back: "Until the day you die you'll be nothing but a hair chopper!" And then I ran home.

Father was constantly at work on our house, as if to compensate for the privations of our refugee life in the country village—the entire family crowded into a single rented room, and before that the many sleepless nights he had spent keeping the children warm in his arms under a bridge or inside a tent. He got rid of our tiny yard, adding a room and a veranda to the house in the way that girls who have just learned how to sew might add secret pockets to the inside of a book bag or the underside of their clothing. And so a mazelike hallway appeared in the house, long and narrow like an ant tunnel.

Along with the hallway there materialized a place where I could hide and no one would find me—the back room next to the toilet, which was filled with old clothing, household stuff and other odds and ends. The day of the ill-fated haircut, I ran inside the house, sneaked into this room and pressed my face against the narrow mouth of a jar, hoping in vain that the sorrow sweeping over my bones like a strong current would empty into it.

Several times after that, usually when I was hunkered down in front of Father's shop waiting for the evening newspaper, I sensed that the young Chinese man had opened his window and was looking toward me.

"Jennie. Time to get up, Jennie—your mom's here," Ch'i-ok said in an affectedly sweet and gentle tone. Jennie opened her eyes and sat up. Ch'i-ok went downstairs and returned with a washbasin full of water. Jennie didn't cry even when the soapy water got in her eyes. We combed her hair, sprayed some perfume on her and changed her into some clothes we had found in the closet. Jennie's father was white and her mother Korean, and at the age of five she still hadn't begun to talk. She couldn't feed herself, much less put on her own clothes, and when she was fed, the food would trickle out the side of her mouth. Whenever the darky was there, Jennie would be moved to Ch'i-ok's room.

Grandmother occasionally saw Jennie on the balcony or outside the house. "Whelp!" she would say, looking at the girl as if in amazement, her eyes filled with the hatred she reserved for animals. She frightened me whenever she stared at Jennie like that. Some time ago our house had become infested with rats, and so we had gotten a cat. The cat bore a litter of seven kittens in the back room, and Grandmother fed it seaweed soup to help it recover. Then she stared right into the cat's eyes and repeated several times, like a refrain, "Kitty had some baby rats, seven baby rats."

That evening the cat ate all seven kittens, leaving only the heads. Then it yowled all night long, not bothering to clean its bloodstained mouth. As if she had been expecting this, Grandmother wrapped the seven tiny heads in newspaper and sent them down the sewer drain.

Mother used to tell me that Grandmother was so fastidious and cold because she had never had children of her own. She was actually Mother's stepmother. I had once overheard Mother whispering about Grandmother to an elderly woman who was a distant relative: "They'd been married only three months when her husband had an affair with his sister-in-law—can you believe it? That's why they separated and she decided to come live with us."

Jennie was like a doll to Ch'i-ok. Ch'i-ok could give her a bath and change her clothes every half hour, and never get a scolding from Maggie. To Ch'i-ok, Jennie was sometimes a baby, sometimes a sick little girl, sometimes an angel. I envied Ch'i-ok with all my heart, and it must have shown on my face.

"Don't you have a sister too?" Ch'i-ok asked me dubiously.

"She's my stepsister."

"You mean that's not your real mother?"

"My stepmother," I lied with a lump in my throat.

Tears gathered in her eyes. "Well, well. Somehow I had a hunch. Don't tell anyone, but I have a stepmother too."

There wasn't a soul in our neighborhood who didn't know this.

I linked my little finger with Ch'i-ok's and we promised to keep each other's secret.

"So, does your mom spank you and tell you to get lost and drop dead?" I asked.

"Yeah, when no one's around." Ch'i-ok lowered her pants and showed me her bruised thighs. "I'm going to run away and be a GI's whore."

How often I wished I really were a stepdaughter, so I could run away whenever I pleased.

Mother was still carrying baby number seven. None of us children in this poor district next to Chinatown believed that babies were brought to earth in the arms of an angel in the middle of the night. And they didn't emerge smiling brightly from their mother's belly button. Everyone knew a baby came out screaming from between the naked legs of a woman.

We were watching some GIs in T-shirts take target practice with knives on one of the tennis courts at the army base. The knives sliced through the air toward the concentric circles on the target. They had a piercing glint, like silver needles, a flash of light, a man's prematurely white hair. Whenever a knife whistled to the black spot dead in the center of the target, the men howled like animals and we gulped in terror.

A white GI had been taking a step back every time he hit the center of the target. He took aim once again, but as the knife was about to spring from his hand, he suddenly pivoted. The knife ripped through the air toward us. We flattened ourselves with a shriek in front of the wire fence surrounding the base. I felt a warm wetness between my legs. A moment later we lifted our pallid faces. The chuckling GI was pointing at something a short distance behind us. We turned and looked. A black cat lay rigid on its back with its legs in the air, the knife stuck in its chest. The cat was as big as a small dog. It was probably one of the strays that were always getting into the garbage cans on the base. Its pointed whiskers were still trembling as we crowded around it. Suddenly my big brother picked up the cat and ran off. The rest of us set out after him. My wet underpants chafed.

Brother stopped, panting, when we were out of sight of the Americans' barracks. Then he looked down at what he was holding. He shuddered and dropped the cat, which fell to the ground with a thud.

"How come you brought that thing?" one of the children demanded.

Thus challenged, my Little Napoleon of a brother

pulled the knife from the cat's chest and wiped the blade on the grass. It was sharp and pointed like an awl. He folded the blade with a snap and put the knife in his pocket.

"Go get me a stick," he said.

One of us snapped off a branch from a tree we had planted the previous spring on Arbor Day and returned with it.

Brother took off his belt and looped it around the cat's neck, then tied the end to the branch. We paraded down the street with the cat splayed out behind him. The cat's paws dragged along the ground, and its weight bent the branch on Brother's shoulder like a bow.

By the time we reached Chinatown the long summer day had begun to wane. As the sun slanted toward the horizon the cat's shadow seemed to grow endlessly from its midsection.

The flour mill workers walked past us on their way down the hill, their hair frosted with flour, their empty lunchboxes rattling.

We walked toward the wharf, treading on each other's gigantic, frightening shadows and the shadow of the long, black carcass of the cat. And then I saw him again. The second-floor shutters were open, and he was watching our procession. I couldn't fathom his gaze, but I thought I saw sorrow, anger, and perhaps a subtle smile.

When we reached the wharf Brother put the branch down and removed the belt from the cat's neck. Spitting in disgust, he cinched the belt around the waist of his pants, which constantly threatened to fall down. Then he dropped the cat into a mass of garbage, empty bottles and rotting, white-bellied fish washing up against the bank.

As we often did when the sun was going down, we decided to go to the park. There we would usually lie on our stomachs on the endless expanse of steps and look up the hoop skirts of the GIs' whores, exclaiming at the bare legs inside the bloated framework of whale tendon. Or we would loll on the grass and bellow one of the old standards that an aging prostitute might sing to herself:

> *When I look back, I see every step of my youth*
> *stained with tears,*
> *When I look back at my regrettable past,*
> *I hear the bells of Santa Maria.*

But this time we walked up silently, one step at a time, toward the sky.

At the highest point in the park stood a bronze statue of the old general whose landing operation here just a few years before was already inscribed in legend. From this spot the entire city could be seen.

Boats and ships were moored at the pier, their flags fluttering like confetti. The jaws of a crane bit into their cargo again and again. At a distance from the pier floated something that looked like an islet or a huge old carp—probably a foreign freighter.

The bell from the Catholic church behind us kept tolling. It was the sound that had been tugging at us ever since—no, even before—we had thrown the cat into the water. Producing endless ripples at precise intervals, confined to a single tone, simplifying every desire and temperament into one basic harmony, the sound of the bell evoked in my mind the awesomeness of a peal of thunder heard on a summer evening upon being awakened from a dream, the mystery of train wheels rumbling through the deep of the night.

"A nun must have died," said one of the others.

We all thought that a nun was dying peacefully whenever the bell tolled on and on like this.

Across the railroad tracks a black stream spewed from the smokestack of the flour mill, surging into the sky above the war-ravaged city like dust rising from a battlefield.

The intense bombardment from the warships during the landing operation would long be remembered in the history of warfare, the grownups liked to say. About the only structures to have remained intact were the old frame houses in our neighborhood, which had been seized from the Japanese at the end of World War II, and the two-story houses on the hill in Chinatown.

The sunlight lingered in the western part of the city, but Chinatown was saturated with darkness, as if the smoke were smothering it. Perhaps it was the dust carried by the north wind from the coal yard, settling there like ash.

Here at the highest point of the city we had a commanding view of Chinatown and the colored blankets and lace underwear on the balconies of the sooty houses seized from the Japanese. These were the scenes, the underside, the mysterious smile of this city. Part of me would always be weighed down by these images. To me, Chinatown and my neighborhood were the flooded stern of a listing ship about to sink.

Torches, lit too early in the evening, flared at the public playfield in the eastern part of the city. The flames swayed as if they were flickering remnants of the wind in the last traces of the sunlight. A crowd of people cried out, "Czechoslovakia go home! Poland go home! Puppet regimes go home!" All summer long, one member from each household would report to the playfield as soon as the sun had vanished, and the throng would shout these slogans while stamping their feet. Grandmother would return from these rallies and groan all night long from the pain in her lower back.

One day at morning assembly our principal had explained why the people were protesting: Czechoslovakia and Poland, satellites of the Soviet Union, had forsworn their obligations as members of the neutral-nations peacekeeping force by digging for U.N. military secrets to pass on to the communist side.

If I buried my head between my knees, the outcry from the playfield would become a distant hum, like the sound made when I blew across the narrow mouth of an empty bottle. It was the sound of the earth groaning deep below the surface, a faint ripple foreshadowing a tidal wave, a lingering breeze licking the roofs of houses.

At home I found Mother retching beside the drain in the yard. For the first time I empathized with the brutish life that women had to live. There was something pathetic and harrowing about Mother's retching, and this symptom of her pregnancy made me plead silently with her to produce no more brothers and sisters for me. I was afraid she would die if she gave birth again.

I couldn't get to sleep until well into the night. My older sister had bound her emerging breasts with a waistband that Grandmother had torn from a skirt. The breasts were sensitive even to the touch of her sheet, so she tossed and turned, embracing them tightly and moaning. As I lay awake, I counted each time the night guards tapped their sticks together to signal their approach, and I tried to count the number of wheels of the freight trains that passed by. At daybreak I went to the wharf. The dead cat was nowhere to be seen among the garbage and rotting fish washing up against the bank, nor was it beneath an abandoned boat I spotted drifting a short distance offshore. Perhaps some children in a distant port were dragging its shapeless body around at the end of a pole.

Autumn drew near, but the bedbugs flourished as never before. When the sun shone full on the balcony, we would take the tatamis outside to dry and scour the wooden floors of our rooms for the eggs. Though our pajamas had elastic cuffs, the bedbugs would manage to crawl inside, making us itch and producing the smell of raw beans. The electricity stayed on until midnight, and so we usually went to sleep with the lights on because they kept the bugs away. But when the lights went out at twelve the bugs would swarm from the straw of the tatamis or from cracks in the floor and launch their all-out attack.

One night, while I was half asleep and scratching away at the bugs, I was awakened by a thunk—it sounded like a block of wood being split. Before I knew it my older brother had thrown on his pants and was down the stairs like a bullet. The sudden hubbub from the street told me something had happened. My heart quickened, and I went out on the balcony. The electricity had been off for some time, and it was pitch dark outside, but I could make out the noisy crowd that had filled the street between our house and Ch'i-ok's. The neighbors' sliding glass doors scraped open, and people appeared on the balconies above, shouting for news. Among the hum of voices the word "dead" came to my ears like a revelation. The word passed from mouth to mouth like a round. Some people reacted by shuddering in disgust, others poked their heads through the layers of on-lookers. My chin trembled as I looked across the street and saw that the door to Maggie's room was open. The darky, dressed in an undershirt, looked down on the street from the balcony, his hands resting on the railing.

A moment later I heard the wail of a siren and saw an American army jeep. In an instant the crowd had separated. Maggie lay in the street, drenched in the brightness of the jeep's headlights. Her long, thick hair covered her face and was strewn every which way, like solar flares. "He threw her into the street," somebody said.

The darky was drunk. The MPs dressed him in his uniform, and as they loaded him into the jeep, his shirt unbuttoned, he chuckled.

The next day I found Ch'i-ok feeding water to Jennie, who had the hiccups. She patiently wiped the moisture that trickled from the corner of the little girl's mouth. But no amount of water would make the hiccups stop.

"They'll put her in an orphanage," Ch'i-ok said. She sounded a bit sulky, as she had the day she told me that Maggie would go to America in the spring—the darky had decided to marry her.

Maggie had looked happy then. Once I had found her washing the darky's feet as he sat on the edge of the bed. Her dyed hair was piled high on her head, and as I stared at the clean nape of her neck she turned to me. Without makeup she seemed to have no eyebrows. She gently beckoned to me, saying, "It's okay. Come on in."

"Jennie went to the Catholic orphanage," Ch'i-ok told me with a fierce scowl two days later. Her eyes were red and puffy. A younger sister of Maggie's had come to pack up the dead woman's belongings. Maggie's room remained empty for quite some time. But I didn't go up there to do homework or to play with Ch'i-ok anymore. Instead I called to her from the street on my way to school every morning.

I became more and more convinced that Mother wouldn't survive another birth, but her stomach continued to swell almost imperceptibly beneath her skirt. As it turned out, the one who failed was Grandmother, whose stinging hands and pungent, vicious curses had seemed to make her healthier by the day. One morning she collapsed while doing the laundry, and she never recovered. My baby brother, who had practically lived on her back, became my big sister's responsibility.

After Grandmother began needing a bedpan, Mother and Father agreed to move her to the countryside, where Grandfather lived.

"A stroke can last twenty years," Mother whispered to Father. "It can melt a rock." And in a slightly louder voice, "When you're old, there's only one place to be, and that's next to your husband, whether you love him or hate him." Finally, in a loud tone, "We'd better reserve a taxi for her."

Grandmother became like a baby. As Ch'i-ok had done with Jennie, I would go into Grandmother's room when no one else was home and comb her hair, feed water to her and sometimes gently feel to see if her diaper was wet.

The day Grandmother was to leave, Mother dressed her in clean clothes. "She still has her figure because she never had children."

Father went with Grandmother to the village where Grandfather lived with Grandmother's younger sister and their children. "I don't feel right about it," Father said falteringly when he returned. He sighed. "I don't think they'll be happy with her. She'll be a thorn in their side. You know, it's amazing—I thought she wouldn't recognize anyone, but then she spread her jacket, took Father's hand, and placed it on her chest. She must have been so frustrated. Makes me wonder what it means to be man and wife."

"There was a lifetime of bitterness inside that woman," said Mother. "But didn't I tell you? We did the right thing sending her there."

Mother decided to open Grandmother's clothing chest. Grandmother had never let anyone else in the family touch it, and so we craned our necks to follow the movement of

Mother's hands. One by one she removed the neatly folded articles of clothing piled inside and placed them on the floor. Out came Father's old long underwear, which Grandmother had hemmed for her own use, and the Japanese-style baggy pants that she had worn around the house. And there were clothes made from fabrics woven in traditional ways, such as sheer silk and rough, thick, glossy silk. As Mother's outstretched hands continued to produce clothing that Grandmother had worn but once or twice in her life, I realized that she wouldn't be coming back, that the days she would wear such clothes were gone, and I felt as if a chill wind had swept through the depths of my heart. When had she worn such clothes? And for what special occasion had she saved them deep in the chest?

The last article of clothing was an otter vest. Mother then groped along the bottom of the chest and took out something small wrapped tightly in a handkerchief. With bated breath we fixed our eyes on Mother's nimble fingers.

With a quizzical expression Mother looked inside the handkerchief. A jade ring broken in two, a tarnished copper belt buckle that seemed about to crumble, a few nickel coins from the Japanese occupation, several buttons of various sizes that might once have been attached to clothing, some pieces of colored thread—these and other things she found there.

"Really, Mother! Saving broken jade is like saving bits of pottery." Clicking her tongue, Mother rewrapped the objects in the handkerchief and tossed them into the empty chest. She set aside the long underwear and other underclothing to use as rags, and moved the rest of the clothing to her own chest. The otter fur was of high quality, she said—she would use it as a muffler.

The next day I sneaked into Grandmother's chest and took out the bundled-up handkerchief. Then I went to the park and walked sixty-five paces from the statue of the general to some trees—one step for each year Grandmother had lived. I found myself beside an alder—the fifth one into the grove—and I buried the bundle deep beneath it.

Toward the end of winter word arrived that Grandmother had died. It had been just the previous summer that she had left in the taxi. Mother, who was in her ninth month, did something uncharacteristic: she began crying while caressing Grandmother's clothing chest, now stuffed topsy-turvy with the children's threadbare clothing.

All evening I hid among the odds and ends in the back room, where no one could find me, and when everyone had gone to bed I went to the park. The sky was black, but I found the fifth alder tree without even having to take the sixty-five steps.

The damp handkerchief, buried for two seasons deep in the ground, stuck to my palm like rotten straw. I brushed the dirt off the pieces of the ring, the tarnished belt buckle and the coins and held them tenderly in my hand. They felt exactly the same as before. They were warm now, but the cold would soon return to them.

I returned the objects to their burial place beneath the tree. After I had tramped the dirt down and brushed off my hands, I started walking toward the statue, concentrating on taking even steps. At the count of sixty I was there. I began to wonder. Surely it had been sixty-five steps the previous summer. Did this mean I would reach the tree in fifty paces the following summer? And a year later, or ten years later, would one giant step take me there?

Since it was still winter and late at night, I could climb up on the statue without any disapproving looks from others. And so I clawed my way onto the pedestal, then climbed onto the binoculars that the general held against his stomach. From there I looked down on the city sparsely dotted with lights. The outcries of the previous summer, swelling like dust from a battlefield, were gone. Now it was still. As I strained to listen to the sounds flowing gently in the darkness, I felt as if I were tapping an undiscovered vein of water in the deepest part of the earth.

The sea was a black plane. I drank in the wind that had been blowing all night from the East China Sea, and the seaweed smell it carried. I saw the oblong light framed by the open shutter of the two-story house on the Chinatown hill, and imagined a pale face revealed there. I felt the soft breath of spring hiding in the chilly air.

Something was budding in my warm blood, something unbearably ticklish.

"Life is... ," I murmured. But I couldn't find the right word. Could it be found, a single word for today and yesterday, with their jumble of indistinguishable, all too complicated colors, a word to embrace all the tomorrows?

Another spring arrived and I became a sixth-grader. My older brother was raising a puppy he had brought home one day. With Grandmother gone, the dog had the run of the house, pooping and shedding anywhere it pleased.

I had grown the better part of a foot in the past twelve months, and since the previous year I'd been carrying around my older sister's Oxford-cloth school bag embroidered with roses.

All winter long my rat pack and I had sneaked coal from the freight trains, and as always we had run wild through the streets. Occasionally I had closeted myself in the back room at home to read popular romances and such.

One Saturday—the day we had no afternoon classes—I was on my way home from school. "Tomorrow's worm-medicine day, so be sure to skip breakfast," our teacher had reminded us the day before. "The worms won't take the medicine on a full belly."

There was much less house rebuilding now, but Corsican weed was still being boiled and the smell still seemed to dye the air yellow.

In the simmering yellow sunlight I frequently stopped to spit. "Feels like the worms are going nuts," I muttered once again.

I saw Ch'i-ok mixing permanent-wave solution in a can in the beauty shop at the three-way intersection. Her father had lost a leg in a conveyor belt at the flour mill and had left the area with his wife the previous winter. Ch'i-ok had remained with the people who ran the beauty shop. Every day I passed by the place on my way to and from school and saw her through the glass door. She would be sweeping the hair on the floor while pulling down her small sweater, which was constantly riding up her back and revealing her bare waist.

I walked past the beauty shop. The yellow sunlight filling the street looked like thousands of feathers soaring up in the air. When was it? Shaking my head in irritation I tried to revive a distant, barely remembered dream. When was it? I continued toward home, and when I arrived I looked at the open window of the two-story house on the hill. He was leaning partway out the window, beckoning me.

I started up the hill, drawn as if by a magnet, and he disappeared from the window. A moment later he heaved open the gate to the house and emerged. His yellow, flatnosed face still wore that mysterious smile.

He offered me something wrapped in paper. When I accepted it, he turned and went inside. Through the open gate I could see the narrow, shaded front walk, the unexpected sight of a sunny yard, and the sunlight dancing and darting on the limpid skin of his feet with every step he took.

At home I went into the back room, locked the door, and opened the package. Inside was some bread dyed in three colors, which the Chinese ate on their holidays, and a thumb-size lantern decorated with a plastic dragon.

I hid these things in a cracked jar that no one used. Mother was in labor in my parents' room, but instead of looking in on her I went upstairs. I sneaked into a storage cabinet, as I did when playing hide and seek. It was midday, but not a ray of light entered. While listening to Mother scream that she wanted to die, I realized that the church bell had been tolling and I fell into a sleep that was like death itself.

When I awoke, Mother had pushed her eighth child into the world after a terrible labor. A sense of helplessness and despair came over me in the darkness of the cabinet, and I called out to her. Then I felt inside my underwear, and finally I understood the humid fever that had been closing about me like a spider web.

My first menstrual flow had begun.

Words of Farewell

O Chŏng-hŭi

CHŎNG-OK CLOSED her eyes and leaned against the sliding glass door to the veranda. She had taken the hard-boiled eggs from the cold water and put them in a cloth-lined straw bag along with a few *ch'amoe* melons from the refrigerator, and was about to step down to the yard. But the very moment she noticed her father, his hair closely cropped, squatting on the lawn as if he were pulling clover and weeds from the tufts of overgrown grass, she thought she saw the fence around the yard receding and a transparent form moving in front of it.

When she opened her eyes the sensation was gone, like a momentary dizzy spell. In the dense, voluminous stillness she noticed only her father's outline, distinct against the board fence, which, long since stripped of its white paint, was damp and rotting from the soaking rains.

What had pierced her vision and disappeared like a fleeting sliver of sunlight was nothing more than a sensation of movement, without apparent shape or texture, but it made Chŏng-ok feel she had viewed the essence of the sudden impulse that had led her here to her parents' house.

What could I have seen? she wondered. Was it simply an illusion caused by water vapor shimmering in the sun? Or could it have been the unseen hand—the unseen power—controlling the unfamiliar figure of her father and his desultory weeding?

She peered toward the yard looking for even the slightest movement that might have caused the illusion. But

231

her attentive stare caught not a breath of wind brushing the tips of the leaves; there were only the sluggish, automatic movements of her father's elbows. The old man's thin shoulder blades looked wraithlike, and his sleaveless ramie shirt was sweaty, as if these simple movements were too much for him.

What was the true character of this sensation that would visit her at unexpected moments, a sensation she felt intimately acquainted with?

It had happened the previous day too. When she entered the front gate, with her boy sound asleep on her back since the bus ride, her mother, who had been watching television on the veranda, came running and took the boy in her arms. At that moment the familiar but unanticipated sensation raked her skin, giving her gooseflesh and startling her, though she realized it was only her father she saw, curled up in an armchair at the front of the veranda. The sun had set some time before, but there he was still wearing dark glasses, leaning slightly forward and staring off into a corner of the yard, which seemed darker for all the roses in full bloom and their heavy scent.

"Why haven't you turned on the light?" Chŏng-ok had asked her parents, touching the back of the armchair. "You're getting bitten by mosquitoes. Won't you go inside?"

"All right. I can't take it anymore. They're biting like the dickens," her mother had complained as she slapped her bare calves and forearms over and over.

The humid night air, thick and sweet with pollen, had stifled Chŏng-ok.

"Is he sleeping?" Chŏng-ok's voice had become a little louder as she struggled to shake off the darkness, viscous and heavy with the fragrance of the roses that ceaselessly bloomed and withered on their viney bushes from spring to autumn. Her mother had shaken her head, her eyes fixed on the television screen.

Chŏng-ok's father had been off in his own world, drawing random figures with his finger on his knee—first a circle, then a square within, and confined inside that a triangle.

It was as if he were sending signals to an unseen place beyond the dark. Like calm water at dusk, he had seemed to blend with the ever-thickening darkness.

Now Chŏng-ok's son was shaking loose the half-ripe fruit of a date tree. His upturned face looked like a kite floating in the air.

The ring of the doorbell pierced the air. Though the gaps between the boards of the fence seemed wide enough for a visitor to see that people were home, the ringing did not stop. Chŏng-ok donned slippers and ran to the gate.

As soon as she released the bolt, the gate was brusquely pushed open and two dark red faces pressed close to her. Propping themselves against the gatepost and blocking the entrance, the visitors stuck out shriveled hands.

Chŏng-ok briefly scrutinized them. Silently they extended their clawlike hands toward her eyes.

"Don't come inside. Stay there," Chŏng-ok said in a choking tone altogether different from her real voice. She took one hundred wŏn from her pocket and dropped the coin into one of the palms. The recipient looked hard at her and grinned. The sunlight glinted on his hairless eyebrows.

"Who is it?" came her mother's voice from inside the house.

"Lepers."

"When they're gone, pour some water on the gate and then sprinkle it with salt."

Chŏng-ok washed down the gatepost with a basin of water and scattered a handful of coarse salt about it.

The boy wrapped his arms around the date tree, shook it some more, retreated a few steps, and looked to see where the pieces of fruit had fallen. He found them hiding among the tufts of grass and put them in his pockets.

The hand of a passerby shot up above the rose bushes that trailed along the fence and plucked one of the straggling sprays.

"Are you ready?" asked Chŏng-ok's mother. She stepped down to the yard.

Chŏng-ok glanced at her and turned away with a weak smile. Her mother was quite the stylish woman with her pink dress in a cloud pattern and her loosely knit summer bag. Her makeup was sumptuous.

"You'll have to take one of the Kangwha buses past Ojŏng-ni," Chŏng-ok's father faltered. He had not looked up even once as they prepared to depart, but had merely continued his mechanical weeding.

"Wouldn't you be better off inside? It's getting hotter by the minute," Chŏng-ok said, extending her arm to him. But he rejected her offer of assistance, gesturing to her to be off.

"Lunch is on the table. Help yourself, and don't go skipping it." But even her mother's hint that their outing might take some time was simply waved off by her father.

As Chŏng-ok's mother opened her parasol, she squinted to see where the sun was. Her dyed hair, a brilliant steel blue in the sunlight, rested firmly on her head like a wig, not a strand out of place, not a telltale gray hair to be seen.

"Are they beggars?" the boy asked. Gently holding the hem of his mother's skirt, he watched the lepers as they pressed other doorbells in his grandparents' alley. Chŏng-ok placed her hand on his head, without really knowing why she did so. Whether the boy took her gesture to mean "Yes" or to mean "Don't be scared" was not clear. But he questioned her no further and instead scampered ahead of them.

Their bus was packed—but not especially because of the weekend, Chŏng-ok concluded, for most of the passengers appeared to be fishmonger women rather than tourists. The empty plastic basins stacked on the floor of the bus reeked of fish and left little standing room. The strong smell of tidewater permeated the women's clothing and hair. Remembering the name of the port where the bus route started, Chŏng-ok guessed the women were on their way home from an early round of peddling. The boats at that port, bearing romantic names such as *Sea Gull*, *Billow*, and *Golden Wave*, would be lying at anchor, smelling of engine oil; from there they would leave for the small islands of the West Sea. The women's loud, immodest chattering would take some getting used to, Chŏng-ok thought.

Chŏng-ok stood clutching the back of a seat near the door, straining to keep from being knocked off balance. Her son's head was buried among the other passengers. She could feel how desperately he was holding on by his insistent grip on her skirt. She wanted to reassure him by saying, "You don't have to hold on so tight. Mom won't ever lose you."

Chŏng-ok occasionally twisted around so she could spot her mother, buried deep within the overcrowded bus. She could still see the back of her mother's hand, its tendons swollen, gripping a handrail. And she could see her nephrite jade ring. The stone was too big to be genuine, its turquoise color too deep and undistinguished.

"Is this your skirt, Mom? Is it you, Mom?"

The boy's small face, unexpectedly troubled, surfaced among the throng. Might the skirt be someone else's? He forced his head back and looked up. His forehead was creased with a few thin wrinkles that made him seem wise beyond his years.

A man sitting in front of Chŏng-ok read her face with a sidelong glance and lifted the boy toward his lap. But then he released him, for the boy had looked at him warily and begun shaking his head obstinately, tightening his grasp on Chŏng-ok's hand. An awkward moment of tension rose from the boy's instinctive wariness and the uncalculating thoughtfulness of the man, who appeared surprised and embarrassed at the little one's stubborn and seemingly hostile rejection. Chŏng-ok dispassionately observed the man's outstretched hands hesitate, harden, and come to rest on his knees.

The arm with which Chŏng-ok clutched the seatback kept drooping from the weight of her bag with its eggs, melons, bottles of soft drinks and other refreshments. "Let us off at the checkpost," Chŏng-ok said, craning her neck toward the bus girl. She had already made several such requests.

"Still a ways to go," the young woman replied without lifting her head. Amid the crush she was somehow able to keep her nose stuck in a magazine.

The bus was passing the Kimp'o rice fields. The rice plants formed a dappled green background beyond the heads of the other passengers. The fresh color caught Chŏng-ok's eye. It looked as if they had been washed clean by the previous day's rain. While this vast green, gently swaying velvet apron sped through her field of vision, a hot, sticky breeze blew up through the windows from the tar of the asphalt road.

Chŏng-ok grew uneasy again when the bus stopped and three youths dressed for a hike boarded, blocking her way to the front. "Is it still far to the checkpost?" she asked, raising her voice and impulsively pushing one of the youths in the back as if she were about to get off.

Only then did the bus girl turn up her small eyes at Chŏng-ok. "I know when to let you off. You don't have to keep asking. I'm not deaf, you know. Really! It's the next stop," she snapped irritably.

Her face burned for an instant, then Chŏng-ok quickly tried to distance herself from her feelings, so easily hurt, by feebly lamenting to herself, "Why do people have to act this way?" She was well aware that her indignation at the bus girl's insolence was accompanied by rage toward herself for lacking the courage to express that indignation, a rage that always seethed deep in her heart, unexposed and festering.

"Mother, come up front," Chŏng-ok called, pushing the strap of her bag higher on her shoulder and seeking the boy's hand. How extraordinarily clear her own voice sounded to her.

Chŏng-ok straightened the boy's clothing by pulling down his shirt, which had crept up under his suspenders. The laces of his sneakers had come undone and his fresh white cotton socks were now smudged all over.

"That way, maybe?" said Chŏng-ok's mother when they got off the bus. She pointed out an unpaved road to the left, which skirted the checkpost. Dust-covered *ch'amoe* melons and tomatoes languished on a low platform in front of a variety store at the intersection.

Chŏng-ok nodded, though she had never been here before and knew little about the area. She covered her mouth against the dust, which obscured her vision like the misty spray from an atomizer.

Dust, there was only dust. The roofs of tiny shops and the vegetable fields beside the road lay tranquil under their coating of the mistlike stuff. How odd, thought Chŏng-ok: it's like chalky ash, or radioactive fallout. The dust had a ghostly aspect and looked dreary to her—as if stilled by the relentless sunlight. She wondered if this dreamlike image was a reaction to the muggy fish smell of the bus, which still pervaded her, or perhaps to the green rice plants swaying vividly beyond the sticky black asphalt.

But this image of barren desolation disappeared as soon as she turned down the unpaved road. She stepped into the dust and saw a bulldozer coated with ocher-colored soil come to a stop on the shoulder of the road. Laborers were digging up deeply embedded rocks from the road. Sparks flew from the blades of their pickaxes. Women were carrying loads of gravel on their heads. The roadway was being scoured in preparation for a coat of asphalt, and only enough space was left for a single row of vehicles to slip through.

Chŏng-ok, her mother and the boy ascended a rise in one of the bordering fields, but here too there was only a rough path of gravel culled from the road. The pricking of the stones hurt Chŏng-ok's soles.

An endless line of honking cars passed by on what was left of the road, leaving no time for the dust to settle. Coolers and mats could be spotted beneath flapping trunk lids. "That's right, it's the weekend!" Chŏng-ok exclaimed to herself. This realization cut to her heart, for reasons she did not clearly understand.

In one of the cars a girl in a sun hat was resting her chin on top of the back seat, which was covered with embroidered hemp. Her gay smile slowly disappeared in the dust. Again Chŏng-ok murmured, "It's the weekend," enjoying the wistfulness of the phrase.

The boy had walked but a short way when he started dragging his feet and whining. Chŏng-ok smiled to herself. She had pretended not to notice his longing glances at the ice cream in one of the small shops, and this must have disappointed him.

Stopping to reason with the peevish boy, Chŏng-ok kept falling behind her mother. The older woman, clopping along a few steps ahead, often removed her sandals and shook the soil from them. She seemed oblivious to the numbing sound of the bulldozer and the gravel being poured on the road. The white parasol held obliquely over her head looked as though it were floating by itself, like a balloon at an amusement park.

The boy looked back. A military convoy had appeared, one troop truck after another. He froze, gaping at the sight. Chŏng-ok gripped his hand more tightly and hastily descended to a path in the field, away from the road. She couldn't keep her heart from pounding the moment she saw the procession of onrushing vehicles. Was it, perhaps, the incongruity and coldness of those bright headlights in the midday sun that bothered her?

The soldiers in the trucks looked down with stony expressions. The tractors and automobiles stopped blowing their horns and moved aside in a jumble, clearing the way for the convoy.

The massive wheels of the trucks, coated with ocher soil from some distant place, rolled by with an earthshaking rumble. Again the boy halted and stood stock-still, watching the gigantic procession with his mouth agape. His hair, now coated with dust, fell across his eyebrows. Streaked with sweat and grime, his face looked pathetic and wretched.

Chŏng-ok turned and lifted the boy onto her back.

Her mother had stopped and was looking at them. "Why don't you let him walk instead of doing whatever he asks," she said with a frown.

"Still far to go?" Chŏng-ok asked, shifting the boy so he sat straight.

Her mother looked around with uncertainty, though she had been here once before. She took the bag from Chŏng-ok, whose hands were clasped beneath the boy's buttocks. "There's a road heading uphill somewhere around here," she murmured. Then she went into a small wayside shop.

The shopkeeper pointed to the road they had been walking, which stretched straight ahead. "Go about a hundred yards more and take the side road on the left."

Chŏng-ok bought an ice-cream cone and planted it in the boy's hand.

"We'll have to walk a good hour or more. And look at the condition of the road." Her mother sounded upset, but she took the lead and set out briskly.

It was hot. Chŏng-ok's arms kept sagging under the weight of the boy, who reacted by pulling on her neck with his sticky hands. Her hair became sweaty and tangled, falling into her eyes and blocking her vision. Unable to watch her step, she would stumble and nearly fall. The unbroken procession of trucks continued.

A girl toting a baby on her back stood in a furrow in the field, waving toward the convoy. A woman with a large bag for carrying gravel squeezed between two trucks, crossed the road, and stepped down to the field. The woman removed the towel encircling her head and dusted off her clothes with it. Then she took the baby from the girl, unbuttoned her blouse, and gave the baby her breast. The girl picked some blades of grass and waved them in front of the suckling baby, laughing brightly. Turning its head to and fro in pursuit of the grass, the child released the nipple and wriggled its arms and legs, trying to grab the flickering blades. At this the girl burst into another high-pitched laugh.

Chŏng-ok's mother covered her nose and mouth with a handkerchief and walked on, then turned and spat a mouthful of saliva.

A column of soldiers appeared behind the procession of trucks as it snaked around a seemingly endless bend in the road. Helmets squeezed their flushed faces, and their green uniforms were stained with sweat. Their insignias, perhaps polished to a luster before the march, had acquired a thick coat of dust.

When Chŏng-ok saw the dull green column marching

by in silent rhythm, the nebulous shroud of anxiety hanging in her chest gradually became heavier and began to suffocate her. To erase her fear, she approached her mother and whispered, "It's a military unit on the move, isn't it?" Without waiting for a response she asked another question, realizing all the while that there was no reason her mother would know the answer. "Where do you suppose they came from? They probably left at dawn."

A bird with enormous wings draped with steel netting, flying through the night in pursuit of the sun and stealing into the gray of early morning. Footsteps treading heavily across her chest every dawn before she woke up.

A black cloud scudded across the sky, veiling the sun. The scattered clumps of reddish brown soil, the green column of soldiers, the vales among the hills and the thickets of tangled brush were all suffused with shade. Then the cloud drifted away.

Chŏng-ok's back was sticky with sweat where the boy clung to her.

"Wouldn't you like to walk for a while?... That's a good boy."

So amazed and curious was the boy at the sight of the column of soldiers, so different from the pictures he had seen of children playing soldier, that he descended without a fuss. The ice cream, which had begun to melt as soon as it left the freezer at the shop, streamed like gruel from the cone, leaving the boy's fingers and mouth soiled and sticky. Chŏng-ok wiped him briskly with her handkerchief, until the area around his mouth was scarlet like new skin. The boy scowled and shook his head furiously.

Chŏng-ok's mother looked back and urged them on: "If you keep poking along like that it'll be sundown before we get there." Her thick face powder, eroded here and there by sweat, had been darkened by the dust. "The man at the store said it was the first side road.... " She seemed flustered that her memory was so hazy. Time had clouded her eyes, and she wondered if she would be able to spot the fork in the road that was somewhere to the left. But she needn't have troubled herself. Across the road, in front of a variety store, at the corner of a side road between vegetable fields, stood a crude signpost: "Entrance to Memorial Park."

Chŏng-ok stood the boy before a pump in front of the store and drew some water. She threw the boy's ice-cream cone in a trash can and washed his dusty face and feet.

The march of the soldiers continued. Perhaps they would see the end of the column when they came down the hill from the cemetery, Chŏng-ok thought. It seemed the tedious march might never end.

Her mother carefully wiped the nape of her neck with a handkerchief soaked in cold water, then slipped the handkerchief inside her dress and mopped the sweat from her chest. Chŏng-ok poured water over her own feet without removing her sneakers. She was about to tell her mother, "If you wash your face, you'll feel much fresher; the water's cold"—but then thought better of it. With her face powdered thick and pale, her hair black like a crow's feathers and the line of her mouth vividly accented by her gaudy lipstick, her mother looked ready for burial. Maybe she would stay mummified when she died. Chŏng-ok smirked at this sudden impertinent thought.

A small group of young people in bright windbreakers and tight jeans passed by carrying guitars. The sunlight resting on the rifles atop the soldiers' packs gave Chŏng-ok a chill. "More people die from futility than fear"—he had said this once, as if he were a terrorist.

The boy moved behind Chŏng-ok and began whining again. It was impossible for him to know the purpose of the tedious military march on this hot day, or the reason his little legs, stumbling over jagged stones, had to tramp incessantly along this parched, hilly road with its weeds and dust and nothing more.

"How about riding piggyback on Grammy?" said Chŏng-ok's mother. But the boy, now on his mother's back, refused to budge. Instead he stared at his grandmother as if he had never seen her before, then averted his face.

"What a funny brat! You think Grammy has thorns on her back?" She clicked her tongue.

Chǒng-ok couldn't blame the boy, for he had never had the opportunity to become familiar with his grandmother, whom he saw a few times a year at best.

Chǒng-ok looked at her watch. It had been two hours since they left the house. Without realizing it they had already walked an hour or so.

She kept thinking they would see the cemetery around the next bend in the hill.

"Let's rest for a bit," said Chǒng-ok's mother. Sitting under a tree next to the road, she shook the sand from her sandals and dabbed at her sweaty face with her handkerchief. Despite the parasol, her face was turning a ripe red in the fierce sun. Chǒng-ok swept her palms across her own puffy, burning face, wondering if the swelling would ever go down.

The tree had a burly base and offered thick shade. The procession of soldiers still caught Chǒng-ok's eye. Though they were quite far off and faint by now, she felt if she opened her eyes wide she could detect even the shapes of their backpacks, filled with emergency rations, bedding and weapons.

He had left as if it were wartime.

"Where are you going?" Chǒng-ok had asked with parched lips. It was first light, and he was about to leave the house, shouldering his tackle bag and carrying a fish net and creel.

"Well, it'll have to be someplace with a lot of fish."

"The keys will be here." Chǒng-ok had him watch as the keys to the front gate and the door dropped with a clink into the mailbox attached to the gate. If he stuck his hand through the slot, he could extract them without difficulty.

"If someone comes looking for you," she asked after a pause, "where should I tell him you went?"

"To Heaven's Pass and the Stream of the Gods," he shot back. It sounded like a password. Immediately he produced a vague smile, as if trying to soften his curt response.

"Don't sleep out in the open if you can help it. It's bad for you."

Bad for you! Chǒng-ok forced a smile as she ruminated

on these words. Tobacco is bad for your health, so let's try to smoke in moderation. Sweets are bad for your teeth. The nighttime dew isn't good for you. She realized that these common sayings, which gave her a sense of routine and comfort, were absurd and laughable.

The entrance appeared: "Anshik Memorial Park." It seemed so sudden, after all of their waiting. The realization that this was their destination took a moment to sink in.

"Here we are."

But for her mother's words, Chŏng-ok could have bypassed the place and walked on forever.

A wide path led between a grove of acacias. There was no sign of the cemetery. Chŏng-ok was briefly disconcerted, perhaps because she had imagined that some positive demarcation between the cemetery and the mundane daily life they saw around them would manifest itself. But the path was merely a connection with the road, merely a part of the hill, lying long and slender like someone's spine. She wondered if she really wanted to see the realm of the departed—the wandering souls—or if she only wanted to sense colors, smells, the stillness of forms she had never experienced before.

The path gradually ascended the hill. They had followed it well into the acacia grove when they came upon a small wooden building with a sign hanging lengthwise from it that announced, "Memorial Park Office." One end of the shabby structure contained the office, the other a small shop that sold incense, candles, liquor and such. The office looked something like a real estate agency to Chŏng-ok. From outside she could see a telephone on a metal desk and a map of the cemetery on the wall that at first glance resembled a detailed map of the capital or one of its districts. Two men were playing chess, one wearing an undershirt and the other a reservist's camouflage shirt unbuttoned from the neck to the waist, exposing his chest.

"Excuse me," said Chŏng-ok's mother. As she poked her head inside the office, the two men simultaneously looked toward the door.

Chŏng-ok's waterlogged sneakers had dried and her

swollen feet felt squishy and uncomfortable inside them. She went to the pump in front of the shop and splashed more water on the sneakers. Then she followed her mother into the office.

"The sale ended a long time ago." The men returned to their chessboard.

Chŏng-ok's mother took from her bag a thin, light brown envelope containing a contract for a lot. "I bought one of the lots."

At that, the man in the undershirt sluggishly turned to look at them.

"I was here once before, but I don't think I can find the lot this time." Chŏng-ok's mother glanced at her daughter, then moved toward the man and gave him an affectedly sweet smile while unfolding the contract.

"Block D, 9-3. It's up on top. Follow the path and take your third right. Then you'll find some steps," said the younger-looking man in the reservist's shirt. His unnaturally dark and thick eyebrows twitched at every syllable he ejected.

"It's a special lot, forty-eight square feet. For my husband and me," Chŏng-ok's mother added impatiently.

"Did your beloved... ?" the man in the undershirt asked, suddenly courteous, trying to determine from their appearance who these two women were.

"No. My daughter happened to be visiting, so I thought I'd show her the lot. We hardly ever see her because she lives in the countryside." She glanced at Chŏng-ok, then produced a shy smile for the man.

Chŏng-ok turned to look at the boy, who was dangling playfully from the pump.

"If the family is bereaved, let us know immediately so we can have the burial mound prepared. It can be quite a problem getting the help. But that's what we're here for. We handle everything."

"I would hope so. That was one of the first conditions when you sold us the lot. And of course you'll take good care of the grave. That was one of the conditions for paying you a maintenance fee."

"All the special lots are in the upper section; you were lucky to get one of them. It looks down, and you've got an open view in front. Can't expect anything better than that. Dead or alive, we've got to be able to look down... "

"And *that*'s why it's special. What a difference in price! We knew what we were doing when we paid extra for that lot."

Chŏng-ok's mother seemed ready to chatter on forever about the lot. But when the men resumed their seats at the chessboard she reluctantly folded the contract, put it in her bag and left the office.

Upon rounding the spine of the hill, Chŏng-ok uttered a low exclamation and closed her eyes, dazzled by the burial mounds spreading across the hill like boiling, seething blobs of lather. Although the cemetery was supposed to be terraced, the closer she approached, the more disordered it appeared. The mounds and their gravestones were of uneven sizes, and most of the mounds were thick with weeds. The epitaphs on the small granite stones, provided by the cemetery office as specified in the contract, were difficult to decipher among the weeds, because their Chinese-ink lettering had been rubbed out, leaving only an indistinct engraving.

The burial sites were separated from the pathways by blocks set in the ground, but because most of the blocks were missing, broken or wearing away, dirt had swept down onto the walks. Perhaps the summer's rain was to blame, Chong-ok thought.

"It's a pretty damn cheap operation," spat Chŏng-ok's mother. "Where's all that maintenance they're supposed to be providing? They want us to pay the fee on time, though." Her tone had been different with the men in the office.

The boy's face turned a bit pale and he said nothing, perhaps apprehensive because of the stillness of the cemetery and the appearance of the graves, heaped up like warts on the back of a hand.

As the man in the office had explained, the path they were to take had steps, or rather the semblance of steps formed by people's footprints and almost buried by soil. In reality, it was no different from a steep mountain trail.

The sun was hot. The boy started sweating again. A mole cricket darted across the whitish path, its short shadows resembling musical notes.

"Where does the path go?" the boy asked Chŏng-ok with an exceedingly doubtful look.

"Well. . . . " Chŏng-ok was momentarily perplexed. The boy was not yet old enough to understand that people have to die and leave everything behind.

"Why haven't you come to see us for so long?" Chŏng-ok's mother abruptly asked.

Her mother had asked the same question when taking the sleeping boy from her upon their arrival at her parents' house the previous night. But Chŏng-ok could not remember her answer. Had it been, "No one to take care of the house"? Or, "I was kind of busy"? Since her mother had not followed up with, "Mr. Yi must be on vacation—where's he off to?" she had probably answered the latter.

"I was kind of busy," Chŏng-ok replied, knitting her brow. Their empty house in Vernal Stream and the empty mailbox with the two little keys inside flashed across her mind. The boy's tricycle would be lying in a corner of the yard.

Chŏng-ok could not explain to her mother that it had been difficult for her to leave home because she was waiting for some brief word from him; that the uncertainty of the situation had made her willing to believe even an unsubstantiated report.

A sense of urgency, unlike her habitual anxiety whenever he left the house, dazed her now, obscuring her vision.

She recalled the sound of the telephone, probably ringing even now in the empty house, and the questions lying in wait inside the silent, unanswered receiver.

"Hello, may I speak with Mr. Yi?"

"He's not home now."

"Do you know where he went?"

The voice inquired after him politely and persistently, without a sign of irritation. A friendly male voice, its sole concern the well-being of the other party, but giving absolutely no hint of what murky, hidden purpose existed at that end of the line. Chŏng-ok became flustered at these calls, realizing instinctively from the speaker's acute professionalism that he would find out what he wanted.

"Hello, may I speak with Mr. Yi?"

"He went to a go club."

"Could you tell me which one?"

"I think it's the Hope Club, but I'm not positive."

"Do you happen to know if he was planning to meet someone?"

"Well, he doesn't tell me anything about his outside affairs, so... "

Although he hardly ever left home, he obstinately refused to answer the phone.

"Did Mr. Yi go out again? Somehow I feel like we're playing hide and seek."

Though its tone was light, almost droll, the unseen voice kept searching tenaciously for any trace of his trail —a trail that might have stopped at a place he had visited.

"He went to the barber shop."

"Is it near your house?"

"Yes, it's called the Springtime of Life."

"A fine name. Ha-ha-ha... "

That day, after coming home with his hair neatly barbered for the first time in a long while, he finally took some scissors and cut the telephone cord. But after he left, Chŏng-ok had the line reconnected.

"Did a burglar do this?" The repairman chuckled as he looked down at the section of line severed so decisively by the sharp blades.

As soon as the line was reconnected the voice crawled out as if it had been hiding in the severed cord.

"Hello, may I speak with Mr. Yi?"

"He's gone fishing."

"Oh? Fishing?"

"He often goes out fishing," Chŏng-ok said, raising her voice to emphasize that this activity was nothing new.

"Did he go with somebody?"

"Well, I'm not sure. Sometimes he goes by himself, sometimes he goes with a group."

"Do you know where he went?"

"He said something like the Stream of the Gods. I think he said he had to walk in quite a ways from Heaven's Pass."

"If he comes home with a big catch, Ma'am, cook up a nice peppery stew with it. I'll come for the meal." The voice roared with laughter.

Although Chŏng-ok distinctly heard the caller hang up, she imagined his laughter still bursting through every little hole in the receiver for quite some time. The man seemed to have been beside himself with delight, but at the same time listening keenly to the sound of his own calculated staccato laughter.

As Chŏng-ok listened to the laughter, her despair at her husband's departure—his figure gradually becoming dim and then vanishing—flashed vividly through her mind, as it always did. "Where are you?" she asked over and over, listening to her voice circling in vain about the empty house.

Where could he have gone?

"There's no reason for them to be looking for me," he had said.

The ocher earth spilled down the narrow trail and found its way between her toes.

The "special" lots, as they were called, occupied the crest of the steep, narrow path. Because they were not marked with serial numbers, Chŏng-ok had to rely on her mother's somewhat unreliable memory to find the correct one.

Chŏng-ok again took the boy on her back, the path being too narrow for two to ascend side by side. Evidently her mother was bewildered by the sight of all the graves. Before, there had been only the burial sites, leveled to be sold.

Taking out the cemetery plan attached to the contract, Chŏng-ok's mother traced their path from its starting point and began matching the graves with the numbers on the plan. While she did this, she repeatedly shook the earth from her sandals, perched first on one leg and then the other, and clicked her tongue. She had been relieved to have arranged for her husband and herself to be buried together here, but now she appeared regretful that the lot had to be in a public cemetery.

The hill that had served as their ancestral burial ground was in North Korea. In the North, Chŏng-ok was told, the family would make a temporary grave in the yard when there was a death in winter; not until the ice melted could they hold a second funeral and a proper burial on the hill.

"To get up here, a corpse would have to stand up and walk," said her mother as she slipped on the sandy ocher soil. She grasped the weeds, grown like tousled hair, and panted as she crawled up the trail.

Stopping momentarily to catch her breath, Chŏng-ok looked back; the path they had crept up seemed far away. Much lower, on a ridge across the valley, seven or eight men with shovels were busily hollowing out a grave—to all appearances a burial.

He had always gone up in the hills at dawn. Chŏng-ok, fast asleep then, never caught sight of him leaving the house and would wonder when he had slipped out. Whenever she heard the clank of the front gate in her fleeting dawn dreams she would be seized with the desperate feeling that she would never see him again. To erase the desolate sensation that she was falling apart, she would soothe herself even while she was dreaming: It's only a dream, she would think, and when it's light and I wake up he'll be back, brushing his teeth at the faucet outside just like always. Her dawn sleep was too short and her dreams disturbing. Once she had considered following him, but she never did. This wasn't just because she liked to sleep through daybreak. Rather, they had an unspoken agreement that dawn was the one time of day when absolutely no one could interrupt him. He had no choice but to spend his days napping, playing go, taking some light exercise in order to sleep at night—fumbling to repair the gutters, say, or pushing the boy along on his tricycle. Since people said a dawn stroll was good for one's health and since she considered it his personal ritual, she refrained from showing the slightest sign that her sleep was ever disturbed.

About the time he returned and stepped inside, accompanied by the cool outdoor air, Chŏng-ok would rub her drowsy eyes. Then, after covering the boy with the quilt he had kicked aside, she would rinse some rice and put it on the stove.

"Why don't you sleep some more?" she would say nonchalantly, as if talking to a patriarch who had diligently swept the alley in front of the house early in the morning. Then she would turn and murmur inaudibly, "I don't know anything. I'm just an ignorant woman. But I've never thought of that as bad luck. I'm a woman who plants flower seeds in the soft, warm soil after the rain and watches the buds and the blossoms in joyful wonder. If I'm not greedy, I can live a mundane existence day by day, like others. And I have a future: our son. But if he hears this he'll probably answer, 'You say, let's plant some seeds and live a simple life, but why do you want to do that? It's because you're anxious to see the flowers, isn't it?'"

It was because they constituted the world in which the boy was to live that Chŏng-ok thought about the time and space that would follow her death—what she called the future. It was because she would leave behind her flesh and blood in that world.

"Goodness! It used to be just a ridge, and now all these people have come to rest here...." Sighing, her mother looked in turn at the map and the graves, then pointed to one of the lots and shouted, "This is it!"

The empty rectangular lot, divided by cement blocks buried among the weeds, was smaller than Chŏng-ok had expected. Perhaps because of the burial mounds heaped around it, this lot, the only empty one in section 9-3, looked more cramped, as if hollowed out of its surroundings. Right beside the lot was a sparsely sodded mound that looked new. Chŏng-ok wondered if a family had recently visited the grave following the third memorial service for the deceased. Collected there were a bunch of withered flowers, a piece of white paper blotted with letters in Chinese ink, leftovers from a meal partially wrapped in newspaper, an empty liquor bottle, paper cups, and other odds and ends. Perhaps a downpour had prevented the visitors from cleaning up. Nothing unusual about a shower in the summer, Chŏng-ok told herself.

Thinking that Chŏng-ok was wondering how two people could possibly be buried in this rather narrow lot, her mother sheepishly tried to vindicate herself: "It's not that small, you know. After all, it's for two people. Look, compare a grave for one and a grave for two—see what a difference there is?"

The flat grave site was a bed of weeds. Chŏng-ok found it hard to imagine that someday the tightly clotted earth, separated only by the weeds' tough roots, would be turned up and a huge mound formed atop it.

The boy's amazing ability to harmonize with new situations and people, a special quality of childhood, made the graves seem no longer strange to him. Chŏng-ok was relieved that she did not have to explain to the inquisitive child this different world in which they were intruders: "Where are we?" "This is where the dead are buried." "The dead? What is dying?" Who indeed were these people called the dead? she asked herself. They were people who had lived in the same era and experienced the same events as she. People she hadn't known, whom she had brushed past indifferently on a street corner, whose eyes had lightly touched hers. They were people who had risen in the morning and fallen asleep at night, people with whom she had experienced sunlight, wind, snow and rain. She had been born at a certain moment in their lifetimes, and at a certain moment in hers they had humbly departed. How awfully fortuitous to have shared the same era with them; yet she hadn't had the slightest premonition or indication of their deaths.

The outskirts of the capital were now visible in the far distance. Though the day was clear, the city looked dim and hazy; it gave Chŏng-ok the impression of a crudely tinted photograph.

Suddenly a breeze gathered. A stream of cool air touched Chŏng-ok's forehead, and she saw a blurry remnant of the city, which the wind seemed to have driven toward her.

A sound carried by the breeze brushed her ears, now disappearing, now returning. So far and faint that she thought she might lose it in just a single instant of inattention, it was like the continuous striking of a gong or a small drum—or a combination of the two.

As soon as the breeze passed, the sound disappeared and the city receded. The sun felt hotter to Chŏng-ok. She watched her mother sitting on an outspread newspaper slapping her calves. Were ants crawling up them? she wondered.

"I wish we had some shade," said the older woman.

But there could be no dense thickets, no trees with thriving roots on this completely denuded graveyard hill. Otherwise tree roots would reach into the burial pits and tangle themselves about the coffins—or so people said.

The sun was directly above them. Their shadows were squashed beneath their feet and their unsheltered, exposed bodies turned crimson.

The cloth lining of the straw bag had become damp. Wondering if something was leaking, Chŏng-ok emptied the bag of its soft drinks, melons and other contents and set them on the grass. A white towel with food spread over it soon became a pleasant picnic table.

Was it because of this? Chŏng-ok murmured to herself. When her mother had casually asked her at breakfast if she wanted to visit the cemetery, had she readily agreed because she envisioned finding there the solitude and absolute peace of the dead? Had she agreed to the trip even though she could barely imagine venturing forth in this scorching weather with the boy in tow?

She uncapped the soft drinks, and the carbonated beverages bubbled and dripped from the bottles. There was only this indifferent fizzing of the froth to break the deathly stillness. After sprinkling a bit of the overflowing foam on the ground to appease any thirsty spirits in the vicinity,

Chǒng-ok took a sip of the beverage and handed the bottle to the boy.

"We should find some shade," muttered Chǒng-ok's mother. But she spoke in vain. There was nothing to make even a spot of shade except the tilted, open parasol. Pointing to the shade provided by the parasol, she said to the boy, "Come here and sit."

The boy's face was the color of a ripe tomato. He took a sip of the soft drink, and after a throaty exclamation of satisfaction he smacked his lips.

"You little rascal, listen to you already," said his grandmother. "You figure on being a big drinker some day? Does your daddy do that?"

Chǒng-ok and her mother burst into a laugh. The boy, pleased with the response he had elicited, repeated the guttural sound—this time louder.

"It looks fairly large," said Chǒng-ok. "I guess it *is* for two people. The location is good, too." Though she thought differently, she said this to satisfy her mother, who had taken pains to emphasize, even to the men in the custodial office, that the lot was especially for two.

"Large? Are you kidding? It's too narrow for two. Even though there's just one mound, they'll be digging a hole for each of us, so they should have made it about as wide as two single lots." Her mother shook her head: this would not do. It hadn't taken long for her to change her tune, Chǒng-ok thought.

"You know, when they bury two people," Chǒng-ok's mother went on, "they make a hole between the graves to connect them before building the mound. We did the same thing when we buried your grandparents. Then we found a better location for the graves, and when we dug up the coffins we found that the holes had been shaped into a nice, smooth passage. You see, the two of them were always visiting each other." Blushing slightly, she broke into a shrill laugh. She had no doubt that a couple buried together would be tied by fate in the next world.

There was a secret game that Chǒng-ok had enjoyed with her friends when she was a girl. It had likely originated in a book of folktales. According to one of the tales, if a girl touched her forehead with one of the ornamental silver knives that women used to carry to protect their virtue, then looked into a round mirror on a moonless night, the face of her future husband would surely appear. And so the girls tried it, despite their apprehension and their disdain at this venture into superstition. It was difficult at their age to resist curiosity and the temptation to see their future mates. No face appeared in the mirror, of course.

Chŏng-ok, however, continued the game for quite some time. As she sat in bed alone and looked into a mirror darker than the room whose light she had extinguished, she earnestly wished to encounter the face of her future husband.

They were now man and wife, he had said after their wedding. He no longer seemed a stranger, and his face had become as familiar as if she had known it in a previous life.

Although she had been seized even then by a vague sense of failure, she had gripped his hand and pledged to be a faithful attendant, to be obedient and true. Yes, we are really man and wife, she had said. And then for the first time she had seen a face in the mirror on a moonless night.

He was walking along a road, raising dust, his parched mouth full of the scorching sun. The sunlight became a fire in his heart. There was no respite from his thirst. He could not remember ever having been free from it. Wishing to rinse the flaring fever from his mouth and soak his burning feet, he glanced around in vain for a cold stream.

On he walked. . . . A path through a field, lacking any trace of human life; the sound of the unripened kernels swelling involuntarily within the verdant, growing rice plants; the sound of new ears of rice drying in the blazing sun.

He wondered where the reservoir could be. He was beginning to feel the weight of his tackle bag with its fishing rods and other gear. The stiff new straps, not yet broken in, dug into the joints of his sweaty shoulders and chafed them.

Surely the girl at the inn had said it was about five miles to the reservoir. While telling him this she had stolen several glances at his new set of fishing gear. Was it simply his imagination that he had read suspicion on her face?

It was almost ten when he woke up that morning; the sunlight had penetrated deep into his room. Upon opening his eyes, he usually listened closely for any movement from outside before getting up. A radio was blaring the latest episode of a soap opera. Otherwise it was quiet.

He got up and opened the door. A girl was wiping the long wooden veranda, her bottom up in the air. She gave him a smile. It was the girl who had brought him dinner after he had checked in the night before.

"Shall I bring you some breakfast?"

He shook his head and, toothbrush in mouth, stepped down to the yard. The girl followed and filled a washbowl for him, as she had done the previous evening.

"Are you going to be leaving today?"

"Where am I, anyway?" he countered, looking at her puffy cheeks. It was strange. Since leaving his house he had become indifferent about the names of his destinations and the places along the way. Every place was exactly the same—was that it? he wondered. But whenever he woke up in a cramped, untidy room in an unfamiliar inn he would shake his head fretfully, trying to remember where he was.

"This is Chinnae-ŭp. You didn't know?" The girl looked at him intently.

Reading suspicion on the girl's face as she tried to detect just who he could be, he revised his question: "I'm wondering if there's a place to go fishing around here."

"About five miles down the road there's a reservoir just full of big fat fish," she responded, her expression quickly softening. "I hear they're swarming because several people have drowned there." Giggling, she pretended to shudder.

Just then an advertisement for a movie thundered from a speaker on the roof of the theater across the street. Listening to the repeated notice of the screening, he suddenly thought it would be all right to take the girl to the movie. He didn't want to be noticed, so having a companion might be safer than being all alone; blending into a crowd would be even better.

"... What's the meaning of that dream you told us about? It's not like the dreams we have. It's difficult to understand. We're not interested in a long explanation." Suddenly the tone relaxed. "Use simple words we can all understand." They burst into guffaws and patted him on the shoulder. But their eyes were not laughing. He abruptly shrugged off the hands. But he couldn't rid himself of the feeling that he was forever caught between the links of a chain that would tighten mercilessly until they crushed his shoulders.

"How would you like to go to the movie?"

"The owner'll give me a hard time if I go out with one of the guests," the girl answered primly. She then turned the radio still higher.

He had had to wait nearly an hour for the first showing to start. Afterward he could remember only a few scenes, such as a speeding car crashing and disappearing into the sea in a mass of flames, and closeups of kabuki actors, their powdered faces white like masks. This proved he had been thinking about other things throughout the film. Even so, he had shed a few tears while watching it. Why?

Before the lights came on for intermission, he looked at the clock next to the red plastic "No Smoking" and "Hats Off" signs. The hands stood at two o'clock. He decided to sit tight awhile; it would still be blazing hot under the midday sun. Skipping breakfast had made his stomach sour, so he bought some pastries and yogurt at the snack bar. The pastries reeked of preservatives.

He also wept a little during the second showing—and at the same scene. Bits of colored paper were being blown about as if in a blizzard, and balloons of various colors rose and filled the sky. Blacks and caucasians in peaked hats holding lanterns decorated with dragon heads shouted in wild abandon, their faces bubbling in laughter. And suddenly he was teary-eyed, overcome by the scene of a woman on the verge of childbirth struggling through a milling throng on a slum street where ragged clothing had been hung out to dry on every balcony.

The colors of the film looked dull on the old screen, and

the subtitles were completely illegible. From the corner a baby cried out in terror. The sound echoed violently from the high ceiling of the dark, nearly empty theater.

He left in the middle of the second showing of the movie. The sun seemed scarcely to have moved. He walked toward it, shaking his head repeatedly in order to dispel the fog in his mind—such a feeling of unreality. The people in the peaked hats dancing in abandon, the shabby, exhausted woman about to give birth, and the crying baby—were they the scenes and sounds of yesterday? Right now? Tomorrow? Walking a road that was indistinguishable from a life he remembered having borrowed for himself and lived—yesterday, the day before that, or much further in the past—for the first time he thought he understood why he had wept. It was because of his son. It was because there was an inevitable beauty to the sight of people making their way through life, even though the life his son would wish for, like the peaceful life he desired for himself, could not in the end be realized.

Chŏng-ok's mother was peeling a second melon. A magpie flapped toward them and alighted on the ground. At the sight of the black form flying into this space filled with sun and stillness, she paused. Chŏng-ok instinctively looked at the boy. He had been sitting bored, blowing into an empty soft-drink bottle with a deep whoosh, but now, his eyes like saucers, he set the bottle down.

The sounds from the ridge across the valley occasionally rode the wind to their ears. Chŏng-ok now recognized them as a gong and cymbals, but so faint and distant were they that she wondered if she might be imagining them.

Her mother briefly squinted at the magpie and resumed peeling the melon.

The boy began creeping toward the magpie. The bird did not conceal its hostility toward the unexpected visitors. Its firm, spry wings had a blue sheen, and its stomach was white as snow. It fixed its glistening, seemingly mocking black eyes on the boy, though it couldn't have seen anything so unusual in him.

The boy sensed the bird's hostility and his eyes grew

tense. He tiptoed closer, clenching his fists and breaking into an amiable smile of childish cunning. But when he was just one step away, the magpie shook its wings and soared away.

The dispirited boy looked at Chŏng-ok as if to complain. She shrugged.

The magpie flew freely in the still white void and then returned to earth, the desolation of midday seeming to weigh heavily on its steel-colored wings. Every time it hopped from one gravestone to another the boy would approach it. He tried his best to muffle his footsteps, but the bird never failed to slip away into the air. When the boy finally gave up and dropped his arms to his sides, the magpie flew near, keeping close enough to sustain its opponent's interest. The bird now had a firm grip on the boy. It was casting its net and entrancing him.

A white bus came up the road in a cloud of dust. It turned at the foot of the hill where they were sitting, then halted at the bottom of the hill opposite them. The doors opened and a funeral party emerged with a coffin. The coffin bearers slowly led the mourners up the hill. As Chŏng-ok had suspected, they were heading toward the open grave far below them where the gravediggers were waiting.

The boy gave chase to the magpie and careened among the gravestones, which towered above him as if they each had a life of their own. Unnoticed by the two women, he had removed his sneakers and socks, enjoying the sensation of the grass under his bare feet. To amuse himself he began embracing gravestones as tall as he and spun himself round and round.

To Chŏng-ok the boy began to resemble the magpie the way he dashed about in the glare of the sun. He seemed to have forgotten that she and her mother existed. For the first time Chŏng-ok saw him from afar as if watching someone else's child. Who was this boy romping around innocently in shorts and T-shirt? Was he the boy she had met so often in her dreams, desires and thoughts before she became pregnant?

Before her pregnancy Chŏng-ok would forever be

imagining children running to her. Although she had no particular face in mind for the baby who would be born after borrowing her womb, the boy bore not the slightest resemblance to any of the children who had run to her from out of the future, some of them halfheartedly and others spreading their arms in joy. Who was this boy of mine?

If he were to walk straight ahead where this paved road forked in three directions, the narrow streets of a town would probably appear. At the left fork stood a board with the Buddhist swastika and an inscription, "Bot'a Temple, 6 miles." The path to the fish-filled reservoir seemed to be to the right.

After hesitating for a moment he saw a variety shop at one of the intersections. On its glass door were advertisements for noodle dishes. He went in. Although the smell of the preservatives in the pastries he had eaten at the theater came up whenever he exhaled, he was still famished.

There were two long tables inside. Hearing him enter, a young woman peered out from the living quarters attached to the back of the shop. Her face was puffy, as if she had just risen from a nap.

"Could I have some ramen?" he asked, looking over the menu.

The woman emerged, buttoning her blouse. "Would you like an egg in it?" She began wiping one of the tables.

"On second thought, could I have some soup noodles instead?" he asked, hastily correcting himself upon recalling the repulsive smell of rancid chicken fat that he associated with ramen.

Without answering she turned toward the shelves, sweeping up her disheveled hair and fixing it with a pin. She took down a bundle of noodles from a shelf where boxes of matches, bottles of liquor and soft drinks, and other goods sat covered with dust.

As he waited for his meal he smoked a cigarette and read in turn every single flyer posted on the wall: a slogan for the government's New Village Movement, a slogan urging increased production of foodstuffs and posters containing photos of the most-wanted fugitives—together with their offenses and the reward for capturing them. All the while he dusted off the basketball sneakers he was wearing by tapping them against the cement floor. A tractor rattled by with an awful din and a succession of housewives and grandmothers with loads on their heads came in to buy candles and incense.

Frogs were croaking in the stillness of the late afternoon. It looked as though it would rain by nightfall.

Finally his meal was ready. The woman served the noodles in their thin anchovy broth, then set some radish kimchi and chopsticks beside them on the table, making a separate trip for each item.

An elderly woman entered the shop with a young woman in mourning clothes who had in tow a boy of four or five. "We'd like some candles."

The shopkeeper gave a faint, knowing smile. "On your way to the temple, I see."

"Today is the forty-ninth day, so it will be the final mass," the old woman whispered, glancing at the younger woman.

The shopkeeper rummaged through the shelves, then brushed off her hands. "We're all out," she said, shaking her head.

The women purchased a fifth of rice wine and some incense and left with worried looks. The woman in mourning had gripped the boy's hand and remained silent throughout.

"If his highness knew there was a mass today, why couldn't he stock up on candles?" the shopkeeper grumbled. "All he ever does is... "

It seemed their business with people visiting the Buddhist temple was far from negligible.

"So the temple's holding a service?" Regretting having requested a spoonful of hot pepper, as if he had set the shopkeeper to a needless task, he tried to ingratiate himself with her. The white skirt of the young woman fading into the distance caught his eye as it moved in and out of sight through the door of the shop.

"Today is the Buddhist All Souls' Day," the shopkeeper replied. "They're on their way to Bot'a Temple, over the hill." Seeing that his eyes were still following the hem of the white mourning skirt becoming faint and far away, she added, "I guess they're finally having their forty-ninth-day mass. They're from the upper village. The kid's father drowned in the reservoir seven weeks ago."

He stirred the hot pepper into the broth, and some insects in the condiment floated to the surface like pieces of white rice bran.

A baby cried from the back of the shop. While the shopkeeper sat looking vacantly outside, her cheek resting against the door frame, liquid saturated the swollen front of her blouse, gradually darkening it and then spreading. When the crying became a piercing scream, she sluggishly rose and went into the back room.

The noodles were plentiful but flavorless. For one so hungry, he now had virtually no appetite.

He payed the woman as she was nursing her child and left.

"Looks like they're opening up the coffin," Chŏng-ok's mother said, squinting, as if all along she had been watching the scene unfolding below. The seven loops of white cotton broadcloth around the black coffin were being untied.

"Why are they opening the coffin?" Chŏng-ok asked.

"So the bones will stay white. That's the way the southerners do it. Apparently the moisture in the wood can stain the bones yellow."

Chŏng-ok gazed at her mother's face. The lines and furrows that crosshatched it stood out clearly in the sun. All the makeup had been wiped away except a touch of blue eye shadow. After slowly chewing several bites of melon the older woman realized she was being observed, and her face hardened a bit. Chŏng-ok got to her feet, stretched her arms high and took a few deep breaths. She could now see the spectacle of the funeral more clearly.

The corpse was being lowered into the grave on a mortuary plank containing seven holes arranged like the Big Dipper. All the bereaved women had prostrated themselves, and now they began wailing in unison. Then some of the men, clad in black and wearing hemp mourning hoods signifying their close relation to the deceased, each scooped a shovelful of earth into the grave and stepped back. Another round of wailing rose from the women, still prostrate in their white mourning garb, their heads lowered. Next, a man in black without a hood respectfully bowed toward the grave and shoveled some earth onto the corpse. He was followed by the women. Chŏng-ok was reminded of officials taking turns with a shovel in a memorial tree-planting ceremony.

The mourners transferred their shovels to the gravediggers, who sprang to work and quickly covered the corpse with soil. Then came the tamping and liming of the earth. The gravediggers, each with a long pole, descended into the grave. Their heads barely rose above the ground. An old man who had been kneeling languidly at the head of the grave began leading a song, and the gravediggers fell into two rows. Alternately face to face and back to back, they stamped the earth hard while responding to his calls in ringing voices. Their tone was sorrowful and slow. Though Chŏng-ok could not hear the words, the melody was distinct.

While the old man, hoarse by now, smoked a cigarette and cooled off, the gravediggers showered the grave with another layer of earth mixed with lime. A lull in the wailing and singing made the sound of the gong and cymbals faintly audible.

Leaving her parents' plot, Chŏng-ok began walking from one burial mound to the next, stopping at each stone to peruse the name and dates engraved on it. Some people had lived almost a century, others barely a decade. In each case she was struck with wonder, for she was alive. There were people still living who had already arranged for their graves. And someone dead at seventeen. Another at twenty. The face of death differing with their ages. But these memories were only shadows in the hearts of those who knew these people at death, and such memories would, in their turn, inevitably become dim and soon be forgotten.

On her next visit Chŏng-ok would stand here again.

The boy would be lanky by then. Would he remember this day? Would he remember their forced march on a scorching summer day buried in his past?

Chŏng-ok was stopped by the sight of some cream-colored roses wrapped in cellophane lying in front of a burial mound. Once fragrant and charming, no doubt, they had withered in the hot sunlight, but their leaves still looked fresh and green because of the water droplets gathering inside the wrapper. Traces of yesterday's shower were evident. Looking closer, she saw some hardened depressions made by high heels in the cramped plot in front of the mound.

Finding here the traces of the rain she had watched the day before while lulling the boy to sleep in her arms on the veranda of her house in Vernal Stream, Chŏng-ok recalled the elusive feeling that had accompanied an image she had seen in that rain—the familiar image of a young woman bringing cream-colored roses to her beloved's grave. But then she shook her head, realizing that rain was virtually a daily occurrence in summertime. The rainy season was over, but the pattern of sudden thunder and lightning followed by clearing had persisted like some celestial prank for a month or so.

"He must have been caught in that rainstorm," the officer at the police substation had said.

The creel, fishing rods, folding chair, and other items the policeman delivered to Chŏng-ok were still damp. The ink had run all over the appointment book and identification card found in his jacket. There was nothing to identify in the photo on his identification card. Like a face from a forgotten past, it was unfamiliar and indistinct, lacking the stamp of his personality. This sensation was accentuated by his short hair in the photo, which had been taken before men started growing their hair long.

The policeman looked Chŏng-ok over as if he were investigating her. He pointed to the boy, who with his hair covering his ears and forehead could not be readily distinguished from a girl. "Is this your... son?"

Chŏng-ok lowered her head. "Yes... " Then she

added, "He's an only child," answering the policeman's unspoken question.

The boy's eyes never left the gun at the policeman's side.

"It doesn't take long for the river to rise when it rains... The island gets cut off and then buried under the water. For all I know he might have swum away, but we're continuing the search. It's easy for outsiders to get into trouble there. If there's no rain, the island's quite safe and there's no problem. It's not that far to shore, and the water only comes up to your waist.... Last year a man was camping there with his kids, and they got caught in a downpour in the middle of the night. He never knew that when the rain comes that island disappears without a trace."

The policeman's explanation lengthened and he spoke more kindly as he sympathized with the young widow.

As Chŏng-ok was picking up the items of fishing gear one by one, the boy shouted with joy: "Aren't those Dad's? When he took me last time...." He remembered having gone fishing with his dad on a long summer day the previous year. The boy hadn't been fishing since.

Chŏng-ok went with the policeman to the scene of the accident, as he called it. The island had been formed by sand deposits in a wide stream that flowed into a river. It lay bare in the water, a flat, small white oval that reminded Chŏng-ok of a fish's belly. It seemed impossible that this solid-looking island could have disappeared overnight in the rain.

The sparkling sands danced under the blazing sun.

The local people all agreed that a lantern had glimmered on the island of sand till late at night. And then the rain suddenly came pouring down.

A man had come fishing. He carried his gear to the island, making several trips through the waist-deep water. At the side of the stream he gave a youngster some change and asked him to get a pack of cigarettes. Early the next morning, worrying about a net he had set in the stream, the boy went outside and found a piece of clothing snagged on a bush. It was the jacket the man had been wearing the previous evening.... The boys who lived along the stream repeated to Chŏng-ok word for word the story they had told several times already to their neighbors and the police.

"He didn't catch anything, not even a chub. We told him the current here is too strong for fishing, but he just laughed."

The next day one of the older boys rowed to the junction of the stream and the river and scooped up a folding chair spinning against a rock and a creel floating downstream.

"It was a wild storm—so windy and rainy we couldn't put up an umbrella," someone else said. "I was out late, and on my way home I saw this light coming from the island."

Some people living nearby had taken a boat downstream as far as a long, rounded dune and searched for his body with long poles. No trace of him could be found.

Chŏng-ok affixed her fingerprint to some forms and was given her husband's belongings by the policeman.

"I understand he teaches at a college."

"Yes."

"Does he often leave home by himself like this?"

"Well, summer vacation started early... and fishing is one of his favorite pastimes."

"Actually, since he's a college instructor I suppose he can do what he wants with his time even when school's in session. But you know, it's quite a ways from here to Vernal Stream, and we're not all that well known for fishing. . . . "

The policeman was obviously trying to uncover the significance of the disappearance of this stranger who had come here on a hot summer day. At that moment Chŏng-ok was seized by a violent urge to tell all. Her throat itched to pour out the flood of words: "He's a lecturer at a provincial college, and we've been married five years now. A while back, everything became off limits to him. He's like someone who's been declared legally incompetent—he doesn't have any rights or responsibilities. And he has to have a regular checkup, like someone with syphilis. He's only allowed to travel during his naps or when he's having a long dream. And so that's why he began sleeping all the time. The way he sleeps with his mouth open—it's just like he's dead, so I get frightened, and several times I've shaken him awake."

But then, pushing these words deep into her heart as she always did, she asked, "Would you happen to know where Heaven's Pass and the Stream of the Gods are?"

The policeman considered the question for a moment, then shook his head. "Never heard of them. I'm sure there aren't any places around here with names like that."

If they're not around here, where could they be, with names like Heaven's Pass and the Stream of the Gods? Chŏng-ok wondered.

After her husband's departure Chŏng-ok had pored over every map she could find—detailed maps that showed cities, towns and townships. But Heaven's Pass and the Stream of the Gods were nowhere to be seen. Since she always expected this sort of thing, she had not been surprised.

Perhaps because of the blueness of that dawn, when she heard those place names from him she had visualized a vertical cliff with no handholds, an azure sky above it that had never opened itself to view, and a blue gorge—the kind where *yŏlmok* trout are said to gather in the chill water to cool their red, feverish eyes.

The tamping feet quickened and the calls and responses accelerated into a quick tune. The gravediggers wheeling about the hole appeared to grow out of it like leeks shooting up from a storage cellar. They were lavish with the lime and stamped the earth hard. Dancing and spinning, their legs almost completely visible now, they were the only people to be seen. The sun had driven the mourners to cover under an open tent.

He sat beside the stream, removed his sneakers, and soaked his whitish, blistered feet in the water. It was astonishingly refreshing.

He bent to look at the various shapes and colors of the stones in the stream bed. His reflection appeared first. The colors of the stones seemed to flow with the water.

He broke his reflection by stirring the water, then collected some stones. Some of the worn, rounded stones lay flat, others were upright. When he took the stones from the water, their colors faded.

"A lizard wearing a pretty flower-print dress said to a baby mouse, 'When the full moon rises, go find me a purple pebble. Make sure it's purple. Then I'll make your wishes come true. . . . ' But the mouse couldn't find a purple pebble no matter how he tried. . . . " Only dimly awake, he was listening to Chŏng-ok's monotonous, mechanical voice as she read to their son. He thought: A purple pebble—if it's purple but not a gem, how pretty and marvelous it could be. . . . "And so? So what happened?" the boy eagerly asked, his legs fidgeting. Chŏng-ok was reading the story without conviction or interest, as if she had told it several times already. . . . So, could that little mouse find a purple pebble? he wondered. Before he could hear the end he began drifting off to sleep. Of course, he told himself, after some impossible adventures, sacrifices and ordeals, that little mouse would obtain the purple pebble and have his wishes come true. That's the formula of a children's story.

He arranged the stones he had taken from the water. As they dried and lost their luster they soon became common and ordinary.

There was a rock in the garden of their house in Vernal Stream that in form and color was difficult to distinguish from a tree root. Brought home some time ago from one of his fishing trips, it had been left alone in a shady corner of the yard, where it was now growing a coat of damp moss. The boy thought the rock grew a little every night. The little rascal's brain was full of stories about magic. He believed that those buried deep in the earth could overcome death and rise from their graves with only a few magic words: *suri suri masuri*. The boy's tiny gestures and expressions, which he had never fully appreciated, pricked his heart with pathos.

"You're putting up a smokescreen. Are you. . . a poet?" they had asked sarcastically. They thought they had discovered his weapon. But this was unfair of them: he had wished to be an advocate of common sense, not so much a poet.

He began to throw the assorted stones back in the water. They struck a large rock rising from the stream, throwing sparks and leaving faint white marks. The last stone whirled into the water, and he rose. The sun was near the horizon. If he set his mind to it, he could probably reach the reservoir before dark. If he walked without stopping he could see the sun become a fireball and make its illusory descent beneath the horizon. Then he could watch the night set in.

A new mound soon rose from the soil that had been hurriedly dug up.

The clanging of gong and cymbals sounded much more clearly and urgently.

It had taken place within twenty minutes at most. The boy had been taking such a long nap. While covering the sweaty boy's stomach with a towel, Chŏng-ok suddenly remembered that she had not picked up the laundry she had taken to the cleaner's right after winter. Before summer was gone, she thought, she would need to have her husband's autumn clothing ready to wear.

After locking the house and gate and dropping the keys in the mailbox, she ran to the cleaner's.

Chŏng-ok was back with the laundry in no time. For a moment she stood outside the wall surrounding their yard and strained to hear whether the boy was crying. Inside it was just as quiet as before. But then she reached into the mailbox. Although the keys were there, something was strange, different. She could not have put it in words, but it was as if a thoroughly familiar sensation had brushed across the back of her hand. Chŏng-ok drew out the keys, which were crudely embossed with the head of a lion, and studied them. They didn't seem twisted or scratched. When Chŏng-ok unlocked the door and entered the house she felt even more keenly that someone had come. It was not that the door was open or that the shoes in the vestibule were disarranged. Nothing had changed. The boy was still asleep with his arms outspread; he had kicked away the towel over his stomach. Only after a look around the house did she understand: it was the faint odor of tobacco.

She flung down the bag of clothing and dashed into the kitchen. She did not know why, but since he had gone, it was always his appetite that came to mind whenever she thought of him. There was no sign he had touched anything, only a tumbler with a bit of water left in it.

But there in the bathroom hamper were the roughly folded clothes she knew so well. It was as if the master of the house were taking a bath.

"Where are you? Where are you?" she whispered, as if wary of others' ears, though she knew he was not there. Finally she picked up the telephone receiver. There was only the incessant dial tone seeming to whir about her ear. Not really knowing what she was trying to find, Chŏng-ok picked up two cigarette butts from the ashtray that were still moist with saliva; she inspected them like a veteran criminal investigator.

As she usually did before starting the wash, Chŏng-ok searched the pockets of the clothes he had left. It was clothing from a restless journey, permeated with the smell of the many places he had been, of the wind, the sunlight, the dew, and the people he had brushed past in places Chŏng-ok had never visited.

The pockets yielded a wrinkled movie stub, whose stamped date was almost illegible, an admission stub to an amusement park, a dirty handkerchief, some flakes of tobacco. Where was the note he might have left?

Then she saw the clear imprint of his lips on the cheeks of the boy, who was fast asleep. There was no need to investigate further.

He was gone forever. Just as he had gone into hiding, leaving only his shell on a pile of sand that had disappeared in an overnight downpour, he had merely changed his clothes and vanished. It had been at most twenty minutes, but that was time enough for him to have been far away by then.

Chŏng-ok put her lips to the sleeping boy's cheek. The boy rubbed his eyes several times in annoyance, tossed about, rolled over and went back to sleep.

The heap of reddish brown soil was being covered with

turf. Chŏng-ok's mother watched, unblinking, as if to fix a mental image of the burial from start to finish that she could review in the future. She had lifted her dress above her knees to prevent it from being soiled and wrinkled, and her legs—once more proud and vigorous than the grass in a meadow—lay there as if cast aside, fleshy but withering, their veins faintly varicose.

The boy appeared from behind the stonework in front of a family plot whose mounds were backed by a semi-circular wall. He ran to Chŏng-ok, settled in her lap and leaned back.

Chŏng-ok passed her fingers through the boy's hair, which stuck to his sweaty forehead. She looked into his eyes. It was precisely when she looked in those eyes that she was conscious of her husband. And in those eyes she saw something new: the piercing eyes of her father-in-law in a faded, yellowing photograph. Despite the round chin that Chŏng-ok associated with her own family, the boy's eyes gave an impression of perspicacity unbefitting a child. She could immediately spot that small face among the jumbled thousands of children flocking into her imagination. But his uniqueness would disappear before long. He would grow and couple with a woman from a different family, and after he had fathered a child, his unique characteristics, inherited from his father and grandfather, would gradually wear away. Later they would be unfamiliar, those faces of children to be born with her husband's surname, as unfamiliar as people buried long ago.

When the mound had been dressed in turf and a simple tray for the offering set before it, the mourners emerged from their tent. While Chŏng-ok was engrossed in the scene, a buzzing swarm of blowflies attached themselves to the melon peels at her feet.

Chŏng-ok looked tenderly at her mother's face. Someday Chŏng-ok herself would be holding a farewell ceremony for her mother on this very spot. She would someday be pouring a glass of wine over her mother's burial mound and burning a piece of offertory paper.

Black smoke rose. The empty coffin was being burned. Her mother sighed.

A moist wind gathered. India-ink clouds billowed up from one side of the sky and covered the sun.

The ceremony below had concluded. The mourners gazed at the sky. Perhaps anxious about the unmistakable prospect of a soaking shower, they hastened to fold the tent, roll up the rush mats and pack the ceremonial vessels.

The gravediggers surrounded the smoldering embers of the coffin and stirred them into flames with sticks.

The jagged row of white and black figures moved steadily down the hill among the burial mounds.

The tall, coarse grass of neglected graves began to tremble eerily in the moist wind, its color darkening in the gray void.

Perhaps sensing a sharp drop in air pressure, a flock of birds filled the sky, their wings fluttering. They seemed to have risen from every ridge and hidden gorge. Suddenly they began swooping in low circles all over the cemetery, cawing back and forth. Chŏng-ok saw that they were magpies.

Now the birds were perched motionless on every gravestone. Chŏng-ok stiffened at the sight of them. For the first time that day she felt panic.

Startled by the enormous gathering, the boy locked onto Chŏng-ok's arm, his face filled with fear.

The mourners had reached the foot of the hill and boarded the bus, which started up with a tremendous racket.

"Let's go," said Chŏng-ok's mother.

Chŏng-ok silently helped the boy with his sneakers, then wrapped the melon peels, eggshells, and other scraps in newspaper and put it all in the mesh bag, together with the empty bottles. She wished to leave no trace in the empty plot. Otherwise, how horrible it would be if the next time she came these remnants prompted her to try in vain to relive the hours she had just spent here.

"Are you planning to go back home today?"

"I'd better," Chŏng-ok replied without really thinking about it. She had intended to stay several days with her parents, but she now sensed in her mother's tone a hint that she should return home. And now that she had responded, she felt like hurrying back, as if something urgent awaited her there, as if she had left the house in Vernal Stream empty forever and not for just a day.

"There might be a path this way too, maybe a shortcut." Chŏng-ok's mother pointed out a ridge opposite the path they had climbed. Along it was the trail to the new grave the mourners had just left.

The sky darkened even more. The path dropped steeply. Chŏng-ok lifted the boy to her back. The clouds were massing overhead.

The more they descended, the nearer the gong sounded.

"No two ways about it, we're going to have a shower." Chŏng-ok's mother folded her parasol, which she had been carrying all the while.

They passed the grave and were eyed by the grave-diggers, who were eating some of the food offered in memory of the deceased. Turning their heads, the gravediggers followed them with drink-reddened eyes until they were out of sight.

They rounded two bends in the path, and a Buddhist temple suddenly appeared at the edge of the hill. The kaleidoscopic tricolor design of the eaves and columns had been touched up; the paint looked fresh enough to smear at the touch of a hand. The incessant sound of gong and cymbals came from a dark sanctuary identified as the Hall of Hades by a plaque hanging at its entrance. It was the sound they had heard all along from the hill.

"Sounds like a mass," Chŏng-ok's mother whispered faintly in her daughter's ear.

Thick raindrops began to spatter on the ground as they entered the temple courtyard. A cast-iron pot was suspended above a fire of pine branches in an outdoor cooking hearth, and acrid smoke was spreading over the ground.

A head poked out from an outbuilding that housed the kitchen. It was a middle-aged woman in a nun's habit. With her short permed hair and long rosary she looked as though she might be an untonsured nun or a shaman.

"A mass, is it?" asked Chŏng-ok's mother in a congenial tone. She had moved close under the eaves of the building and now took a seat at the edge of the veranda. A sly, artful smile—the kind Chŏng-ok associated with the elderly—appeared on her face now that she had achieved her ulterior motive of escaping the rain.

Through the open door of the sanctuary they could see colored lanterns hanging everywhere from the ceiling. They would have been the ones displayed on Buddha's birthday a few months before.

"It's the mass for Paekjung," the woman replied without interest, having determined that the new arrivals were neither supplicants to Buddha nor regular benefactors of the temple.

"Well so it is," said Chŏng-ok's mother. "That's right, it's July fifteenth." She turned to Chŏng-ok, who was sitting beside her, and said loudly, as if this news had taken her completely by surprise, "We'll see a full moon on our way home."

The lines of rain became a driving wall of water. The runoff from the eaves bounced off the ground to form new lines in the air, leaving small grooves in the earth.

Was it love? Chŏng-ok thought with a faraway look as she listened to the gong and the chanting of the scriptures. The sonorous sounds penetrated the rain more clearly now. What could have drawn her here?

Chŏng-ok looked at her watch. The night would be well along by the time she and the boy returned to Vernal Stream after a three-hour bus ride. Would the clouds have lifted and the moon come up?

"We're going to see a full moon," her mother said again.

Chŏng-ok turned to her, wondering if she had heard correctly. Her mother was gazing absentmindedly at the rainy courtyard.

The faint smell of incense lingered in the rain. It was Paekjung, the fifteenth of July. A mass for the dead, a day for the departed. A full moon, a lambent night. Taking the boy on her back, Chŏng-ok would walk the steep, dark road to her house in Vernal Stream, which was already the stuff of memories.

A Note on Romanization

The romanization of Korean names and words in this book follows the modified McCune-Reischauer system, which is used in scholarly writings in English on Korea and in the Korean government's English-language publications. In general this system spells Korean words as they sound. The only diacritical mark not used in the English alphabet is the breve (˘), which sometimes appears above *o* and *u*. Romanized Korean vowels are read as follows:

ŭ: similar to *oo* in English bᴏᴏk
ŏ: similar to *u* in English rᴜn
u: similar to *oo* in English mᴏᴏn
o: similar to *aw* in English lᴀw
a: similar to *a* in English fᴀther or *o* in pᴏt
i: similar to *ea* in English lᴇᴀp
e: similar to *e* in English sᴇt
ae: similar to *a* in English sᴀt

The two-letter vowel *oe*, as in the Korean surname Ch'*oe*, may be approximated by pronouncing the *e* of English rᴇd while rounding the lips as if pronouncing the *o* of English hope.

An apostrophe distinguishes aspirated consonants (consonants produced with a strong puff of air). Thus, *Ch'*, as in the Korean name *Ch'oe*, is like *ch* in English chalk but is pronounced with a stronger puff of air. *Ch* (without the apostrophe), as in the Korean name *Chŏng*, is also like *ch* in English chalk but is produced with a weaker puff of air. (The apostrophe is also used to indicate division between syllables whose differentiation would otherwise be ambiguous, as in *Wan'gujŏm*. Without the apostrophe, this word might be read either *Wan-gujŏm* or *Wang-ujŏm*.)

There are a few instances in which McCune-Reischauer romanization departs from the general prnciple of spelling Korean words as they sound. *Hye*, as in the name *Hye*-yang, is pronounced as if it were romanized *He; Hŭi*, as in the name *Hŭi*-jung, is pronounced like English hee. Also, certain place names retain idiosyncratic spellings, such as the capital city of Seoul, which is actually a two-syllable word that would be spelled Sŏul in McCune-Reischauer and prounounced sŏ-ul.

Finally, it should be noted that the names Myŏng, as in Myŏng-hŭi, and Kyŏng, as in Kyŏng-ok, are one-syllable words.

About the translators

Bruce and Ju-Chan Fulton are well known for their translations of Korean fiction and have received a number of awards for their published works, including a prestigious prize from the Korean Culture and Arts Foundation. They live in Seattle.

International Women's Writing from Seal Press
Selected Titles

To Live and to Write: *Selections by Japanese Women Writers, 1913–1938*, edited by Yukiko Tanaka. $9.95, 0-931188-43-1.

The House With the Blind Glass Windows by Herbjørg Wassmo. $9.95, 0-931188-50-4. The story of a young girl's struggle with incest by one of Norway's most important authors.

Egalia's Daughters by Gerd Brantenberg. $8.95, 0-931188-34-2. A hilarious satire on sex roles by Norway's leading feminist writer.

Two Women in One by Nawal el-Saadawi. $7.95, 0-931188-40-7. A novel of sexual and political awakening by a well-known Egyptian writer.

Angel by Merle Collins. $8.95, 0-931188-64-4. A vibrant novel from the island of Grenada.

Nervous Conditions by Tsitsi Dangarembga. $8.95, 0-931188-74-1. A novel of growing up in Zimbabwe by a brilliant new voice.

Seal Press, founded in 1976 to provide a forum for women writers and feminist issues, has many other titles in stock: fiction, self-help books, anthologies and translations. Any of the books above may be ordered from us at 3131 Western Ave, Suite 410, Seattle WA 98121 (include $1.50 for the first book and .50 for each additional book). Write to us for a free catalog or if you would like to be on our mailing list.

Printed in the United States
4361